NIGHT MARE

→   →

"THIS BOOK IS A KILLER.... Dorner's novel succeeds on many levels: as a heart-stopping novel of suspense, an examination of difficult moral questions and a study of characters in the grip of complex social issues, all written in clear and subtle prose.... *Nightmare* goes far past the typical who-done-it into the 'why,' as well as portraying the chilling emotional aftermath experienced by people following a crime. MARJORIE DORNER HAS WRITTEN A GRIPPING AND THOUGHT-PROVOKING NOVEL THAT MAKES THE READER HUNGRY FOR HER NEXT BOOK."

—St. Paul Pioneer Press Dispatch

NIGHT MARE

A NOVEL BY
MARJORIE DORNER

WARNER BOOKS

A Warner Communications Company

For my daughters,
Sumitra and Jaminie,
who have given my life its center

Acknowledgments

For information about legal matters and courtroom procedure, I am deeply grateful to James Forsythe, a good lawyer and a good friend.

Prologue

Linda Hammond stood looking up at the house at 7 Carimona Street, wondering why a monster's home should look so ordinary. The feeling of panic she had experienced for more than a week was now overlaid by a faint, recurring nausea. She took note of this nausea only occasionally and wondered once, idly, if it could be attributed to the fact that she had eaten so little in the past eight days, or if the dramatic change in the weather over the weekend might be making her feel sick. It was still early June, and this sudden, oppressive heat was unexpected in Minnesota, where the journey into summer was usually more leisurely. Then, too, Linda was exhausted. A deep bone-weariness struggled against nerves stretched tighter than a high wire; since last Monday, sleep, like food, had eluded her except for some dream-tortured snatches.

Linda had parked her car at the end of the short block and walked downhill to find the address, having rightly guessed that the number signified a house close to the river; number seven was the last house on the right before the street dropped away to the railroad tracks and, beyond, to the river itself. Once this neighborhood had been decidedly middle class, early residents of Holton finding the riverfront an ideal location for large, expensive houses. But since the new railroad line had been routed out of the city's center to follow the river for the whole length of the town, these old houses had been abandoned by the class that built them and cut up into apartments for laborers hired at the new industrial park. The more units per building, the more profit for landlords, who often saw improvements to these buildings as self-defeating, preferring instead to use the decaying structures as tax write-offs.

Nothing was moving in the neighborhood—no cars, no animals, no people. Linda had vaguely noticed on the drive over that the whole town seemed deserted, preternaturally quiet, as if the heat had bludgeoned every living thing into a stupor. The humidity was so high that the air looked hazy, especially so near the river. The house before her seemed to swim out of focus as Linda looked at it, and she swallowed hard to suppress a wave of nausea. She looked all around at the drowsy, seedy street, feeling a hysterical urge to scream, to wake up everyone on the block and bring them tumbling into the street, their faces registering alarm and curiosity. Then she could shout at them, tell them what no one seemed able to believe in this cosy, picture-postcard little town.

"A madman lives here!" she would scream. "A sadistic maniac has walked among you and you didn't know it. And he's coming back, maybe even today. We have to do something."

Do what? What was there to do, she wondered dully. She wasn't even sure why she had come here to stand staring at this house. Was it because she had some notion that she could learn more about the monster by seeing his lair, gain some knowledge that would provide the key to stopping him? What was there in this place that the police hadn't already found? The police. Even they didn't know what they were dealing with, couldn't be made to see that evil might sometimes take up residence even in a town like Holton, filled, they thought, with people just like themselves. So they were smugly blind, just like the citizenry they were sworn to protect. Except for one, the tall, hawk-faced outsider. Linda felt sure he knew, had intuited from the beginning that horror had been loosed on the sleepy river town, had worked its poison in secret, undetected until it had closed around her daughter, her little Dana—

But Linda couldn't let her thoughts run that way. She would collapse if she let herself think about it too much, and she mustn't give in. She felt again the urgency that had brought her here, the need to do something, if only to watch and wait for the monster to make some move that would finally make the disguise drop away. She turned her attention to the house again, moving closer along the short, cracked front walk.

Number seven was a large, two-story frame house with an open wooden porch all along the ground floor front;

the posts were now rotted and discolored by streaks of rust extending downward from the sagging eaves' troughs. The cheap white paint was cracked and peeling and so soiled from passing trains that it was no longer white at all. The door facing the street was at the extreme right side of the porch and it, too, was much painted and cracked from its base to the doorknob. Linda noticed that this door was standing slightly ajar. She walked quickly up the three concrete steps and pushed the door open.

What had once probably been an elegant foyer was now a narrow, short, wood-paneled hallway with a stairway at the end and one door in its left-hand wall. On the right-hand wall were three cheaply made aluminum mailboxes. The first one had a card taped to it which displayed two names, one above the other: DWAYNE SCHWANKE and ROBERT LUHMANN. The third was labeled with a piece of masking tape with the name William Cromett printed on it. But it was the center mailbox from which the label leaped upward into Linda's eyes. The words J. RYTER were scratched into the cover, the letters jagged and deep enough in places to perforate the aluminum. After another glance at the door, Linda assumed that there must be only one downstairs apartment, shared by Schwanke and Luhmann.

At the top of the stairs, Linda found that a hallway had simply been walled off with more paneling. On the left, two doors faced her; the first one had a metal 2 tacked to it and the second one had only a faint impression in the paint where a 3 had once been. This door also had a notepad and pencil in a little frame. Someone had written

"Bill, don't forget to pick up the battery" on the top piece of notepaper.

Linda knocked on this door, first a light tap, then harder. She knew the police had already questioned Ryter's neighbors, but she felt somehow that they might be more willing to talk to her than a policeman. When no one came to the door after three knocks, Linda went back downstairs and knocked on the door in the lower hallway; again, no one answered. They must all be at work, Linda thought. This big, formerly posh house was as empty as her own home.

Once outside again, Linda walked to the side of the house which faced the river. She had to walk around a high untrimmed hedge which extended from the left edge of the front porch to a driveway. The hedge hid a graveled parking lot which had obviously replaced a spacious side lawn. There were no cars in the parking lot. An enclosed staircase had been built onto the side of the house, the quality of both the lumber and the workmanship showing it to be a later, inferior addition to the house. Linda supposed that the city fire codes demanded a second exit for second-floor apartments and that this staircase was the crude response. A long window and a side door opened from the ground floor apartment under the staircase, which had been built slanting toward the front porch in order to avoid blocking this door. The opening of the staircase was only about three feet from the hedge. Linda walked all the way to the backyard, which was unkempt and overrun with dandelions. A high unpainted fence separated the yard from the neighboring property. Linda couldn't even see the house next door.

Curiosity drove Linda to return to the foot of the outside staircase. She looked around to see if it were possible for anyone to notice her. To her left was the parking lot and then the railroad tracks; behind her was the towering hedge which screened her from the street. Hitching her purse higher on her shoulder, Linda ascended the narrow, shaky stairs. At the top, a rough shed with only one small, high window surrounded a fine old bay window so that anyone inside looking out would have only rough boards as a view. The window jutted out so far that the passageway past it was wide enough for only one person. On either side of the window, a doorway had been cut into the wall and on each flat, hollow-wood door someone had simply written a number with a magic marker. The first door, at the head of the stairs, had a 2 on it and the one on the other side of the bay window had a 3.

Not quite sure what she intended to do, Linda went back to the first of these doors and turned the knob. It was locked. She turned to the side of the bay window; it slanted outward from the door and obviously had sheer curtains on the inside. Linda put her hands on the window frame and leaned her face up to the screen, trying to see inside. The screen window moved under her hands. For a second, Linda let go and stood back. Then she pushed at one side of the screen; the other side came out of its frame just enough for Linda to get hold of it with her fingertips. She pulled slightly and, after sticking a little, the screen came out very suddenly, falling onto the floor of the little shed with what sounded like a terrible crash.

Linda took a minute to calm herself and to listen for any sounds from outside which might indicate that someone besides herself had heard the noise of the falling screen. After a moment, she moved the screen to one side, leaning it up against the center section of the bay window. The inside glass window was closed, but Linda could see that it wasn't locked. She crouched down and pushed upward on the window's frame with one hand on either side of the glass. At first she thought that the humidity had stuck it fast, but a little motion of her weight from one hand to the other finally produced some movement. At last the window was raised enough for Linda to get her fingers under it and then, with one lift, she had it all the way open. She considered for a second only; then she picked up her purse and crawled through the window.

Linda stood up next to the window inside Ryter's apartment, squinting a little in nervousness. She found herself in a large, long room that was living room, dining room, and kitchen all in one. Just inside the bay window was a large chair whose brown corduroy upholstery was badly worn and even torn on the padded arms. To her left, a television set rested on a metal frame, and next to it was an old-fashioned stereo with a large cabinet. On her right was a sofa, its back to a set of three windows which faced the street. At the end of the room, across the expanse of a braided rug, was a small dinette set with only two chairs and behind it, against the wall, a counter, stove, and refrigerator all lined up in a row. In the far right corner of this wall was a closed door. The room was fairly clean and utterly devoid of anything which might characterize its occupant—no pictures on the walls, no books, no magazines in view. The size and location of the room suggested that it might once have been the master bedroom in the days when the house was a single-family dwelling.

Linda stood near the open window, her heart thumping, beads of sweat beginning to form on her upper lip. The other windows were closed and the heat of the day seemed captured and intensified in the still air. What was she doing here? What did she expect to find? When Lieutenant Willman had told her of his failure to get a search warrant, she had suggested that the apartment might contain enough child pornography to make it clear that Ryter was a deviate, but nothing could look more impersonally normal than this room. Had she imagined that there might be a diary describing past crimes? One look at this room convinced her that Ryter was not the sort of person likely to leave such a clue. Perhaps Willman had seen this too when he came to arrest Ryter and so had not pushed for a search warrant.

Still, Linda felt she could not leave without trying; she had, after all, broken into someone's apartment and to just turn around and leave again seemed to make a mockery of the gesture. She went straight to the left, to the stereo cabinet, not only because it was the only piece of furniture in the room which might conceal something, but also to avoid the front windows whose plain cotton curtains were open. In the exact center of the cabinet's sliding top door was a 35 mm camera with a fitted leather case. The brand name suggested what Linda had already guessed at first glance: it was an expensive camera, seeming wholly out of place in these surroundings where everything else looked second hand or cheap.

Linda squatted and slid open the doors of the record cabinet. About ten albums, all country and western music, were leaning up against the left side of the compartment. To the right was a small stack of magazines, all popular news and gossip publications. There was nothing else. It struck Linda that she had half-expected to find a photograph album or a box of loose color prints. What would Ryter's family photos look like? What would he take pictures of?

Linda went on to the kitchen cupboards. Some of them were just empty; others held small and mismatched sets of dishes, silverware, and kettles. The cupboard under the sink revealed two bottles of liquor as well as the usual cleaning supplies and garbage bags. Linda even opened the refrigerator, not so much that she expected to find anything incriminating as from a certain curiosity about what someone like Ryter might eat. The refrigerator was almost empty; several cans of soda, some wilted lettuce, and a covered bowl with some unidentifiable casserole remains inside provided no further insight into the man Linda so much loathed and feared.

She opened the door in the right-hand corner of the room to find an old-fashioned bathroom. A high, footed bathtub stood near the facing wall; the stool was on the right, both its cover and rim leaning up against the tank; a pedestal sink was on the left, topped by a mirrored medicine cabinet. Linda looked inside the cabinet and was again struck by the absence of personal things; one bottle of aspirin, toothpaste and brush, shaving cream, and a cheap, plastic-handled razor did not fill even one shelf. A small radiator was next to the sink, and another door which opened into the bathroom from the left-side wall was standing ajar. Linda pulled it open and found herself in Ryter's bedroom.

It was a very small room, shaped like an "L" to fit around the bathroom. The size of the room and the cheap wood paneling suggested that this had once been part of a spacious upper hallway. The wall to the left was crowded with a small dresser and a wardrobe. Almost immediately to the right of the door, the room took a right-angle turn to form a small cubicle with a window facing the street; the curtains were drawn, making the room semidark. This cubicle had just enough room in it for a single bed which was neatly made, its pink chenille spread making an unattractive contrast with the orange-and-brown indoor-outdoor carpeting on the floor. Next to the bed, along the wall which must have faced the inside stairway, was a small bedside stand topped by a lamp and an electric alarm clock. This wall also contained the door Linda had seen from the outside when she had climbed the stairs inside the house. It seemed odd that anyone would admit front-door guests into one's bedroom and then escort them through the bathroom before arriving at what were normally considered the "public rooms," but Linda could see that the partitioning of the second floor had made any other arrangement almost impossible.

By this time, Linda was feeling discouraged and depressed, in addition to uncomfortably warm. This room, too, looked austere and blank, as if no one lived there at all and the apartment were ready to show to a prospective tenant. Still, she felt compelled to complete the ritual of searching, as if otherwise she wouldn't be able to justify her actions to herself. She turned on the small lamp on the bedstand, confident that this light could not be noticed through the thick draperies that were closed over the window. The bedstand had two small drawers. In the first one, Linda found an assortment of men's socks, rolled into tight balls, and three crumpled neckties. When she pulled open the lower drawer, her hand leaped away as if she had found a snake inside.

On the plain wooden bottom of the drawer rested a gun—a flat, short-barreled pistol with a long black handle. Next to it was a little box, looking rather like a box of old-fashioned kitchen matches, except that this box was black and had no top label. There was nothing else in the drawer.

Linda stood with her hand against her mouth, staring at the gun. She had at last found something that characterized the occupant of the apartment, and it seemed to confirm in one shocking impression everything she had feared about Ryter. Gleaming black, well tended, and deadly looking, the gun was a fitting symbol of the madness and evil she had seen in Ryter's eyes and heard in his voice. She had never seen a handgun at close range before, having been raised in a household where the refusal to own guns was looked on as a symbol of moral superiority—a mark of status, almost. This lack of experience made the sudden appearance of this particular gun even more horrible to Linda. In her imagination, she could see the gun in Ryter's hand, could see him stepping up to a child on the sidewalk and showing her the short barrel; she could hear his soft, almost feminine voice saying, "Just get in the car and don't make any sound. Smile and make it look as if you know me."

Without any further thought, Linda reached into the drawer and picked up the gun. Holding it by the barrel and keeping her fingers well away from the trigger, she slipped the gun into the center compartment of her purse. She picked up the box and gave it a shake; when the sound confirmed her suspicion that the box contained bullets, she slipped it into her purse as well.

Quite suddenly, Linda felt a terrible need to flee, to get out of the stuffy apartment. Without closing the drawer, she ran back through the bathroom and across the big room. She opened the back door and pulled it shut behind her. Only now did she pause, noticing the screen leaning against the middle of the bay window. She slid the inner glass window down as far as she could, and then snatched up the screen and pushed it back into its opening, pounding with the heels of her hands to wedge it in place. Then she ran down the rickety stairs. Once outside, she paused to pull long breaths into her lungs. Somehow she felt it was not safe to return to the street, so she crossed the little parking lot and walked down the steep embankment to the railroad tracks. Then she followed the tracks to the right until she came to the next street heading away from the river; then she turned right again and circled the block to her car, walking quickly, the purse clutched in her right hand, its shoulder strap dangling against her leg.

Part One

Chapter 1

Across town, in the Holton County Jail, a big police officer was escorting a short, sandy-haired man back to a cell. They had been to the basement office where the short man had just completed a call to his ex-wife, a supervised call for the sole purpose of giving her instructions about the bail bondsman. When the cell door swung open, the short man turned to his beefy companion.

"How about coming in for some cards?"

"No way, Ryter," the big policeman said. "You got me in trouble once already this time around. I don't need any more."

"I'm sorry I fibbed to you about that other phone call, Olson," Ryter said, his voice soft. "But I explained why I had to do that, didn't I? You and me go way back, don't we? And you're not in such very big trouble."

"You didn't hear Willman Friday night. I thought for a minute he was gonna have my badge."

"He's an overreactor, didn't you tell me that? It's over now, and haven't I been a good boy ever since? Didn't I get a nice haircut and a shave and these pretty clothes just for you?"

"Just for the judge, you mean," Olson snorted, but he was beginning to weaken under the cajoling questions. He had known Ryter, on and off, for several years, had watched him sobering up in a cell after "one of his beauts," as the other officers called his drunken bar brawls. When he was sober, he was always a lamb, quiet and docile, and he was a worthy opponent at gin rummy, watching the cards with his hooded eyes and keeping his gloating to a minimum when he won. It was hard at those times to imagine that this plain little man could have been the cursing, raging handful of the night before. And this new charge! Well, Olson didn't believe it. Ryter had been off the sauce for a while now, had shaped up. It didn't make sense to Olson that he would pull something as bizarre as the charges said. "Hysterical women," Ryter had said in his soft, matter-of-fact voice. "Women imagine all sorts of wild things, especially where sex is concerned." And Olson believed him.

"Come on, Olson," Ryter way saying. "There's nobody else in these cells. Who's gonna know if you play a few hands of gin? I ain't gonna tell."

"Okay, for a while," Olson said, leaving the cell door open and easing his bulk onto the cot while Ryter slid the one chair over to form an "L" with the open part of the mattress. "I'll deal first," he said, and took the cards from the prisoner's hands.

Ryter watched the big hands mashing the edges of the cards into each other in the crude shuffle that had always made him seethe with anger. But he never showed any irritation with people like Olson, having learned over the years that stupid people were no challenge to him and could easily be handled by soft words and a pretense of friendliness. Olson wasn't worth his anger anyway; to expend energy on him might blunt the other—the deep rage. Besides, it was hard to tell when fools like Olson might be useful. Friday night, for instance, that slack-jawed gullibility had got Ryter an unsupervised phone call. And right now, cards would help the time to go faster until the bail ticket arrived. Then he would be out, and then, then—

Ryter dropped his eyes onto his cards. He had learned to hide his eyes when he wanted to fool people. Even dummies like Olson might read something there if they looked hard at his eyes, especially when he was thinking what he was thinking now. He had seen the woman in court again, the Hammond woman; she had come to gloat at the first hearing, but this time she had come to try to pretend that she wasn't afraid of him, to try to face him down. Well, he hadn't been faced down, had he? She was the one who had cut and run.

Thinking of her made a wave of fresh hatred sweep through him, which caused a slight tremor in the hands that held the cards. The stuck-up bitch with her slick clothes, dressing up like a man to try to show she was as good as a man. Thinking she was so smart, looking down

at him as if he were some sort of a bug, when he could
rip her in shreds if he let himself, if he could get his
hands on her. He had been so careful, so thorough, but
people listened to bitches like Linda Hammond—bowled
over by her high-toned ways, probably—and that's why
he was here. That's why he had gone through the
humiliating hearings, had to listen in silence to all those
fairies in suits, because of the Hammond woman and her
juicy little brat. Oh, those dark curls, that pink little
mouth—but that was another entertaining meditation,
something for another time, plenty of time to remember
that little girl.

It was the tall cop who listened to Linda Hammond, of
course, the big-city transplant who was so sure of his
own smarts. That first night, last Monday night, Ryter
had seen that Lieutenant Willman wasn't like these other
flatfoots. He was quiet, cool, gave nothing away, but
there was a brain behind those bright, dark eyes, an
arrogance that came from knowing he was smart. Whenever he met someone like Willman, Ryter didn't hide his
eyes, didn't pretend as he did with Olson. He liked to let
such people know—in a subtle way, of course, without
really giving anything away—that they were dealing
with someone as smart as they were. Smarter. It was a
pleasure to let the smart ones know that he was beating
them, was winning. No matter how educated they were,
no matter how uppity, they would have to see, sooner or
later, that the shrimp, the dropout, had beat them, was
smarter than all of them.

Where was Willman now? He had been in court, but
that was two hours ago. Probably sniffing around all over

town trying to find out something. Well, let him sniff. It wouldn't do him any good. There were no tracks to find. If Willman searched his apartment, he would find nothing illegal, nothing to connect him to the Hammond brat, nothing about the others. The evidence was unreachable, except by his own reach, and no one else would ever know where to look for it. It would take an act of God, he thought with a smile that pulled his soft lips away from his teeth. Or a train wreck.

"What you smiling about like a damned cat?" Olson said. "You one card away from gin?"

"More than one," Ryter said, his smile widening. "But I bet I can count on you to give them to me."

When Ryter lost the hand, he just shrugged his broad shoulders, looked down, and carefully gathered the cards together.

Chapter 2

Lieutenant Arnold Willman waited in the locker room of the packing plant, his aquiline nose still twitching from the smell of blood and feces which had poured into his nostrils from the kill floor when the foreman left the room to summon George Pomeroy. Willman was tired; bags of skin hung below his dark eyes, his thin shoulders sagged forward as he leaned against the row of lockers. He had been working nonstop on the Hammond case for days now, following tiny leads and digging up people only tangentially related to the case. There were no big leads, never had been from the beginning. And Willman hated to be rushed. He was such a meticulous detective, so scrupulous about details, that he really needed more time for his investigations.

He smiled wearily to himself at the irony. During the twenty-five years he'd worked for the Chicago police force, his schedule had been demanding, even hectic, most of the time. One of the advantages, he had thought, of moving to a town like Holton was that there would be fewer investigations and he would, therefore, have more time to sift through evidence in the way that would satisfy his passion for certainty, for solutions. Now the first big case that really demanded investigation was rushing him and pressuring him in ways he would not have thought possible. Oh, there had been one murder last year, but the shooter had walked into the station to surrender before the body was even cold. This time, it was the very smoothness of small-town life that was demanding such speed on his part. In Chicago, he could count on the overcrowding of the court dockets to give him at least two weeks between arrest and arraignment. But in Holton District Court, room could easily be made for a "big case" like this one, and the machinery was about to spring Ryter before he, Willman, could find enough stuff to prove how dangerous it would be to spring such a man.

The thought of Ryter made his eyes narrow slightly. Willman was a man without many illusions. He had never imagined that the move to Holton would remove him completely from the varieties of human scum he had dealt with in his years on the Chicago force. The big city might provide creeps in greater numbers, but it couldn't claim any originality in criminal types. Everything from Peeping Toms to sadistic killers—probably every town had at least one of each kind. He had met guys like Ryter once or twice before and was not really surprised to find one here in the sleepy northern town he had adopted and where he was still treated like a stranger. But Ryter chilled his blood just the same. The smoldering hatred, the barely controlled violence, the exalted ego—all combined in a man with obvious native intelligence and cunning—were pretty formidable. He was dangerous all right, because he really believed that he couldn't be stopped, couldn't be held to account for his behavior. And so far, he was very nearly justified in his confidence. It was the sort of thing that made Willman even more determined. And, of course, there was the child, the poor little girl. Willman had always felt fiercely protective of children, their vulnerability evoking in him a deep response that had nothing of the sentimental in it and that had never yielded before the cynicism which clouded almost everything else in his experience.

George Pomeroy brought the smell with him when he finally came into the locker room, looking wary and a little scared, like a schoolboy called into the principal's office.

"What's so important you had to call me away from work?" he asked gruffly after Willman had introduced himself.

"Well, I've got an ongoing investigation on my hands," Willman said smoothly. "You must have read about it in the paper."

"Yeah, but it don't have nothing to do with me."

"You used to live at 7 Carimona Street, didn't you?" Willman asked, flipping open his notebook.

"Sure," Pomeroy said, "but I been gone from there a while now."

"Yes, it seems the turnover in that building is pretty

brisk," Willman said with a little smile. "But you were Ryter's neighbor for quite a while longer than the present tenants. Cromett, the one in your old apartment, has been there less than two months, and the men downstairs not much longer."

"Look," Pomeroy said, leaning forward so that his blood-spattered apron came alarmingly close to Willman's jacket, "I was no friend of Jack Ryter's. Whatever trouble he's got himself into ain't got nothing to do with me."

"I'm not saying it has. I'm only hoping you can tell me something useful about the ways he lives, about his habits."

"His habits used to be getting drunk and making noise, though that stopped a few years back. After that, I didn't see or hear much from him, and I was just as glad."

"Did he have people over? Did you hear him with anyone in his apartment?"

"No, sir." Pomeroy was calming down now, beginning to feel a little self-important in his role as informant. "He never had nobody over at all that I know of, even when he was a drinking man. Did his drinking in bars or alone in his bedroom. Then he played his stereo real loud and screamed at me when I pounded on the walls. He was a real loner, I guess. Ain't that always the way with them perverts, though?"

"Do you know anything about any interests he might have had, any groups he might have been associated with, the names of any of his associates?"

"I don't think he had no associates," Pomeroy said.

"Couldn't seem to get along with anybody very long. Let's see. There was that camera business."

"Camera business?"

"Coupla years ago. Ryter got some fancy camera, Lord knows where, cuz he never got any money. Then, first thing you know, he's using part of the basement for one of them darkroom places, to develop his own film. Landlord was pissed when he found out about it, cuz the chemicals was eating up the old sinks down there. But, you know, old Jack talked him into letting him keep it up, told him all about how he'd took a course special at the Vo-Tech just so he could make his own pictures, how it was helping him behave, stay sober."

"So, he went on developing pictures?" Willman was finally interested, his keen eyes alight.

"Sure. At least till the time I left. I don't know about after, cuz I ain't seen Ryter or that house since."

"Did he take lots of pictures?"

"I don't know."

"Did you ever see any of these pictures?"

"No, sir. Not a one. Like I said, Jack Ryter was no friend of mine."

"And you have no idea what he took pictures of?"

"No, I don't. His kid, maybe. Or maybe he got all artsy-craftsy and was chasing butterflies and clicking away at wild flowers down by the river. I got no idea."

"Anyone else you know ever see the pictures?"

"Not that I know of. I heard the landlord saying the room in the basement was always cleaned up real good, though, nothing laying around down there—not a scrap."

"Okay," Willman said. "Can you think of anything else?"

"Nothing."

"Well, thanks. If you think of anything at all, give me a ring, will you?" He handed Pomeroy his card. "My home phone number is on there, too."

As Willman turned to leave, Pomeroy said to him, "So, do you think he did it?"

"That's what I'm trying to find out," Willman said tonelessly, without turning around again.

"Hard to believe, though," Pomeroy said. "Here in a place like Holton, I mean. The guy was a drunk, sure, and he could talk plenty mean, I remember, but *this*—I mean, he's got a little girl of his own, don't he?"

"That doesn't always mean anything."

"Well, I don't know if I believe it," Pomeroy said, shambling back toward the door. "This sort of thing happens, I guess, but not around here."

Willman compressed his lips, holding back any reply. When he stepped out of the air-conditioned locker room into the street, the oppressive heat settled on him again, seeming to bend his tall frame even more forward as he headed for his car.

Chapter 3

After Linda left Ryter's apartment, she drove around aimlessly for a while, her heart slamming, sweat collecting in the hollow of her throat. What should she do? Should she drive out onto the bridge and throw the gun into the river? Should she take it to the police? Perhaps Ryter had stolen the gun and that would be something else to charge him with, to keep him in jail. But how on earth could she explain having the gun herself? Ryter could just deny that he had ever had it, and she would have admitted to breaking and entering. She might be arrested herself.

Without consciously choosing it, Linda suddenly found herself on her own street, the car already turning into her driveway. She hurried into the house, a powerful impulse to hide the gun making her feel panicky, as if she expected someone to appear at her side door asking if he could search her purse. She pulled out the little kitchen ladder and climbed up onto the countertop, gasping a little from the heat concentrated so near the ceiling. Without examining the gun, but handling it gingerly, she slipped it behind her best crystal glasses in the narrow top cabinet. Then she dug out the box of bullets and put it next to the gun. When she finally sank down onto a kitchen chair, her head was buzzing, her hair soaked with sweat.

What had she come to? Who would have imagined that a life so conventional as her own could so quickly deteriorate into a furtive half-life in which she would steal and hide guns?

Nine days. Just nine days ago, in what seemed now like another century, she had been a normal, ordinary woman in a tidy middle-class home, preparing dinner like any other homemaker and mother. It was the fish she remembered most clearly, the fish filets—and the clock, the Early American kitchen clock which had first brought the nagging edge of fear on that Monday afternoon in Linda's other life.

It had been almost 6:20 when Linda began to feel faintly uneasy that Dana hadn't come home from her Girl Scout meeting. Summer vacation had already begun and the Scout leaders needed only a short planning session for a midsummer trip to an amusement park. Dana Hammond was a responsible, serious eleven-year-old who would not dawdle past a time when she knew her mother would begin to worry; the short walk from the Wardens' house should have brought her home by 6:10 at the latest.

Linda was washing fish filets and running her thumbs over the pieces, checking for bones. She was a tall, self-contained woman who never exhibited any of the flapping, semihysterical behavior that she found so distasteful in other people. Her concern expressed itself now in a slight squinting of her hazel eyes as she glanced at the kitchen clock. By 6:30, the fish was ready for the oven and Dana still wasn't home. From long habit, Linda decided that a quick phone call was preferable to further worry, particularly since she was a woman whose imagination manufactured graphically frightening scenarios which the more rational side of her was almost powerless to banish. Such phone calls, Linda suspected, had gained her something of a reputation as an overprotective mother, but she was willing to accept the charge if it meant that scenes of madly careering cars, gathering crowds, and approaching ambulances stayed out of her head.

"No, she's not," Pam Warden said in her chirping voice. "The meeting was over a little before six, and all the girls left right away. Maybe she went over to the Wielands' with Jenny."

"I'll give them a call," Linda said, but her stomach was knotting and a familiar tingling at the back of her scalp announced the onset of panic. By the time she had called the homes of all six of the other girls in the troop, it was almost 7:00; no one had seen Dana since 5:55.

Linda stood with her hand on the phone, swallowing convulsively and struggling to control her breathing. If she called the police, what would they say? Even in a town the size of Holton, the police must be hardened to stories of eleven-year-olds who were late for dinner. They would probably tell her to wait an hour or two and then call back; maybe they would even suggest that Dana was a runaway, a phenomenon so ordinary that the police would not even be very interested. But she knew she would have to call; waiting another hour alone was out of the question, and the police, at least, knew about accident calls.

The dispatcher, a woman, said, "Just a moment, please," after Linda had explained her reason for calling. There was garbled talk in the background, and then the dispatcher said, "Two officers will be right there, ma'am."

"Has there been an accident?" Linda gasped, stunned by this ominously prompt response.

"No accident, ma'am. The officers are on their way."

In the seven minutes it took for the squad car to arrive, Linda sat in the chair next to the front door, her hands pressed against her short hair, thinking dully that it would be easier somehow if she had another adult to talk to, to worry at; one of the hardest things about being a single parent was that there was no one to say, "You're being silly. Don't overreact."

Both of the police officers were very young, both looked away from Linda's questioning eyes.

"We got a report about six-fifteen from a lady on Seventh Street," one of the policemen said, looking steadily at the band of his hat which he held in his hand. "She saw a man take a child into a car and drive off, and she said it looked like the child didn't want to go."

When Linda could breathe again, she said, "My daughter has short dark hair, and she was wearing a red windbreaker over her Girl Scout uniform."

"That fits the description the woman gave," the other policeman said. "The man was short, brown hair, maybe about thirty the woman said, driving a tan car; she didn't know what model." He looked questioningly at Linda.

"I have no idea who that might be," she said.

"We thought it might be the father. You know, a child snatching."

"No, not possible. Dana's father lives in California, and I assure you he would not snatch her. We've been divorced for five years and he seldom takes advantage of his regular visiting privileges. My daughter's been kidnapped and I want to know what you're doing about it."

Linda had taken refuge from her panic in anger, instantly convinced that Dana was the child the woman had seen; nothing else would explain her failure to come home.

"There's an all-points bulletin out," the dark-haired policeman said. "The lady said the car went west on Seventh, so that's where we're starting."

Linda sank down onto the chair again, numb, feeling nauseated.

"That was more than an hour ago," she said. "How can you find them? She could be anywhere."

"We're doing everything that can be done," the blond officer said—they seemed to take turns talking—but he must have recognized the hollowness of his reassurance because he blushed when Linda looked up at him.

"If it's a kidnap for ransom, there might be a phone call," the dark policeman said. "We'll stay here with you to monitor the call if it comes in. Do you have an extension?"

"In my bedroom," she murmured, lifting her hand to point. "First door on the right at the head of the stairs. But you don't think it's for ransom, do you? School-teachers don't attract that kind of kidnapper, do they?"

The officers looked at each other briefly and then down at their hats again. The phone rang, its sound like an explosion in the room. Linda sprang to her feet as one of the officers sprinted up the stairs. The other stood ready to signal Linda when to lift the receiver, which vibrated under her hand with the third ring.

"Linda?" a man's voice asked in answer to her "Hello."

"Yes."

"This is Hal. You didn't sound like yourself."

Hal Lawrence was a counselor in the junior high school where Linda was a special education teacher.

"I can't talk to you now, Hal," Linda said. "We think Dana's been kidnapped and I have to keep this line open in case someone tries to call."

There was a short pause, and then Hal said, "I'm coming right over," and he hung up. One of the things Linda liked about him was his steady calm.

Linda made coffee, got the young officers to sit down after one of them had called in to headquarters from the squad car. She herself kept moving from room to room, stashing the fish in the refrigerator, wiping the countertop, carrying the coffee pot out to the living room to serve more coffee to the policemen; her hands did not shake.

Hal Lawrence arrived about 8:00, and Linda pulled the door open for him before he had a chance to ring the bell. He was a nice-looking man with pleasant wrinkles around his pale blue eyes; at forty-three, he had patches of silver in his hair, a reassuring fullness in his well-muscled torso. When he took Linda's elbows in his hands, she could look almost even into his face, for he was only slightly taller than she was.

"No news," she said. "Would you like some coffee?"

"I'll come with you to get it," he said softly, his face and eyes expressing the concern and sympathy he did not voice. He stood with her in the kitchen while she told him what little there was to tell, and though he didn't touch her again, he stood close, the coffee untouched in his cup. With no more than nods and small murmured sounds, he poured a sort of balm over Linda's raw nerves.

They had worked together in the same school for four years. Linda's students were Hal's most frequent clients, for Linda taught the learning disabled who, by the time they got to junior high, had often developed emotional problems that sent them to a counselor on a regular basis. He was a good counselor, too, patient and kind, but firm in providing guidance. When his wife had died of cancer two years earlier, Linda had watched with bemused detachment as the single women in the school district began to hover over the widower, bringing him food, inviting him over for dinner. Always a deliberate, reticent person, Linda had held herself aloof, if anything becoming even more formal with Hal in an effort to disassociate herself from the predatory behavior which embarrassed her. Gradually, she had come to see that, under his unfailingly polite exterior, Hal was also embarrassed, even angered, by the overt attentions of these women.

Then, in the past few months of this school year, he

had found more and more cases that he needed to discuss with Linda, stopping by her homeroom three and four times a week, lingering to visit even when there was no more to be said about the student he had come to discuss. Still, it was only after Linda's friend and colleague Susan Fisher began to tease her about her "beau" that Linda began to wonder if the attraction she felt for Hal Lawrence might be reciprocated, so slow was she to hope in matters of the heart. Her divorce had done that to her, among other things. Now Hal stood next to her at the kitchen counter as if it were his place to be there, and she felt a certain wonder that it should seem so normal to her, too.

On the other side of the house, the front door slammed loudly and, even in her numbed condition, Linda felt a flash of irritation at the young policemen; if they must be in and out, they could move more quietly, she thought, show some respect for a person's nerves.

"Ma'am?" one of the officers called, sharp, peremptory.

Linda crossed to the dining room and stopped short as the scene in the living room registered with her like a freeze-frame shot at the end of a movie: the two policemen standing in the middle of the room holding bright blue and yellow coffee mugs and between them, wide-eyed and rumpled, Dana.

Chapter 4

For three of four seconds—the time it took for Dana's glance to find her mother—no one moved. Then Dana began to run and Linda found that her legs would no longer hold her up. She sank to her knees on the rust-colored carpet, her arms thrown out in front of her. The child jumped across the last two feet and landed against her mother's chest and shoulders.

Linda sat down on her heels and pulled Dana onto her lap, trying to cradle all of the angular preadolescent body against her breast and stomach. In her anguished relief, she found that what she wanted to say, to cry out, was, "Why did you ever learn to walk? Why did you ever separate yourself from my body, get so far away that I couldn't protect you anymore?" But she only said, "Baby, baby, my baby," over and over, rocking Dana back and forth while the three men stood helplessly by. Dana cried, but quietly, without hysteria.

At last, Linda let Hal raise her to her feet, but she wouldn't set the child down; she carried her to the sofa and sat down with Dana in her arms.

"Are you hurt at all, baby?" Linda said. "Tell me if you're all right."

"I'm not hurt," Dana whispered. "I got away. I jumped out of the car, and I had to hide for a while, and then I ran home." She made a gasping sound, the aftershocks of crying, and then said, "It was Chrissy Ryter's father."

Linda blinked for a moment, her brain struggling to focus; she had been so sure the man would be a stranger.

"The Ryters live in the yellow house at the corner of Cass and Eighth," Linda said to the policemen. "At least the mother and daughter do. They're divorced and I don't know his address. I don't even know his first name."

The blond policeman headed for the squad car while his partner sat down to face Linda and Dana.

"Just try to relax, little lady," he said. "In a few minutes, you can tell us everything that happened, so you'll only have to do it once, okay?"

Dana nodded, blinking gamely through her tears. Now that she had absorbed the fact that she was safe, that policemen and her mother were in control, she was beginning to take an interest in the fact that Hal was there and that she was the undisputed center of attention. She sat up without letting go of Linda and said, "I'm kinda thirsty."

"I'll get some milk," Hal said.

"Kool-aid, please," Dana said, and all the grownups laughed, much too loud and much too long for just Kool-aid.

"Glasses are in the first cupboard to the right of the sink," Linda said, looking up gratefully at Hal.

When the blond policeman came in again, he said, "Lieutenant Willman is on his way. We can get some preliminary information before he gets here."

"How well do you people know Chrissy Ryter's father?" the dark-haired officer asked Linda.

"Hardly at all," Linda said. "I think I've seen him only once, from a distance. The Ryters were already divorced when Dana met Chris, the daughter. They played together sometimes during the third and fourth grades, after we moved to this neighborhood. Dana always tries to befriend kids who seem shy or out of it." Linda paused to stroke her daughter's face, to straighten her hair with her fingers. "Sometimes the father was visiting when Dana played over there. Then the girls grew apart this last year. That happens at this age. Chris isn't in Scouts and doesn't skate, so they didn't get together after school. I've seen the mother shopping at the Kwik Trip, but I've never actually met her." Linda felt numb; these people were neighbors.

Dana drank the Kool-aid Hal had brought her, gulping it all in a few seconds. Then she looked up at her mother half-guiltily.

"I didn't get in the car on purpose, honest I didn't, Mom," she said. "I said, 'No I don't need a ride' and I tried to walk away, but he pulled me."

"Oh God, I know that, honey," Linda said, hugging

her hard. "It's not your fault, none of it is your fault. A lady saw him pulling you into the car and called the police. That's how we knew you'd been—taken." At the last second, Linda edited out the word "kidnapped."

An awkward silence fell. Everyone seemed embarrassed by the unnatural postponing of questions and answers, yet all seemed constrained to wait for the lieutenant, to keep to the young officer's notion that Dana should have to tell it only once. When Lieutenant Willman arrived, the blond policeman let him in. Linda remembered reading about him in the newspaper when he had first come to Holton three years earlier. Arnold Willman had been a Chicago policeman for twenty-five years before "retiring" to become an investigating detective on the Holton police force. Linda saw now that he was a tall man in his early fifties, almost bald, with sharp dark eyes that looked out of a lean face; he wore casual but well-pressed clothes. He introduced himself all around, moving slowly and deliberately, handing his jacket to the blond policeman before he sat down at one end of the sofa. The dark-haired officer went out to the squad car while the blond one took out a notebook and pencil.

"Well, Miss Hammond," Willman said gently to Dana. "Do you think you feel up to telling us what happened?"

Being addressed in such a formal way seemed to make Dana aware that she was still sitting on her mother's lap; she slid down onto the sofa, but remained close up against Linda as she straightened and arranged herself. Her heart-shaped face and hazel eyes made her resemble Linda despite her much darker coloring. There was something in the strong-jawed lifting of her head that also suggested her mother's control, a habitual composure only rarely shaken by the weeping from which she had now recovered.

"I suppose I should start right at the beginning," she said.

"That would be a good idea," the lieutenant said, smiling with his eyes even though his thin face remained otherwise unchanged.

"I was walking home from Scouts along Seventh Street, the way I always take. A car went past and then stopped. Mr. Ryter got out and came around to the sidewalk to ask if I wanted a ride. I told him it was just a little ways and that I always walk. He said again that he wanted to give me a ride and he stood in the sidewalk in front of me. When I tried to walk around him, he grabbed my arm and pulled me toward the car, saying all the while that it was a nice car and that I should like a little ride."

Talking about it seemed to take the child back to the experience; she snuggled against Linda, resting her head on her mother's shoulder.

"I suppose I should have yelled or screamed or something, but he just kept on talking, real quiet, and pretty soon I was in the street on the other side of the car. Then I jerked to get away, but he kinda threw me into the front seat and jumped in. The car was still running and he just drove off, but not this way. He turned at the next block. I told him it was the wrong way, but he laughed and held onto my arm when I tried to slide over to the other door."

"Did he say anything else to you after that?" Willman asked.

Dana looked down at her hands and tugged at her thumbnail for a moment.

"He said I was a pretty girl and that we were gonna have fun."

There was no surprise in this for Linda, but even so it took an effort of will for her to control her breathing.

"Did you notice where the car was going at this time?" Willman said.

"Yes. We were down to Second Street by then and going out towards Pilsen's Landing. Whenever we came to a stoplight, he would grab onto my arm. Then, when the light turned green, he would let go to start the car going again."

"You mean to shift?"

"Yes, shift. Most of the time there were lots of cars on both sides of us, but I didn't yell. I don't know why."

"Did he ever touch you except to grab your arm?"

"Sometimes he would hold me here," Dana said, indicating her left thigh. "And then he would put his hand between my legs—up high. I kept pushing it away and he would laugh."

"Any other touching?"

Dana looked down again and breathed a shuddering sigh.

"At one stop sign where there were no other cars, he held the back of my hair real tight and he kissed me."

"On your mouth?"

She nodded and then turned her face to Linda's ear to whisper, "He pushed his tongue in my mouth."

Linda looked up at Willman to see if he had heard. He nodded, his eyebrows puckered into the kind of frown Linda remembered her father making if anyone used foul language in his presence.

"Was anything else said?" Willman went on.

"I was telling him I had to go home, for him to take me home right away. Then he said, 'You can get that idea out of your head, cuz you're never going home again.' "

Willman's frown deepened and he exchanged a puzzled glance with Linda.

"Those were his exact words?" he asked.

"I think so, yes," Dana said. "Is it important?"

"You're doing fine," Willman said, smiling for the first time. "What then?"

"I could see that the next stoplight was the last one before the street gets out of the city—you know, out by the hockey field—so I figured I had to do something. When he let go of me to shift, I jumped for the door. He caught part of my jacket, but the car swerved a lot, so I could pull loose. I got the door open and jumped out. I fell down and rolled over. My knee is scraped a little."

She pointed to her right knee where a patch of dried blood showed above her knee socks.

"I ran into the hockey field and behind that hedge that runs along the street. I could see the car where he had stopped it. Then he turned around, right in the street, and started driving along the hedge. I ran all the way to Laird Street where the bleachers are and I hid under them. Jenny and I play there sometimes when I visit her, and we know the best places. I saw the car go around the block a coupla times."

She wiped her face quickly, embarrassed to have the tears starting again.

"Then he stopped again on Laird Street and just stayed there for a long time. I don't know how long, but the sun finally went down. I thought I should try to run again, but I guess he saw me cross the street, because I could hear the car start up again real fast, you know that squealing that tires make. I hid in that new housing development where nobody lives yet until he drove past. Then I ran to the next building to hide again. It went on like that for a while."

"He was looking for you all this time?"

"I guess so. He was driving around and around. I ran down to the river where there's all that tall grass, and I just kept following the river back and hiding whenever I heard a car."

"Did he keep hunting for you in his car?"

"I don't know. Cars went by, but most of them had their lights on by then, so I couldn't tell who it might be. I just ducked down whenever I heard a car."

"Why didn't you try to go to somebody's house when you got back into town?" Linda asked softly.

"I don't know," Dana said after a little pause. "I guess I was scared to talk to anybody. I stayed in backyards mostly because I thought he might see me if I went to the sidewalk. I knew the way home and that's what I wanted to do—just get home."

"It's more than two miles from that project to here," the blond officer said. Linda buried her face against Dana's hair and rocked her back and forth for a while.

"You've done very well, young lady," Willman said at

last. "You're a very brave and resourceful girl. You did just what I would have done under the circumstances."

Linda looked up at Lieutenant Willman, her eyes stinging with tears of gratitude. It struck her that he knew exactly what he was doing, deliberately using the weight of his title, his authority, his public persona to reassure a frightened little girl that she had done right, had no reason to feel ashamed or somehow implicated in the crime of which she had been the victim.

The dark-haired officer stuck his head in at the front door.

"They got him," he said. "It just came in on the car radio. He was just sitting in his apartment when they knocked."

Again Willman frowned; it was clear that he had not expected this.

"I'll want to question him right away," he said. "We're finished here for now," he added, and he stretched himself up to his full height, reaching behind himself for his jacket without looking at the young officer who held it.

Linda followed Willman out onto the porch.

"You were surprised that Ryter said that to her about never coming home again, weren't you?" she asked.

"Frankly, yes," he said. "I've been around child molesters before, lots of them. They usually keep right on trying to reassure the kid that she—or he—will be home soon, that everything is sort of normal. This sounds, I don't know, kinda—sadistic."

Linda felt her heart lurch, for it was exactly the word

which had occurred to her when Dana had been telling about it.

"Anyway," Willman went on, "he sounds like a bad lot. Did he ever make a move for Dana in the past that you know about?"

"No," Linda said, "and I *would* know about it, Lieutenant. Dana tells me things. We've talked often enough about touching and privacy; she would know enough to tell me if he had even made her uncomfortable by the way he looked at her."

"Well, I'll keep you posted." Willman started down the steps. "We should probably arrange a lineup to have Dana identify him, just to be on the safe side. I'll let you know."

"Thank you, Lieutenant," Linda said. "I'll want to know about every step involved in putting that monster behind bars."

Willman glanced back up at her and smiled slightly before heading off at a sloping gait toward his unmarked car.

Hal stayed for another hour and a half when Linda asked him to. They made French toast for Dana after Linda had washed and bandaged her knee, but drank only coffee themselves. When Hal left, Dana was watching a sitcom on television. Linda stood on the porch with Hal for a few minutes.

"I don't think I can tell you how glad I am that you were here," she said, looking down at the wrought-iron railing.

"I hope I was some help. Elaine and I never had

children"—he paused, clearly debating with himself about whether or not to confide further. Deciding, he added— "*could* never have children, but I can imagine what you must have been going through. I'm just glad I happened to call when I did."

"I never did ask you why you called in the first place," she said, smiling and looking up at him.

He shrugged and looked away.

"I called to talk to you," he said. "School's been out a week and I was missing you."

"Good," she whispered, talking hold of the lapel on his soft corduroy jacket. "I was missing you, too."

He looked back at her with a little smile and covered her hand with his own.

"I'll call you tomorrow, okay?" he said.

"Okay." She didn't go back inside until his small blue economy-sized car had pulled away from the curb.

For the first time in years, Linda sat in Dana's room while the child fell asleep. During the months following the divorce, she had done this often, for Dana, then only six, had been constantly worried that her mother might disappear, too. Now Linda sat on the straight-backed chair she had painted white to match the desk and watched Dana's sleeping face. Only now did the mother react to the events of the evening, absorbing them enough to form a mental and emotional stance toward them. She had always been slow to react, giving the appearance of being calm in a crisis when really she was only emotionally numbed. It wasn't that she froze; she was able to function normally at a physical level, adding to her reputation for being "good under pressure."

Once when she was in college, she had been struck by a slow-moving car as she hurried across the street on her way to a class. The impact had sent her sprawling onto the pavement, her books and papers flying all over the grass in front of the library. She remembered clearly that her only reaction had been to say "Oh," in soft surprise as the car struck her legs. The driver was another coed who became so instantly and so thoroughly hysterical that Linda had to comfort and reassure her, and then drive the girl's car to the health center so that someone could repair her torn knees. Only when she was sitting on an examination table did she begin to feel the physical symptoms of fear and shock; the nurse found her shaking and perilously close to throwing up.

Now sitting in the semidarkness, she was shaking hard, for she was beginning to imagine what that two hours had been like for Dana; she was feeling along her own nerves the terror, the confusion, the revulsion. Tears coursed down her cheeks, but she made no attempt to wipe them away. She tried to remember how she would have felt about all of this at Dana's age, but she realized at once that when she was eleven, kids like herself didn't realize there was such a thing as the sexual abuse of children. Yet she could remember the dread she had felt thinking that "bad people" might take her away from her parents; sometimes that dread had made her afraid even to go out of the house.

Now her stomach twisted with rage as she considered what effect this experience was likely to have on Dana's future; she knew her daughter well enough to know that Dana would struggle against her fears, her shaken confidence in the safety of her world, but the shadows had closed on her and the sun could not shed the same assurance that it had warmed her with yesterday. Linda saw already that she would have to help Dana by repressing her own terrors, by resisting the impulse to tie the child to her side. She stood up and crossed the room to close the window; in the northern regions of the Midwest, late spring still brought chilly nights. But she was not ready yet to leave Dana's room.

When she sat down again, she pulled an afghan up around her shoulders. She remembered suddenly that she had been rinsing fish filets at the very time Dana's ordeal was beginning; how odd that she could have been so obliviously occupied while horror was stalking her child. That simple task seemed to have happened years ago. It belonged to a past that was now irrevocably gone, to a world that she had suddenly lost and over which she now shed tears of real grief and longing. She felt betrayed, as if everybody and everything in her life had been lying to her for all of her thirty-four years. The quiet middle-class upbringing in Minneapolis had told her, "You're safe." Her kind, well-educated parents had implied that she was immune to those sordid things they heard about on the news. Her education had promised that the world would give her a humane and ordered existence; even if her work brought her into contact with some people who came out of those places where parents beat their children or drunkenly slashed at each other with kitchen knives, she herself would not be touched. When she took the job in Holton after getting her M.A., everyone said what a nice town it was, what a good place to raise children.

It was not that life had never disappointed her, never presented her with unexpected shocks. There had been her divorce with all its attendant feelings of failure, loss of sexual confidence, guilt about Dana. And her father had died suddenly of a heart attack the next year, her beloved father who had always been the fortress from which she could sally forth with the assurance that she was "covered" by protective cannon at her back. When her mother had moved away from Minnesota a few months later, she had struggled against the terrible sense of aloneness, of feeling abandoned. But never before had she felt that pure evil had reached out to touch her, had risen up from its warren to blow its foul breath into her face. She felt both outraged and terrified, exposed as she used to feel in those childhood dreams where she tried to run from some creature so awful that she didn't dare to look around at it, those dreams in which her legs wouldn't move or the door to safety wouldn't open. In less than two and a half hours, a nightmare had come true, had made itself a real place in the snug, comfortable world she used to think was so invulnerable.

She wanted to run into the quiet street shouting, "You've got to make it right! You've got to fix it!" But she only reached out to push a dark curl to one side of Dana's forehead.

Chapter 5

On the morning after the kidnapping, Linda had made a big breakfast for the first time since summer vacation started: bacon, eggs, muffins, and juice. Dana liked to help with breakfast, and it gave them both a safe feeling to be working together in this way. They ate mostly in silence. Neither felt ready yet to discuss the events of the night before. Dana reported that she had slept well with no dreams, but she seldom remembered her dreams anyway. Linda said that she had slept "sort of okay," but this was not true; she had slept hardly at all.

After breakfast, Linda felt an urge to clean, to make the already tidy kitchen sparkle, to vacuum carpets and polish tables. Dana seemed to understand almost instinctively and pitched in without a grumble, though she never grumbled much about that sort of thing, being a compliant, easy-going child. They worked for two hours, always in the same room with each other, often close enough to touch or for a pat or an elbow squeeze. Neither one of them even suggested going outside, though the beautiful June day looked in at them with its sunshine and yellow-green new grass.

The house was special to both of them because it was a fairly new step up from the tiny apartment they had left two years ago, and also because Linda had made the down payment with part of her modest inheritance from her father. Dana still had strong memories of her grandfather, who had adored her and played with her when her own father was already a distant and somewhat forbidding figure. The money, along with the divorce settlement, had also seen them through Linda's master's degree program, so she could finish all at once instead of struggling with night classes and summer school for five or six years. When Linda thought about her job in Holton or, especially, when she looked at this "two-bedroom dollhouse" (as the real estate ad had called it), she thought of her father taking care of her even from the grave. Doing her work well, taking pride in it, was a way of honoring him, and so was keeping the grass trimmed or washing woodwork as she was doing right now.

Linda didn't realize how tightly wound she and Dana still were until the phone rang, and both of them jumped as if it had been a firecracker. It was Hal.

"No, we don't know a thing yet," Linda said in answer to his questions. "Nothing since you left last night."

"Surely you have a right to know whether or not he's in jail," Hal said.

"Lieutenant Willman said he would keep me posted."

"Maybe you should call him."

"Maybe I will if we don't hear anything before lunch."

"Would you two like to get out of the house for a while this afternoon? I could drive you to the lake or something."

"Thanks, Hal. I think that would be nice, but Lieutenant Willman said something about being available for a lineup and I think we should wait to hear from him."

"And it's a little too soon yet, isn't it? To go out, I mean?"

"Yes, a little too soon." She was happily surprised that he understood so easily what she was feeling.

"Can I call tonight?"

"Please do. About ten-thirty?"

"Sure. After Dana is asleep?"

"Yes."

By 11:30, Linda was feeling anxious and irritated enough to call the police station. Dana sat next to her, wide-eyed and quiet.

"The lieutenant is with District Attorney Gordon," the dispatcher said when Linda had identified herself and asked for Willman.

"Let me speak to someone in charge then," Linda said.

"Sergeant Olson," a laconic voice said into her ear with a slight rising inflection at the end, as if his name served the double purpose of identifying himself and asking, "What can I do for you?"

"This is Linda Hammond. My daughter was abducted yesterday, and I'm interested in knowing what has happened to the man who did it."

"Oh yes, Mrs. Hammond." The voice was now animated; apparently the case had livened up the whole police force. "He's right here in a cell, ma'am. Lieutenant Willman is getting the D.A. to bring the charges. He should be getting back to you pretty soon, now."

"Thank you," Linda said. "Should I wait for his call?"

"I think he'll come over there, ma'am."

Willman arrived at 1:00, alone this time, his tall frame seeming to fill the screen door as Linda went to unlock the inside front door.

"We made the arrest last night," he said, sitting in the chair Linda indicated. "We can do that on something called 'police presumption of guilt' without a warrant."

"Has he confessed?" Linda said, putting her hand onto Dana's knee. The child sat forward, eager to hear, her trust in Willman obvious; surely he would be able to make bad people tell the truth.

"Not exactly," Willman said, keeping his alert eyes on Linda's, not looking away in embarrassment as the young officers had done when they felt they were giving bad news.

"Meaning?" Linda asked, confused.

"He doesn't deny that Dana was in his car. He says he was just driving through the neighborhood to see if his own daughter might be playing outside. When he recognized Dana, he says, he offered her a ride home and she accepted. He says he left her off a few minutes later at the end of your block.''

''Liar!'' Linda cried. ''What about the witness? What about the fact that Dana came home bleeding and frightened almost two hours later?''

''He says Mrs. Denser misinterpreted what she saw, that he was only holding Dana's arm as he escorted her to the driver's side.''

''Why would he take her around the car at all? And she was struggling to get away. Didn't this Mrs. Denser say so? Wasn't she sure enough to call the police?''

''Yes, that all impresses District Attorney Gordon. But Ryter says he just has a habit of taking 'ladies' to the driver's side, and Mrs. Denser must be somebody who has nothing better to do than to look out her window and make up fantasies about what she sees. He says that it's not his fault if a kid comes home late and then makes up wild stories to keep her mother from yelling at her.''

''You believe me, don't you?'' Dana spoke for the first time, her face pale and her eyes moist.

''Yes, Miss Hammond, I do,'' Willman said, turning his dark eyes onto Dana. ''But I think you have to know what he's saying, so that it won't upset you when you hear it in a courtroom later. I talked to him for a long time and *he* never got upset.''

''Okay,'' she said softly. ''I see what you mean. I have to be calm, huh?''

''That's right,'' he said and smiled, a seemingly rare event that brightened his face and made him look very different.

"Will there be a lineup?" Linda asked.

"Not much use to it," Willman answered. "He doesn't deny being with Dana or being seen by Mrs. Denser."

"So what's next?" Linda was bringing her anger under control again.

"Well, I need this young lady's help for about an hour," he said. "That is, if she feels up to showing me where she hid in the hockey field and in the housing project."

"Sure," Dana said brightly. "Are we gonna look for clues?"

"As a matter of fact, we are," he said, obviously pleased by her quickness. Then to Linda he added, "Gordon would be happier if we can verify Dana's story with some physical evidence. That was sort of my specialty in Chicago, gathering physical evidence, I mean."

"Mom gets to come along, right?" Dana said.

"Right," Willman said, standing up.

Linda found the excursion harder than she thought she would. Dana seemed unperturbed in the bright sunshine with the towering policeman at her side, but Linda found her imagination reenacting the scenes all over again as she saw where they were originally staged. Under the bleachers at the hockey field, Dana pointed out the place where she had knelt in hiding, and Willman, armed with a flashlight and pocketknife, carefully dug out a small patch of grass that was stained with blood from Dana's scraped knee. The blood had dried to a dark brown, but Linda's stomach still lurched at the sight of it. At the housing development, they walked around for a long

time before Willman found some threads from the knitted
cuff of Dana's jacket; she had pointed out a pile of
lumber where she had crouched for a few minutes, and
the fibers were tucked neatly inside a splinter on one of
the boards. They also looked all along the soft shoulders
of the road, but found no tire tracks other than those
made by heavy construction machinery.

When they were home again, Linda sent Dana upstairs
"to read for a while" because she wanted to speak to
Willman alone.

"What we found today will help?" she asked.

"Very much. It will confirm that Dana was out there,
that her story is credible."

"Story?" Linda said, an edge in her voice.

"Look, Mrs. Hammond," Willman sighed. "I'm on
your side, on Dana's side. I absolutely believe she is
telling the truth. It's the D.A.'s job to convince a jury
that she is, though, and this John Charles Ryter is one
cool customer."

"What does that mean?"

"I talked to him for more than three hours last night,
and he never budged an inch, never got excited, even.
He did his 'concerned father' act for me, too. Didn't he
have a child of his own, just Dana's age, and didn't he
know what a worry kids can be? Why he often came
around just chancing that he could have a little extra chat
with his girl, because kids growing up without fathers
have a tough time nowadays. He only gave Dana the ride
because he knows she's in the same boat—worse, because she almost never sees her father."

"So," Linda said, her eyes narrowing. "He means to

and decent and kind, like Hal or Jerry Fisher or Lieutenant Willman.

"Or Grandpa," Dana said.

After dinner that night, Linda began to wonder if she should call her ex-husband. Was it something he had a right to know about immediately, not just in a letter? Would it help or comfort Dana to talk to him? And could it be misinterpreted later in a courtroom if Dana could be made to say, "No, we didn't tell my daddy right away"? Linda shivered a little when the question came into her head; already, they must begin to think of how things would sound in court. Dana had seen her father only twice in the past two years, spoken to him on the phone perhaps a half-dozen times. The distance was all of Daniel Hammond's making. When Dana was supposed to go out to Sacramento to visit, he would force a cancellation at the last minute, arguing that his accounting firm kept him too busy for long-range plans. His phone conversations with Dana were short and brisk. He had remarried a young woman with two small children, and seemed determined to break almost completely with his first family.

When they had finished the dishes, Linda said to Dana, "I think maybe we should call your dad and let him know what's going on."

"Sure," Dana said. "Just a letter would be kinda cold."

Linda looked hard at her daughter. She was open-faced and eager, not a trace of resentment in her face or voice. Her remark about the letter was utterly sincere, the irony unconscious—Dan seldom wrote more than a quick note in answer to Dana's letters. Thank God for this kid, Linda thought, and hugged her for a long minute.

"They oughta castrate the bastard!" Dan said after Linda had briefly explained what had happened to Dana. Linda thought the outrage sounded a little forced, stagey, but she was willing to admit to herself that her ear might be tainted by her own resentment.

"There's going to be a little hearing soon, and then the trial, I guess," Linda went on. "The police are sure of a conviction."

"Well, I should hope so," he said. "Poor little mutt." The last part was muffled as if he had shifted the phone from one hand to the other while he was saying it.

"She's right here if you want to talk to her."

"Gee, babe, I'd like to, but we're getting ready to go out here, just going out the door, as a matter of fact."

The "babe" was a new development, just since his move to California, and Linda wondered if his new wife was listening to his side of the conversation.

"Just give her my love, will you," Dan went on, "and tell her I'll be calling real soon. Will you do that for me, babe?"

"Certainly, Daniel," Linda said, keeping the worst of her anger out of her voice in order to spare Dana. "I'll give her that message."

"Daddy had an appointment he was already late for," Linda said after hanging up. "Remember, it's two hours earlier in California." She recognized that the last sentence sounded pretty lame. "He says he'll call you soon."

"It's okay," Dana said, but her face was clouded.

"Look, honey," Linda said, taking Dana's chin in her right hand. "Your dad can't be here for us. Now that's too bad, but we can be just fine by ourselves, too. We have each other to pull ourselves through, right?"

"Right," Dana said and smiled again. "Daddy can't help it that his job is in California. Should we call Grandma, too?"

"No, honey," Linda answered. "I'll write her a long letter tomorrow. And you know we'll have to play everything down, or else Grandma will think she should do something, and there's nothing she *can* do from so far away. It isn't a good idea for her to travel, especially in the summer, but she'll think she has to come unless we make her think everything is under control."

Linda's mother had moved back to her home state of Georgia, where her brothers and sisters all lived, within a year after her husband's death. "Without your father, I could never stay warm in Minnesota," she had said tearfully. She now suffered from emphysema, the sad result of thirty years of chain-smoking, and seldom left her air-conditioned apartment in the summer.

Later, when Dana was asleep, Linda sat in the living room and thought through her call to California. Finally, she had to admit to herself that the real reason for her decision to tell Dan on the phone was her own residual hope that it might change him, might reverse his growing indifference. She still harbored, somewhere, a reflex need to lean on him, to demand his protection. Maybe she had even had an unconscious hope that the crisis would bring him to Holton to see them through the trauma. She remembered how, during the divorce, she had even sometimes fantasized that she would contract some terminal disease and Dan would come back, repentant and transformed. She had believed that all her reconciliation dreams were long dead, but now she realized that there were still some that needed drowning. Dan's lack of response on the phone had provided a big drowning tank.

She had married the handsome man-most-likely-to-succeed Daniel Hammond while they were both at Macalaster College, and had loved him fiercely almost until the end. She realized now what an incredible naïf she had been, projecting the model of her parents' marriage onto all marriages, believing simply that the late nights and long silences were to be expected of a man building his own company. She had missed completely the exchanged glances of friends, and so she had remained wholly unsuspecting until the night she had caught her husband with Dana's babysitter, a college girl Linda had hired for her one-night-a-week psychology class. The class was an effort to finish her interrupted graduate study without inconveniencing Dan; he had to work late, he said. When the eight-week class was dismissed an hour early, Linda had returned home to find them on the sofa.

Remembering, she could see again the image she had spent almost six years trying to banish from her mind: Dan's head coming up from inside the girl's opened shirt, his mouth still open, a fine strand of saliva connecting him to her breast, and above his dark hair, the girl's smug little face, looking neither surprised nor guilty.

In her outraged innocence, Linda had, in the view of some of her friends, "overreacted." But as the divorce proceedings went forward, she began to learn more and more about his other affairs: his secretary, a woman he had met at his tennis club, the wife of one of his partners. The humiliation was worse with each new disclosure. Each time she would confront him with a story, he would confirm it, saying over and over, "I can't help it. I just can't help myself," as if she must accept this as a given and take him back. But, at the same time he was smashing the trust she had invested in him, he was also planting in her head the notion that some men were apparently unable to control themselves sexually, and you could not tell ahead of time which ones they were. So it was that, even six years later, when she was trying to reassure Dana that there were decent, good men in the world, her list was so pathetically small and did not include the child's own father.

When the phone rang at precisely 10:30, Linda felt embarrassed that she had forgotten almost completely that Hal was going to call.

"How is Dana doing?" he asked. "Did she get to sleep all right?"

"Yes, fine," Linda said, thinking that, within thirty seconds, Hal had expressed more concern for Dana than Dan had done earlier in the evening.

"And how are you doing?" he said, and the balm of his voice seemed to enter her head from the telephone receiver.

"We had quite a day," she said and told Hal all about it, right through the call to California. They talked for more than an hour.

"How about if I take you ladies to lunch tomorrow?" he said at last. "And if it's a nice day, we could go to the park after that."

"We'd love to," Linda said, feeling girlish and a little giddy. "What time should we look for you?"

"About twelve-thirty?"

"Fine. We'll be all gussied up."

"See you then."

Linda went to bed and slept soundly for four hours. Then she wakened to find Dana standing beside her bed, her white nightgown luminous in the dark.

"Can I get in with you?" Dana whispered.

"What is it, honey?" Linda asked, making room and pulling Dana down beside her. "Did you have a bad dream?"

"I don't know." The child's voice was shaking. "I just woke up feeling scared, real scared."

Chapter 6

Willman had called the next day just as Linda was writing "Wednesday morning" on the top of the letter to her mother.

"The hearing is at ten-fifteen tomorrow morning in county court," he said. "Fourth floor in the courthouse."

"Thank you for telling me," Linda said. "Have you come up with anything new from his apartment or his car?"

"Haven't looked at either one."

"Why not?"

"He admits that Dana was in his car. He used no weapon of any kind. The D.A. says a search warrant wouldn't help—whether anything could be used as evidence, I mean."

"Do you mean he could have an arsenal in there or

three tons of pornographic material and nobody can look for it?''

"You see, Mrs. Hammond," Willman said, using his patient voice, "a search warrant must state specifically what we're looking for, and that specific something must be related to the alleged crime or crimes. Otherwise, it's illegal search and seizure. Besides, while I was in his apartment the other night, he invited us to look around, said it would be all right for us to look in his closets and drawers. I don't think he would have dared that if he had anything illegal in there. We're all right, though, don't you worry. This is just the first hearing, and I'm still checking out leads, interviewing people. This is an ongoing investigation, as we say in the business."

"I'm sorry, Lieutenant. I'm being overanxious, I suppose. I shouldn't try to tell you your job."

"I understand," he said, and he sounded as if he really did. "No need to apologize. I'll see you tomorrow morning."

"Oh, will you be there?"

"Oh yes, ma'am. The arresting officer files a report for the record."

Dana watched a game show on television while Linda finished her letter and called her friend Susan Fisher.

"My God!" Susan gasped. "It was Dana? The paper didn't give the child's name."

"It's in the paper?" Linda said. Since Monday night, she had not been out the side door of the house where the paper girl always left the newspaper. She had not even thought about papers for two days.

"Front page," Susan answered. "I tell you, I had another of those 'talks' with Erin as soon as I read it, about screaming blue murder if anyone ever tries to grab her. Who would have thought it would be Dana?"

"Could you take Dana for a while tomorrow?" Linda said, cutting straight to the point. Susan was a dear friend, but a born chatterer who would go on commiserating for an hour if given her head, and Linda had not begun to get ready for Hal's arrival. "The creep goes to court in the morning and I plan to be there."

"Of course, certainly." Susan was eager to help.

"I'll bring her over about nine-thirty. Maybe it will help Dana to talk to another child so near her own age. You know how she is; I don't think she'll scare Erin by talking about it."

"A little scaring wouldn't be a bad thing."

"We can talk when I pick her up." Linda's tone said that it was time to end the conversation, and Susan had a keen ear for her friend's signals.

Linda dressed carefully, pairing her green silk blouse with a fawn-colored skirt she hadn't worn in years. All the time she was fussing over her makeup, one part of her mind was wryly amused over a thirty-four-year-old woman getting ready for a "date" with a man she had known for four years, a date that included her daughter. But still she applied the mascara carefully, highlighted her cheekbones with blush, pouted a little at herself in the mirror after brushing on a coppery shade of lipstick. Her short, naturally curly hair looked shiny and fashionably fluffed around her face; once blond, it was now a pale brown. All in all, she thought, surveying herself in the mirror, not bad, not bad. Her father had always said she had "good bones," and it was true; she might not be a knockout beauty, but she was likely to age well.

"You look gorgeous," Dana said when she came downstairs.

"Thank you, ma'am. So do you."

Dana had only one skirt, preferring to live most of her life, at home or school, in jeans and knit tops, the "uniform" of school children in Holton. A ruffled white blouse, bought at the same time as the skirt, completed her outfit, and she had painted her toenails to show off her new sandals.

Hal pronounced them both "lovely" and took them to a smart little basement restaurant downtown. He looked all brushed and polished himself, in a navy blazer and gray slacks, his open-collared shirt faintly redolent of a musky after-shave lotion. Linda watched him during lunch, seeing him with new eyes. Wasn't it odd, she thought, that they had seen each other every working day for all these years without particularly noticing each other's clothes? At least *she* had not noticed what he wore. And now they were dressing for each other.

He spent much of the time in the restaurant charming Dana. He was attentive to her, almost courtly, listening seriously to what she said, talking easily about rock groups and sticker collections. Of course, his work exposed him to such preteen obsessions, but Linda found herself marveling that a man who had no children of his own could be so natural and relaxed with an eleven-year-old. Linda remembered that Daniel had always seemed awkward around Dana from the time she was an infant, as if she were some family pet he thought might suddenly bite him. Dana glowed under Hal's attention, becoming animated in her conversation, giggling behind her hand.

Linda wondered if Hal was aware of how much he was winning the mother by wooing the daughter. Crazy modern world, she thought, when a man courts a woman, not with flowers and candy, but by being nice to her children. But it was working. Once, when Hal looked across the table at her, Linda's face must have been so eloquent that he blushed almost immediately and looked away.

After lunch Hal drove them to Nelson Park, a picnic and playground area that fronted the river. Only after they had walked around for fifteen minutes did they realize how overdressed they were for the setting. Then Dana spotted Jenny Wieland, her best friend, and was soon running and playing despite the skirt and ruffles. Hal found a bench from which they could see all the playground equipment and wiped it down with his handkerchief before motioning Linda to a seat.

"She had a bad night last night," Linda said. "Had to crawl in with me. But you'd never know it to look at her now, would you?"

"Well, you look pretty wonderful yourself," he said, "and you must have had a bad night, too, if she was having nightmares."

"You are gallant, sir." She laughed. "Come to think of it, I haven't slept much since Monday night. Dana is doing better in that department than I am."

"I guess kids don't have to worry as much. That's what they have mothers for."

"I'll do better, I think, when I can see this Ryter character is being kept off the streets," Linda said. "I suppose I also just want to see him, to make sure he doesn't have a tail and cloven feet, that he's just a man after all."

"Have you always gone to look instead of running away?"

"Are those the two 'types'?"

"Pretty much. Adrenalin makes you attack or run. I'll bet you never were one to hide under the covers when you heard a noise."

"No, I didn't," she said, looking at him in mild surprise that he should have such accurate insight into her. "I used to get up to see what it was, even when I was a kid. It wasn't that I didn't feel scared, because I sure did, but I always figured that I'd get more scared if I just had to imagine what the noise could be."

"Yes, that's what I would have guessed about you," he said, smiling at her. From this close vantage Linda could see the fan of nice laugh lines forming around his eyes, eyes which looked bluer outdoors than they did at school. "I think you're right to take that approach. You'll probably find that you're dealing here with one of those pathetic creeps who will finally admit that he needs help and just pleads guilty to avoid a trial."

"I wish I could believe that," Linda said. "Lieutenant Willman described him as a 'cool customer' and even used the word 'sadistic' about him. He hasn't wavered a bit in his story."

"A few days in jail might melt his cool, don't you think?"

"Well, he's been in jail before. He's no stranger down there."

"But this is much more serious trouble than he's been in before. He's never been looking at a prison sentence until now."

"Why do you think he would suddenly try something like this, with no history of it before? And he wasn't even drinking."

"Well, I'm no psychiatrist," Hal said, "but I sometimes work with parents like this in some of my toughest cases at school. Men who relate badly to adults, who are suspicious loners, sometimes turn to children for their emotional needs when there's some crisis in their lives. It's a typical pattern in incest cases, at least."

Linda shivered a little despite the sun.

"Let's talk about something else, okay?" she said.

And they did. Hal talked about his late wife, how they had been best friends as well as "old marrieds," and told Linda about his boyhood on a Wisconsin farm where, as one of six children, he had been "blessed" with a sense of responsibility and a love of the outdoors, which he still indulged by gardening and hiking.

"I'm an avid walker myself," Linda said.

"I know," he said and blushed a little. "I used to watch for you in the parking lot until Susan told me you always walk to school. Walking is so much saner than all this jogging and running, don't you think?"

"And easier on the arches," she laughed.

"There," he said. "That's the laugh that looks so good. You have very nice teeth." Then he flushed. "Good God, what a dumb thing to say!"

"No it isn't," Linda said, touching his arm. "It's very sweet. I *should* have nice teeth. My father was a pediatric dentist and half of his friends were orthodontists. No kid's teeth ever got so much attention."

"Well, it's all paid off," he said. "You know, I don't know why I'm having so much trouble making small talk. I guess I'm pretty rusty at—" he paused, groping for the words, turning red again. "In this area of life," he finished lamely.

"You're doing just fine," Linda said. "Just fine." And she gave him a smile that showed even more of her expensively straightened teeth.

When Jenny's family left the park, Linda and Hal collected Dana and started back for the car. When Linda almost tripped on the shaggy terrain, Hal offered her his arm, and they walked the rest of the way to his car with her forearm resting against his side, her fingertips reaching almost to his wrist.

Chapter 7

At the same time that Linda, Dana, and Hal were walking across the park, John Charles Ryter was finishing a phone call to his ex-wife. He had tried to be subtle, to work the subject gradually around to his need for a lawyer, but Sandy had short-circuited his plan by saying, almost immediately, "You should get a lawyer, Jack."

"You say that like you think I done it," he said, instantly offended.

"I'm not saying any such thing."

"That Hammond brat is lying, that's all. You remember what a stuck-up little puss she was when she used to come over there with Chrissy. Didn't she dump Chrissy? Didn't you tell me that? Well, this is just a scam to get herself out of trouble. She ran off and was late, and she don't want that tight-assed mother of hers to be scream-

ing at her, so she makes up a story about my taking her
for a ride."

"Okay, Jack."

"You believe me, don't you, Sandy?"

"Sure I do." The voice was the same tired sigh he had
grown so weary of in the seven years they had been
married.

"Well, maybe I do need a lawyer, being that this is a
teacher's kid telling the lies. The thing is, I don't have
the bread to hire no lawyer."

"That's too bad, Jack, but don't they give you a
lawyer if you can't afford one?"

"I don't want none a them court-appointed shysters,"
he flared. "I been there before. Do you think you could
scrape up something to get me a real lawyer? I got some
hearing coming up tomorrow."

"I got less than you do, Jack. You ain't even sent the
support checks lately."

"I'm drowning here and you're talking about support
checks."

"I got nothing, Jack, not even anything I can hock."

On the way back to his cell, Ryter remembered all
over again the reasons he had divorced Sandy. Every time
he saw her, with her washed-out, rabbity face, or heard
that whining voice, he was amazed that he hadn't just
killed her instead. But she was the mother of his child—
he actually thought the phrase whenever he got especially
sick of Sandy, or wanted to smash in her spiritless face—
and the phrase stopped him. From the time Chrissy was
born, there had been no sex with Sandy—the thought of

it made him gag—and it was a relief to be relieved of the duty. It was hard for him to believe that he had ever felt obliged to marry her just because she was pregnant. Moment of weakness. But he felt a confused warmth for Chrissy. That was why it maddened him so much to see her becoming more like her mother every day.

When the door clanged shut, he flung himself onto the cot and covered his eyes with his right forearm, the one with the tattoo. He had to concentrate hard to steady his breathing, to keep his teeth from grinding. This was the feeling he hated worst in the world—the feeling of helpless rage. When some guy cut him off in traffic or somebody lipped off to him in a public place where he couldn't make a scene, his stomach boiled with this rage, the desire to smash and bloody the offender who remained maddeningly beyond his reach or too powerful to challenge safely. At these times, his head would feel like it was swelling, a pressure at his temples that almost made him dizzy.

It was the very earliest feeling he could remember. At three and four and five, when his father would beat him, sometimes so hard that blood would come up in the welt marks from the belt, this rage was already growing in him. His father had seemed like a giant then, so toweringly enraged that any display of anger or defiance from his son might have pushed him over the edge into murder. So the boy had learned to pretend passivity, to avert his eyes and still his panting chest. But the rage was eating him up inside.

By the time he was a teenager, he was already trying to escape through drink. Whenever he was made to feel powerless, whenever the pressure in his head got to be too much, he would simply drink himself into unconsciousness. At seventeen he left his parents' house for good and wandered from job to job, from state to state, never in any one place for more than a few months, investing his earnings in liquor and prostitutes. A brief stint with a carnival had brought him to Holton, where the river and the quiet streets and the pretty houses called to some deeply buried image, something absorbed from television and never part of his own experience, something he would have laughed at if anyone else had talked about it—a notion of home.

But the drinking was starting to get him in trouble by that time. What used to be a relief to his rage had begun to aggravate it. When he had just a certain amount of whiskey, he seemed to give himself permission to bash people for the smallest annoyance; sometimes he even picked the fight himself. And, when he was in this state, he felt he could beat anyone to a pulp, no matter how big or mean-looking. Half the time he took the worst of the beating himself. Most of the time he woke up in a cell the next morning feeling worse than ever, having to grovel to the stupid cops because he had taken a swing at one or two of them while they were bringing him in. The pressure in his head had tripled with a hangover and the prospect of courts, fines, and more swallowed rage.

And here he was again, only in much bigger trouble than when he'd been a heavy drinker. What made his anger even deeper was that he had been fouled up by such a little slip: he had imagined that the kid was too scared to try anything. Who would have thought she would make a break for it from a moving car? And he had been so careful, so patient, so ready—all gone in a second! He had followed her for months, learning her habits, finding out about her music lessons and her Scout meetings, watching what routes she walked, observing when she would be with friends and when she would be alone. And the advantage, of course, was that she knew him slightly, had met him when she used to play with Chrissy. She would not take immediate fright, because she would recognize him. And it had worked, just as he had planned, except for the nosy old dame poking her nose out from behind her curtains—but she didn't get a license number, so she wouldn't have mattered if only the kid hadn't got away. After all his plans.

The first one hadn't been planned at all. It had just happened.

After the last bar fight, the one that had got him into such a mess that he hadn't done much drinking since, he had left Holton to look up an old buddy who had moved to Louisiana as a construction foreman saying, "If you ever need a job, Jack—" Somehow he felt there might be something good about starting all over someplace where he wasn't known, where people weren't such jerks as they were in Holton. He had tried not to notice that the old buddy, Terry Goltz, didn't seem exactly thrilled to see him. For three days he stayed in a motel, the money going fast, driving over to Goltz's nicely trimmed little neighborhood every day to see if "something" had turned up. On the fourth day, Terry had not even let him into the house.

"I'd like to help you, Jack," he said through the

latched screen door. "But there just isn't anything on my crew right now. Doesn't look like there will be for quite a while, either. You know how it is."

"Sure," Ryter had said. "Sure, Terry. Things are tough all over."

And he walked away with his temples throbbing so much that he thought he might scream. At the end of the block where he had parked, he found a crying child standing next to the bike she had just crashed into the side of his car. A long, fresh scratch ran along the lower half of the door and the bicycle was a wreck, its front fork bent against the wheel.

"What the hell you done to my car?" he said to the little girl.

She cowered away from him, but showed no disposition to run.

"I wish you wouldn't fuss at me," she said. "I didn't mean to hurt your car. My bike is ruined and I hurt my leg." Her lips trembled and she looked close to tears. She was pale and blond, with close-cropped hair and a pouting mouth; the Southern accent sounded foreign to him, like some ugly alien language.

Before he could stop himself, Ryter had grabbed her arms and was shaking her, shaking her so hard that her head wobbled and fear came up into her eyes, fear that made him feel glad. He could see her poising herself for a shriek, so he clamped his right hand over her mouth. She struggled madly, but he wrenched her around and got his left arm around her waist. He looked all around himself. The street was quiet, no traffic in this after-dinner hour. A lawn slanted sharply uphill to a hedge, behind which he could see only the roof of a house. He lifted the child—she was no more than ten—and carried her quickly around to the driver's side of the car. He started the car and put it in gear before letting go of her mouth. As the car pulled away, he could feel the back wheel going over the bicycle.

He drove until it was dark, never letting go of the girl for long. He didn't hear what she was saying through her blubbering; oh, he knew she was talking all right, but the words didn't register with him. Finally he turned off the road into a winding gravel lane and stopped the car.

"Now," he said. "You are going to find a nicer way to talk to me. You surely are."

She made a jump for the other door and he grabbed her. She kicked at him, lashed out with her little fists. It was a pleasure to attack her, to violate her, a sexual pleasure he had never known before in his life. As long as she struggled, or cried, or pleaded, he renewed his assault, and it gave him a feeling of exaltation, of power that was almost as good as the sexual release, that heightened the sexual release. He enjoyed her screams, wanted to hear her beg. Finally he heard something that stopped him. Just as she was nearing numbed shock, she whimpered, "I'll tell. I saw you at Mr. Goltz's house, and they'll know who you are."

He sat up among the scattered clothes, his mind still. He had felt anonymous here, so far from his usual haunts. When he left Terry's house, he had thought that he might get some dynamite and just blow up the whole block. Then he could drive out of the state. No one knew him. No one could touch him. Now the brat had said,

"I'll tell," and she actually knew something she could tell. He reached for her face in the darkness, feeling her try to twitch away from him. He caught her jaw and then closed his other hand around her thin throat. When he had finished strangling her, he was surprised to find that he had another erection. He used her still-warm body to take care of it. Then he pushed her out of the car and threw her clothes out after her.

When he reached a gas station, he used the self-service island and just drove off without paying; he had no money anyway. He drove all night. When it was light enough the next morning for him to see the blood on the plastic upholstery, he stopped long enough to get a ragged shirt out of the trunk and wipe the seat clean. Then he threw the shirt into the ditch and started for Holton. For a long time, he was frightened that he would be found out, but nothing ever happened, and that was three years ago now.

Chapter 8

Lieutenant Willman was driving north on a country road outside Holton. He had spent much of the morning on the phone, talking to people in Illinois who had known Ryter, or known of him, while he lived there. It had been a depressing few hours for several reasons. He learned nothing of value about the suspect. And the voice of a woman police dispatcher had reminded him uncomfortably of his ex-wife.

It had been twenty years since the divorce, and he had not seen Marilyn more than three or four times in all those years, but there was still some pain somewhere inside whenever he thought of her. The youthful passion they had started with carried them through the first years of marriage, but it couldn't hold against the growing bitterness she felt about his work. The unpredictable schedules, the overtime, the all-night stakeouts, the vice squad duty in sleazy places, and, above all, the constant fear for his life turned her first querulous and then sullen.

The conversation he remembered best had taken place after he had made sergeant and was assigned, more or less permanently, to crime-scene evidence gathering. Encouraged by the raise in salary and the relative stability of his assignment, he had again raised the subject of children. He had campaigned for years to get Marilyn to agree to have at least one child, but she had always put it off with, "Not now. When we're more settled—when you decide if you're going to stay on the force or not." He had always ignored the implication of blackmail in the latter excuse, pretended he hadn't understood the trade she was suggesting. But after the promotion, he had renewed his case.

"We're not getting any younger, Marilyn," he had argued. "We want to be around when the kid graduates from college, don't we?"

She had turned to him, her grey eyes cold and hostile.

"I don't think it's such a good idea to bring a child into this marriage," she said. "A baby won't change anything."

After that, the silences grew longer, and then Marilyn finally moved out. No quarrel, no blowup. Just a silent dissolution of what was already dead. Willman had settled quietly into an austere bachelor's life, but a certain tone, a certain down-state Illinois accent on the phone could still make him wince.

After the calls, he had gone to the plastics factory where Ryter had worked since the previous August to interview co-workers at the lunch break. The foreman had looked angry at the mention of Ryter's name, but he told Willman that a man named Scott Fitak was "about the closest thing to a friend Ryter had around here." After the usual protestations about not being very friendly with the accused, Fitak had loosened up and talked about a time earlier in his acquaintance with Ryter when they had gone duck hunting together.

"It was last fall, after he'd just started here, when he was still working the day shift with us. Coupla us guys got a hunting shack in the wetlands up past Pilsen's Landing—good spot for ducks. So we took Ryter along a few times. He was a lousy shot, didn't know beans about shotguns, though he said he'd hunted before. We didn't believe him much, even before that."

The reference to Pilsen's Landing was the only lead Willman took away from the interviews at the factory. It was the road to Pilsen's Landing Ryter had started on just before Dana Hammond got away from him. Willman got Fitak to give him detailed instructions about how to find the shack, and he had started out after grabbing a quick sandwich for his own lunch. After a few wrong turns, he finally came upon the ramshackle building, tucked away among the scrub trees that bordered the swampy wetlands. There was no other building for miles around.

Fitak had told him there was no lock, so he just walked in, not pausing to scrape off the wet clay that stuck to his shoes once he had left the graveled lane. It was a windowless, cramped place with chinks of light showing through the walls. There was a small wooden table in one corner and four metal folding chairs leaning together against the wall next to the table. The rest of the floor space was taken up by a cot, whose sagging mattress was covered by a clear plastic sheet. The roof looked snug enough against the rain, but a smell of damp and mold permeated the shack anyway. Willman guessed that the worst of the smell came from the mattress; the ticking, which had once been a blue and white stripe, was now an almost uniform grey. He had to hold his breath as he bent to look under the cot, where he found several coils of light rope and twine.

The floor, he noticed, was stained in various places, dark patches on the unpainted boards. Was it blood, he wondered. Duck blood, probably. It was easy to imagine the hunters just dropping their kill onto the floor before going out to hunt again. If he were to call in the state lab boys, what would they find? Ryter's fingerprints? But that would be useless; Fitak had told him that Ryter had been here several times. It wouldn't prove that he had been here recently or that he had been preparing this shack for some evil purpose. Willman sighed and went back outside.

At the car, he scraped his shoes back and forth on the gravel, trying to get rid of the clinging mud. Then he stood up and looked all around again at the thin white birch and the scrub pine, at the waist-high weeds which grew up from the acres of wetlands that stretched all the way to the river. The sun had gone behind some clouds and the wind was still chilly on that early June Wednesday. Willman pulled his jacket tighter around himself, his stomach knotting a little as the breeze brought the marshy smell of the swamp into his nose. God, what an awful place! What if Ryter *had* planned to bring Dana Hammond here? She would immediately have seen the hopelessness of her situation, for she was clearly a bright girl. She might not even have bothered to scream—except in pain. Willman shivered again. And afterwards? What would have become of the child afterwards? There were so many places around here to dispose of a body. Such a little body would be no trouble, no trouble at all.

But it would be best to keep his suspicions about this place to himself. Probably no hard evidence existed to support his theory, anyway. And he didn't want the child to think about the man actually *planning* her abduction in advance. The mother didn't need any more worries, either. She was an intelligent woman, brave and calm— Willman had admired the way she handled the child on Monday night—but she had had a bad shock and didn't need another. He just wished he had more solid evidence for the hearing in county court on the next day. It was the hearing where bail would be set, and Willman wanted the bail to be high, very high. He had a bad feeling about John Charles Ryter, a deep intuition that the threat of punishment meant nothing to the sneering, cocky little man. Yes sir, jail was the place for that guy.

Chapter 9

*L*inda had always admired the Holton courthouse as a piece of architecture. It was a massive five-story structure built with various colors of local sandstone in what was called "Prairie Gothic" style, its round turret making it look somewhat like a medieval castle. It had sometimes seemed to her that the building reflected Holton's siege mentality, the townspeople standing fast against anything they would have called "newfangled," raising these walls to intimidate any outsiders who might try to bring changes.

Linda had arrived early and found the county courtroom quickly; the sign next to the door said "Judge Dennis O'Reilly." She waited on a bench outside until she saw Lieutenant Willman coming down the hall, his tall frame sloping forward a little as he walked. He smiled when he saw her and, once again, the hawkish features were transformed into a pleasant face.

"You can just go on in," he said. "Take a seat anywhere behind the railing."

Linda followed him inside and, although she was aware of a few other spectators already in the gallery, walked past them without glancing to either side. She sat down in the first row behind the railing, on the aisle where she could look straight up at the judge's bench, which was unoccupied at the moment. Standing at a table inside the railing was Paul Gordon, the district attorney. Linda knew him slightly because his son, Jason, was a student at the junior high, a bright kid who was also a "little stinker," as Hal said, one of those class clowns who try to overcome both brains and small size by entertaining the regulars. The father was a short, bald man, who had the habit of holding his glasses against the bridge of his nose while he talked. He dressed expensively and was said to have political ambitions. Willman went through the little swinging gate and began a whispered conversation with Gordon.

The remodeling which had been going on at the courthouse ever since Linda and Dana had moved to Holton had not yet reached the fourth floor. The gallery seats were old and hard, and the room was not air-conditioned. Two large fans stood at the front of the room, but the morning was still cool enough to make them unnecessary. Linda sat very straight, her shoulder blades resting lightly against the wooden chair back, her hands folded loosely in her lap. Her slight squint was the only betrayal of her nervousness.

A door to the left of the judge's bench opened and a uniformed policeman brought in John Charles Ryter. As the police had first told Linda, he was a short man, about five feet six, with nondescript light brown hair cut in the shaggy way that suggested home barbering. He wore blue jeans and a tan, short-sleeved shirt. His chin was almost on his chest, and he didn't lift it until he sat down at a table with his back to Linda, so she got only a vague impression of his face—blunt nose, clean-shaven jaw, no view of his eyes at all. He did, after all, look quite ordinary—a little, square-built man with slumped shoulders. No swagger, no cloven feet.

A bored voice intoned "All rise," and Judge O'Reilly swept in saying "Be seated" before anyone could stand all the way up. He was a large, square-faced man who looked as if his judicial robes annoyed him, got in the way of his headlong rush to get the court dockets cleared. He glanced quickly through the brief in front of him and then, snatching off his glasses, asked Gordon to proceed.

In his public voice, which was very different from his ordinary voice, Paul Gordon read the charges, "kidnapping and criminal sexual conduct in the second degree," and went on to say that the charges were based on "the incidents occurring on the night of June 11, Monday." Then Lieutenant Willman, speaking clearly but quietly and referring frequently to his notes, outlined those incidents. To Linda, the officialese was more horrifying than a simple description would have been; when Willman read "oral and genital contact," she twitched as if someone had poked her between the shoulders. She calmed herself by reasoning that such jargon must save time in these brief hearings.

When Willman had finished, O'Reilly turned to Ryter, who might, up until this moment, have been invisible.

"Do you understand the charges against you?" the judge barked.

"Yes." Ryter spoke so softly that Linda could hardly hear him.

"Have you retained counsel?" the judge said.

"No, I really can't—"

"Speak up, please." O'Reilly was almost shouting now.

There was a pause and when Ryter spoke again, it was louder and, Linda thought, with a certain edge.

"No. I can't afford no lawyer."

"Do you wish to have counsel appointed for you?"

"Yeah. I guess."

"Counsel will be so appointed. Anything else?"

"Your Honor," Gordon intoned. "The state requests that bail be set at fifteen thousand dollars."

"Pretty steep, isn't it?" O'Reilly seemed not to like District Attorney Gordon.

"Not in this case, Your Honor," Gordon went on, oblivious to the irritation of others. "The nature of the crime is such that the release of the defendant would be inimical to the public safety. Moreover, Your Honor, in a previous assault charge against the defendant, he is known to have threatened the complainant and several witnesses; those threats caused the complainant to refuse to testify."

Linda looked sharply at Willman and caught him just looking away from her.

"Both the victim and the witnesses in this present case should expect the state's protection," Gordon concluded solemnly.

"All right," the judge said. "Bail is set at fifteen thousand dollars. Mr. Ryter, you may post bond or have some licensed bondsman post it for you. Your first appearance in District Court will be within ten days of this hearing at which time you will enter a plea to the charges outlined here today."

And that was all. The policeman stepped forward to escort Ryter from the courtroom. As he stood up, Ryter turned his head and looked straight into Linda's face as if he had known all along that she was there, known all along who she was. Linda felt the breath knocked out of her as surely as if she had been punched in the stomach. Ryter's eyes were set deep inside a prominent brow ridge; they were very pale, almost colorless eyes, and the look in them struck instant terror in Linda. It was not that the look was a standard narrowed-eyes look of hatred or malevolence; he held his eyes very wide open and his forehead was smooth. It was just that his eyes looked so cold and yet so *knowing* that Linda thought they didn't look human; they looked insane. It was not a long glance, perhaps no more than four seconds, but Linda felt her hands beginning to tremble before Ryter had looked away.

Willman was coming through the gate now, and he stooped to take her elbow. She walked numbly beside him into the hallway.

"You're shaking," he said.

"He looked at me," she said. "Ryter looked at me so—" She broke off because she couldn't think of the words to describe it without sounding like a hysterical woman. Willman had a worried frown when she looked up at him.

"It gave me a chill, I guess," she said dismissively. "What did Mr. Gordon mean by Ryter threatening people in the past?"

"I told you about the time he was charged with assault in a bar fight," he said, but he looked embarrassed and couldn't meet her eyes.

"You didn't tell me that he got out of it by threatening people," she said evenly.

"Well, just the victim that we know about for sure," he said.

"How do you know?"

"The guy told one of the officers who went back to talk to him."

"Told the officer what?" Linda's voice was getting edgier all the time.

"He said that Ryter promised to kill him if he testified." Willman came out with it at last, looking straight back into Linda's eyes.

"And you couldn't do anything about that?"

"Well, I wasn't here at the time," Willman said with a wry smile. "But the officer couldn't do anything more than urge the man to go ahead and to add the threats to the charge. There were no witnesses to the threats, though, and the man just flatly refused to testify, so the charges had to be dropped."

"John Charles Ryter must be a very frightening man," Linda said, searching his eyes.

"Not necessarily," Willman said gently. "You've got to remember what kind of a person this so-called victim is, too. Not exactly a solid citizen, you know. It would have been hard to prove who started the fight. I don't think it would take much to make this guy back off. He may have exaggerated the threats to get off the hook with the D.A."

"But you didn't tell me about it."

"You already had a lot on your plate, Mrs. Hammond. No sense my adding to it for no reason."

"Now listen to me carefully, Lieutenant," she said, looking at him hard. "I do not wish to be 'protected' by ignorance. Not knowing things brings me no reassurance. So, please, from now on, no secrets, no minimizing, no fudging. Deal?"

"Deal," he said. "You're a pretty tough lady, aren't you?"

"Not so tough," she said, managing a little smile as she remembered her conversation with Hal. "It's just that I find hiding scarier than facing the bogeyman."

Willman's smile broadened, showing a row of surprisingly small, even teeth; he looked younger when he smiled.

"Is this District Court appearance going to be the trial?" Linda asked as they started toward the elevator. "Will Dana have to be there?"

"Oh, no," and he chuckled at the thought. "That *would* be a speed record. First appearance in District Court is when the defendant enters a plea to the charges, and motions are made by both sides. The prosecution presents a 701 file, which includes any statements made by the defendant to law enforcement officers and any evidence which might be subject to constitutional question. Then the district judge decides if the accused should be bound over for trial.''

"I had no idea this was all so complicated," Linda said, shaking her head.

"You asked for the truth, so here it is," Willman said. "It could be months before the trial. Even a court-appointed attorney will use all the stall tactics."

Linda stopped short to look up at him.

"Why should his lawyer want to stall?"

"For things to quiet down, for people to forget. And now that he's getting a lawyer, it will be Dana's turn to be investigated, you know."

"Investigated?" Linda's jaw dropped.

"Sure. Her friends and her teachers will be interviewed; your friends, too."

"What for?" Linda couldn't contain her outrage. "To find out if she has a history of seducing older men?"

"No. To find out if she had a history of fantasizing, of making up attention-getting stories. To find out if her family life is stable."

"Well, I promise you, Lieutenant, such an 'investigation' will reveal a very well-balanced, mature, feet-on-the-ground little girl."

"You don't have to convince me," Willman said. "I never had any kids of my own, but if I had one, I'd want her to be just like your kid."

Then he actually began to blush, as if he had suddenly

realized how much he had revealed about himself. He turned away and adjusted his tie.

"You're a kind man," Linda said softly. "I'll bet you don't hear that very often, huh?"

"Hardly ever," he said, grinning at her. "Now you go take that little girl home and try not to worry. Ryter doesn't have enough assets to raise ten percent of his bail, so he's safely inside a cell for a while."

"That's a good thing to know," she said, stepping into the elevator. "You'll tell me when the District Court hearing is going to be?"

"You bet," he said as the elevator doors slid shut.

Linda and Susan sat over coffee among the remains of lunch while Dana and Erin played in the backyard. Erin was a somewhat overweight, bubbly ten-year-old who idolized Dana and allowed herself to be gently bossed around whenever they were together.

Susan was Linda's opposite in almost every way; a tiny, dark-haired, intense woman whose emotions were always very close to the surface. She laughed easily, cried easily, flared easily, but was generally so good-natured that her friends had little trouble dealing with her talkativeness, especially because she had a disarming self-awareness about it: "I've got no clutch between brain and mouth," she would often say, and then laugh raucously. She taught social studies to the eighth-graders, who loved her and thought she was "fun."

"So you think he might be crazy," Susan said, "just by the way he looked at you?"

"It's hard to explain, Susan," Linda sighed. "And I

can tell that the lieutenant doesn't think of Ryter as just some creep, some ordinary molester. God, listen to me! Talking about ordinary molesters as if they would be easier to handle. But I can tell you that I'm glad Ryter's in jail and that he's likely to stay there until he's transferred to a state prison."

"You should try to get this all off your mind for a while," Susan said, picking at the green grapes. "The law will provide. Your trouble is that you always think you gotta handle things yourself. Now you know that's true, Linda, and that I say it to you as a friend. You've got a compulsive side."

"You're right," Linda laughed. "It's the Protestant Ethic, I guess. You're lucky to have been spared it. It makes me nervous to leave my fate in other people's hands. I did that once, with Dan, and you know how that worked out."

Susan patted Linda's hand and clucked sympathetically.

"We're going up to our cabin next Friday," she said. "Why don't you come along? We've got plenty of room, you know, and the kids would have a ball. Think how nice it would feel to just wallow around on the dock with a beer in your hand. You'll come back all tanned and sexy, and Hal Lawrence will fall over in a faint."

Linda laughed but blushed a little, too.

"You're a doll, Susan, but I can't. The next hearing could be anytime in the next ten days."

"So? They can have it without you, can't they? The wheels will keep on grinding away without you pushing at them, won't they? Come on. Hal's going off to his convention of counselors, isn't he? So why shouldn't you go away, too?" Susan had a habit of speaking in rhetorical questions.

"I couldn't relax," Linda said, feeling a little sad that this should be true. "I'd be wondering what was going on, what motions were being made, who his lawyer was talking to about us. I want to *know* every step of the way so that I can deal with what's coming. You know the trial isn't going to be easy for Dana. She'll have to tell it all in public and she'll be cross-examined. You've heard what that can be like."

"You watch too many movies, my dear," Susan said. "Do you really think any Holton lawyer is going to be mean to Dana?"

"It's his lawyer's job to bring her credibility into question," Linda said, feeling a little irked by Susan's breeziness.

"Where do you pick up that kind of talk?" Susan laughed. "You read too much, too."

"Lieutenant Willman warned me about it."

"So? Willman is a big-city cop, an alarmist," Susan sniffed. "When he's been here a little longer, he'll find out what a difference it makes to live in a place like Holton."

"A place like Holton?" Linda said. "A place where your kids are safe on the streets?" Her voice was sharp.

"I'm sorry, pal," Susan said. "This is rough on you, I know. You do what makes you feel better, okay? I won't be a pest."

"You're not a pest, Susan. I'm grateful as hell to have you around."

* * *

When Linda and Dana turned into their own driveway, they noticed a woman standing on the front porch. Before Linda could look at her carefully, Dana said, "That's Chrissy Ryter's mother." Linda drove the car straight into the garage and hurried Dana into the house through the side door.

"Could you go upstairs for a while, honey?" Linda said. "Maybe listen to your radio or something?"

"Sure, Mom," Dana said, understanding immediately.

Linda walked quickly through the house and pulled open the front door, but she made no move to unlock the screen door. The woman on the porch turned at the sound of the door. She was several inches shorter than Linda and younger by about four or five years, a colorless, drab woman with a narrow, pinched-looking face. She wore knit slacks and a sleeveless blouse which had once been white, but had acquired the yellowed look that synthetic fabrics get after many washings.

"What can I do for you?" Linda said.

"I'm Sandy Ryter." The voice sounded scared, like one of Linda's students when a homework assignment was late.

"I know who you are," Linda said. "What do you want?" And Linda folded her arms tightly across her chest.

The woman paused, seeing from Linda's gesture that she was not going to open the door, not going to let her into the house.

"I seen you in the courtroom today," Sandy said, looking at the mailbox, stalling, putting off the real reason for her visit.

Linda was surprised; she had never looked at the other spectators, never imagined that Ryter might have some friend or ally there.

"I didn't see you," she said simply.

"I been waiting here for a while," Sandy said, turning her gaze to the wrought iron porch rail.

"What exactly did you want to say to me?" Linda asked, keeping her voice carefully neutral, refusing to be drawn into chatty explanations of where she had had lunch.

"I came to ask you, to beg you, not to do this to Jack," Sandy said, not looking at Linda even now.

Linda took half a beat to recognize the reference. She had come to think of Ryter by his full, formal name, John Charles Ryter, the way she always thought "Lee Harvey Oswald" or "James Earl Ray," so the use of this unfamiliar nickname produced a blank stare on her face.

"My husband," Sandy said helpfully, looking up at Linda.

"Don't you mean your ex-husband?"

"Yes, my ex-husband."

"And what is it you imagine I am doing to him?"

"These charges, these lies. I don't know why your girl would say those things, but you got to get her to stop saying them."

"My daughter does not tell lies," Linda said, keeping her voice icy calm.

"Jack might be rough sometimes, but he wouldn't—he ain't like that." The voice was soft, wheedling.

"You apparently don't know your ex-husband very well," Linda said flatly.

"Think about us, then," Sandy said, an edge of hysteria coming into her voice. "Chrissy and me, we gotta live here, our family is here. What is something like this gonna do to us? You got a kid. Think of what it would be like, living with a thing like this."

"I *do* think of what it's going to be like for my child to 'live with a thing like this.' It may take her a long time to get over the terror of it."

"He didn't hurt her none," Sandy cried, her thin voice going up in pitch to an unpleasant whine, half accusing, half supplicating.

"Didn't hurt her?" Now Linda's voice clearly registered her outrage. "She's already been having nightmares. She may never wholly trust people again. She may have to battle her fears every time she has to walk down a street alone, even in broad daylight. He told her she was never going home again. Can't you imagine how terrifying that is for a child?"

"And what about *my* kid?" Sandy was near tears, but angry, too. "Can't you think about her for a minute, about the hurt this is gonna do to her?"

"Perhaps you should think more about your daughter yourself!" Linda found herself shaking with fury. "You'd better ask her some questions about her relationship with her father. She may have been his victim long before he dragged Dana into his car."

"What does that mean?" Sandy looked stunned, breathless.

"Aberrations like his don't just suddenly appear. Child molesting is a habit, and it sometimes begins at home."

Sandy Ryter flushed, her throat and jaw becoming mottled into irregular patches of white and deep red.

"You got a awful dirty mind," she whispered.

"No," Linda said, much more loudly than she intended. "You have an awful, dirty ex-husband."

Sandy turned and walked down the concrete steps, holding the rail as if she might fall otherwise, and then hurried off down the sidewalk. Linda stood in the doorway for a long time, breathing hard and shaking. When she finally unfolded her arms, she saw bright red marks inside her left elbow where she had been gripping it with the fingers of her right hand.

For the rest of the day, Linda felt depressed and faintly nauseated. Sometimes she would remember Ryter's eyes—the icy stare with its glint of madness, or evil, or both—and sometimes she would remember Sandy's pinched face. Each time, her stomach would contract and the back of her throat would burn slightly. Dana, who seemed to have radar when it came to Linda's moods, tried to cheer her up, offered to play Casino, a game the two of them enjoyed and often played for pennies. But when Linda had missed simple combinations four or five times, Dana gave up.

"You think maybe you should talk about it, Mom?" she said, putting the cards aside.

"That's what *I* always say, isn't it?" Linda smiled wanly. "I'll be fine, darling, really I will. It's just that talking to Chrissy's mother upset me a little."

"I feel sorry for her," Dana said.

"You would," Linda said, reaching over to mess

Dana's dark curls. "You're a peach, kid, one in a million."

That night, when Dana was asleep, Linda called Hal. He wanted to hear all about the court appearance, would have gone with her had it not been for a morning meeting with his supervisor about travel funds. She told him the surface facts, but didn't try to explain about Ryter's eyes; even in her own mind, it was beginning to seem silly, a bizarre overreaction. What she really wanted to talk with him about was the visit from Sandy Ryter and how rotten it had made her feel. She described the whole scene to him.

"I was just awful to her, and that's not like me, really it isn't."

"I know it isn't," he said soothingly. "You're one of the politest people I know. She really had no right to come to you like that, trying to shift the responsibility from where it properly belongs. I think it's considered improper, even under law, isn't it?"

"Well, it's certainly improper for an accused person to try to contact the victim's family," Linda said, "but I don't know about the accused person's family trying to do the same thing. Anyway, that's no excuse for the way I acted. That poor little mouse of a woman has never done anything bad to me or mine, and I was rude to her, worse than rude; I was really vicious to her."

"Stop whipping yourself, Linda. It doesn't sound to me as if you said anything to her that wasn't true and even sensible. She *should* consider his relationship with their daughter pretty carefully."

"I suppose," Linda said, still unconvinced. "But it was the way I said it that's still bothering me. I was shaking, I was so angry, and she didn't deserve that."

"You've been under a great deal of strain since Monday," Hal said, his voice gentle and full of sympathy. "Try to remember that and give up on this self-flagellation stuff."

"You see, Hal," Linda said. "I think what I've really wanted to do ever since Monday is to smash in Ryter's face, to pound him into a pulp, but I can't get at him and I'm not much good at pounding anyway, or even screaming, which might help me. So I think I took it out on her. I just turned all that rage on her. I was *trying* to hurt her, to say whatever would give her pain, would humiliate her. And that's just awful."

"No, my dear," he said, "that's just human. Now put it out of your mind, get some rest. What have you decided about Saturday night?"

"Well, if you don't mind, Hal, I think I'd rather not leave Dana with a sitter just yet. I thought maybe you could come here for dinner about seven. There's a good movie on Channel Nine at ten o'clock, something with Jimmy Stewart in it. What do you think?"

"Dinner and a movie sounds like an ideal Saturday night date to me," he laughed. "I'll bring some wine."

"It's good of you to understand," she said.

"Hey, I'm a good guy," he said.

"I know you are."

She tried to take his advice about getting some rest, but found herself wide awake at 2:30, turning over in her mind the events of the day. Sandy Ryter's blotched face kept coming back into her head even when she tried to think about Hal, about how he had called her "my dear" on the phone. And at 2:30 A.M., her reaction to Ryter's pale, chilling eyes no longer seemed so silly. She began to think she would be better off if she were the sort of person who could cry easily.

Chapter 10

Fridays in the summer were busy days for the Hammonds. They spent part of the morning doing laundry and part of it grocery shopping. Then they ate lunch at one of Dana's favorite fast-food places and went window shopping until the open swim at the YWCA; Dana called this their "mother-daughter day."

On that Friday's excursion to the grocery store, Linda had Saturday's dinner very much in mind. She had a few specialities, but had never developed her mother's passion for cooking, partly because, from childhood, she had been an avid reader and would always choose a good book over planning and preparing complex meals. She even rather enjoyed reading cookbooks, but couldn't seem to apply their brisk advice about how to prepare "forty-eight one-hour gourmet dinners." Dana helped her pick out the freshest produce for a salad and suggested that, if they couldn't grill hamburgers, a good second choice would be chicken cacciatore. Linda agreed and quickly finished the menu by picking up the things she would need to make dill bread, the one homemade bread she found foolproof.

Over lunch, Linda gently raised the subject of Ryter and the trial. Without using Willman's words, she helped Dana to understand that Ryter's lawyer would try to make it seem as if she were making up stories about Mr. Ryter, that he would even be asking her friends about her. Linda knew that Dana would respond better if she were prepared for this ahead of time instead of having one of her schoolmates blurting, "Hey, some guy is trying to find out if you're a liar." Linda also told Dana that she would have to tell in court all of the details of what had happened, including where and how Ryter had touched her.

"I don't want to do that," Dana said, "not in front of all those people. Do I *have* to, Mom?"

"Yes, honey, you have to." Linda's voice was firm. She had never been one of those mothers who told their children "It won't hurt a bit" when they were about to get a shot. "It won't be easy, I know, but you must try to remember that it is nothing for *you* to be ashamed of. He's the one who should be ashamed. And, unless you can help the court to convict him this time, he might do the same things, or worse, to other girls. We can't let that happen, can we?"

"I guess not," Dana said. "But it's going to be so embarrassing."

"I know, darling. But I think it might help if we do

what I sometimes tell my students to try when they have to do a demonstration for the class. As soon as we know when the trial is going to be, we'll go over what you're going to say, and I'll pretend to be the other people, to ask you the questions they might ask. After you say it out loud lots of times, it won't sound so embarrassing. It always helps to try to imagine ahead of time what it will be like; then you can be ready for it. Okay?''

"Okay," Dana said, pushing a french fry around on her plate, but she didn't sound convinced.

It was the first hot day of summer, so the swim was especially nice. Dana was a strong swimmer and let some of the clownish side of her personality out when she was in the pool. Linda had learned early some of her mother's terror of water and preferred the shallow end, always grateful, when she saw Dana hurtling off the diving board, that she had been able to keep from conveying this fear to her daughter. The hour and a half in the chlorine-blue water seemed to wash away, for both of them, some of the strains of the past few days. Linda felt tired when they got home, but fresher somehow.

The weather forecast that night told them that the next day would see temperatures in the high 80's, so Linda decided to bake her dill bread that night to keep from having to light the oven the next day. The bread was rising for the second time when she put Dana to bed, sitting next to her for a few minutes to chat before going back downstairs. She had brought up the fans from the basement and put one in each of the bedrooms. The third one was blowing the oven heat away from the dining room when the phone rang at 10:45.

Thinking it might be Hal, Linda carried the phone to the sofa arm and set it down before answering it.

"Hello," she said brightly.

"Oh, teacher, teacher." The voice was very soft, almost a whisper. "You should never have said what you did to Sandy."

"Who is this?" Linda said, her voice catching as she sat up straight. The words were just a reflex, for she already knew who the voice belonged to.

"People like you always think they can treat people like me like shit, don't you? You're so high-toned and fine, aren't you, that you can say ugly things to the likes of me without any fear at all. Ain't that right?" There was no anger in the voice. It was singsong, almost playful, and very quiet.

Linda could not make her voice work to fill the pause after the last question.

"Well, you ain't right about that, teacher," the voice went on. "You sure ain't. Cuz you will regret for *all* your days the day you said such a thing about me. You think you got me where I can't do a thing about it, so you can spread garbage around about me. But you are wrong, wrong, wrong, teacher."

"Where are you?" Linda managed to gasp.

"Where I won't be for long." There was a small laugh then, a "heh, heh, heh," toneless and without mirth. "I don't think I'm going to prison on this one, but even if I do, it won't be for long. No sir, not for as long as you think. And as soon as I get out, I'm gonna hurt you. I'm gonna hurt you in the worst way there is. Do you hear that, teacher?"

"You can't threaten me like this," Linda said, knowing how clichéd it sounded, knowing she should just hang up, but her hand was frozen onto the receiver which she was holding so tightly against her ear that the cartilage was already beginning to ache.

"This ain't a threat, teacher. This is a promise. And what is the worst way I can hurt you, do you think? Huh, what do you think? No answer? Well, I'll tell you what I think. I think that little black-haired bitch of yours is the answer. She's what started all this, anyway. I'm coming for her, teacher, that's what I'm gonna do. No matter if I go to prison or not, I'm coming back for her first chance I get."

Linda let her breath out in a shuddering gasp.

"You don't like that too much, do you, teacher?" The voice didn't sound gloating, only interested. "You might think to yourself that the cops can protect her and that you can watch her real good, too. But cops protect people just so long, and even a mama can't watch her little darling every minute of the day. Sometime, someday, she's gonna be walking home from school, or taking her bike to the park, or something like that, and then she'll just be gone. There won't be no witnesses, you can bet on that. Even if you move away, I'll find you. I'm gonna have lots of time, all the time in the world."

All the while the soft, insinuating almost feminine voice was coming into her ear, Linda could feel a chill settling over her mind, as if someone had opened the top of her skull and was pouring cold water over her brain.

"Now, I bet you got a pretty good imagination, huh, teacher? I want you to imagine all the ways I'm gonna entertain myself with your brat before I'm through with her. I'm a pretty imaginative guy myself. I think it will take me days and days to use up all the things I can think of. And then do you know what? Can you guess?''

"No," Linda whispered. She was numb with disbelief and could manage only the one syllable.

"Her body will never be found," Ryter said. "Nobody'll ever be able to pin it on me. You can believe what I'm telling you, teacher. I know how to do it."

The soft singsong paused for a moment.

"You believe me, don't you, teacher?"

Linda was past any power to speak. She was not breathing, but only holding air in her lungs. She had taken no breath since the matter-of-fact voice had said, "Her body will never be found."

"Remember, you heard it here," Ryter said, and then there was a soft "cluck," the sound caused by a finger depressing the phone button rather than hanging up the receiver.

Linda sat with the receiver against her ear, listening to the complete silence, her mind cold and numb, unable to form any thought at all. When the dial tone began again seven seconds later, it made her jump as if it had wakened her from sleep. She drew a gasping breath and dropped the receiver next to herself on the sofa. For another ten seconds, she stared at the phone, listening to the dull buzz of the dial tone as if it were something she had never heard before.

Then her mind lurched, formed a purpose. Simultaneously, she snatched up the receiver and pushed the 0 on the phone's face. All emergency numbers had been frozen from her memory.

"Give me the police, quick," she said, and she hardly recognized her own voice.

"I want to talk to Lieutenant Willman," she told the dispatcher.

"Lieutenant Willman is not on duty tonight," the dispatcher said. "Could another officer help you?"

"Anyone who can tell me why he's out of jail," Linda said, but she was not hysterical, not shouting.

"And who is 'he,' ma'am?" the dispatcher said.

"Ryter. John Charles Ryter."

"Just a minute, please."

The phone clicked to "hold" and Linda waited, breathing in short, shallow gasps, hearing her heartbeat inside the ear with the receiver against it.

"This if Officer VanderKellen," a deep voice said after another click. "What can I do for you?"

"I want some explanation of why John Charles Ryter is out of jail."

"And what is your name, ma'am?"

"I'm Linda Hammond." When she had said the words, Linda thought what an unfamiliar ring her own name had.

"Oh, yes, Mrs. Hammond." Apparently all of the police force knew who she was. "Someone has given you some misinformation, I'm afraid. Ryter is here, in his cell."

"He just called me."

"That can't be, Mrs. Hammond. I know he hasn't been released."

"He called me," Linda said more firmly. Her breath was beginning to steady. "And he made the most awful threats, said such terrible—" She couldn't go on because a sob had surprised her.

"Somebody must be playing a nasty joke on you, ma'am. Ryter is locked up tight as a drum."

"I know it was him," Linda said, though she could not have explained how she knew, for she had heard his voice only once before, for a few mumbled words in the county courtroom. "Somehow, he called me."

"Now, try to be calm, Mrs. Hammond," the officer said, but his voice had assumed the tone used to placate a child or a senile patient.

"I am calm, officer," Linda said, and she was. "Someone has allowed that man access to me, and I wish to have it investigated. I want Lieutenant Willman involved at once." It was her "teacher voice," and it was effective.

"We'll look into it, Mrs. Hammond," VanderKellen said, "and we'll get back to you."

"Tonight," Linda said. "You'll get back to me tonight, before I go to bed."

"Yes, Mrs. Hammond, tonight."

Linda hung up and sat very still for a long time. Her head was buzzing and prickly; she could feel that her arms were cold and clammy despite the heat. Shock, she thought; one part of her mind was detached and calmly observing her own condition. It was really self-protective, shock, she thought; it kept you from flying apart in a bad crisis, dulled your senses so that you could face whatever it was later, only a little at a time instead of all at once.

And she didn't think about Ryter's call, didn't go over it in her mind. She only thought about her skin and about how icy the back of her head felt. Did it mean she might faint? Should she lie down or put her head between her knees? Which was it?

She began to smell something sharp and acrid, something burning. She stood up thinking that the house must be on fire, that someone had set the house on fire. Only after she had turned around twice in the center of the room did she remember the dill bread. She ran to the kitchen, narrowly missed toppling the fan, and snatched open the oven. A little cloud of smoke billowed out and the fan carried it to the open window over the sink. Linda turned off the oven and reached for the hot pads, her body following the patterns of a habitually careful person even though her head felt like a detached balloon floating somewhere near the ceiling.

The bread was black, split open, smoking. Linda set it in the sink and let cold water run over it for a few minutes. Then she turned the fan up to high. The smoke alarm in the dining room had made only one little warning beep and then settled down and was silent. Oddly, Linda didn't feel upset that the bread was burnt; she felt relieved. It had distracted her, given her something to do, presented her with something she could handle.

Standing in the middle of the kitchen, Linda began to think about locks. She knew the doors were locked—that was just a big-city habit she had brought with her to Holton—but were the locks any good? What was it the public service messages on television were always saying about dead-bolt locks? What was a dead-bolt lock, any-way? She tried the side door just to make sure it was locked, and then crossed the house to the front door. She slid the chain onto its bar, but she couldn't help noticing how flimsy it looked, how weak. Her eyes followed the windows all around the ground floor of the little house; all the windows were open and only the slightly rusted screen stood between her and the warm night air. "If someone really wants to break in—" She could hear that sentence repeated by almost all of her adult acquain-tances when they were going away on vacation or talking about a bicycle theft. "If someone really wants to kill the President—" Linda shook her head to make the sentence go away. Then she took the chain back off the bar and went to the sofa to wait.

It was almost midnight when the doorbell rang. Linda had expected a phone call, had several times considered calling the police station again, so the doorbell frightened her, but she swallowed hard and went to switch on the porch light. Lieutenant Willman was standing outside the door. When Linda let him inside, she noticed that he looked untidy, something she would not have believed possible. He was wearing blue jeans and a baggy shirt, and his lean jaw was covered with beard stubble. His eyes looked tired and a little guilty.

"It *was* Ryter who called you," he said as he sat down.

"I knew that. How?"

"Well, this particular officer sort of knows Ryter," Willman said, looking away from Linda's eyes. "Ryter's ex-wife visited him at the jail this afternoon, and Ryter told the officer she was very upset, that he was worried about her. So could he call her privately just to check up on her, keep her from maybe doing something foolish? I told you how convincing he can be.''

"So this officer just let him make an unsupervised call?"

"Yes. He even let him use the office down there while he waited outside.''

"Well, that's just wonderful,'' Linda said, making a snorting, mirthless sound. "He threatens me with the police standing by and says he called his wife. She'll probably back him up, too.''

"He doesn't deny calling you.''

"What?''

"I've just come from a little talk with him. He says he lied to the lockup man because he just had to talk to you, had to try to persuade you to believe in his innocence, to get you to help his ex-wife who is so upset that he's worried what she might do to herself.''

Linda sat for a moment with her mouth agape, stunned by the sheer audacity of the man they were trying to deal with.

"Lieutenant Willman,'' she said at last, "that man is a dangerous lunatic.''

"Why don't you try to tell me exactly what he said to you,'' Willman said, taking a small notebook and pen out of his shirt pocket.

Now Linda had to turn her mind to it for the first time, to think directly about the voice and its terrible words. First she told him about Sandy Ryter's visit, and then she went on to the phone call. Though she had to swallow often just to keep her stomach from turning over, she managed to get through it all while the tall policeman jotted things down in his notebook, his long face averted from hers. When she had finished, he looked up at her, and the professional mask broke down when he saw her face.

"Do you have any liquor in the house, whiskey or something?" he asked, putting his hand on her arm.

"Some brandy, I think," she said. "Why?"

"Because I think you'd better have some. Where is it?"

"In the kitchen."

He followed her out into the kitchen and took the brandy bottle from her hand when she lifted it from the cupboard. He poured about four ounces of brandy into a glass, an old Mickey Mouse water tumbler that Dana had loved when she was younger.

"Now you just sit down and drink all of that," Willman said, pointing at a kitchen chair. "And I'm going to tell you a few things from my great fund of experience as a cop. Okay?"

Linda sipped the brandy as he pulled another chair around to face her.

"Now, listen close," he said, folding his long frame onto the chair. "I have come across all sorts in my time. Plenty of guys get all steamed up when their bad behavior finally lands them in jail. I've met very few who were willing to admit it was their own fault and that they should really be steamed at themselves. They think they gotta blame somebody else, and lots of them say some pretty wild things about the somebody else they decide to blame. I've heard threats you wouldn't believe. I've *been* threatened so many times myself that I can't remember them all. Now here is the important part. I've known very few of these guys to ever try to carry out those threats. They feel caught and humiliated and they want to make somebody else feel bad, too, so they lash out with their mouths and that's the end of it."

"Always?" Linda said. "Is that always the end of it?" He shook his head, looking a little angry.

"Nothing is 'always,' Mrs. Hammond. I'm trying to tell you, though, that the odds are with you on this one. He gets all done being Mr. Monster Man on the phone, and then he settles down and takes his lumps."

"You did not hear his voice, Lieutenant. I can't describe that voice," Linda said, staring over the rim of the glass, not looking at Willman but at some place in the middle distance where horror past description lived. "When he asked me if I believed him, I knew I did. I believed him all along, and I still believe him no matter what you say about the thousands of ordinary crooks who scream things they don't mean. He means it. He means to kill Dana."

"He might think he means it," Willman said, standing up and beginning to pace. "But he's gonna be sitting around in a cell for quite a while and eventually he's gonna cool off."

"Or just get more angry and obsessed," Linda said.

"Look, Mrs. Hammond," Willman sighed. "Don't go borrowing trouble."

Linda had finished all of the brandy and her stomach

felt very warm, but the chill in her mind was still there. She set the glass down and watched Willman pace for a while.

"You know for yourself, Lieutenant, that Ryter is not an ordinary person. You said so. You said he sounded sadistic. You said he was a 'cool customer.' "

"Looks like I said too much."

"Why didn't he run away after Dana got away from him? You know you were surprised when you heard that he was just sitting in his apartment waiting for the police. And why didn't he just deny that he had seen Dana at all? He didn't know about Mrs. Denser then. And he didn't bother to deny that he called me either. He thinks he can handle anything that comes his way. Isn't that called megalomania? Doesn't it mean that he's a clever and dangerous madman?"

"I don't know what megalomania is, Mrs. Hammond," Willman said, stopping for a moment to look at her. "Ryter has stumbled onto the insight that a successful lie sticks as close as possible to the truth. It doesn't take a genius, or a maniac either, to figure that out. And he does like to fool cops, that's obvious."

"Because policemen are authority figures. You said he has a problem with authority figures. Doesn't that mean he resents and rebels against anyone who threatens his delusions of grandeur? Well, teachers are authority figures, too, Lieutenant. I think that's why he kept calling me 'teacher' on the phone tonight, saying 'people like you.' Now he's focused all that resentment on me. I believe he means to try what he says."

"For that, he'd have to be stupid," Willman said.

"And that argues against what you've been saying. He must know he'd never get away with it."

"I'm not worried about his getting away with it, Lieutenant. I'm worried about his doing it. If he's really as crazy as I think he is, he doesn't believe he'll get caught; he's not rational enough to consider real consequences."

"Nobody is as crazy as you think he is," Willman said in exasperation. "At least the way you're thinking right now. Tomorrow, when you've had some sleep, you'll start to see the sense of what I'm telling you. In the meantime, I'll add threatening you to the charges against him, which will keep him locked up even longer. And I have personally seen to it that Mr. Ryter will make no more unsupervised phone calls. Now, will you believe that we're doing all we can? I'm still asking around about him, too, to see what else can be added to his list."

"Yes, Lieutenant," Linda sighed. "I believe you're doing all you can. I pray it's going to be enough. Thank you for coming over on your own time, too."

She walked him to the door and watched his car pull away. The breeze that came through the screen door into her face was warm, but she still shivered slightly. She didn't even consider going up to bed, but made her way to the sofa instead. For the rest of the night, she sat there, cross-legged, with her elbows propped on her knees and her hands against the sides of her head, an unconscious effort to warm the inside of her skull.

Chapter 11

When Dana shook Linda awake at 8:15 on Saturday morning, Linda grabbed out at her as a drowning person might reach desperately for a rescuer, pulling her down next to herself on the sofa. Linda had been asleep, slumped against the sofa arm, for less than two hours, and she was in the middle of a frightening dream when Dana came downstairs.

"Why are you sleeping in your clothes?" Dana said, her voice muffled a little by having her face held so close against her mother's shoulder.

"Oh, I just fell asleep down here last night, that's all," Linda said, letting Dana sit up again.

"You mean you never went to bed?" Dana was aghast as such an irregularity.

"I guess not," Linda said, "because here I am in yesterday's clothes."

119

"Want me to fix you some breakfast?" Dana asked, looking up with some concern into Linda's face.

"We'll rustle up something together," Linda said, deliberately brightening her tone as she saw the little frown forming on Dana's forehead.

In the kitchen, Dana found the waterlogged bread in the sink. The fan was still blasting away on high, and Linda turned it off as she passed.

"What happened to the bread?" Dana was beginning to look as if the sky was falling, so unaccustomed was she to any display of carelessness from her mother.

"I just forgot about it while I was reading," Linda said crossly. "Could you carry it out to the garbage can for me and just dump it? Bring the pan back in. I think I can scour it clean."

Dana went outside quietly and Linda watched her through the window over the sink. In her dream, Linda had been inside an immense room with doors in every wall. She knew or sensed that Dana was behind one of the doors and that some sort of menace filled the whole place. There was no specific danger, only the empty, cavernous room, but Linda felt Dana calling for her, needing her. She began to open doors. Some of the doors led to long corridors which looked hygienic and well-lit like a hospital; some of them opened into the air, high up, so high that Linda couldn't see the ground below, but clutched at the door frame to keep herself from falling. Behind one door, she saw a tightly bunched group of people, as if a crowded elevator had just opened, though the door had looked ordinary enough when she touched it. One of the people was Daniel. He was looking up at something that Linda couldn't see, and he looked frightened. Most of the doors opened onto complete blackness, nothingness. As Linda moved faster and faster, the number of doors began to multiply; the room became a corridor of closed doors and there was no end to it. By the time Dana had wakened her, Linda was very close to panic.

Now, alone for a moment in the kitchen, Linda summoned all her resources, knowing that she was going to have to spend a busy day on almost no sleep. And she saw that one thing she could do for her daughter, in her waking state if not in her dreams, was protect her, at least protect her from knowing anything about the phone call of the night before. And that meant protecting her, too, from the bad effects that phone call was having on her mother. By the time Dana came back with the charred loaf pan, Linda had pulled herself together.

"I'm sorry I barked at you," she said, giving Dana a hug. "I guess I got up on the wrong side of the sofa," and they both laughed.

For most of the day, Linda kept to her disciplined effort to keep Ryter's voice out of her consciousness. She showered and changed after breakfast, washed up the dirty dishes, vacuumed carpets while Dana dusted. Before lunch, they both hopped in the car and went to a neighborhood grocery to pick up a heat-and-serve loaf of garlic bread. On another, earlier day, Linda would have left Dana at home while she ran such an errand, or even sent her on her candy-apple red bicycle to get the bread by herself. Dana liked such tasks, felt grownup when entrusted with grocery money.

Only once, while she was scouring the bath tub, did Linda let herself think about John Charles Ryter. It crossed her mind that before last night, she had wondered why Dana would let herself be led off the sidewalk and all the way to the driver's side of Ryter's car before she tried to pull away, had been taken off in broad daylight without a scream. But now she knew why. She could easily imagine that soft, hypnotic voice saying, "It's a nice car. You'd like a ride, wouldn't you? You know who I am, so the rule about not riding with strangers doesn't apply, does it?" never letting Dana answer or take fright. Like a snake charming a mouse.

And only once during the long night before had Linda lost control enough to let her imagination turn to what it would be like for Dana if Ryter succeeded in doing what he had threatened, had promised, on the phone. Within two minutes, Linda had become so shaken that she had to wrench her mind away from the horror by walking up and down, from the dining room to the living room and back again, literally counting her steps out loud. She was going to have to find ways of blocking her imagination until Ryter was safely convicted and in prison, or she would have to begin to fear for her sanity.

Hal was exactly on time. He had brought not only wine, but flowers and a roll of stickers for Dana; he had remembered her preferences from their chat over lunch, and Dana looked positively adoring as she thanked him. While Linda was reaching for a vase on a kitchen shelf, he said softly next to her ear, "Is something wrong? You look awfully pale."

"I'll tell you later," she whispered, afraid to look at

him, afraid the sympathy would make her cry on the spot.

The dinner was a success and Hal said he was particularly fond of Italian food. When the table was cleared, they all played board games at which Hal was good-naturedly inept. He lost most of the time, but seemed to enjoy himself anyway. Dana teased him when he had missed an obvious move in Aggravation, and he went into a mock dejection that made them all laugh.

When Linda was tucking Dana in upstairs, the child said impishly, "If you marry him, Mom, we'll have to teach him all about games."

"Do you like him?" Linda asked seriously.

"Sure," Dana said. "He's funny and he listens."

"Yes," Linda said with a little smile. "Those are two things that can go a long way."

Hal was in the living room with a glass of wine when Linda came back down.

"Come tell me what's bothering you," he said, patting the sofa cushion next to him. "I've got your wine here, too."

"It seems every time I see you lately, I've got some new tale of woe to tell," she sighed, sitting down and crossing her long legs. "You'll begin to think I'm a chronic whiner."

"Nonsense," he said briskly. "You're the least whiney person I know. Now Donald Carver—*there's* a whiner."

Linda giggled in spite of herself. Donald Carver was the assistant principal at the junior high, and he never seemed to have a cheery word to say to anyone.

"Come on, now," Hal said more seriously. "You'll

feel better if you talk about it, and I want to help any way I can.''

Linda kept her control intact while she related the call in detail and Willman's effort to calm her fears. Before she had got well under way, Hal reached out to take her left hand. He held it while she repeated the awful words Ryter had used. He didn't speak until she had finished and taken another sip of wine.

''Why didn't you call me?'' he said softly. ''I'd have come right over and you wouldn't have had to be alone.''

Why hadn't she called him? Linda looked at the kind, concerned face and then at the warm hand that was closed over her own, and she wondered why it had never occurred to her to do just that. As soon as she considered, she knew the answer.

''I guess I thought it would be unreasonable to call anyone after eleven o'clock,'' she said with a rueful smile.

''That's just silly,'' he said.

''I know it is,'' she answered. ''But you weren't raised by a southern lady like my mother; her idea of what was rude or unreasonable corresponded almost exactly to what she thought was morally wrong.''

''Well, in future—'' he began and then broke off at once. ''Please God, there'll never be such an occasion again, but if there's any crisis at all, you pick up that phone no matter what time it is.''

''Okay,'' she said. ''One part of my genteel upbringing gladly scrapped.''

Hal looked thoughtful for a moment.

''Of course, Willman might be right,'' he said. ''It

could all be bluff, but he does sound pretty sick, close to losing control. But it seems so odd, so inconsistent."

"Inconsistent?"

"Yes. You said he has a history of drinking and brawling. That's one way of exorcising one's demons, a fairly typical one, in fact. But to switch so suddenly to another pattern; it seems like two different men we're talking about here."

"Well, the brawling business seems to have died down a bit lately. Lieutenant Willman says that Ryter hasn't been in that kind of trouble since he—Willman, that is—came to Holton, and that's almost three years now."

Hal frowned, a little vertical crease forming between his brows.

"What is it?" Linda asked.

"Well," he said. "This is just my undergraduate psychology major talking here, of course, but it seems odd that he could be a good boy for that long and then suddenly break out in a new antisocial pattern. Especially since he seems so close to psychosis now. You'd think there would be clearer warning signs."

"What are you thinking?" Linda asked. "There's something else, isn't there?"

"This is all idle speculation," he said, patting Linda's hand. "But I think you might have hit pretty close to home when you suggested that he had an incestuous interest in his own daughter. Suppose he had repressed that interest because it was too horrible for him to face. That would explain why he reacted so violently to what you said to his ex-wife—if it were something he must keep hidden, from himself most of all."

"But why suddenly reach out for Dana the way he did? That's what you're puzzling over, isn't it?"

"Not exactly. Dana is a substitute child, obviously, one he can give himself 'permission' to molest. No, what seems strange is that he's done this only once, that there haven't been earlier incidents. If he's so near to a breakdown now, to flagrantly announce to you his deviant intentions about a child, then it must have been pretty strong for a long time, maybe for years."

Linda suddenly sat up straight, snatching her hand away to clap it over her mouth, but the words "Oh, God!" had escaped before the hand arrived there.

"What is it?" Hal said.

"He said he knew how to do it," Linda whispered from behind her hand.

"What do you mean?"

Linda put her hand back down on top of Hal's.

"Right after he said Dana's body would never be found, he said 'I know how to do it.' Those were his exact words. He said something about not being caught because he knew how to do it."

"What are you driving at?" Hal was looking even more worried.

"What if he meant that he had already done it? That he knew he could get away with it because he had already hidden a body, even several bodies? What if those things he said to me on the phone were not just a description of what he *planned* to do, but of something he had already done?"

"Now, come on, Linda," Hal said. "Aren't we making a pretty big leap here?"

"No, no," Linda said, lifting her forefinger to make an imaginary count in the air. "You said it's unlikely that he could have been, as you put it, 'a good boy' for three years only to suddenly grab a child now. And he quit the bar fights after a few scrapes with the law, one of them serious. That ended in his threatening the victim into silence. No counseling or help in between. So all that hostility is still there inside him anyway, but he cuts out the drinking because it makes him too *openly* aggressive. What's been happening in those three years that might not be so open, that he might have learned how to get away with?"

Hal's frown deepened, but he didn't say anything.

"Oh, Hal," Linda said despairingly. "You're not trying to talk me out of it. You think it makes sense, don't you?"

"Not necessarily," he said. "There could be another explanation. Maybe his incest fantasies are *not* fantasies. Maybe there was real incest in the family, but the separation from his wife cut him off from the daughter, so he turned instead to Dana."

"No," Linda said, shaking her head. "They were divorced when Dana met Chrissy and that was when we first moved to Holton four years ago."

"Well, there are always visitation rights," Hal said.

"I don't know," Linda said. "He was so outraged over what I said to Sandy. Could he be that vengeful if what I suggested were actually happening?"

"We're neither of us psychiatrists, Linda, and I think it's time we stop playing this game. You're just getting more scared. Whatever went on in the three years, the guy is where he belongs now and he's going to stay there for a long time. No matter what he said to you on the phone, he can't do anything about it; he can't get at you or Dana. Try to relax and let the system work. The law is going to protect you in the best way it can, by removing the threat from society.''

''I can't help thinking it's my fault,'' Linda said, tears welling up in her eyes.

''What is your fault?'' Hal had the same exasperated tone Willman had finally come to.

''His threats, his turning all his weird hostilities against Dana. If only I hadn't been so cruel to that woman. If only I had kept my big mouth shut. He might have forgotten about us, or thought it wasn't worth bigger trouble to harass us.''

She was weeping now in earnest, tears streaming down her face. It was the first time she had cried since the whole mess began.

''Come here,'' Hal said gently and pulled her against his chest. ''You have a good cry. You deserve one. But cry over the right things. Cry because you're scared and tired and because a nasty little man has put you and Dana through a little version of hell. Don't cry from guilt because you don't have to have any about this. Put the guilt where it belongs, on Ryter.''

He tightened his arms around her and rocked her back and forth, raising one hand to the back of her hair and stroking downward to her neck as he went on murmuring soothing words into her ear. His hand, where it touched the skin of her neck, was warm. After a while, she stopped sobbing and just rested against his blue shirt, feeling the muscles of her shoulders beginning to relax.

"I'll tell you what," he said after almost a minute of silence. "I don't have to go to that convention on Tuesday. I'll stay in town and we'll take in a few movies, maybe go golfing. Do you like to golf?"

Linda lifted her head to look into his eyes.

"Don't be silly," she said. "You've been planning all spring to go to that convention. You're on a panel, for God's sake."

"So, the panel can get along without me," he smiled. Up close, he smelled nicely of wine and after-shave lotion.

"You're a very nice man, Hal Lawrence," Linda said, sitting up and brushing the palms of her hands under her eyes. "But you're going to go to your convention."

"Look," he said, taking her shoulders in his hands. "You're determined to go to that second court appearance, and I don't want you to go alone. If that little bastard looks at you again, I want him to see somebody else looking back. I can look pretty scary, too."

Linda laughed, a genuine, amused laugh. The thought of Hal looking fierce or threatening was really funny to her, but the laugh was also from relief, a giddy feeling that she could set the burden down if she chose to, and he would take it up. She hadn't felt that way in six years.

"Oh, Hal," she said. "You're wonderful, but the hearing isn't likely to happen until after you get back. 'Within ten days,' the judge said and that's probably working days, so I'd guess next week sometime, not this week."

"You're going to be okay in the meantime, though?" he asked. "Promise me."

"I promise you," she said. "I know it's hard to believe lately, but I'm not usually a hysterical lady. I'll snap out of this and be my usual hardy self as soon as I get some sleep. I must look a fright." And she dabbed at her eyes again.

"You're not a fright," he said. "You always look wonderful to me."

"Thank you," she said, and she meant for much more than just the compliment. She leaned forward impulsively to kiss his cheek. He still had his hands on her shoulders, and he held her when she tried to sit up again. When he leaned forward, his lips came to rest against her forehead at the hairline. His surprisingly soft, warm mouth began moving slowly down her head to her ear and then her jaw and throat. Linda turned her face toward the seeking mouth which grazed her chin before finding her lips. She lifted her arms under his and folded them behind his broad back, feeling the bands of muscles move as he wrapped his arms around her. He kissed her cheeks and eyes and then her mouth again. Then they looked at each other from a distance of about eight inches.

"One of these days," Hal whispered, "when you're a little less vulnerable, I'm going to ask you if I can spend the night."

"One of these days," she said, smiling up at him, "when I'm a little less tired and ugly from crying, I'm going to ask you to stay."

"So, who do you think will ask first?" he laughed.

"I'm not taking any bets on that," she said. Somewhere in her mind, she was amazed that they were having this conversation so easily, so naturally. A week ago, she wouldn't have thought it possible.

"I think we'd just better forget about Jimmy Stewart, don't you?" he said.

"Who's Jimmy Stewart?" she asked, kissing his chin where a small diagonal scar slanted toward his lower lip. She would have to ask him someday how that had happened.

"I mean," he said, chuckling, "you had almost no sleep last night, so I'd better pass on the movie and let you get to bed." And then he blushed. Linda thought she had never seen anything as charming as Hal Lawrence blushing at the mention of her bed.

They held hands as she walked him to the door, where he pulled her into his arms once more and kissed her, a long kiss. Linda thought how nice it was to feel the entire length of his body against hers; they were so nearly the same height that everything seemed to correspond perfectly: breasts, thighs, knees.

"I'll call you tomorrow," he said. "But not until after lunch because I expect you to sleep till noon."

"Okay," she said.

Linda didn't go to sleep immediately as she thought she would. She thought about Hal for a long time, went over every word and touch several times in her mind. It was a way to hold on to it, to make herself believe in it. It was not easy for her to accept that a relationship as promising as this one seemed could be for real. She hadn't had a man in her life for more than four years and had got used to thinking of herself as out of circulation, a matron of sorts.

During her divorce, she'd had a brief affair with one of Dan's friends. It was a gesture of pure revenge on her part, for she didn't really like the man. He was only one of several men who propositioned her during that time, but he was single and good-looking, someone who regularly beat Dan at tennis, so she found him the ideal candidate for her purpose. Then, in graduate school, she had spent several months in a relationship with one of her professors. He had helped her to explore and eventually really enjoy her own sexuality—Dan had always lacked imagination where sex was concerned, at least in his marriage—but the professor was married and Linda couldn't reconcile herself to the role of the other woman. So recently hurt by a philandering husband herself, she felt guilty and a little sordid about helping someone else's husband to philander. It didn't help much that he said his wife had "friends of her own."

Linda broke it off, and found that the formerly gallant man of letters had an ugly, spiteful side. After repeated efforts to get her to change her mind, some of them during drunkenly maudlin late-night visits, he apparently told other members of the faculty that Linda was a "hot number" who traded sex for grades. Her major professor, a kind and fatherly man, had told her about it and had also put a quick stop to the rumors, but the situation had frightened her badly. That she could, once again, have so misjudged a man she went to bed with made her wary and skittish around any man who showed an interest in her.

And now, after all this time, here was this wonderful surprise. Hal Lawrence had sneaked up on her out of a solid friendship during which she had seen his character from many sides: faithful and loving husband; capable professional; decent, generous, self-effacing colleague. Could it be that she had finally picked a winner, and that, even more wonderful, he had picked her? The thought of it warmed her all over, and she fell asleep almost happily about midnight.

Chapter 12

*L*inda had awakened at a little after seven on Sunday morning feeling anxious, even alarmed. For a few seconds, she couldn't focus the feeling or connect it with anything; then she thought of Dana, and all of the nervous terror of the past week swept over her. Had she been dreaming? She could remember nothing in particular, but she had a vague memory of being startled in her sleep by a noise. Whether it was a real noise outside or a sound in a dream, she couldn't tell. The only certainty was the present feeling of anxiety. She tried to think of Hal, of his arms around her and his lips on her face, but all she seemed to remember clearly from the nigh before was the conversation about Ryter.

All that analysis, she thought, all that effort to figure him out as a psychological case study, how useless it was and how enervating. Every human being was an enigma

to a certain extent, and Ryter seemed much more
undecipherable than most people. But even if some of
what she and Hal had speculated about his psyche should
be true, what did it achieve, except as an effort on their
own part to neutralize him, to tame him into some sick
person who might be cured, even pitied? In the clairvoy-
ance of early morning, on this bright, already hot June
Sunday, Linda thought of Ryter simply as evil: a potential, or even actual, killer. She suddenly remembered a
sentence she had read somewhere, maybe in college, that
she had dismissed at the time as old-fashioned thinking,
something about how the devil's greatest wile was to
convince us that he doesn't exist. Maybe that's what all
this psychoanalyzing was about; it was a trick to make
people think evil doesn't exist. When Ryter was whispering
his poison into her ear on the phone, she had *felt* herself
in the presence of evil, and now, lying quietly in bed, she
was beginning to feel that the only part of last night's
guessing that might be true was her suspicion that Ryter
had already committed the horror he was describing.
What did motive matter? It was deeds that were the
measure of people, after all, and anyone capable of such
a cruel violation of innocence was evil.

Linda made up her mind to get Dana up by 8:00 so
they could go to church. They hadn't been to church
since Easter and were never regular in their attendance.
Linda's mother had come from a Methodist background
and her father from a Lutheran family; they had apparently agreed not to struggle about the religious upbringing of
their daughter, so Linda had grown up sampling churches
and had formed no strong bonds to any particular denom-

ination. Because Daniel had business friends in the Congregational Church, she had gone with him. Both she and Dana liked the young pastor at the Congregational Church in Holton, so they regarded it as their church.

Dana was a little bemused at being wakened briskly so early with no warning the night before, but she liked the dress she'd got for Easter and didn't mind getting into it again to go out on such a fine morning. At the church, Linda noticed heads turning when they came in, and several times before the services began she saw people whispering and then turning to look at Dana. Of course, she thought, it would have been too much to expect that Dana's identity as the victim of an attempted kidnapping could be kept a secret in a town the size of Holton, where word of mouth was more efficient than the newspaper in spreading information. Still, she hoped Dana wouldn't notice the stares and whispers. How was her daughter going to react to the kind of attention she was bound to get for a while? With a child as serious and sensitive as Dana, it was hard to judge what was going on under the dark curls. Linda had meant to pray, but she spent her time worrying instead.

In the parking lot, Betty Lindstrom caught up to them. She was a neighbor whose son had been one of Linda's toughest cases during the past year, and the mother, Linda thought, harbored a lot of resentment, looking to blame the school for her boy's learning problems. So Linda was surprised to be greeted in such a friendly manner until she realized what Betty was really up to.

"What a shock to find out that your Dana was the girl the papers are talking about," she burbled, her face more friendly than her eyes. "It must have been an exciting few days for you."

"Exciting isn't a word I would choose for it, Betty," Linda said.

"No, probably you wouldn't. Well, half the people I've talked to just don't know what to make of it."

"What to make of it?"

"Well, you know. You hear about things happening in other places, or about strangers coming in from the outside to make trouble, but when it's somebody that people know—well, I mean, this fellow has lived here for donkey's years. It's hard to know what to believe." And she turned her eyes sideways at Dana, a sly smile spreading on her face.

"You can believe that it happened just as Dana said," Linda said coldly.

"Well, of course I can, my dear," Betty gushed. "But you know some people. Some of them say that kids just know too much nowadays, altogether too much, what with television and sex education. Some people say it just stirs up their little imaginations. Not that they mean to lie or anything, but just that they imagine something has happened when it really hasn't. Of course, I don't doubt that Dana has remembered accurately. Mind you, I'm just telling you what some people say."

"That's very good of you, Betty," Linda said, taking Dana's elbow and piloting her away. Her heart sank at the prospect of Dana testifying before a jury chosen from among the people Betty Lindstrom was describing, because she knew all too well that the description was fairly accurate. A crime like this one, committed by a local, seemed to them like a bad reflection on their town, a threat to their view of themselves. So they preferred to disbelieve, to blame the victim, just as Betty Lindstrom preferred to believe that the school was to blame for her son's dyslexia.

When the phone rang after lunch, Linda jumped to answer it, thinking it must be Hal, but it was Dan's voice which said, "How're you doing?"

"Fine," she said. "Here's Dana." And she handed the phone over to their daughter.

Linda had no lingering wish to tell her ex-husband how she was feeling, and that, she thought, was progress, something to be glad about. She listened intently to Dana's side of the conversation, but only to learn what she could about what her child might be feeling.

"Sure I was scared, but he didn't hurt me, you know."

"We don't know yet when the trial is gonna be, but Mom says we'll get ready for my part before it happens."

"Well, there'll be another witness, the lady who saw him grab me, so I guess I won't be the *star* witness."

"I'm doing pretty okay, I guess, but I don't think I'm gonna like having to tell about it."

"Sure I do. Otherwise he might get out of jail."

"Nothing much. Staying home a lot. One day, we went to the park with Hal and then he came here for dinner."

"A friend of ours. He works at Mom's school."

"Yeah, he's nice. He got me stickers."

When, after less than ten minutes, Dana announced

that Dan wanted to talk to Linda again, she sighed and took the phone.

"Now, I don't want you to take this in the wrong way, Linda," he began, pausing for her reassurance. She remembered the tone as the one he used to convince clients to be "reasonable."

"Go ahead, Dan," she said. She would judge how to "take it" after he had said it, not promise anything ahead of time.

"I hope you're not going to be overprotective of Dana because of this unpleasant business," he said. "Sounds to me as if you've kept her attached to your hip ever since it happened. She's gotta get back up on the horse sometime, babe."

"I *have* thought about what you're saying, Dan," Linda said, her voice calm, even detached. "But I'm the one on the scene and I have to play it by ear. I assure you that I'm as eager as you are to see Dana develop independence."

And she said no more: no defensiveness, no snide digs, no self-justifications. She was both surprised and pleased with herself. Dan asked her nothing at all about Hal, and Linda put the phone down fifteen minutes after it had rung.

Hal called about an hour later, and they talked for a long time while Dana got into her bathing suit and went into the backyard to run through the lawn sprinkler. Before long, some neighborhood kids joined her and Linda could hear squeals through the dining room window, while Hal scolded her mildly for getting up so early, told her he couldn't find his best white shirt to pack for the convention, and asked if she wanted him to drop by on his way to the airport on Tuesday. She did.

The phone rang often the rest of that day and the next day, too. Friends who had finally heard that the kidnap victim was Dana wanted to say how awful they thought it was and to ask how Dana was handling it. Pam Warden wanted to say how terrible she felt that it had happened right after Dana had left her house, and wasn't it just frightful that such a thing could happen in Holton; no place was safe anymore. Monday afternoon, Linda's mother called to ask if she should come to stay for a little while. Dana handled it perfectly when she took over the call on the bedroom extension, finding the right tone to reassure her grandmother.

"You don't have to worry about me, Grandma. I'm just about over being scared, and we're doing fine. The trial won't be for a long time yet, so I've decided to forget all about it for a while."

Linda fervently hoped that this would happen for Dana, but she herself felt an additional strain having to talk about Dana's ordeal so often, especially as she had to hide the worst of her suspicions about Ryter because Dana was around during most of the calls. Instead of having the effect of making the incident less painful, the rehearsals of it—which of necessity took on a certain sameness after the first two calls—made Linda resent the need to trivialize the experience, to minimize it. She began to feel that she was simply reassuring other parents when she was so badly in need of reassurance herself.

* * *

On Tuesday morning, Hal stopped by for an hour before he had to leave for the airport. He confessed to being a little nervous about flying, without any apparent need to play the hero for Dana and Linda. He asked Dana what she would like him to bring her from St. Louis, and she said she didn't know what was *in* St. Louis to ask for. Just before he left the house, Hal kissed Linda goodbye, a circumspect little kiss, while Dana looked on wide-eyed. From his car, he called, "I'll call you as soon as I get back on Saturday afternoon," and Linda waved and smiled, suppressing a sudden urge to cry out and tell him not to go. She watched the back of the little car until it was out of sight down the tree-lined street.

In the afternoon, Linda let Dana walk over to the DeKasters' house six blocks away to play with Trina DeKaster, a member of Dana's Scout troop and her classmate at Edison Elementary School. The warm spell had become a genuine heat wave, and Linda was uncomfortable the whole time she was weeding the flower bed and mowing the lawn, but she had to do something to keep from watching the clock, to prevent herself from calling Lois DeKaster and saying that she would pick Dana up. At quarter to five, fifteen minutes before she had promised to be home, Dana came walking into the backyard where Linda was sitting in a deck chair, pretending to read.

"You're early," Linda said, trying to sound breezy.

"I didn't want you to worry," Dana said simply.

"Are you sure you're not a thirty-five-year-old midget in disguise as a child?" Linda said, giving her a hug.

* * *

At 6:15, just before Linda was going to begin preparing a chef's salad, the doorbell rang. Lieutenant Willman was standing on the porch when Linda went to the door, and the sight of him brought back the chill of Saturday night. Poor man, she thought as she unhooked the screen door to let him in, it wasn't his fault that she associated him with bad news. Perhaps that was always the case with him and accounted for his looking solemn most of the time.

"I thought I'd just stop in for a minute after my shift," he said. "You wanted me to tell you when Ryter's appearance in District Court is going to be."

"Yes?" she said.

"Well, it's tomorrow afternoon at one," he announced. He had opened his tie and there were sweat stains on his shirt.

"So soon?" Linda was caught off guard, felt frightened.

"Well, Judge Landis starts his vacation on Friday and he didn't want to pass this case on to his substitute," Willman explained. "New guy wouldn't know the background. Besides, cases like this are rare, even in District Court in Holton County." And he smiled his wry little smile.

"If you have a few minutes, Lieutenant," Linda said, "I'd like to talk to you about something else."

"Sure," he said.

Linda looked at Dana, who was a step ahead of her.

"I suppose I have to go upstairs," the child flared. "Whenever people want to talk about interesting things lately, I have to go away."

Linda knew part of this was play-acting, showing off

for the policeman, but she could also see that she would have to be more firm than usual.

"Please, Dana, do what I ask you to do. It'll be just for a few minutes."

"All right," Dana said, pouting a little. "But I want to talk to the lieutenant sometime, too."

"Maybe next time," he said, smiling at her. She went upstairs, but she stomped a little as she went.

"There's something else I should tell you, too," Willman said. "The threats Ryter made on the phone aren't going to be added to the charges."

"Why not?"

"Gordon worries whenever he's got a case of one person's word against another's, with no other witnesses, I mean. But he plans to use it as an argument against reduced bail." Willman was following Linda to the kitchen while he was speaking.

"Could that happen?" Linda asked, alarmed. "Could his bail be reduced?"

"Well, his lawyer will almost certainly argue for it," Willman said. "The judge appointed Steven Hahn, a young hotshot eager to make a name in his firm. But it's not likely to happen, especially now after Ryter's threats, so don't you worry."

Linda got iced tea for Willman and herself, and they sat down at the kitchen table in front of a fan.

"What's the latest in your investigation, Lieutenant?" Linda asked, searching his face for any sign that he might try to hold out on her.

"Not a lot," he sighed. "I've checked Ryter all the way back to his home in Illinois. Not many surprises there. He got kicked out of high school three times before he finally quit for good. Violent father. About what you'd expect.''

"Nobody can shed any light on his being a child molester? No other incidents?''

"I'm still working on his known associates here in Holton," Willman said. "But so far, I've got nothing concrete.''

"I've been thinking, Lieutenant," Linda said, sitting forward on her chair, "about what he said on the phone. You remember when I told you he said that I could believe him about not getting caught? And then he said, 'I know how to do it.' Do you remember that?''

"Yes," Willman said. "It's in my notes.''

"I've been thinking he could have meant that he'd done it before, gotten rid of a body, and that's why he could be so confident.''

"I thought of that myself, Mrs. Hammond," he said and took a long swallow of tea. "I called in all the files for missing children for the whole area.''

"And?" Linda had not tasted her own tea.

"There are two unresolved cases," he said and then hurried on. "That's not so out of the ordinary when you consider I got the files for five counties.''

"Just tell me about the cases, please.''

"One was here in Holton about two years ago. A thirteen-year-old. She was babysitting her cousins and when her uncle and aunt got back, she was gone. The kids were asleep upstairs and there was no sign of a struggle.''

"I don't remember reading about that," Linda said. "And we were living here then."

"It never made the papers, at least not the front page, because the parents believed she'd run away."

"Why?"

"She was a rebel. It was a tough family situation, too. She didn't get along with the father, and the mother admitted there was some family violence. The girl had often threatened to run away. They never heard from her."

"Is there any connection between Ryter and this family?" Linda asked, and she was hardly breathing.

"His wife's brother was dating an older sister in the family at the time. Ryter and the brother stayed pretty chummy, even after Ryter's divorce."

"My God," Linda said. "*He did it*. He took that child and he killed her. How could her parents just write her off like that? How could they?"

"Mrs. Hammond," Willman said, looking at her with a stern frown between his eyebrows. "There is no evidence whatsoever to support that assumption."

"But you believe he did it, too," Linda said, her wide hazel eyes fixed on his lean face. "You know you do. Ryter found out about that poor girl from his brother-in-law and he killed her."

"What I believe or what you believe doesn't matter," Willman said, setting his glass down on the table. "The only thing that matters is what can be proved in a court of law. Now I'm working on that. The trail is cold, of course, but I'm looking, you can believe me."

"Tell me about the other case," Linda said. She could feel the chill settling over her mind again.

"Mrs. Hammond," he said, shaking his head.

"I told you once, Lieutenant, not to try to protect me with ignorance. Just tell me."

"A twelve-year-old in Bakerville last fall. She left school on a Friday afternoon and never arrived home."

Linda gasped and put her hand to her temple; the hand was icy from holding the glass of tea.

"He said, 'Someday, she'll be walking home from school, and then she'll just be gone.' I can hear him saying it."

"The police over there still don't know what to make of it," Willman said. "The mother is convinced that the girl was kidnapped, but nobody saw anything and there are houses all along where she would have walked, people watching for their own kids. It's a busy time of day. And, again, there's some indication that she might have been a runaway. There was a messy divorce and a custody fight. The kid's friends said she'd been depressed. At first, the mother thought her ex-husband might have taken the child, but the investigation showed that wasn't the case."

"Bakerville is less than twenty miles from here," Linda said.

"I know what you're thinking, Mrs. Hammond," he said quickly. "But as far as I've been able to check, there is no connection of any kind between Ryter and this family."

"But the patterns are so clear," Linda said, her voice getting a desperate edge. "He looks for girls, all about the same age, whose disappearance might be seen as a case of runaway, girls in 'tough' or broken families. I'm sure you would have considered Dana's disappearance from that angle if she hadn't got away and if Mrs. Denser hadn't seen Ryter trying to take her. Well, wouldn't you?''

"It would be a possibility we would have to consider, yes,'' Willman said.

"There's a Bakerville connection. I know there is,'' she said. "You know what Ryter said to Dana. He told her she was never going home again because he meant to kill her even when he pulled her off the street. He knows how to do it because he's done it twice before.''

"Or,'' Willman said, pausing for effect, "we could have three completely separate cases here with only one superficial coincidence connecting two of them.''

"You tell me what you believe, Lieutenant,'' Linda said.

"No, Mrs. Hammond,'' he said, and his jaw set firmly before he continued. "I'll tell you what I know. That's our deal.''

Linda could see he meant it, but she put her trembling hand onto his arm anyway. He flinched a little because her hand was very cold.

"The trial is a long way off,'' he said. "And before it gets here, I'm going to know a lot more about John Charles Ryter. You can bet on it.''

"I *will* bet on it, Lieutenant Willman,'' Linda said, taking her hand back into her lap. "I'm going to count on you to put him away for a long, long time, because I frankly don't see anyone else who can do it.''

"Well, that's what I get paid for," he said, getting up.

"Would you like to stay for some chef's salad?" Linda said. She didn't feel odd about this invitation because she felt she knew Willman as a friend, but he looked flustered and embarrassed. "You're off duty, aren't you?"

"Officially, yes," he said, looking at the door. "But guys like me do our best work sometimes when we're off duty. I'll just grab a sandwich somewhere."

Linda let him out, feeling sorry to see him go at the same time that she was heartened by the idea that he was going away to continue working on the case, to keep digging into the past of that ice-eyed man.

That night, Linda lay awake for hours, thinking about the woman in Bakerville, the mother who was trying to cope with the worst nightmare a parent could face. She wished with all her heart that Hal was not in St. Louis, that he was right next to her in the bed, that he could go with her to District Court the next day, for she was really afraid to see Ryter again, even to look at his back. She found herself thinking about her father and weeping for him as she hadn't done in more than two years. And just before she finally fell asleep, she thought about Arnold Willman nosing around Holton asking questions, and the image of his tall, sloping figure and his piercing eyes gave her a strange sense of comfort.

Chapter 13

Jack Ryter enjoyed his supper the evening before the District Court hearing. In fact, he had felt much better ever since his phone call to Linda Hammond. His outrage and frustration had peaked on that Friday afternoon when Sandy had told him what the Hammond woman had said, that she had as much as accused him of incest. He had gone pale and very quiet, so much so that Sandy got scared. She had seen that look before and much preferred shouting and cursing.

Back in his cell, he had sat rigid on the edge of his cot, rocking slightly back and forth. At the first hearing, the one in county court, he had glimpsed Linda Hammond on his way into the room, the only spectator in the front row. Of course, he had seen her before, during the months he had been watching the child, had seen her climbing in and out of her car, dressed in that red coat

149

and those tall leather boots. He could tell even at a distance that she was one of those cool, "put-together" women, whose hair was always clean and whose underwear probably matched like the models in magazines, one of those high and mighty women who would look through him as if he weren't even there. Most of the time he could tell himself that he didn't care about women like that, but she had come to the courtroom to gloat, to see him squirm, and he hated her for that with a fierce hatred. She hadn't kept her cool when he looked at her, though, when he showed her that he knew all about her and why she was there. He had seen the fear in her eyes then. But she hadn't learned her lesson; on the very same day, she had said that awful thing to Sandy, acting like she thought he belonged to another species or something, keeping Sandy out on the porch as if she were the Avon lady and witch-bitch Hammond didn't buy from door-to-door stuff. That's who she thought she was, all right—one of the people who can keep other people waiting on the porch. Well, she wouldn't keep *him* on the porch if he decided he was going inside.

But he was helpless, locked up, and he couldn't get at her to rip out that clean, perfumed hair. But the phone call had been wonderful, had cheered him up immensely. He wished he could have seen her face because he could tell from her voice what it must have looked like. It made him feel good that people were terrified of him; it gave him a sense of power that warmed his guts better than liquor had ever done. When stupid old Pete Roblicki had tried to get him charged with assault, it had gladdened his heart to see that baboon's face when it had finally dawned on him that this was no joke, that he could take it as gospel that one Peter Roblicki would die if the charges ever came to trial. Yes, Linda Hammond was scared now, and she couldn't do a thing about it—just her word against his, no witnesses. She wouldn't come to court the next time.

Planning how to call her privately, and what to say, and how to tell Olson about it after she complained had been almost as much fun as the call itself; he had used up most of Friday afternoon and evening thinking it through, refusing food because he didn't even feel hungry. When the helpless rage got as bad as it was earlier on that day, when his head felt like an overripe melon ready to explode, planning how to do something always made him feel better, more in control. Fantasizing about revenge wasn't enough; he had to construct a real plan that could work without his getting caught. If he didn't have a plan, his rage would be followed by black depression, and the next step would be drunkenness. Getting drunk was too dangerous, and he had come to loathe the sensation of being out of control, of turning himself over to the rough hands of bar toughs and, eventually, the police. No, much better for *him* to be in control and other people to feel terror, helplessness, rage, humiliation.

He had made this discovery more than two years ago now, in March, when he had been fired from the lumberyard. Normally, he would have gone on a royal drunk, but seeing all the cars in the parking lot, just sitting there with no one around in the middle of the shift, stopped him somehow. All those jerks who thought they were too good to work with him, that stupid foreman who liked to throw his weight around—these cars were their pride and joy. He considered slashing the tires or scratching the paint, but guessed that the link would be too obvious; they would get him back for that. He strolled around looking in car windows until he saw the camera, sleek and expensive, just sitting on the console inside a red Malibu; he didn't know whose car it was. With his jacket covering his hand, he tried the door. Sure enough, the jerk hadn't bothered to lock up. He just lifted the camera up by its leather strap, closed the door, and strolled away. After he had driven off, he found he didn't feel like getting drunk anymore.

Eventually, the guy came to his apartment, one of the crew he hardly knew.

"I had my camera stole on me the day you got fired," he had said.

"So?"

"That's it, right there on your cabinet."

"No, it's not."

"It sure as hell is my camera."

"Can you prove that? You got serial numbers or something?"

"I'm just gonna take it back!"

"You could try."

"Then I'll call the cops."

"Go ahead. You got nothing on me. I bought that camera."

He had looked at the man, just stared at him the way he had stared at Pete Roblicki, until he could see the confusion and fear coming up. Of course, there was no police report. Guys like that didn't register their belongings; they didn't have the sense to lock them up. Idiots.

It was the same month, that March, that he had first heard about the Schacht girl. Sandy's brother, Don, was dating a bimbo named Lou Ann Schacht at the time—a big, loud broad with a laugh that would curdle milk. He and Don were old drinking buddies; in fact, he had met Sandy through Don in the first place. Now Don would talk about Lou Ann and her family whenever they got together for a few beers. Lou Ann's mother was a witch, Don would say, and her father was worse, a loudmouth who, Lou Ann said, beat up everybody in the family, especially the kid sister, Cheryl. This girl was about twelve or thirteen and didn't have the sense to keep her mouth shut around the old man, had to lip off at him when he was in a stew about something—a rebellious and wild kind of a kid.

Finally a day came when he had gone with Don to pick up Lou Ann for a movie. The house was a mess: socks and dirty dishes strewn on the living room carpet, the rooms smelling of cigarette smoke, spilled beer, and old dirt. Cheryl was there, curled up in a corner of the sofa, dressed in one of those long tee shirts that kids Chrissy's age wore for nightgowns. She was a thin, brown-haired, sullen-looking child, small for her age with no adolescent development visible through the dirty yellow shirt. She didn't even look up when the men came into the house.

"Hello there," he had said to her while Don stood nervously waiting for Lou Ann to come downstairs. She turned her dark eyes up at him and just stared, blank, no expression at all.

"Man is talking to you, Cheryl," the father snarled. He was a huge man, flabby and unshaven, padding around in his socks. Ryter saw the girl's eyes flare as she looked sideways at her father, but she didn't speak.

"It's all right, Mr. Schacht," he said smoothly, putting on his best face. "I got a girl about that age myself, so I know how shy they can be sometimes. She don't have to be nice to me."

He had begun to watch her after that, stopping his car in the neighborhood at odd times, in places where he could see the house. For the rest of the school year and on into the summer, he began to learn her habits—when she had to be back inside if she played outside, who her friends were in the neighborhood, where she went to babysit. And he was planning all the time. He drove out into the country looking for back roads and lanes, for areas that looked relatively untraveled. It took him awhile, but at last he found the abandoned farm house, its windows boarded up, its front porch rotted into a sagging wreck. After he had found a back way in, he dug a hole behind the house, one that he could hide easily with the tall weeds that grew all around the old foundation of what had once been a barn. And he had gathered his supplies: plastic sheeting, ropes, some sharp knives. And film. He bought a roll of 35 mm film with thirty-six exposures.

Later, when he had used the entire roll, he realized that he couldn't have it developed anywhere. It was then that he had decided to take the film-developing class at the Vo-Tech, one of those short summer extension classes in the Adult Education Program.

Chapter 14

The District Courtroom was on the first floor of the courthouse and, as usual, Linda was early. She had taken Dana to the Wielands' so that she and Jenny could go swimming at the outdoor pool. It was still very hot, so Patty Wieland, Jenny's mother, had decided to go with them and had invited Dana to stay through dinner. "Probably just burgers at some place that's air-conditioned," Patty had said.

Linda had prepared herself for this afternoon by carefully showering and "dressing up" in white cotton slacks, a bright print blouse, and her best high-heeled sandals. Even while a side of her knew that this was silly, another, deeper, level of her mind understood that she felt more confident when she was dressed up, and confidence was something she had been feeling in need of lately. It would be harder, somehow, for her to look at Ryter again if she were wearing jeans and some old shirt.

When she walked into the courtroom, she thought it looked more like a small lecture room in a college, its spectator seats fanned out around a lower area where the judge's bench, raised on a platform, faced two simple tables. Everything looked either refinished or new and the room had been air-conditioned to an almost uncomfortable chill. This time, Linda looked carefully at the other spectators, but Sandy Ryter wasn't there. After hesitating for a moment, Linda chose a seat about halfway between the bench and the back door.

Paul Gordon was already at the prosecution table, sorting papers into two stacks. A young man in a tan lightweight summer suit sat at the other table. He was very blond, compact, and thin—like a distance runner, Linda thought. He, too, was looking through papers, but unlike Gordon, who seemed to do everything at a ponderous pace, his movements were quick, nervous. This must be Steven Hahn, Linda thought.

A door on the right opened and a policeman brought John Charles Ryter to the defense table. As in his county court appearance, he walked with his head down and his hands folded in front of him, but he looked very different. He had had a haircut, a professional job by the look of it, and he was wearing a sport coat and tie over dark slacks. Even his shoes, Linda noticed, looked newly polished. Again, she was struck by his ordinariness; he might have been any man in Holton dressed for a date or even for church. He looked harmless.

Lieutenant Willman came down the center aisle past

Linda just seconds before a young woman came from the chamber's door to say, "All rise. Tenth District Court in the county of Holton is now in session. Judge Wayne Landis presiding." Another woman entered from the same door to take up a position behind a desk with tape recorders on it.

Judge Landis was a slight man of about sixty, very grey, with round glasses. He was so pale that he looked ill and he moved slowly as he climbed to his bench. For a long time after he had told everyone to be seated, he paged through the papers that the first young woman had brought in and put down in front of him. Then he cleared his throat and, in a high, reedy voice, read John Charles Ryter his rights and the charges against him.

"How do you plead?" the judge said.

Steven Hahn popped to his feet and said, "My client wishes to plead not guilty, Your Honor." His voice, like his manner, was brisk and earnest. Linda hadn't expected Ryter to plead guilty, and yet she felt a strong wave of disappointment when he didn't.

"Mr. Gordon," Judge Landis said, "have you prepared a 701 file?"

"Yes, Your Honor," Gordon said, handing stacks of papers to the judge and to the young defense attorney. "This is an outline of the statements made by the victim and the witness. It also contains statements which the defendant made voluntarily to law enforcement officers. There is a description of the physical evidence gathered by the police. With the help of the investigating officer, who is also the arresting officer, I can summarize the material for the court."

"Proceed, Mr. Gordon," Landis said.

Once again, Linda had to listen to a description of how her daughter had been terrorized. As she heard a summary of Mrs. Denser's statement, she suddenly realized that she hadn't yet thanked this woman for calling the police, for being willing to testify. That was unlike Linda, who was usually polite, thoughtful. She would have to ask Gordon or Willman if such a contact would be appropriate before the trial. Most of the time that Willman was describing the lab tests done on the grass and fiber samples he had found, Linda watched the back of Ryter's head. Occasionally he would move slightly, so that she could see part of his profile, but he didn't react much to what was being said about him. Once, he picked up a pencil and began to draw short diagonal lines on a legal pad in front of him. The way he moved his hand, with a kind of controlled force, seemed menacing to Linda.

The oddest part of the hearing, Linda thought, was that no one else seemed to take notice of the defendant. He had allowed his lawyer to speak for him on the plea, so no one had yet even heard his voice. The judge and the young defense attorney looked intently at Gordon or Willman while they were speaking. Ryter seemed officially invisible. Linda wanted to shout, "Look at him! Make him talk, so you can hear that voice. Look into those eyes so you can see what I've seen there." But all she could do was sit there in the comfortably padded seat and pretend to be invisible herself.

Gordon ended by formally requesting that John Charles Ryter be bound over for trial. When he had finished speaking, Judge Landis sat up straight and asked, "On the basis of the material in the file, is there any need for an omnibus hearing?''

Steven Hahn jumped to his feet again, holding a stapled set of papers in each hand.

"Yes, Your Honor," he said. "At this time, the defense wishes to file a motion to dismiss the charges for lack of probable cause." And he walked forward quickly to present one set of papers to the judge and the other to Gordon.

Judge Landis looked down at the papers for a few seconds.

"Very well, Mr. Hahn," he said. "Let the record show that a formal motion to dismiss the charges for lack of probable cause has been made. Such a motion in itself becomes the subject for an omnibus hearing, which will formally consider whether, on the basis of the evidence, there is probable cause to bind the defendant over for trial. The omnibus hearing will be scheduled within fourteen days of this appearance. Is there anything else?''

"Yes, Your Honor," Hahn said, getting to his feet again. "I would like to request a reconsideration of bail in my client's case. The original sum seems exorbitant, and my client is unable to raise the necessary capital to post bond. He has a family to support, Your Honor, and the time he has already spent in jail has jeopardized his job. We request that he be released on his own recognizance on condition that he sign a waiver of extradition."

"Your Honor," Gordon intoned; "bail was originally set in county court on the basis of Mr. Ryter's past history of threatening his victim in an assault charge some time ago. Since that time, Mr. Ryter has telephoned the mother of the victim in this case and made threats against the victim.''

"There were no threats, Your Honor,'' Hahn said. ''My client admits that, in a moment of weakness, he persuaded police officers to let him call the alleged victim's mother, but it was only to beg her to believe in his innocence and to ask her to stop harassing his wife.''

"The victim's mother was *being* harassed by Mr. Ryter's ex-wife,'' Gordon said loudly. ''It was the former Mrs. Ryter who went uninvited to the Hammond household to try to have these charges dropped.''

"Your Honor,'' Hahn said in a patient, insinuating voice. ''These families know each other. The children are in the same grade at school and have had a falling out. Then the mothers have a quarrel over these charges which are simply the fantasies of a rejected little girl.''

"Your point, Mr. Hahn?'' Landis asked.

"Well, don't you see, Your Honor?'' Hahn said. ''The mother of the alleged victim has a vindictive wish to keep my client in jail, so she responds to his pleas for understanding by creating a story about threats, a story based on what she overheard in the county court appearance—some unsubstantiated story about my client threatening someone in the past.''

Linda had to clasp her hands tightly to keep herself down in her seat. She felt a strong urge to scold Steven Hahn as if he were one of her students, to say to him, ''How can you think anyone will believe such fantastic stories!''

Judge Landis considered in silence for a moment.

"Mr. Gordon," he said at last. "Are there any corroborating witnesses to either of these alleged threats?"

"No, Your Honor," Gordon said.

"Well then, is there any *other* reason why bail should remain at $15,000?"

"Yes, Your Honor," Gordon said quickly, but he was beginning to look and sound uncertain. "Mr. Ryter is not a native of Holton and his employment record shows no strong ties to any position in this community. The probability of his fleeing to escape prosecution is high."

"Not true, Your Honor," Hahn said, smiling at Gordon. "My client has resided in Holton for twelve years and has the strongest tie a man can have—his own child. He has already agreed to sign a waiver of extradition, and if the Court pleases, will agree to report weekly to the county sheriff."

"Your Honor," Gordon began.

"Hold on," Landis sighed. "We'll compromise. Under the conditions outlined by defense counsel, and the additional proviso that the defendant make no effort, either direct or indirect, to contact anyone connected with this case, bail is reduced to five thousand dollars."

Linda was too stunned to move. Neither Gordon nor Willman seemed able to look at her. As the hearing ended, she had to will herself to her feet, hanging on to the seat in front of her as if her legs had suddenly fallen asleep and threatened not to support her. During the argument between Gordon and Hahn, she had forgotten to look at Ryter, who had now risen to be escorted out of the courtroom. She turned her head back to find him already looking at her. His eyes were the same as she remembered them—cold, knowing, inhuman—but this time a tiny smile turned up the corners of his mouth.

Linda felt the awful sense of cold settling over her brain again and had to lock her knees to keep from falling back into her seat. All the time that Ryter was being led by his elbow like a blind man, he continued to look over his left shoulder into Linda's eyes. His face never changed; except for the intensity of the eyes, it might have been made of wax. When he had disappeared through the door, Linda found herself running up the aisle and through the swinging doors at the back of the courtroom. She didn't stop until she had reached the short set of stairs leading to the outside door of the building, and there she leaned on the railing, holding on until her knuckles turned white. Paul Gordon and Lieutenant Willman caught up with her a minute later.

Linda swung around on them, her eyes blazing.

"You told me he wouldn't get out," she cried. "You said the judge was likely to raise the bail amount even higher."

"I'm sorry, Mrs. Hammond," Gordon said. "I always thought Landis was soft, but even I never imagined he would be this soft. Maybe it's not so bad, though. Maybe Ryter won't be able to come up with five hundred dollars."

Linda turned her gaze to Willman, who had already been looking at her. He blinked twice, but he didn't look away.

"I think he can raise the bail," Willman said. "He's got a little property he can hock, and he's already been after his ex-wife to help him. My officers have been supervising his calls, so we got a pretty clear idea of how much money he thinks he can pull together.''

"Is this possible?'' Linda said, her voice cold with fury. "Is it possible that this scum is going right back out on the street, just as if nothing had happened?''

"Well, Mrs. Hammond,'' Gordon said in his public voice, "there *are* conditions on his release. He won't be able to come near you or your daughter, for instance, without landing back in jail. So I don't think you need to be so upset. And the charges are still pending against him.''

"That's another thing,'' Linda said. "What is this omnibus hearing the judge was talking about? It's not the trial, is it?''

Here, Gordon felt on safer ground, and his voice became even more pompous.

"No. It's a hearing before the judge, no jury involved, to weigh the available evidence. We present enough of our case to convince the judge that there is probable cause to believe that the defendant committed the crimes included in the charges. Then the judge can rule on the defense motion to dismiss.''

"How is that different from what happened today?'' Linda asked.

"Well, it'll be more like the trial itself,'' Gordon explained. "The rules of evidence aren't as strictly observed, but the witnesses will testify and be cross-examined.''

"Dana will have to be there?'' Linda was shocked.

"Yes, Mrs. Hammond,'' Gordon said. "It won't be so bad. It'll be like a rehearsal for the trial.''

"Then comes the trial?" Linda demanded. "Are there any other possible hearings I should know about?"

"Well, Mrs. Hammond," Gordon began.

"It still can be very complicated," Willman interrupted. "The judge doesn't have to rule on the defense motion at the omnibus hearing. He can take the motion and the evidence under consideration before deciding if Ryter should go to trial. Landis is notorious for taking motions under consideration for two or three months. Then Ryter's lawyer is likely to ask for a change of venue. That will have to be ruled on, too."

"And then the trial could still not be for months after that?" Linda asked.

"That's right," Willman said simply.

"But I'm confident, Mrs. Hammond," Gordon said, "that Ryter will be bound over for trial. And I wouldn't be pursuing the case if I didn't think I could get a conviction."

"But everybody was confident he wouldn't make bail," Linda said, looking accusingly at Willman.

"He'll be convicted," Gordon said confidently. "And the maximum penalty for these charges is twenty years in the state prison." He said it with rolling satisfaction.

"Let's talk about the real world, Mr. Gordon," Willman said, and he sounded angry. Then he turned to Linda and took her arm. "Now this is the truth, Mrs. Hammond. Under the sentencing guidelines of this state, the criminal sexual conduct charge is more serious than the kidnapping charge, weird as that sounds, especially since this charge includes a severity level of three. That means it's more serious criminal sexual conduct because the victim was under thirteen and because the circumstances caused her to have what the law calls a 'reasonable fear of imminent great bodily harm.' But Ryter has no previous convictions on similar charges. He's never even been *charged* with crimes like this before.''

"What are you trying to say to me, Lieutenant?'' Linda said.

"Even is he's convicted on both of the charges,'' Willman explained, tightening his grip on Linda's elbow, "the sentencing guidelines call for no more than twenty-four months in prison. If it's all good time, that is if he behaves himself, he'll be out in sixteen months.''

"Sixteen months!'' Linda gasped.

"And he might be convicted of lesser charges,'' Willman went on, relentless in his honesty. "If he's found guilty with a severity level of two, he'll get probation.''

"My God, he was right,'' Linda said numbly. "He told me on the phone that he wouldn't be put away as long as I thought he would. He might even be acquitted. That's possible, too, isn't it?''

"Yes, it is,'' Willman said. "If his lawyer can make a jury believe that Dana might have made it up to get even with his daughter for something that happened at school, he'll walk.''

"Now, that's not going to happen, Mrs. Hammond,'' Gordon said.

Linda pulled her elbow out of Willman's grasp and walked down the stairs; she pulled open the door and went outside without looking back at them. She was opening the door of her car when Willman caught up with her.

"Mrs. Hammond."

She turned to look at him, but he just stood there without saying anything more. His face looked haggard, sad, and a little embarrassed.

"Can you protect Dana?" she said, and her voice was no longer angry; it was pleading.

"If you mean, can I assign an officer to watch her all the time," he answered, "or to watch Ryter all the time, then the answer is no. We're understaffed as it is and even if I made such an assignment, the chief would countermand it."

"So what's to be done, Lieutenant?" she said. "You know Ryter will try to get at her, maybe not this week or even next month, but sooner or later. Everything he said to me on the phone is true."

"Is there some way you could get Dana out of town for a while? Some safe place? I can let you know when the omnibus hearing is going to be, and you don't have to be in Holton until then."

"What good will it do to run for a few days?" Linda said. "He'll still be on the streets when we get back."

"Our best bet is to make the case stronger," he said. "To find out about any other crimes he may have committed so that he can be put away for a longer time. I can't be doing that if I'm worrying about protecting you two, spending my time parked in front of your house on my off-duty hours."

"You would do that, Lieutenant?" she asked.

"If I had to," he said, looking away. "But I'd rather not have to."

"There is a way to get Dana away," Linda said,

suddenly thoughtful. "Some friends of ours have a lake cabin and they've invited us to go up there with them. They're leaving Friday morning, in fact."

"That's good," he said, brightening a little. "You get away with your friends and leave your forwarding address with no one but me."

"Oh, I won't be going along," Linda said.

"Why the hell not?" It was the closest thing to an outburst she had ever heard from him, though he was not shouting.

"He's not after me," she said. "And I've already told you I can't stand not knowing what's going on. I want to know the exact minute he walks out of the jail. And I want to hear the second you find out how Ryter knew that family in Bakerville."

"Be reasonable, can't you?" he said, half pleading, half exasperated.

"Look, Lieutenant," she said, "I've been trusting to the system all along. You and my friends have been telling me to relax, not to worry, let the law take its course. Well, the law is letting that monster out of jail, and I'm one of the few people who realize what a monster he is. I can't go play in the water while he makes his plans, scouts my house. I can't."

"All right, all right," he sighed. "I'll take half a loaf. Just get the kid someplace safe, will you?"

"I intend to," she said. "And will you let me know exactly when Ryter walks out of jail?"

"Yes, I will," he said.

"Lieutenant," she said more softly. "I know it sounds like I'm blaming you, but I'm not. I'm very angry and

very frightened, but I *do* know it's not your fault that
Ryter is getting out."

"Okay," he said, his sharp eyes softening, a tired
smile turning up the corners of his mouth. "And one
other thing. You find it so easy to believe that Ryter
means what he says. Well, you can believe that I mean
what I say, too. I'm not going to let up on this guy until I
nail him."

"Godspeed, Lieutenant," Linda said. "I do believe
you. I can see how tired you are and I know it's because
you've been working on this case when you're off duty.
We're grateful to you, please believe that."

"All part of my job," he mumbled, and then he
walked away toward his own car.

Linda drove straight to the Fishers' house, her hands
gripping the wheel as if she were driving on ice and
afraid of losing control of the car. Her head was buzzing,
her mind racing from one sensation to another: rage, fear,
a deep sense of foreboding, but rising above it all, a
horrible guilt, a conviction that she could have prevented
the worst of her fears if she hadn't lost control during her
conversation with Sandy Ryter. She seemed to see Ryter's
face looking at her from the windshield, his deadly eyes,
his waxen smile. She could almost hear the whispering
voice saying, "Oh, teacher, teacher. You should never
have said what you did to Sandy." So she, Linda, was
responsible for bringing all of his twisted rage and
perversity to focus on Dana, a victim whose helplessness
made her the preferred target anyway. If she could only
take back what she had said! Never before in all her life

had Linda felt such an aching longing to turn back the clock so that she could undo something. If she had been kind to Sandy Ryter, he might have turned his paranoid hostility somewhere else, perhaps onto Mrs. Denser for calling the police.

As soon as this thought crossed Linda's mind, she was horrified by it. She was actually wishing that Mrs. Denser would be the object of Ryter's vengefulnesss, wishing terror onto a woman who, a few minutes ago, had been the object of her sincere gratitude. Yet, against this shock at her own motives, Linda heard another part of her mind crying, *Anybody but Dana! Let anyone else be dragged off and tortured and killed, just so it isn't Dana.*

Susan Fisher looked hard at Linda's face when she opened the door.

"You look like you've seen a ghost," she said.

"Close," Linda said, moving past Susan into the living room. "I've come straight over here from the courthouse."

"What happened?" Susan said. Then, noticing Linda's nervous glances, she added, "It's all right to talk. Erin's playing next door."

"They're letting Ryter out of jail," Linda said, sinking down onto the sofa. "At least as good as letting him out because his bail has been reduced so that he'll be able to pay it."

"You're kidding," Susan said.

"No, I wouldn't kid about this, believe me. It didn't

make any difference that he'd said those awful things to me on the phone."

"What awful things on the phone?" Susan said with a puzzled frown, and then Linda remembered that Lieutenant Willman and Hal were the only people she had told about Ryter's call.

As quickly as possible, Linda told Susan about the call, about her fears that Ryter might have been responsible for the disappearance of two other girls, and about the court hearing. Susan listened with growing sympathy, her small, pretty features reflecting every emotion. Every now and then, she would say, "Damn," softly under her breath. By the time Linda had finished describing the proceedings in court, Susan was fairly bouncing with anger.

"So, the kid lawyer made it sound like a cat fight between two women, did he?" she said. "Nothing for the big guys to get upset about. I'll lay you odds that the judge wouldn't have been so quick to accommodate the defense if the threats had been made against a man. So the boys let this creep go when he should just be gassed like a cockroach."

"Lieutenant Willman is trying to find evidence linking Ryter to the two other cases," Linda said. "He's really an ally in this, Susan. He thinks it would be best for Dana to get away from Holton for a while so he can get on with his investigation without worrying about protecting her."

"Good idea, just on general grounds, I'd say," Susan answered.

"So could Dana go to your cabin with you on Friday?"

"Of course," Susan was saying even before Linda had finished the question. "Both of you come along. I already invited you, didn't I?"

"I won't be coming along," Linda said and then held up her hand to forestall Susan's protests. "Please don't try to talk me into going, because it's a waste of time. Dana won't be staying for the whole three weeks, either. I'll have to come get her when she has to testify at this omnibus hearing thing. That will be sometime in the next two weeks."

"All right, if you're going to be stubborn," Susan said. "Of course Dana is welcome to come with us. We'll be glad to have her, you know that."

"I know, Susan," Linda said, taking her hand. "You're a good friend. Now listen, it's important that no one else knows where Dana is. That way, if Ryter starts asking around about her, he can't get any information."

"God, Linda," Susan said. "This is like some movie."

"I know," Linda said. "But we have to take precautions where somebody like this is concerned. Don't even tell Erin that Dana is going along until I bring her over here on Friday morning. Erin might tell some neighborhood kid and that would spread fast, especially since Dana is something of a celebrity now."

"Okay." Susan nodded. "We're planning to leave very early, though, so maybe we could just come over to pick her up."

"No, no," Linda said, "I don't want anyone in our neighborhood to see Dana going off in your camper. It wouldn't take Ryter many questions to find out where she'd gone."

"How do you think of these things?" Susan asked. "I'd be a basket case, and here you are thinking through just what has to be done."

"You can develop a paranoid imagination pretty fast when something like this happens to you," Linda sighed.

"I guess," Susan said. "But I think you're better at it than I would be."

The notion of a competition between them over who had a better paranoid imagination struck them both funny at the same moment, and they laughed out loud. Linda's laugh had a faintly hysterical ring to it, even in her own ears. Susan asked her to stay longer, but Linda was too restless to sit still, too haunted by the feeling that she should be doing something to help Dana.

Linda drove around for a while, trying to focus on some plan of action. It was too early to pick up Dana, yet she felt a terrible sense of time slipping away. Maybe she could try to help Lieutenant Willman get something conclusive on Ryter. But where to start? She had heard the court reporter read back Ryter's address—7 Carimona Street. She brushed the sweat from under her eyes and swung the car around to the north. Maybe there was something the police hadn't found at that madman's house.

Part Two

Part Two

Chapter 15

*L*inda sat slumped against her kitchen table thinking about the gun hidden among her wine glasses. All the way home from Ryter's apartment, she hadn't been able to focus her mind on any clear idea; she had felt only an intense sense of panic, and it had taken a tremendous power of will to keep herself from speeding, from racing the car through stop signs. Now she was becoming aware of how thirsty she was, how dry her throat felt. She got up and drank two glasses of cold tea, pouring it straight from a refrigerated pitcher without bothering about ice. Only then was she able to think about the consequences of what she had done.

What difference did it make that she had taken one weapon away from Ryter? There were so many weapons. How often had she heard people in her own social set lamenting how easy it was for people to buy guns, any kind of people? And a gun was not the only threatening object which might force a child into a car; a steak knife would serve the purpose. So what had she done? She had broken into a man's apartment and stolen a gun. It was entirely possible that Ryter owned the gun legally, even that he had registered it. He had never been convicted of a felony, so it was probably not illegal for him to own a gun.

When he got out on bail, what would he find? Linda turned more pale as she imagined what Ryter's apartment looked like at this moment: a light on in the bedroom, the drawer of the bed table standing wide open. If Ryter really was a "cool customer," as Lieutenant Willman thought he was, he might very well suspect her and call the police to report the theft. And her fingerprints were everywhere in that apartment, in every room, on the door, on the window frame. She might find herself arrested just as John Charles Ryter was getting out on bail; she felt sure he would take great delight in the irony.

What if she were just to call Lieutenant Willman and tell him about the gun? Maybe Ryter had stolen it and then they would have, at last, some other crime to charge him with. Could the police use the gun as evidence, though, now that she had taken it away? Couldn't Ryter just deny that he had ever had the gun, just say she was once again trying to create evidence to keep him in jail? He was so good at that, so convincing, as Willman had said.

What other alternatives were there? She could put it back, just go back to 7 Carimona Street, climb through the window, and put the gun back into the drawer. It wouldn't be too hard to remove any trace of her presence in the apartment. Almost as soon as she thought about returning the gun, Linda felt a deep revulsion. She might be putting back into Ryter's possession the very instrument with which he would murder her daughter.

Suddenly Linda was shaking with rage. A man who had kidnapped her eleven-year-old daughter with intent to rape her, who had threatened to take her again and then to kill her, who had probably already killed other children, was going to be released from jail, perhaps very soon. He was allowed, apparently, to have this ugly, deadly weapon which the police hadn't even looked for, never mind confiscated. And because she had taken the gun away from the criminal, she was now in danger of prosecution herself. She wouldn't put it back. No matter what else happened, she couldn't turn that killing machine back into those hands and then have to wonder what he was doing with it, what he planned to do with it. He might get another gun, but she had *seen* this one, and so putting it back was out of the question.

The dinner hour came and went, but Linda didn't think about food; the tea had filled her stomach and quenched her thirst. She paced from room to room and then sat for a while in front of the fan in an effort to cool off. It was too early for this damned heat, she thought irritably. On top of everything else, to have to drip with sweat, to have to feel your brain fogged by the pressure of the humidity! Finally, she realized it was time to bring Dana home from the Wielands'. She would have to pull herself together, to hide from her child the worst of her nervous terror.

Dana was quiet on the ride home, sensing with her

usual radar that something was bothering Linda. By the time they got into the house, Linda had summoned a mock cheerfulness she hoped would fool her sensitive daughter.

"I've been visiting at the Fishers' for a while this afternoon," Linda said. "How would you like to go with them to their lake cabin on Friday? Swimming, waterskiing, all sorts of good stuff."

"That's great," Dana said. Then she looked suspicious. "You're coming, too, aren't you?"

"No, darling, I'm not," Linda said, taking her arm. "I've got lots of things I have to do in town."

"What things?" Dana said.

"Grown-up things," Linda said, closing the subject with her tone of voice. "Now, let's get your things together and see what needs washing."

"I don't want to go if you're not going," Dana said in a rare display of stubbornness.

Linda suspected that Dana's reluctance had a lot to do with her recent experience. She wasn't ready yet after her trauma for a separation from her mother, even though she had spent a week at camp the previous summer and enjoyed it immensely. All the while Linda was helping Dana select clothes to take along, she had to keep up a reassuring stream of talk about how much fun the cabin would be and how Dana might even learn to water-ski before Erin did.

Later, when Linda had come up from the basement where she had started a load of laundry, she saw Dana picking up the phone in the dining room.

"Who are you calling?" Linda asked sharply.

"Jenny," Dana answered.

"You just spent half a day with her," Linda flared. "Why on earth do you have to call her?"

"I want to tell her I'm going with the Fishers, so she won't wonder why I'm *not* calling her."

"Don't do that, honey," Linda said, taking the phone out of her hand. "I'll tell the Wielands where you've gone. Come play cards with me for a while."

Dana came into the living room, but she looked confused, worried. Linda thought, *We can't live like this. We can't go on living like this for very long, or we'll both be crazy.* They played cards until Dana's bedtime.

When Dana had been upstairs for more than an hour, Linda could resist no longer; she climbed back up onto the kitchen counter and brought out the box and the gun. She had begun to cross the dining room when the phone rang, startling her so that she almost dropped what she was carrying. She looked at the phone while it rang again. Who could be calling her? Hal was in St. Louis and, besides, it was after 11:00. Finally, she forced herself to walk to the phone and pick up the receiver with her left hand; her right hand was holding the gun by its short barrel.

"Hello," she said tonelessly.

"Mrs. Hammond? This is Lieutenant Willman," the by-now familiar voice said.

"Yes, Lieutenant."

"I'm calling to keep my promise," he said. "Ryter has raised ten percent of his bail."

"When will he be out?" Linda asked, no longer surprised by this information.

"Tomorrow morning," Willman said. "Well, closer to noon, I'd say. I know the habits of this particular bail bondsman and he doesn't conduct business before eleven A.M. The processing will take another hour, so Ryter should be walking out of here about noon tomorrow."

Linda looked down at the gun and turned it over in her hand so that the handle glinted in the light.

"Thank you for calling, Lieutenant," she said.

"Is it set for Dana to get away?" he asked.

For a second Linda didn't understand the question; the afternoon already seemed weeks away.

"Oh, yes," she said, her mind clicking at last. "She'll leave with my friends on Friday morning. No one else will know where she's gone."

"Good," he said. Then after a pause, "Are you all right, Mrs. Hammond? You don't sound like yourself."

Again, Linda glanced down at her right hand.

"I'm fine, Lieutenant," she said. "Just tired. I haven't been sleeping very well lately."

"Well, try to get some rest," he said. "And lock your doors."

"Oh, I always lock my doors," she said, and she smiled a bit at the irony.

When Linda hung up the phone, she felt a little dizzy and her head was beginning to throb dully. Was it exhaustion, she wondered, or all the strain? Then she remembered that she hadn't eaten anything since breakfast. For someone as regular in her habits as Linda, skipping two meals could easily cause the symptoms she was now feeling. But she didn't feel hungry at all. Well, she would have to force herself to eat something, then, and going into the kitchen to hunt for food would distract her from the gun and keep her from thinking about Ryter going back to his apartment the next day.

She warmed up a can of soup and made some toast. Sitting at the kitchen table, she ate mechanically, her mind blank and cold. Before the soup was half-finished, she found she couldn't force another spoonful into her mouth. Still holding a half-eaten piece of whole wheat toast, she carried the bowl to the countertop where the breakfast dishes were still stacked up. Linda reflected briefly, without emotion, that her kitchen had never before looked such a mess. Then she walked back out into the living room and put the box and the gun onto the coffee table.

Not until she had pulled the drapes and lowered the shade over the three narrow windows in the front door did she go back to sit down on the sofa. First, she opened the little black box, confirming her suspicion that it contained bullets, bright, shining bullets whose pointed ends were a different-color metal from the side casings. Were some of these bullets already in the gun? The box didn't look full. Linda became more afraid to touch the gun. On closer inspection, she saw that it had several features she hadn't noticed before. In a recessed half-circle above the trigger housing there was a tiny lever, and on the handle just behind the trigger was a small button that had next to it a short groove, suggesting that the button was supposed to slide in that direction. Linda thought she recognized the metal extension at the top of the handle as the hammer. She could tell that the gun was not a revolver, but beyond that she had no idea what kind of weapon it was or how it worked.

Suddenly Linda heard footsteps in the hallway upstairs. She had just enough time to scoop the box and the gun under a throw cushion in the corner of the sofa before Dana appeared on the stair landing.

"I keep waking up," Dana said. "It's too hot to sleep."

"I'll put the fan right next to you," Linda said, rising unsteadily.

"I don't want to go with the Fishers on Friday either," Dana said, and she looked as if she might cry.

Linda went upstairs with her to set up the fan and then sat on the floor next to Dana's bed, talking to her about her own experiences at summer camp and visiting on her cousins' farm. She remembered how her own mother had often done this same thing, sitting beside the bed and talking to her when some childish fear or disappointment had kept her awake. After about a half hour of this reassuring drone, Dana fell asleep.

Linda didn't leave the room, but sat there just looking at her sleeping child, looking at the dark eyelashes where they spread out like fans on the softly rounded cheeks, at the little mouth opened in sleep, at the graceful curve of shoulders rising and falling slowly with her breathing. The thought of anyone assaulting and violating that tender body brought tears streaming down Linda's face. And so she kept her watch all night, memorizing her daughter's features as if this were the last time she would see them, occasionally touching her sleeping face, pulling the single sheet back whenever Dana turned over in her sleep. It seemed impossible that she could ever have scolded Dana or been angry at her for any reason.

At about 6 in the morning, Linda dozed off, her head against Dana's mattress, her legs curled up next to the bed. She slept undisturbed for only an hour, and then she began to dream. All of the features of the room appeared in realistic detail, none of the usual distorted landscape of dreams. She was making corn on the cob, stripping away the leaves and corn silk and placing the golden ears in the wire basket that fit inside her biggest stainless steel kettle. Soon, the basket was full, enough corn to feed a big crowd, though Linda didn't have a clear idea who she was cooking for. Then she carried the basket, straining under the weight, to the stove where the big kettle was steaming over a burner. Slowly, she began to lower the basket into the boiling water. Only when it was already half-submerged did she see that the basket contained not corn, but Dana—Dana as she had looked when she was a few months old.

Linda's head jerked upright from Dana's bed, her eyes wide and staring, her mouth opened as if she might scream. Her left arm had fallen asleep from being pressed against the side of the bed and she rubbed it for a few minutes as she looked around the room, satisfying herself that she was awake, that they were both safe. After a glance at her watch, she got to her feet, feeling the stiffness in her legs and a dull ache in her right side. Then she went downstairs to make some coffee and think about breakfast. And to move the gun back to its hiding place.

Chapter 16

*I*t was Dana who saw him first. She came racing into the kitchen just after lunch, her face gone pale under the new tan, her mouth trembling.

"He's out there," she whispered in a desperate hiss.

"Who?" Linda said, but the terror in Dana's eyes answered her question before the child could speak again. "Mr. Ryter. Chrissy's father."

"Where is he?" Linda found that she was whispering, too.

"On the corner across the street, in front of the duplex."

Linda didn't even pause to dry her hands but ran through the dining room to the front door. Despite the heat, which was as bad as the day before, they had kept the inside door closed and locked. With Dana clinging to her waist, Linda pulled the sheer curtains aside so she could see clearly through the narrow windows of the door.

Ryter was standing perfectly still, his arms folded across his chest; he stood on the grass between the sidewalk and the street, almost as if he wished to be out of the way of any pedestrians who might be happening by. He was staring fixedly at the Hammond house. Even at the distance of seventy feet, that short, tense body and rigid head seemed threatening to Linda; his very stillness seemed like a taunt.

Linda automatically dropped her hands onto Dana's shoulders and moved the child behind her, as if she thought those no-color, crazy eyes could pierce the house and wound her daugher. The sense of cold inside Linda's head was by now almost familiar. She felt sure Ryter had gone back to his apartment the minute he was released on bail and had found the empty drawer in his bedroom. So convinced was she of Ryter's maniacal cunning that she believed without question that he knew she had stolen the gun. He had come here to show her that he knew, to show her that she had put herself squarely in the wrong, had reduced rather than heightened her ability to protect Dana.

"I want Lieutenant Willman," Dana whimpered from behind Linda's hip. "He'll make him go away. He can make him go away."

"Don't worry, darling," Linda said, her voice absurdly contradicting her words. "I *am* going to call Lieutenant Willman, but not until Mr. Ryter goes away. We have to watch him until he leaves, to see what he intends to do, if anything."

"He's after me," Dana cried, and by raising her voice, she frightened herself into sobs.

"He can't hurt you," Linda said, drawing Dana around to hold the child against her stomach, but she didn't bend down, wouldn't risk taking her eyes off Ryter. "He's just trying to act tough, to see if he can scare us into giving up on the trial. But he daren't come any closer than the corner, don't you worry."

"How do you know?" Dana asked, her voice muffled against Linda's apron.

"Because the judge said so," Linda said, aware of how hollow that reassurance really was. "If he tries to get closer or to talk to us, even on the phone, he'll have to go straight back to jail. He knows that, so he won't try to do anything else except stand there looking like a stupid statue."

As she spoke, Linda knew that she was trying to convince herself as much as Dana. It was an effort to keep her voice from shaking. The terrible sense of guilt she had felt after the court hearing was doubled now. Not only had she focused Ryter's vengeful lunacy on Dana by being spiteful to Sandy Ryter, but now she had intensified it by breaking into his apartment and stealing his gun. She felt like a snared animal whose every move to escape engages another coil of the netting, until the struggle is finally paralyzing. Do netted baboons and tigers have to endure the added horror of watching their babies carried away by the triumphant poachers?

Of course, she had no idea how long Ryter had been standing there before Dana saw him. In just the few minutes Linda had been watching him, he already seemed like a fixture on the corner, like some obscene gesture carved in stone and set into place over the protests of the shocked citizenry. And yet, she knew he would look utterly harmless to anyone else looking out of a window; to passersby, he would seem to be some laborer waiting for his ride back to work after lunch: a composed, normal-looking man whose presence in the Holton landscape would pass unnoticed. No treat here. Surely only a hysteric could object to such an innocuous picture.

For ten more minutes, Ryter stood without moving while Linda made soothing sounds to Dana and felt her own nerves stretching tighter and tighter. The sun was still on the front of the house, and the heat through the glass was making sweat pool in the hollows of Linda's throat. An occasional car would go by on the quiet street, never wholly obscuring the watching figure, and Linda found herself wishing with all her being that she had telekinetic powers so that she could will a car to drive over John Charles Ryter. She even imagined the horrified driver saying, "I can't understand it! I couldn't steer. Something must have gone wrong with the steering," while she and the other neighbors watched the ambulance start off for the city morgue.

Quite suddenly, Ryter dropped his arms to his sides and started walking across the street. Linda jumped as if she had been poked, then craned her neck to follow Ryter's movements as far as the door would permit her to see. Just before she lost sight of him, she disengaged herself roughly from Dana's grasp and ran to the side window. From here, she could see Ryter disappear behind the Hardwicks' house, not hurrying and not strolling either, reappear on the other side of the Hardwicks' driveway, and then cross to a tan car. He got inside and drove away to the west. Linda sprinted across the house to the back of the dining room where she could watch the car until it was out of sight. Behind her, Dana was saying, "What's he doing? Is he trying to get in?"

Linda called the police station immediately.

"Lieutenant Willman is out in his car," the dispatcher said.

"You can reach him by radio, can't you?" Linda asked.

"Yes, of course."

"Well, please do that and tell him that Linda Hammond wants to see him as soon as possible. It's very important."

It was more than half an hour later when the phone rang.

"He was here," Linda said when Willman had identified himself, never even considering that she would have to explain who "he" was.

"I know," Willman said.

"What do you mean, 'I know'?"

"I followed him there from the jail just as soon as he got out on bail. He had his car in our impounding yard."

"You saw him watching us?"

"I saw him standing on the corner across from your house, yes. For almost half an hour."

"You're sure he didn't go to his house first?" So convinced had Linda become that Ryter knew about the missing gun that she couldn't wholly register what Willman was saying.

"Of course I'm sure. Why do you ask?"

"Nothing. Never mind. Why didn't you arrest him if you followed him here? The judge said it was a condition of his bail that he couldn't come near us."

"No, Mrs. Hammond," Willman said in his patient voice. "He said Ryter couldn't try to 'contact' you or Dana. As long as he stays at least fifty feet from your property and doesn't say anything, he isn't contacting you."

"That's absurd!" Linda was almost shouting. "It's obvious that he's trying to intimidate us."

"I know, I know," Willman said. "If he does this often enough, it will establish a pattern of harassment and then we *can* get his bail revoked."

"Often enough?" Linda blustered. "What the hell does that mean? Do we have to be prisoners in our own house for weeks, peeking out of windows to see if Ryter is lurking around? Don't you know what that would be like? Dana saw him and she's terrified." Linda couldn't keep the hysteria out of her voice any longer.

There was a pause at the other end of the line and then Willman said softly, "Is she with you now?"

"Yes."

"Could I talk to her?"

Linda handed the phone over to Dana without speaking.

"Dana?"

"Yes." She was still whispering.

"I don't want you to worry about Mr. Ryter because I'm watching him. Do you hear me?"

"Yes, Lieutenant," Dana said out loud.

"You go to your friends' cabin tomorrow and don't tell anyone else where you're going. That way, Mr. Ryter won't have any idea where you are and you'll be safe. Until you leave, I'm going to make sure Mr. Ryter stays away from you. Okay?''

"Okay," she said, more confident. "Will you take care of my mom, too, while I'm away?"

"Yes, I'll take care of your mom, too. And she'll take good care of herself. Try not to be scared."

"I'll try."

"Now, let me talk to your mom again."

When Linda got back on the phone, Willman said, "He's in his apartment now and I'm calling from a place where I can see his car. Maybe you could get Dana to your friends this afternoon while we know Ryter isn't watching you. Then she can leave tomorrow without him suspecting a thing—your car will be there at your house if he should drive by later."

"That's a thought," Linda said, her mind numbed by the information that Ryter was even now in the apartment she had broken into, was perhaps staring at the empty drawer. "I'd like to know why he isn't at work. Didn't his lawyer make a big deal about his losing his job if he missed any more work?"

"He works the graveyard shift, Mrs. Hammond. I thought you knew that."

"I think you did tell me that once, but what exactly does that mean?"

"That plastics factory runs twenty-four hours a day, never shuts down the vats. The last eight-hour shift is from one A.M. to nine A.M., and that's the one Ryter works."

"I see."

"I'm going to keep my eyes on Mr. Ryter for the time being and I'll check in with you again about three. Do you think you can have Dana stashed by then?"

"Yes," Linda said, almost moved to a smile by the word "stashed." "Thank you for being our guardian angel."

"Yes, thank you," Dana said, putting her mouth next to Linda's. "I'm gonna be brave."

Linda called Susan Fisher to clear the early arrival. Then she and Dana packed hurriedly, Dana now wholly cooperative, obviously convinced of the wisdom of getting out of town. All the time Linda kept up a reassuring patter to Dana, she was thinking about Ryter in his apartment. If he would come straight from jail to glare at them, what would he do if he figured out who had taken his gun? What was going through that twisted mind even now? She could hear again the poisonous voice on the phone saying, "As soon as I get out, I'm gonna hurt you. I'm gonna hurt you in the worst way there is."

Chapter 17

O f course Ryter had meant for the Hammonds to see him. He had waited patiently until he saw the curtain move inside the door and then stayed long enough afterwards to make sure the Hammond bitch had a good scare thrown into her, but not long enough for the cops to roust him. He was too smart to let the law get in his way now. He had watched this house before, many times, but this was the first time he had let himself be seen; his purpose was different now, of course, his sense of caution almost completely routed by his anger.

But he had always felt dull anger and resentment while watching the Hammond house; the whole neighborhood made him seethe with a sense of injustice—all these people who owned their own houses and who had credit cards and savings accounts, while he had to live with other people's cast-off furniture and could barely maintain a checking account. He had accepted without question his father's conviction that there was a direct causal connection between these two states—it was *because* people like Linda Hammond had these things that he couldn't have them. It was their fault that he had to drive a twelve-year-old car and buy gas for it five dollars' worth at a time; it was because their kids had braces that his kid had crooked teeth.

Ryter often found himself thinking about things his old man had said, found himself accepting the assumptions he had made, for, despite the hatred, it was his father's view of the universe which had stuck, had become his own. He never thought about his mother at all. She had ceased to exist for him emotionally from that moment in his early childhood when he had finally realized that she couldn't protect him from his father. So the equations had been set: gentleness equals weakness and must be despised; cruelty equals strength and must be imitated.

He had plenty of time to think and plan while he waited for the Hammonds to see him and then for them to be frightened. There would be a trial but not for quite a while yet. All he would have to do would be to grab the Hammond kid sometime soon, strike quick as lightning when they would all think he was only trying to scare them. No witnesses this time—he would have to be very careful about that. He had the advantage, of course, because he already knew Dana Hammond's habits so well, and no one suspected that. He wouldn't be able to keep her for very long, just a few hours at Fitak's hunting shack, but it would be long enough for pictures, lots of pictures. And because the cops would never be able to find the body or prove that she had been with him—he had already buried one car vacuum and bought another— it would do no good for that smart aleck Chicago cop to arrest him; it wouldn't even mean anything if he had no alibi. Then the trial for kidnapping would be a joke—no victim to testify, no conviction. It was going to be wonderful to settle that luscious little brat's hash, jumping away from him like that, and bring that smart-ass Willman down on his head. Pity he couldn't keep her longer.

Then he would have to figure out a safe way to send the pictures to Linda Hammond, one at a time. With that, he could take all the time he wanted, months or even years, could watch her come out on her porch to get her mail—no law against that. It would be best if he could arrange to have the pictures arrive from different parts of the country, lots of different postmarks. And he *did* have some connections now, men who wouldn't dare to question why they were being instructed to re-post sealed envelopes—who wouldn't dare to tell anyone. The first pictures had seen to that.

At first, he had developed the pictures of Cheryl Schacht just for himself, carefully wrapping the negatives in two layers of plastics bags and hiding them under the stones between the railroad ties. He had done the same with the pictures themselves when he wasn't looking at them, never leaving them in his apartment when he was out of the house, bringing them upstairs only in the middle of the night when he couldn't sleep. Just as the planning stage had been a pleasure in itself, the pictures prolonged the experience for months after the Schacht girl was buried. He would go over all of them in order, reliving the events, almost rehearing the girl's cries. He had his favorites among the pictures, especially some of the close-ups, and he found release all over again by masturbating while he looked at his favorites.

But gradually the images lost their power, became just lines and curves on pieces of paper. It was as if he had used them up, had taken all meaning out of them. It was then that he began to think there might be money in selling the pictures; he was always hurting for cash and had heard that there were underground mailing rings that specialized in S&M kiddie porn. The problem was how to find a safe way into such a mailing list. The answer came easily enough when Nancy Birkin, a prostitute he saw from time to time, asked if there was any fantasy that was a real turn-on for him. He made up a fantastic lie involving racially mixed groups of women and then asked if she knew where people could get pictures like that; were there outlets she knew about where people could sort of special-order the sexual fantasy of their choice in pictures? Dumb old Nancy had produced an address without a murmur.

The rest had involved his getting a post office box in a neighboring town, writing to ask for child pornography, and then suggesting by return mail that he had pictures for sale. He never kept any of the stuff that was first sent to him; it didn't particularly interest him and he considered it dangerous to keep it around. Soon, he began to get orders. Plain envelopes would appear in the post office box, envelopes containing cash and an address. He would get out the negatives, print a set of pictures, and send it out in a plain manila envelope. The orders were never frequent enough to provide him with much more than pocket money, but it was something. It gave him a definite sense of satisfaction. Of course, he didn't print all of the pictures for his customers—he never sent the ones he had taken after Cheryl was dead.

But his new business wasn't enough to keep him content. The old restlessness and anxiety began to build again, the feeling that he was losing control, that his life was flying apart. He lost another job and had to go on welfare for a while. Welfare! God, his old man would spit on him if he knew. When summer rolled around again, he found work doing road construction for the county—hot, back-breaking work that bored him almost as much as it exhausted him. But there he met Frank Conrad from Bakerville, a garrulous, grizzled crew chief, fifteen years with the county and loved every minute, to hear him tell it. During breaks, Frank would talk and the men would listen, the hot stink of asphalt still burning in their noses.

At last, Frank said something interesting. He began to talk about his next-door neighbors who were getting a divorce—"God knows why!"—and were wrangling over property and cars and pets, and especially, over the custody of their little girl—"purty little mite, but quite a bit spoiled." Subtly, over many days, Ryter asked questions that made old Conrad even more expansive on the subject of his neighbors: their names, their friends, even the makes and models of their cars. It was no problem at all finding the address in the Bakerville phone book or confirming it by looking up Frank Conrad's address—417 Sanborn must surely be next door to 419 Sanborn.

It was a tidy little house, beige stucco with dark brown shutters. He would drive over to Bakerville in the mornings before his shift began, so he could begin his watching. The wife was a full-figured blond—probably a dye job— who drove a tiny foreign import that seemed too small for her. Once or twice he saw the husband coming over for a visit or maybe a fight. Poor jerk was probably stuck in some dinky apartment now, while the cow got his house and half his worldly goods. But Kristin Allen was a beauty, all right, eleven or twelve, strawberry blonde hair, dimpled elbows, the faint suggestion of breasts inside the sundresses and halter tops she wore as she flew around the neighborhood on her bright blue bicycle.

Before the summer was over, Ryter was "between jobs" again and so had plenty of time to spend in Bakerville, learn habits, and make his plans. When he got the job at the plastics plant in August, he thought of it as only a temporary delay. The mother, he had noticed, was watchful; maybe she was afraid her ex-husband would try to grab the kid. Well, that would work right into his plans, would give him time before a kidnap alarm was sounded. School began, Ryter went hunting with Scott Fitak, and he got booted to the night shift. None of those stupid jerks supected that he preferred to work at night; it left his days free to watch Kristin. He especially watched her on her way home from school. Her pattern was always the same: for the first two blocks, she walked with three other girls; at the next corner, one of the girls split off to the right; after three more blocks, Kristin turned left and the two other girls kept straight on; in the next block after her turn, Kristin walked diagonally across the fenced-in parking lot of a locker plant—only a tall, blank wall faced that parking lot. It was just a matter of waiting until there were no other cars around. And of moving very fast, of course.

He had kept Kristin for three days. The hunting shack was so isolated he didn't have to worry about anyone coming across her while he went to work as usual, and he had made very sure she wouldn't get out of the ropes. On the fourth day, he could see that she was almost unconscious from dehydration—he hadn't thought about giving her anything to drink—and she had no spirit left at all. So he had finished her quickly and put her body in the wetlands; it was easy to make a deep hole in that swampy ground. He had already vacuumed the inside of his car after taking her out of it to put her in the shack because she had thrashed around quite a bit in the car, and now he buried the car vacuum with her. He remembered reading that the guy in Atlanta had been convicted on the basis of fibers found in his car. The plastic sheeting he had used in the shack he buried in a separate hole.

He had taken lots of pictures of Kristin, many more than he had taken of Cheryl, but he found that he had used up the pictures faster this time; even before Christmas, they no longer did anything for him. By spring, he had already sold four sets of them to his mail customers. But he wouldn't sell any pictures of Dana Hammond. If they surfaced anywhere, for any reason, that sharp-eyed cop would find a way to trace them back here to Minnesota, and he would have pictures of his own to show to postal employees. No, only Linda Hammond would get the new pictures and the cops wouldn't know how to trace them. It made him feel happy to think of her getting the pictures, of what her face would look like when she saw the color prints. Imagining it made the time on the corner pass very quickly for him, brought a little smile to his face.

He smiled as he walked to his car knowing she must be watching him, smiled as he drove away having broken no laws. There was nothing the snotty bitch could do. He was only two blocks from his apartment when he noticed the tall policeman in the car behind him, and then he stopped smiling.

Chapter 18

When Linda and Dana arrived at the Fishers, the camper was parked in the driveway and Erin was waiting next to it, dancing with excitement as the Hammond car pulled in. She had obviously just found out that Dana was going along. Jerry Fisher waved at them as he came out of the house. He was a tall, plain-looking man, as easy-going and quiet as Susan was volatile and talkative. He said little beyond hello when Linda and Dana stepped out of the car, but Linda could tell from his face that Susan had told him everything. He patted Linda's shoulder clumsily and carried Dana's suitcase into the house.

Erin's enthusiasm was mildly contagious and soon Dana had joined her in the kitchen to look at the "goodies" they were taking along. Susan appeared from the basement carrying a small cooler in one hand and a folded chair in the other. Linda hurried forward to help her.

"You'd think there were no stores up at Lake Wheaton," Susan said, "the way we always take so much food along. But we really need something to munch on in the camper on the way."

When she had handed the deck chair over to Jerry, whose job it was to find room for it somehow in the camper, Susan looked up into Linda's face.

"You look pretty awful, kiddo," she said.

"Thanks," Linda said with an attempt at a smile.

"You know what I mean," Susan said. "I wish you'd change your mind and come with us. It's not too late."

"Thanks, Susan, but my mind's made up."

"But what are you going to do alone here in Holton while we're gone?"

"I don't know. I really don't know." Linda felt too tired to try to create a story.

"All right, Linda, all right," Susan sighed. "Here, I made you a map. It starts at Warner, which, of course, you can find on a regular map. The phone number is on there, too."

And she handed Linda a piece of paper of which she had carefully drawn in county roads, dirt roads, and finally the short road to a square labeled "Fishers' Folly." All along the route, Susan had penciled in chatty descriptions of landmarks to watch for. Linda folded the paper and slipped it into her purse.

"Thank you, Susan," she said. "Thank you for everything."

"It's nothing," Susan said dismissively, reluctant as

usual to have her kindness acknowledged. "I'll sit on the kids to keep them in the house today. That way, nobody around here will know Dana is with us. And we leave very early tomorrow morning, before the neighborhood is stirring."

"That's good," Linda said numbly. "That's what's important."

"You just don't worry about Dana, you hear?" Susan said, giving Linda a hug. "Try to get some rest. Oh, and could you remember to come over and take our garbage bags to the curb tomorrow night? The truck doesn't come until Saturday morning and I hate to encourage the neighborhood kids to play chicken with the bags on those dirt bikes of theirs. Sometimes, they scatter garbage for half a block."

"Sure," Linda said. "It's the least I can do. Count on it."

When it was time to say goodbye, Linda couldn't hold back the tears as she hugged her daughter for a long moment. Dana, too, had wet eyes when she looked up at her mother.

"Aren't we being silly?" Linda said, trying to laugh. "We'll see each other in a little while. And I'll call you every few days."

On the way home, Linda heard again in her mind Susan's question, "What are you going to do alone here in Holton while we're gone?" It occurred to her now that she really had no clear idea about any course of action beyond waiting for Lieutenant Willman to call. She had begun living from moment to moment, she, a woman who was usually so organized that she had her Christmas shopping done before Thanksgiving. This new sense of helpless drift was an agony to her, making her alternately angry and terrified.

Willman checked in at 3:00 as he had promised.

"Well, that's taken care of," he said when Linda told him the Fishers would leave at dawn. "Now you take normal precautions for yourself until Ryter goes to work."

"What if he doesn't go to work? I'm exhausted, but I don't think I'll be able to sleep tonight if I have to imagine that he might be prowling around."

"I'm going to check on him tonight to make sure he goes to work."

"Will you call to tell me?"

"At one o'clock in the morning?"

"I won't sleep until then, anyway. I want some assurance that he's otherwise occupied for eight hours."

"All right, Mrs. Hammond, I understand." His voice was gentle again. "I'll give you a ring."

By 4:00 Linda thought she might try to get some sleep to make up for the near sleeplessness of the night before. But the heat had been compounded by another sharp rise in the humidity, and even the fan blowing directly into her face didn't seem to relieve her discomfort very much. More importantly, because exhaustion might have overcome discomfort otherwise, she couldn't shake the feeling of foreboding which had settled on her at the courthouse the day before, the nervous certainty that it was only a matter of time before something terrible happened.

Stretched out on her bed with all her clothes on, Linda began to imagine that she heard noises downstairs. Twice she turned off the fan to listen, her ears straining, her shoulders rigid. Finally, she gave up the effort to sleep and went downstairs where she sat in front of another fan trying to read a magazine which had been unopened since its arrival four days ago. The refrigerator began to run, its sound startling her so that she jumped. She began to realize that without Dana in the house, she was more afraid than she had been before.

When she was in college, she remembered now, she had read a novel in which a character had to testify at somebody's trial. The character was trying to explain the actions of the defendant, to justify those actions—Linda seemed to remember that the defendant had been accused of cowardice of some sort—by saying that it's easy to be brave when everyone else is watching you and expecting you to be brave, but not so easy when you're alone. Until now, she had thought that the witness meant that it was easy to *pretend* bravery when people are watching. But here in her empty house, Linda could see the real meaning. There was no pretense about it. She had actually *felt* braver when Dana was there, needing her to be brave, expecting her to be the grown-up. Now that she was alone, the fear was closing in on her.

At 5:30, she gave up the pretense of reading and went into the kitchen. She got the gun and bullets back down from the cupboard and carried them into the living room. Placing the objects carefully in the center of the coffee table, she sank down onto the sofa.

She sat still with the fan blowing into her face until 7:00, but her mind wasn't still. While the sky became overcast outside and the humidity became even more intense, she took no notice of any of it, but focused her eyes on the gun. Her mind darted from one impression to another, but found no coherent course of action. Her defenses were weakened by sleeplessness and lack of food and, in this condition, she couldn't hold her imagination away from graphic images of Dana in Ryter's hands, of Dana bleeding and terrified, of Dana's body buried in some far-off woods. When she tried to wrench her mind away, there was the gun and the two courses of action she seemed to have left: put it back or be arrested for stealing it. Oddly, one idea kept circling in her mind, fading to the edge of consciousness and then coming back again, like someone vaguely familiar on a Ferris wheel that she was watching from the ground. It was the idea that had come to her before she originally rejected the notion of putting the gun back: it would be fairly easy to erase the evidence that she had been in Ryter's apartment; a dust cloth would do it.

At 7:00, a course of action emerged into the front of her consciousness, almost like a completed sentence that someone else had spoken to her: she had access to Ryter's apartment and Ryter's gun, so when he came back from work the next day, she could be waiting for him and kill him.

Linda recoiled in horror from the idea, actually whispered the word no out loud. At the same moment, however, a deep emotional satisfaction filled her and brought with it a flood of accompanying arguments. It would solve everything. Dana would be safe forever. The horror of waiting for Ryter to act would be removed from both of them. There would be no trial. If she could make it look like suicide, the case would be closed. The last clause resonated in her head like a bell: the case would be closed.

She stood up and began to pace, walking back and forth as fast as she could without actually running. Her mind was racing so fast that ideas fell over each other. She would have to fire at close range—that was what everybody in the cop shows talked about—and she would have to wipe everything she had touched; no one else was likely to be there because they had all been away when she was there yesterday; the house was screened from the street and she wouldn't actually have to look at him after he was dead, just drop the gun and get out; if both doors were locked, the police would think he had killed himself—he might not even be found for a long time—she would have to wear gloves. At last, sweat began to roll down her back and she made herself sit down.

Immediately, the rational, careful Linda took over. She would never get away with it. There were hundreds of things that could go wrong. She might be seen by the neighbors, perhaps had already been seen yesterday. Lieutenant Willman was such a good policeman, so thorough. He would just keep asking questions until he found someone who had seen her. She would make some mistake, maybe even lose her nerve at the last moment, miss him or only wound him slightly. And then Ryter would certainly kill her. She had never fired a gun in her life, and she had no idea of how to load this one or fire it even if it was already loaded. Even if she succeeded in killing Ryter, if the gun would simply go off when she pulled the trigger, there would be errors she wouldn't be aware of committing. She would be caught, and this would be first-degree murder. The scandal and trauma would be unbearable for Dana and, of course, the child would lose her mother to a long prison term.

The fan turned and turned, and Linda sat very still. The rational side had won out for the moment, but it brought with it all the foreboding she had been feeling before 7:00. Try though she would to shake the feeling, she couldn't rid herself of the belief that inaction on her part would bring disaster more certainly than *any* action she might take. The certainty that she had no control over what might happen was profoundly depressing. And, irresistibly, the notion kept sneaking back into her consciousness that Ryter's death would solve the problem. Once it occurred to her that she might throw the gun away and go back to Ryter's apartment just to remove her fingerprints. But immediately, she was overwhelmed by the same feeling she had had while she was searching the apartment: why risk a return trip, with a chance of being seen or caught, to accomplish so little? As long as she was already there—

Linda broke off the thought and went to the bookshelves to take out several volumes of the encyclopedia. She wouldn't really do anything, she told herself, but she was curious about how the gun worked, and reading was something to take her mind off depression. She carried the books to the coffee table and put them down next to the gun. Then she began to look up "gun," "pistol," "firearms," and "weapon." All of the articles were very general and none of the pictures looked exactly like the object lying next to the books. Yet, oddly, she felt somewhat cheered by her reading. She was used to approaching problems by reading books about them. When she was pregnant with Dana, she had calmed her anxieties by reading every book she could find on pregnancy and childbirth.

More and more often, as the skies darkened with clouds and the sunset, Linda kept coming back to her plan to kill Ryter, telling herself always that it was only an exercise to keep herself from being depressed, that she would never really attempt such a thing. She paced. She made herself some coffee. She ran upstairs and rummaged through a box in her closet until she found a pair of white nylon gloves that she had once worn with an Easter suit, a lovely lilac-colored suit she had long ago given to Goodwill. She dropped the gloves onto her bed and went back downstairs.

Linda alternately paced and sat down, her mind seething with conflicting thoughts and plans, all of which seemed to go nowhere. About midnight, a strange thing happened: Linda actually physically felt it occurring inside her head. It was as if a bureau or other high piece of furniture had begun to totter and then fall, slowly at first and then rushing to meet the floor with a terrible crash. Afterwards, her head felt light and a little giddy, but she was very calm. It was as if she had emerged on the other side of exhaustion and terror into a place where she no longer felt any emotions at all, only a determination to act, to do something besides agonizing. She stood up quickly and fished her car keys out of her purse. Then she picked up the gun and held it in her hand. There was at least one thing she could do. She must wait now until Willman called to tell her that Ryter was safely at work, and then she could learn how to use this gun.

Chapter 19

Willman was waiting for Ryter when he came down to his car at 12:45. The tall policeman had originally planned simply to follow the tan car from a safe distance until he could confirm that Ryter had gone inside the plastics factory. But, almost at the last moment, an odd impulse to confront the little man made him get out of his own car and walk into the graveled parking lot. His own emotional involvement in this case was a constant surprise to him. As he watched Ryter's slightly rolling gait change to a cocky strut when he had obviously spotted the policeman next to his car, Willman felt a wave of something close to hatred sweep through him. Somebody ought to just plug the little bastard and make Holton a whole lot cleaner.

"Well, well, well," Ryter called across the last ten feet. "Slumming, are we?"

"Oh, no. Just working late," Willman said, straightening up to his full height, waiting for Ryter to get close enough so the dim glow of the street light would show him the simian face. "I just have a question or two."

"Better be quick," Ryter said, deliberately coming up close to the tall policeman, obviously determined to show some aggressive bluster. "I gotta go to work."

"This won't take very long," Willman said blandly, swallowing his distaste for the little man. "Just a few little details."

"Well then, fire away," Ryter said, rocking back and forth on his heels.

"I understand you're quite a photography buff," Willman said, noting with satisfaction that Ryter's eyes flared open and then darted sideways.

"What's that supposed to mean?" Ryter said, but Willman could hear that the macho sneer had gone out of his voice.

"Got a nice camera, I hear. Just like a camera one of your co-workers at the lumberyard used to own. Even develop your own pictures, I'm told, right in the basement over there."

"So?" Ryter looked back at Willman now, defiance lighting his eyes like fire. "I guess even people like me can have hobbies, can't they?"

"Certainly." Willman kept his voice mild, but his eyes were alert, his nerves tight. "But, funniest thing. Nobody seems to have seen any of your pictures. Yesterday, I talked to your old neighbor and he never saw any of the photos, and late this afternoon, I interviewed your ex-wife again. She didn't even know you owned a camera.

No pictures of your daughter, no photographs of your hunting trips with Scott Fitak.''

This time, Ryter almost staggered backward and his head dropped toward his chest. He didn't answer for a long time. Then Willman saw the thick shoulders stiffen and the head lift slowly to look straight up into his face. Willman could see at last what Linda Hammond had meant about Ryter's eyes—they were pretty scary all right—blank and crazy.

''I guess you could say I'm something of an artist,'' Ryter said, and the voice was the singsong, whispery voice Linda had heard on the phone. ''I'll just snap away at things that appeal to me, but I don't flatter myself that the pictures would interest my old neighbors or my ex-wife.''

''Well, maybe you could let me have a peek at some of them.''

''I didn't keep any.''

''None at all? All those developing sessions in the basement and no prints to show for it?''

''Not a one.'' Ryter was almost purring now. ''I'm still learning, you know, and I don't want to keep my mistakes around me. Some people might settle for less than the best, Lieutenant, but that's not me. I destroy things that aren't perfect. I just tear them up.''

Willman thought it was really a marvelous trick to get so much venom and threat into that soft, almost lilting voice. He found himself unable to say anything in response.

''You don't want to make me late for work, do you, Lieutenant?'' Ryter went on in that crazy, Romper-Room-hostess voice. ''Wouldn't that be police harassment? I

have a very important job, you know. Can you guess
what I do?''

''No,'' Willman said, feeling absurdly like a child
being quizzed by his kindergarten teacher.

''I make toilet seats,'' Ryter said, and a smile spread
across his blunt lower face. ''The rings and the covers for
toilet seats. Where would America be without me, Lieutenant? I'll tell you where. America would be in the shit.
May I go now?''

Crazy as a loon, Willman thought as he walked back
toward his own car. And dangerous. He knew that more
surely than ever. He also knew he had struck nerves more
than once in that interview, but the little scuzz hadn't
broken. If anything, he'd emerged the winner, a confidence born of lunacy carrying him above the sane man's
carefully barbed questions. As Willman opened the door
of his car, he could hear gravel stones flying and tires
grinding as Ryter's car sailed out of the parking lot and
sped away down Carimona Street.

Willman followed the car out to the industrial park and
watched as it swung into a parking place. Only after he
had seen Ryter disappear behind the double glass doors
of the plastics factory did he drive to a phone booth to
call Linda Hammond.

''He's at work, Mrs. Hammond,'' Willman said, hearing the weariness in his own voice. ''You can relax now,
for a while at least.''

''Thank you, Lieutenant,'' she said, and the by-now
familiar voice sounded hollow and dulled. ''That's what I
needed to know.''

Chapter 20

Ryter stood just inside the doors of the factory, off to the left, his forehead leaning against the glass. He watched Willman's car come to a stop at the end of the parking lot. His eyes were wide and blank, the whites showing all around the irises, like the eyes of a skittish horse. Behind the eyes, he felt his brain was boiling; the familiar pressure in his temples was almost unbearable. Even at night the parking lot seemed to shimmer with the heat under the arc lights. The rows of cars looked like animals huddled together. But the plain gray sedan was separate, watchful, its headlights like the eyes of some big cat waiting for something to move, to show itself by moving, so it could pounce.

After a few minutes, the sedan moved; it backed around the end of a row of cars and then rolled slowly down the slight grade to the parking lot entrance. Ryter watched the tail lights receding toward town, his eyes unchanged as if he had never even blinked since coming inside the building. Finally, he let his eyelids fall and held them closed.

Behind him, the noises of the factory came through the heavy inner doors, muffled but still familiar. And of course the smell was there. The smell of heated plastic drifted even to the far reaches of the parking lot. It clung to his clothes when he left work. He had begun to think it seeped into his refrigerator and got into his food. The temperature inside the factory was always hot, even in the winter. On a night like this one, he knew it would be over a hundred degrees at his work station.

Now Ryter opened his eyes again, but the blank stare was gone. His colorless irises were almost obscured by the widely dilated pupils. The light reflecting from the surfaces of his eyes made them appear to glow from within like heated coals. Whatever he was thinking, it brought a slow smile to his lips, pulling his mouth away from his stained teeth until the pointed canines were fully exposed. In that moment, anyone coming on him unaware would have thought he looked like a grinning demon in a Renaissance painting of hell.

But no one saw him. He was already late for his shift, so the short entrance hall of the factory was deserted except for him. He moved back to the center of the doors and pushed on the long bar. One door swung noiselessly outward, and he closed it softly behind himself once he was outside. Then he trotted across the parking lot to his car and drove off into the hot sticky night.

Chapter 21

When Linda hung up the phone it was 1:15 A.M., but she was wide awake. She knew she must learn how to use the gun, and that it would have to be by trial and error. Of course, she couldn't experiment at all with the gun in the house. If it were loaded and accidentally discharged because she touched the wrong thing, the neighbors would hear and a bullet hole could be found somewhere in her living room. She felt strangely elated and energetic as she went into the kitchen to get a flashlight. Then she went back to the coffee table, and brought out her car keys.

She drove for a long time after leaving Holton, drove south along the river until she came to County Road H, where she turned to the west. At first, she saw other cars and some of them passed her. What were these other people doing out so late on a Thursday night, she wondered? What would they think if they knew what was in the purse beside her? She opened her car window as far as it would go, letting the night air rush against her face, but that air was hot and sticky.

Linda had driven this route to take Dana to Scout camp last summer, and she remembered a large tree farm that took up several miles of this road, just rows and rows of straight, tall pines with all the underbrush cleared away, no buildings anywhere in sight. Once she had arrived at the tree farm, she slowed down and began to look for some firebreak or other lane that might lead into the trees. Sure enough, after almost two miles of driving at twenty miles an hour, she spotted a graveled lane on the right side of the road. She checked her rearview mirror for headlights, but saw none, so she turned in and drove until she was satisfied that her car couldn't be seen from the road.

When Linda got out of the car, she left the headlights on. She carried the flashlight and her purse around to the front of the car. When she'd taken out the gun, she paused, listening for any sounds of traffic behind her; the silence was broken only by the sounds of small animals moving away from the disturbance she was causing, for the muggy air was so still that no plant life was moving at all. At any other time, Linda would have been afraid to be there alone, but now she felt grateful for the solitude. She pointed the gun into a gap between the rows of pines and pulled the trigger.

Nothing happened. The trigger didn't even move when she squeezed it. Turning the gun flat on her hand, she trained the flashlight onto its side. When she moved the little lever above the trigger housing, she noticed that in one position, the lever revealed a tiny orange dot, while in the other position, the lever covered the dot. Accustomed as she was to appliances which were clearly marked with words like ON and OFF, Linda found this lack of signals mildly annoying. When she had moved the lever to the opposite of its starting position, she again pulled the trigger. This time, the trigger moved, but there was no shot. The lever, she deduced, must be the safety.

Perhaps the gun needed to be cocked in order to fire. She pulled the hammer back, surprised at the strength of the spring; when the hammer clicked into an open position, she aimed and tried again. The hammer snapped forward with a smart "click," but there was no shot. All right; the gun wasn't loaded. Linda turned up the butt and examined its base in the light from the flashlight. It appeared that the lower edge was not fused to the handle. Linda tried pulling it, slipping her fingernails under the edge, but there was no give at all. She put the light back onto the handle where she had first noticed the small button. She pushed on the button and slid it into the little groove. The bottom part of the handle fell onto the hood of the car, making a cracking sound that Linda first mistook for a shot. When she picked up the object, she saw that it was a rectangular case made of metal; one end was the base of the gun handle and the other end had an opening in it through which Linda could see a metal platform of some sort. The opening was shaped like the bullets.

Now Linda put flashlight and gun on the hood of the car, stooping into the headlights to work with both hands.

She got out the box of bullets and pushed four of the shiny pellets down into the opening which looked made for them, noting each time the pressure that answered her push. The little platform was obviously spring-loaded. While she worked, she could hear a distant rumble of thunder. Standing upright again, she pushed the case back into the handle of the gun until she heard a click. Again, she pointed the gun and pulled the trigger, and again there was no sound.

Now what? Linda felt a flash of anger. She wasn't going to be able to make the damned thing work, so everything else would have to be scrapped. Think, think. Why wouldn't it go off? Because the bullets were in the handle and not in the place where the hammer fell. There must be some other operation to get the first bullet into that place. She looked the gun over carefully, but there were no other levers or buttons. A glimmer of lightning brightened the sky over the pines, and this time, the thunder sounded closer.

Linda leaned against the car for a moment, searching her memory for movies or television programs where she had seen men using guns. An image swam into focus: a bearded man hiding behind a pillar on a parking ramp, holding a gun next to his head with the barrel pointing upwards; then, just before a car came hurtling down the ramp, pulling the whole barrel backwards toward himself and letting it snap forward again.

Linda moved the gun into her left hand and cupped her right hand over the barrel; then she tightened her grip and pulled hard. A casing over the barrel slid backward with a grating metallic sound and when she let it snap forward, the hammer was cocked. This time when she pulled the trigger, the explosion ripped into the silence and the end of the barrel leapt into the air. At the same time that Linda heard the bullet tearing across the trees, her eye caught a movement off to the right of her hand. She turned the flashlight onto the ground and saw the shell casing where it had fallen after popping out of the gun. She would have to remember to pick them up, she thought calmly as she cocked the hammer and squeezed the trigger again. Lightning streaked across the sky at the same time the shot exploded. So, only the first bullet had to be put into the chamber by moving the barrel. This time, the thunder shook the ground under her feet, but Linda wasn't ready to leave yet.

Would she have to cock the gun to fire it, or would it now fire by itself when she pulled the trigger? She raised the gun level with her eyes, aiming at something definitely for the first time. She remembered reading that aiming a gun was like pointing; pretend that the barrel is your finger and just point it quickly at what you want to hit before you pull the trigger. Linda pointed quickly at a tree some ten feet from where she was standing, and squeezed the trigger. Again the tearing "cr-a-a-ck" sounded in her ears and again the barrel jumped, but not so much this time because she was expecting it and was holding her arm more steady. Lightning streaked across the sky and the answering thunder came much more quickly than it had before. The storm was almost upon her.

Linda had one more test to make. She clicked the safety lever and tried to pull the trigger; it didn't move. She clicked it back and fired away the last shot. A wind was kicking up all around her as she used the flashlight to retrieve the four shell casings and put them into her pocket. Multiple flashes of lightning made the path as light as day while Linda slipped the gun and bullets back into her purse and turned off the flashlight. She had reached the door of the car when the first few drops of rain were blown onto her arm and face. Then, in the next flash of lightning, she saw a figure walking toward her car, approaching the circle of light made by the headlights.

Linda stood frozen with her hand gripping the door handle.

"Who's there?" It was a man's voice.

Linda couldn't speak, couldn't move, though her mind was screaming at her, "Get away! Get away!" She felt irrationally convinced that Ryter had somehow followed her, had got around her on this narrow lane.

The figure advanced into the headlights, his arm raised to shield his eyes. It was a young man, tall, gangling.

"I thought I heard gunfire," he said, tilting his head to one side as he tried to get a look at Linda.

"I did, too," Linda said in a voice she herself didn't recognize. "I drove in here to have a look. The shots seem to be coming from over there," and she pointed into the woods.

Another brilliant flash of lightning lit up the young man's face as he turned to look where she pointed. She recognized him. It was David Polson, a boy who had been in one of her classes the first year she taught in Holton. She turned her own face away as fast as she could, pretending to shield her eyes from the thunder.

"Must be somebody trying to get a deer out of

season," he shouted over the thunder's aftershocks. "My girl and me been parked up here aways. I guess we better get out of here."

"Yes," she said, keeping her face down.

"You, too," he said. "No sense getting shot by some nut who doesn't look what he's shooting at." And he began to walk away.

Linda sprang into her car and backed all the way to the road, the wheels spitting dirt and stones under the car as she barely kept it under control. By the time she turned the car back the way she had come on County Road H, the skies had opened and rain was pelting through the open window. She had the car moving forward at the same time she was rolling up the window. It poured all the way back to Holton, the rain moving across the road in sheets, sometimes so heavy that the windshield wipers could hardly keep up with it. The lightning created the illusion of shapes moving in the ditches, and the thunder was sometimes almost deafening; one crack was so loud and followed so instantaneously on the lightning that Linda was sure something had been struck very near to her passing car.

By the time Linda pulled into her own driveway, the rain had almost stopped, and only distant rumblings signaled where the storm had gone. When she stepped out of her car, she was amazed at how much cooler it was, almost chilly. Inside the house, she found wet carpet under the west and south windows, which had, of course, been wide open, but not bad enough to require sponging. It would dry again in a few days. She sat down in the kitchen to consider what it meant that she had seen David Polson.

Had he recognized her? She didn't think so, for he'd never got a good look at her face. In all that noise, it was unlikely that he would have recognized her voice. David Polson, frankly, was not the sort of boy anyone would ever think of as quick. So he had heard shots and seen a woman next to a car. He believed that the gunfire had come from somewhere else and that it signified an illegal hunter. Was it possible that he would read in the newspaper of the death of John Charles Ryter and, eventually, connect the two events? No. At least, it was highly improbable. And, unless somebody could make the connection, no one would be going out there to dig bullets out of pine trees. She would have to take the chance and go ahead as if David Polson's amorous adventures hadn't put her plan in jeopardy.

Just this quickly did Linda dispense with a potential obstacle in the way of her plan. A day ago, the encounter in the pines would have been more than enough to arouse in her a panic so thorough as to make impossible any attempt to use the gun again. But ever since that thing had tipped over in her mind, she had felt calm, almost suprarational, considering action exclusively in terms of its practicality. Everything seemed simple, clear; it was or it was not too risky to proceed now that someone she knew had intruded on her gun practice; either she would be painstakingly careful, or she would be caught; either she would kill John Charles Ryter, or he would kill Dana. In her imagination, there was no continuum of possibilities, only a stark choice between mutually exclusive opposites.

Standing up now, she fished the spent cartridges out of the pocket of her jeans and put them into a small plastic scrap bag; twisting the top shut, she set the bag next to her purse on the counter. Then she opened the drawer in which she kept a neatly folded stack of rags, the remains of old cotton dish towels which had been bleached and laundered until they were too thin to be much use in drying dishes. With one of these rags, she carefully wiped all the surfaces of the gun and the box of shells, and placed both next to the plastic bag. Then she went upstairs to change clothes.

The breeze coming through Linda's bedroom window felt almost cold; the storm had obviously brought behind it a mass of air dramatically different from the one it had pushed to the east. Linda stripped off her clothes, checking her shoes carefully for any signs of dirt; except for being wet, the shoes were unmarked. She found an old sweat suit that she had given up wearing in public months ago; the shirt was hooded and had a roomy pouch in the front. When she had put on the sweat suit and clean socks, Linda got from her closet a pair of tennis shoes whose frayed condition had made her consider them worth saving only for jobs like painting or gardening.

Finally, she picked up the white nylon gloves and slid her hands into them. They fit snugly and had a sheer ruffle just at the wrist. Linda spread her hands and looked down at them, faintly aware of how ludicrous the gloves looked next to the faded navy blue sweat suit. But overriding this vestige of her saner self was another

Linda, the one who simply reminded herself that she mustn't take the gloves off again until everything was over.

She trotted back downstairs and made a pot of coffee. Then she carefully loaded two bullets into the gun, snapped one into the chamber, and made sure the safety lever would prevent an accidental discharge. Finally, she sat down at the kitchen table, her gloved hands wrapped around a steaming coffee mug, and waited for dawn.

Chapter 22

At 7 A.M., Linda was crouched behind some bushes along the railroad tracks, watching the parking lot at 7 Carimona Street. On her way there, she had overshot the block so that she could approach the house from the north along the tracks. If someone had noticed her Wednesday, that same person must not see her today. She had walked all the way from home, grateful that the blustery, unseasonably cool morning had made it seem normal to have the hood of her sweatshirt pulled tightly around her face. She kept her gloved hands inside the front pouch where they now closed over the gun, the bullet box, and the dust rag she had used to remove the fingerprints from both. On the way over, she had dropped the little bag of spent cartridges into the dumpster that stood behind a darkened shop on Main Street.

She had chosen the bushes because they provided the

best screen from any prying eyes that might be busy in the neighborhood. She couldn't know that John Charles Ryter had long ago chosen them for the same reason— that she was crouched less than four feet from two railroad ties he had marked with long scratches, that the white stones between those two ties covered all the evidence that would ever be needed to send Ryter to prison for life. Her attention was focused elsewhere, and even her most terrified imagination couldn't have conjured up the horror that lay so close to her now.

There were three cars in the parking lot, two near the street and one near the back of the house, and a conspicuous space was left where Ryter's car must usually be parked. At 7:10, a young man walked around the hedge from the front of the house and got into one of the cars near the street; he had backed the car into his parking space and so was able to drive straight out of the lot onto the street. At 7:20, another young man appeared from the same direction, trotting a little, and got into the second car. He backed up, swinging the car into the center of the lot. When he went forward, the back wheels spit stones almost as far as the last car. Late for work, Linda thought, and she smiled a little. She assumed from the position of the cars in the lot, and from the fact that the men had come from the front of the house, that these two must be the occupants of the downstairs apartment, Schwanke and Luhmann.

Linda shifted position, easing the ache in her legs, for she didn't want to sit on the damp grass. She had a long wait before the owner of the third car appeared. It was almost 8:00 when he came out of the enclosed staircase at the side of the house and took a sharp right turn to cross the lot to his car. Linda could hear the crunching noise his work boots made on the gravel. He must be Bob, she thought, the occupant of apartment three. If he used this side staircase, he must walk straight past Ryter's door and the bay window which separated it from his own door. Had he noticed anything odd about the replaced screen? Had Ryter noticed that the inside window wasn't completely closed? Linda watched the car leave.

Five minutes later, she stood up and looked around. Then she walked up the embankment to the parking lot and crossed to the side staircase. In the little shed at the top of the stairs, not everything was as Linda had left it. Through the badly rusted screen, she could see that the lower window was fully open. Ryter must have been trying to get as much outside air as possible into the apartment before the storm broke; or maybe he had deduced that this was how the gun thief must have got into the apartment. No point worrying about it now, though. When she had removed the screen, Linda took out her cloth and carefully wiped it, and then the window frame and sill. Before she stepped through the window, she remembered to wipe the outside doorknob and the wood around it.

Once inside the apartment, Linda paused to mentally retrace her movements of Wednesday. It was a little stuffy in the room, but much cooler than yesterday, a lucky break, Linda thought, because her mind worked much better in cooler temperatures. The front windows were now open and a breeze was stirring the curtains. Methodically, beginning with the window behind her, she began to wipe every object she could remember touching, going around the room in the same direction she had followed two days ago.

In the bedroom, she found the room as it had first appeared to her: semidark, bed carefully made, curtains drawn. And the drawer of the bed table was closed. What had Ryter made of the fact that the gun was missing? Would he have told anyone that it was gone, anyone at work? That would be bad for her plan to make his death look like a suicide, but she was committed now and felt no disposition to turn back. If people knew the gun had been stolen, they would conclude that Ryter had been murdered, but they wouldn't be able to prove that *she* had done it. And Ryter would still be dead, which, she reasoned, was the important thing. She wiped down the light switch, the lamp, and the closed drawer. Then she replaced the bullet box in the drawer. She went back into the living room, opened the side door, stepped into the little shed, and replaced the screen. Now, if Ryter came up the side stairs when he got home from work, everything would look to him the way he'd left it.

Linda had already thought about where she must stand to wait for Ryter. If she could hear him coming up the side stairs, she would wait in the bedroom, and if he came up inside the house, she would wait next to the refrigerator facing the bathroom. She tried both places. The space next to the refrigerator was narrow and somewhat exposed; anyone with reasonably good peripheral vision would notice her almost immediately after coming through the door. She would have to be ready, would have to act very fast. The site in the bedroom was much better because the room formed an "L" around the bathroom, making it possible for Linda to hide in the alcove which contained the bed; from that position, she would be able to extend her right arm to the edge of the bedroom door. She noticed that the light switch was to the left of the door, so, if the room were darkened, anyone coming through that door would already be turning to the left as he came in, giving her just the right amount of time to lift her arm and have the gun in position.

Linda practiced this maneuver, raising the gun to the level she judged would be the height of Ryter's temple. She knew he was shorter than she was—she was almost five-nine—so she wouldn't have to lift the gun much above her shoulder. Only when she had lifted the gun twice did it occur to her that the plan would work only if Ryter were right-handed. A left-handed man wouldn't shoot himself in the right temple. She dropped her arm to her side and walked back through the bathroom to the kitchen. There was no place at all to hide on the other side of that door, and the placement of the bathroom mirror made it too risky to try to hide in the bathroom itself.

Linda leaned against the refrigerator, thinking. The majority of people were right-handed, she knew, but did she dare to count on Ryter's belonging to the majority of anything? It was useless, she thought, in this barren apartment. She closed her eyes and tried to call up the three occasions on which she had seen John Charles Ryter. At first, she could remember only the eyes looking

out from under the thick brows, those sinister, pale eyes,
and she could remember the little waxen smile. Then
suddenly, she could see in her mind, as clearly as if the
courtroom had been transported into Ryter's living room,
the hand reaching for the pencil and making those short,
meaningless lines on the legal pad—the right hand. Linda
sighed with relief, feeling elated and even proud of
herself for solving what might otherwise have been a
serious difficulty.

Glancing down at her watch, Linda noticed that it was
almost 8:30. Lieutenant Willman had said that Ryter
worked until 9:00, so she must begin to prepare herself
mentally for his arrival. As soon as she thought of
Lieutenant Willman, Linda felt a qualm, a combination
of fear and something like pity. He was such a clever
policeman—those sharp eyes spotting the tiny fibers from
Dana's jacket—that she would have to be extremely
careful about what she did in this apartment. But she
simultaneously remembered his kindness, the tired face,
the way his eyes blurred sometimes when he talked about
Dana. Poor man. It wasn't his fault that he couldn't do
this for her, couldn't just walk up to Ryter and execute
him. She believed he would have liked to, would have
been almost as relieved as she to have the threat to Dana
removed.

Quite suddenly, right in the middle of thinking about
Willman, Linda was struck with a completely new idea.
It came to her as a question, clearly formed, and very
alarming. What if Ryter should not be alone when he
came home? If he came up either staircase with someone
else, she couldn't go through with her plan. The thought

of having to kill anyone else besides Ryter was simply insupportable, so she would be discovered in his apartment holding his gun in her hand, and he would even have a witness to her crime, not just a case of his word against hers.

Obviously, she had to find a place to watch for his arrival, to see if he were alone or not. If she saw someone with him, she could wait to see what staircase they used and then leave by the other door. At least Ryter could no longer prove who had taken his gun. It would mean that she'd have to come up with another plan—inconvenient, but not impossible. Linda considered the bedroom window as a place to watch; it faced the front of the house, but wouldn't allow her to see the parking lot. She crossed back into the larger room and approached the front windows from the right, staying along the side wall as she moved. By sitting sideways on the arm of the sofa, she could see past the drapes into the street below and could easily see the entrance to the parking lot.

Here Linda took up her vigil, the gun still held loosely in her right hand. This vantage point, she now realized, would help her plan even more, because it would give her an earlier indication of which staircase Ryter would use. Even if he drove into the parking lot, she'd be able to see if he walked around the hedge to the front door or along the hedge to the side stairs. If he came alone, she would spring instantly into action, getting to her hiding place before he even began to mount the stairs. Once inside, he would eventually have to pass where she was waiting for him. Linda assumed that anyone just getting home from work would want to bathe and change clothes, because, of course, that's what she would have done at once. Her wait wouldn't be long, she reasoned, and, after that, she had planned every move she would make.

She would put the gun in Ryter's lifeless hand, chain both doors from the inside—she had already noted that both doors had chain locks—to make it appear that Ryter had locked himself inside, and then leave by the window again. No house was close enough to this one that she needed to worry much about someone hearing the shot. In the woods, the "cr-a-a-ck" hadn't sounded very loud to her and she'd been holding the gun that made the noise. Then she'd cross the parking lot to the embankment and the tracks, and walk home by a completely different route from the one she'd taken to get here today and on Wednesday. At no point did Linda let herself think about the actual moment of pulling the trigger, but she calmly reminded herself that it would probably not be a good idea to look at Ryter's head afterwards.

Ten o'clock came and went, then eleven o'clock. At 11:15, a long freight train set the house trembling and clanking for seven minutes. By noon, Linda was wondering out loud why it had never occurred to her that Ryter might not come straight home from work. Because *she* would, under similar circumstances, have come home to hide herself from any unnecessary conversation, she assumed that everyone must react in the same way. That there might be people in the world who were not ashamed to have been in jail, who could go walking or driving around their towns without any apparent embarrassment, was something she'd never thought possible.

Linda began to pace from the sofa to the bay window and back again. She'd already observed that no cars came this far on the dead-end street, so she felt confident that she would hear any car that approached the house. With this confidence, she'd already made one trip to the bathroom. It was not much warmer in the apartment than it had been at 8:30, but Linda was beginning to perspire, her hair sticking to her forehead as she paced. What on each could Ryter be doing? Could he have gone to the police station to report a stolen gun? But surely he would have done that yesterday when he first discovered the theft. Could he, she wondered suddenly, stopping midway between sofa and window, could he be trying to find out were Dana was? Could he, even now, be questioning the Hammond neighbors to find out who Dana's friends were, who Linda's friends were? Might he already have discovered that the Fishers were out of town and that they had a cabin at Lake Wheaton? Perhaps he never meant to come back here at all, but was so obsessed that he would not rest, literally, until he'd done what he threatened on the phone.

Linda could feel the terrible chill settling on her brain again as she considered this possibility. She might be waiting here in this silent house, in an apartment that looked like nobody lived in it, while John Charles Ryter was stalking her child. Her carefully worked-out plan might be just a mental game, after all, while a much more experienced killer went about his deadly routine with an efficiency she couldn't begin to imagine. Linda lifted her right hand to her forehead and almost struck herself with the gun she was still holding.

Somehow the sight of the gun settled her nerves. Could Ryter go on about his ugly business after learning that someone had been in his home, going through his things? If he suspected her, he might go to her house again to stare or even to try to get inside. Would he do that, with the car sitting there in the driveway? It was impossible to judge what such a man might do. Well, she didn't much care if he *did* break into her house; he would find nothing—no child and no gun. In her present state, nothing else mattered much to Linda. And if he did violate her house, it would only add additional credence to the portrait of a desperate, sick man—a man who might easily become suicidal. And he would come back here eventually, when he found nothing to vent his rage on.

Somewhat calmed, Linda sat back down on the sofa arm and stared out at the street. As the hours passed, she alternated pacing with sitting, self-reassurance with panic. She began to see all of her plan as pure folly, lunacy—the word echoed in her mind a few times: lunacy. How could she have imagined that she could stop someone like Ryter? She should just get out of here and tell Lieutenant Willman about the gun, tell him that Ryter might already be after Dana. Or she could just drive straight to the Fishers' cabin with the gun and wait for Ryter to try something so she could shoot him in self-defense. Or she should be calm, she told herself over and over, and wait for him to come to the apartment so that she could go through with her original plan. If not knowing where Ryter was for a few hours could make her this anxious, what would it be like to go on for months and months, before the trial and maybe even after the trial, wondering where he was, what he was planning, where he might strike? Faced with that prospect, she no longer thought of her plan as lunacy; it seemed the only sane alternative.

At one point, Linda thought her watch must have stopped, at least for a while, so she crossed the room to the wall phone next to the kitchen cabinets and dialed the number for the correct time; her watch was right. Holding the phone in her hand, she considered calling the Fishers, but realized it would mean calling information first—the paper with the number on it was in her purse which she'd left at home—suddenly, Linda gasped aloud. She had left her purse at home, on the coffee table! What if Ryter *had* broken into her house and found the purse? The map to the Fishers' cabin was in her purse!

Linda was gathering herself for flight when she heard a car. She darted to the window and looked out. Two cars were turning into the parking lot, one behind the other, the two cars which had left at 7:10 and 7:20 that morning. Good God, Linda thought, they were home from work! It was impossible. Then she glanced at her watch again; it was 3:37. A shift that began at 7:30 could end at 3:30. She watched numbly as the two young men got out of their cars, greeted each other, and walked around to the front of the house. She stood motionless as she heard the door downstairs close.

What could she do? She had to get out of this house and she didn't even know if she dared to cross the floor. In these old houses, you never knew which floor boards might creak. She'd taken no notice of these things when she was walking around earlier because she hadn't thought it would be necessary. Sweat began to trickle down the middle of her back. She was mentally measuring the distance to the side door when the blare of rock music startled her so much that she almost screamed. The floor under her feet had actually begun to throb with the bass from what must surely be quadraphonic stereo in the room directly beneath her.

How long would it take Ryter to drive to the Fishers' cabin if he had left this morning? Should she just forget her own risk and call from here to warn Susan and Jerry to get out of there? The trip was almost eight hours, Susan had said, so the Fishers and Dana were already there, but Ryter couldn't have made it there even if he'd left Holton right after he got off from work. So she had some time. With that rock music shaking the whole house, she could get out without the men downstairs hearing her. Keeping close to the walls on the theory that the boards might be less likely to creak there, Linda crossed the large room toward the side door. She had almost reached it when she heard the sound of gravel grinding under car tires; even the music couldn't wholly obscure that sound. She darted to the window and saw the tan car pull into the parking space she had guessed belonged to it. When the man stepped out, Linda knew at once that it was Ryter; even from above, the short figure and the sandy hair were unmistakable.

Trapped! No way out where she wouldn't be seen. Linda's brain raced at a panicky rate. She had to hide, here in the apartment. But where? Ryter was sure to discover her. In the bedroom? That was where she had planned to wait for him anyway. Suddenly, a revised plan struck her all at once. She could do what she had planned all along. If she could get away unnoticed afterwards, it would make the suicide theory even more plausible; the downstairs neighbors would have seen Ryter come home alone and would have noticed no one else around the place. The music might even be loud enough to cover the sound of the shot, but what if the young men *did* hear it? Well, what would *she* do if she thought she heard a shot in an overhead apartment? She would open her own door, go up the stairs and knock at the door. She would call through the door to find out what the noise might be. If she were with another adult, she would consult him as to the best course of action. If the men behaved normally, there would be enough time for her to get away down the side stairs before they could decide what to do next.

All the time these thoughts were racing through Linda's mind faster than she could have expressed them, she was watching Ryter walk unsteadily across the parking lot, along the hedge, and toward the side staircase. She moved quickly now, tiptoeing along the wall, past the kitchen, and through the bathroom. She crossed the little bedroom and slid the chain onto the bar of the front door. Beneath her feet, the rock music was throbbing as she recrossed the darkened room to the doorway leading from the bedroom to the bathroom. She clicked the lever off safety, moved the gun back into her right hand, and took up her position.

Chapter 23

When Ryter had sneaked back out of the plastics factory, he'd had a brief moment of gloating over Willman's error. Cops! Even the smart ones like Willman had no imagination—thinking that going through the doors meant going to work! But depression closed on the little man before he'd driven many blocks, a depression he'd been fighting since early afternoon.

From the moment he'd first spotted Willman following him on the way home from the Hammond house, Ryter had begun a rapid slide into the blackest of his moods. He'd become so accustomed to being the watcher, so confident that he could remain unobtrusive while he sized up other people, that it had never occurred to him that others could successfully watch him. The cop must have followed him straight from the jail, must have been sitting there all the while he was on the corner watching the Hammond house. So his plan to snatch the girl fast, sometime very soon, wasn't going to be a snap. This sharp-eyed cop wasn't as easily fooled as the others into thinking he was harmless, scared by the threat of prison into being a good boy.

It made him furious to be followed. He toyed with the idea of not going home at all, but just driving aimlessly around town until the bulldog got tired and let go. But he intuited that it might be better to let Willman think the tail was still a secret; then it would be easier to plan behavior to mislead the cop, to lull him into thinking he could give up a bit. A few hours of staring at an apartment house might convince him there would be no more action today. So Ryter had driven to his house, parked his car, and gone upstairs without turning his head to right or left.

He discovered almost at once that the gun was missing; the table lamp seemed to be actually spotlighting the open drawer. Ryter was badly shocked. He sat down abruptly on the bed and ran his hand around inside the drawer, thinking simultaneously how silly the gesture was, yet he couldn't seem to absorb the obvious fact. He made a circuit of the apartment, found the back door locked, and checked the windows, which were all closed. All the time, he panted from the stifling heat of the closed-up apartment.

The gun meant a great deal to him. He had bought it a year before from a barroom acquaintance who was desperate for cash to make his car payment. Ryter had recognized the gun's quality and delighted in getting it for so little money. He had fired it only six times, just target practice and to get the feel of it, in the wetlands past Pilsen's Landing. He'd polished it, and he handled it frequently when he was in the apartment, but he'd never used it to threaten anyone, never even considered using it to intimidate Cheryl Schacht or Kristin Allen or Dana Hammond; he had enough confidence in his own physical strength where these children were concerned. Besides, guns could be far too easily traced, he knew.

No, he didn't have to use the gun for it to have the emotional weight it had for him. It was his great last resort, his ultimate fallback position; it symbolized the final power to control, to rout helplessness, to vent his rage against all his enemies. There was a part of his mind that sensed the direction in which his life was spinning, that recognized the acceleration in his need to commit the crimes he photographed. While his everyday consciousness remained irrationally convinced that he would never be detected, that he could go on fooling all the stupid jerks in the world, some deep intuition whispered that it couldn't last, that the forces in his own mind and soul would bring disaster crashing down on him. And then he would need the gun. Then he would blast into bloody pulp all the people who would come to get him, to humiliate and trap him, to make him feel small and helpless. They would know who he was before he went out, before the other guns found him and sent his own brain into a fiery explosion. That would be an end his old man could at least respect. Hadn't his father spoken admiringly of John Dillinger and other guys who had died in a hail of bullets when the cops closed in? So he had petted and stroked the gun and kept it close to his bed while he slept. It had to be ready when the time came.

And now that goddamned cop had taken it away. His instant conviction was that Willman had got a passkey from the landlord so he could search without a warrant and, finding the gun, had deliberately carried it off. And he had left the light on and the drawer open to taunt him, to flagrantly sneer at him. It was as if the tall policeman had calmly kicked him in the groin and then said, "See what you can do about it, ass-face. I got the power here."

Ryter raged and cursed, pacing back and forth from room to room. There were laws! No cocksure Chicago bull could get away with theft. But that cop was too smart to leave any prints behind, so what was a man to do? Besides, he wasn't sure if it was legal for him to have the gun without a permit. Those things varied from state to state. If he complained, it would have to be to the police, and then they would have something else to nail him with. That cool son of a bitch had searched his apartment without a warrant, and now he could just say, "I'm sorry to hear you were robbed while you were in jail, but these things happen. Even small towns aren't what they used to be."

Ryter could feel his mind numbing in the stifling heat and humidity. He paused long enough to throw open all the windows, even the one that faced the shed, but the air outside was little better than the air inside. He scanned the street for a sign of Willman's car. But, of course, he wouldn't leave it in sight; he would walk to where he could watch unseen. Ryter began to pace again, recognizing the onset of depression by his sudden thirst for liquor. But he knew he mustn't drink, mustn't lose the little control he had left. That cop would like nothing better than to have him try something now; he would slap him right back in jail until the trial, and then it would be prison. Prison was the one thing he couldn't let himself think about.

He went on pacing and cursing, losing all track of time. Finally, something seemed to short-circuit in his brain and he felt completely exhausted, so worn out that he could barely drag himself to the bed, where he lay down on top of the spread and fell asleep. Often, in his childhood, when the fear and helplessness had become too much for him, he had found escape in sleep, a kind of willed oblivion that he somehow hoped would bring him out into some other life.

When he woke up, it was already after midnight. It took him several seconds to remember what had brought him to fall asleep with all his clothes on. When it came back to him, he could feel depression closing on him again. But he roused himself, got up, and went into the bathroom to splash water over his face. They would not get him yet, he thought. So the cop had the gun. That didn't mean anything. He had never used that gun in any crime. If he kept quiet about it, just pretended he hadn't noticed anything out of the ordinary, the cop's gesture would have gone for nothing. It was meant to get a rise out of him, but he wasn't going to rise, and that would mean he had won after all. And he could always get another gun, maybe not as fancy, but one that would do the job. He went back into the bedroom, smoothed the bedspread and changed his shirt. Then he rummaged through the kitchen for something to eat. Soda crackers and a canned soft drink were all he could find that didn't look spoiled, but he felt refreshed after eating anyway. He decided to go to work; breaking routine might give that cop an excuse to maneuver him back into jail.

When he first saw Willman in the parking lot, he felt a surge of glad energy; here was a chance to show the thieving bastard what Jack Ryter was made of. By the time the interview was over, though, he was shaken to the core, pushed over into a state where he himself didn't know what he might do next. The surface cockiness was pure sham, a reflex, the retreat into pretended calm when his brain was whirling like a Fourth of July pinwheel.

On the way to the factory, he knew Willman was following him. How much did the cop know? The questions about the pictures were clearly a fishing expedition, but the remark about hunting with Fitak was terrifying, had caught him so much by surprise that he had almost cried out. One thing was very clear now: most of his plans for the Hammonds would have to be scrapped. He wouldn't dare try to develop any more pictures at all, for fear that Willman might be standing outside his makeshift darkroom. The old pictures and negatives would have to stay in their hiding place forever now, because he could never be sure when someone might be watching him. He would have to snatch the Hammond kid and kill her fast, no fun ahead of time, and he would have to work some sort of alibi, too. And when it all blew over, he would have to leave Holton for good.

He ground his teeth with rage at having his plans
thwarted like this. The Hammond bitch would lose her
kid, but it didn't seem enough to him. Somehow, he felt
that all this attention he was getting from Lieutenant
Willman was her fault, too. He had seen the contempt in
the hawkish face, imagined Linda Hammond telling the
tall policeman, "Of course, he's the kind of scum that
lusts after his own daughter." She deserved the worst,
but he would have to regroup, give himself time to
arrange a new plan.

When he left the factory, he drove around aimlessly for
a while, watching for any sign of Willman's car. He was
beginning to feel the terrible pressure in his temples, the
ballooning sensation that made him think his head might
explode. When he was pretty sure that Willman was off
the trail, it occurred to him that he had almost eight hours
to work with: the cop thought he was at work, so the cop
would stop guarding. Maybe there was some way he
could get at the Hammonds tonight—old Nancy Birkin
would give him an alibi later, if he leaned on her hard
enough; he knew she was more than a little afraid of him.

He drove to the Hammonds' quiet neighborhood and
cruised slowly past the house on the other side of the
street, an old trick from the days of watching Dana. The
house was dark, as he'd expected. Only when he'd
almost passed did he see that the car was gone. He was
so stunned that he brought his own car to an abrupt stop
and just sat there, staring at the empty driveway. Where
were they in the middle of the night? What was going
on?

It came to him suddenly. That cop had told them to

hide until the trial. They had left home, maybe to stay with friends. Maybe they had even left town. The thought terrified him. The Hammond bitch and her brat had taken themselves away from the habits he already knew so well, had taken themselves out of his control. It might take him days, even weeks, to find out where they were. A teacher didn't have to work in the summer, so they could be almost anywhere. And that cop would be watching him, following him. He was shaking now in rage and frustration. Think, think. He had to make himself think clearly. After he got calmer and rested in his mind, he would be able to plan again. But he just couldn't go back to the apartment, to the empty drawer and the empty cupboards. That would only make him more depressed.

He smashed his foot onto the gas pedal and the car screamed into motion, leaving a trail of rubber on the street in front of the Hammond house. He drove straight to Nancy Birkin's apartment. She had no other customers— Thursday nights were not so busy—and she let him stay all night "for old time's sake." The satisfaction he got from prostitutes had never been much more than a release of physical tension, and this night was even more unsatisfactory than usual. Nancy had to use all her tricks to get him ready, and after two times, she just settled down to chat nervously at him. The noise of the storm finally made conversation almost impossible. When Nancy fell asleep at 4:00, he paced around her two-room apartment, chewing on his lower lip, trying to make his mind focus on what he ought to do next. Willman's face kept swimming up before him: the cool eyes, the disgust curling his mouth even when he tried to pretend indifference.

When he left at 8:00, Nancy was still asleep, snoring quietly in the stained sheets. Some bars opened at 8:00, he knew, and he had decided that a little controlled drinking would soothe his brain, would let him rest until a time when he could think clearly again. In the morning, he stuck to beer and walked from bar to bar to test his own steadiness. After a greasy hamburger lunch served right on the bar at Shorty's Tap, he switched to whiskey. He kept a careful count and he still walked when he thought it was "time to change the venue," as he would say to the bartender. But by 3:00, he could feel the fire coming up in his head, the onset of the recklessness that used to land him in jail. After a dangerous flare-up with a bartender he'd never seen before, he decided it was time to call it a day.

He could hear the blare of the rock music as he drove into the parking lot at the side of his building. How he hated rock music! How he hated those jerks who lived downstairs! Probably pansies. But he warned himself not to make a scene. All he had to do was get upstairs and have a few more drinks alone. Then he would blank out completely and not have to think for a long time. He crossed the parking lot with the studied care of a drunken man and slowly climbed the rickety side stairs, which seemed to moved even more than usual under his feet.

Chapter 24

*L*inda didn't hear the side door open, but she heard it close loudly, almost a slam. She held her breath, listening. There were footsteps and then, closer to her, the sounds of cupboard doors opening and closing. The refrigerator door slammed shut. Next came a sound she didn't recognize at first, a cracking noise followed by several sharp bangs. Then it came to her—ice cubes being twisted out of a plastic tray and falling onto the countertop. For a while, Linda could hear nothing more. She tensed her right arm, waiting for any sound in the bathroom. Her breath was just a short shallow panting now.

The sound of the television set startled her. Ryter had turned it on very loud to be heard above the music from downstairs, and Linda recognized the voice of a popular game show host. If he sat down to watch a whole television show, Linda thought, she would not make it. Breathing as she was, she was certain to faint or get so dizzy that she wouldn't be able to function. The fingers on her left hand were already beginning to feel numb. Her right hand gripped the gun handle, her forefinger held out carefully, away from the trigger; if she should squeeze from sheer nervousness, she would shoot off her own foot. Several minutes passed.

Then there were footsteps again, quick footsteps approaching and crossing the bathroom. Linda stopped breathing and moved her finger onto the trigger. Ryter came through the door already half-turned to the left, away from Linda. He switched on the light as she raised her arm. Some slight sound or perhaps the tactile sensation of movement near him made him turn his head back quickly to the right. Linda's pupils had contracted with the coming on of the overhead light so that, at first, she saw only a shape. In a frozen second, she was able to refocus and, at the same time, see recognition dawn in the no-color eyes just three feet away from her—not fear or surprise, just recognition. Then she squeezed the trigger.

What shocked Linda was the noise. In the open expanse of the pine forest, the gun had sounded not much louder than a cap pistol, but with walls to reverberate the sound, the explosion of the shot seemed almost deafening. It took her almost two seconds to recover, to notice that Ryter had fallen away from her onto the orange and brown carpet. He was lying on his side and he wasn't moving. Linda willed herself into motion, looking down at the gun so that she could move the lever onto safety.

With one long step, she was close enough to Ryter to crouch down next to his right arm. She took his hand and closed it over the handle of the gun; even through her gloves his skin was surprisingly warm, almost hot to the touch. Then she pressed his index finger against the trigger before clicking the lever off safety again and leaving the gun under his hand. She had gone over this a hundred times in her mind, so she hardly had to think about what she was doing, and she did it all very quickly.

But some force she couldn't control turned her eyes up at Ryter's face. The eye she could see, the right eye, was open, the light from the overhead fixture glinting off the wet surface. Above the eye and a little to the left was a dark blotch with blood welling out of it. Several trickles of blood had already begun to find their way down the face, one pooling against the side of the blunt nose; another had detoured around the other edge of his eyebrow and was descending slowly into the beard stubble on his jaw. His mouth was open slightly and, for a second, Linda thought she saw it move.

The sound of the rock music stopped abruptly, almost in midnote, shocking Linda into standing straight up. They had heard the shot, she realized, and were just now reacting, trying to listen for any other sounds coming from the floor above them. In the other room, the television set was blaring, a loud commercial jingle. Linda stepped carefully into the bathroom and out the other side into the larger room, taking long strides and setting her feet down very carefully. She circled the big room along the walls, imagining the two men below would very soon be mounting the inside staircase. The fact that more than fifteen seconds must have passed from the shot to the turning off of the stereo demonstrated how slowly most people reacted in circumstances like these.

When Linda got to the side door, she saw that Ryter had already put the chain lock in place when he came home. She turned immediately to the window; holding the screen on one side with her right hand, she gave the other side a little pop with the heel of her left hand. The screen swung outward and she caught it before it had a chance to fall the four or five inches to the floor of the little shed. Without letting go, Linda ducked through the window and carefully turned with the screen in her hands. She was just about to place it into the frame when she heard voices directly beneath her feet.

"He probably just dropped something, I tell you," one voice said. "You know how he's always banging things around up there."

"That didn't sound like something dropping," the other voice said.

Linda had forgotten about the side door on the ground floor, the door which made it necessary for the staircase to face so awkwardly forward. The men must have been in the room directly below Ryter's living room and so had chosen this side door rather than their front door to begin their investigation. Linda stood motionless, afraid that the slightest movement in this rickety shed would be heard below her.

"Well, the TV is still going," the first voice said.

"That don't mean nothing."

"Well, whatta ya think we should do, then?"

"You go around the front and see if he'll come to the door, and I'll go up these stairs."

"To do what?"

"To knock, ya idiot. To see if he can come to the door."

"Okay."

And Linda could hear shoes crunching across the gravel stones. Next she heard a tentative step on the stairs below her. In one swift motion, she pushed the screen into place; it didn't fit snugly, but she couldn't risk pounding on it. The man on the stairs advanced another two steps; he was obviously not eager to fulfill his part of the plan he'd suggested. Linda waited, not breathing, until he moved again, taking advantage of his noise to step around the bay window and flatten herself against the door marked with the number 3. Unless the man looked directly across the bay window, through rusted screens and sheer inside curtains, he wouldn't be able to see her. She mustn't move, though, or even breathe very loud; no panic could break out now.

At the head of the stairs, the man Linda couldn't see, because it would have meant moving her head, pounded on the door marked with a 2; she could feel the vibrations in the back of her head. After a pause, he knocked again and called, "Jack!" Only the sound of the television set answered him. Soon Linda could hear a muffled pounding from the other side of the apartment and a voice calling, "Open up, Jack." Again, only the television noise served as a reply. The man near Linda tried one last, tentative knock. Now there was another sound, the distant rumble of an approaching train; a slight premonitory tremble was beginning to shake the little shed. It was too much for the man opposite Linda; he turned and ran down the steps, shaking the whole staircase in his haste to be away. Linda could tell that he'd stopped in the yard below, so she remained motionless. Soon, she heard the other man returning to the side of the house.

"What now?" the new arrival asked as he approached.

"I don't like this," the other man said. "I think he's in trouble in there."

"Well, then, what're we supposed to do about it?"

"I think we should call the cops." He was beginning to shout because the train was getting closer now.

"Ain't he had enough trouble with the cops already?" the other man shouted back.

"Well, what if he offed himself up there, huh? Are we just gonna wait 'til we start smelling him?"

"Okay, okay. We'll call the cops."

Linda heard the door close just before the train bore down on the house, roaring as the diesel engine passed, quieter as the rhythm of the freight cars set the whole house shaking. She began to move cautiously around the bay window and towards the stairs. Any noise the boards might make under her feet would be covered by the sound of the train. Linda paused to pat the window screen firmly into place and then, staying at the inside surfaces of the stairs and easing herself down with her hand on the side of the house, made her way to the bottom, where she paused to pull the hood of her sweatshirt up around her face.

Remembering the sound of the gravel under the men's feet, Linda went straight forward to the narrow strip of grass along the hedge. She had to take several steps away from the house before she could see around the staircase. The door of the downstairs apartment was indeed closed and had no glass in it. With four more steps, she could see into the downstairs window, the long picture window that faced the river. She could just glimpse the shoulder of one of the men; he had his back to her. Linda walked sideways, her back to the hedge, never taking her eyes from the window. Nothing inside the lower apartment moved. At last, just as the caboose of the train clanked past the parking lot, Linda was able to duck around the end of the hedge and walk across the street, angling to the right so that no one could see her from the front windows of 7 Carimona Street. She walked down the embankment and turned south along the railroad tracks. Head down, gloved hands jammed inside the pouch of her sweatshirt, she followed the retreating freight, forcing herself to walk—mustn't run; somebody might remember a running figure.

As she walked, Linda stripped the gloves off her hands and balled them inside her right fist. At the corner of Main and Seventh Street, she dropped them inside the litter basket which stood next to the postal drop box. Only now did she realize that she didn't have the cloth she'd taken with her to Ryter's apartment; she had meant to bring it away and drop it with the gloves. She simply couldn't remember where she'd left it, but her feelings were so numbed that she felt no alarm over this over-sight. What difference would an old rag make, she thought? She began to walk again, pulling the hood off her damp hair and letting it fall onto her back.

When she got home, Linda went into the house through the side door—that morning, she had slipped her spare house key into the pocket of her sweatpants. She locked the door again on the inside and walked straight upstairs. She stripped off all her clothes except her bra and panties and rolled everything up into the sweatpants, including the tennis shoes. Then, deliberately and carefully, she put on fresh clothes and her sandals. When she had run a brush through her short hair, she picked up the bundle and went down to the kitchen where she took out a garbage bag and stuffed the bundle inside. All of this was automatic, planned ahead of time, because she wasn't really thinking about anything at all.

Scooping up her purse in one hand and carrying the bag in the other, she walked out to the car and drove straight to the Fishers' house. The garbage cans were next to the garage. Linda stuffed her own bag in one of the bags inside the cans. Then she tied the bags with their self-ties and carried them to the curb. Tomorrow morning, Susan had said, these bags would be taken to the landfill, and any fibers she might have left behind in Ryter's apartment wouldn't help Lieutenant Willman because he wouldn't be able to find their source. Again, this was part of the planning and replanning she had done during the long sleepless night that now seemed months ago; it required no present exercise of the imagination, something Linda wasn't capable of in her state of mind.

Back in her own house again, Linda took a long soaking bath. She sat there with her arms draped loosely over the edges of the tub, her mind blank. She felt numb and rather peaceful. The massive overload of her emotions and her desperate thinking seemed to have caused some circuit-breaker effect in her mind. If someone had asked for her name, she might not have been able to give it. At last, she stood up and dried herself slowly, patting the skin along her arms as if it hurt her. She paused to clean up the tub, the reflex of a habitually neat person. Then she walked naked into her bedroom and crawled into bed. It was 6:05 P.M. She fell asleep at once and slept like a stone for fourteen hours, a deep sleep without any dreams.

Part Three

Part Three

Chapter 25

*L*inda woke to the sound of pounding, a distant
thudding that made a slight vibration in the bed-
stead next to her ear. She came to consciousness
slowly, unaware even after she opened her eyes of what
day it was or what time of day. Sunlight was slanting
across her windows from the east, that angle and that
brightness which on another day would have made her
think, gladly, that it was going to be a fine summer day.
She felt drugged, unable to focus her mind except to
wonder vaguely why she was naked under the sheets. It
was only when she had already sat up that she realized
what the pounding was—someone was knocking on her
front door.

A little chill passed over Linda's exposed flesh as she
stepped from the bed. She groped in the closet for her
bathrobe and pulled it on as she walked into the hallway.

It was not until she reached the stair landing that the memory of the day before came over her, all at once, and it almost knocked her to her knees. Feeling dizzy and nauseated, she clutched the railing to steady herself. At the same time, another side of her mind was saying calmly, "I haven't eaten in two days. I'll feel better when I've had some breakfast." But who could be at her door? What time was it? Finally, she pulled herself up straight and went down the rest of the stairs.

Lieutenant Willman was peering through the windows of the door. Linda's mind wasn't moving fast enough for alarm, so she pulled open the door. Willman's face was almost exaggeratedly relieved at the sight of her.

"You're all right," he said, not as a question, but as a fact of which he was very glad. He looked rumpled and unshaven.

"Yes," she said. "I'm all right. What is it?"

"I rang the bell over and over," he said. "And I tried your side door. Then I just started to knock."

"The bell is in the kitchen," she said. "It's hard to hear upstairs, and I was very sound asleep." She was still finding it very hard to think—making her mind move was like trying to run underwater—so she confined herself to responding directly to whatever he was saying.

"I know it's early," he said, and he looked a little sheepish. "But I was worried about you."

"Why?" Linda was genuinely puzzled.

"May I come in for a few minutes?" he asked.

"Of course," she said. "I didn't mean to keep you standing there. I'm not thinking straight yet." And she opened the screen door to admit him.

Just inside the door, he turned back toward her and said quietly, "Ryter is dead."

"Dead?" She said it with some real surprise because she hadn't really known that the shot was fatal; she thought she had seen his mouth move in that moment of horror when she'd looked at his face.

"Yes. Yesterday afternoon," Willman said.

Linda turned away from him, trying to force her sleep-drugged mind to alertness. How must she respond? How could she best keep those hawk's eyes from seeing her guilt? She must try to act as if all of this were news to her. She must do and say what she would do or say if she had no idea at all of what had happened yesterday in Ryter's apartment.

"How?" she finally managed to say.

"Shot." He was going to give very little away, apparently.

She turned back to him, tightening the sash on her robe.

"So. Did one of his sordid acquaintances gun him down in some bar?" she said, her eyebrows arching upward.

"No. He was in a few bars yesterday, but he died at home," Willman said, meeting her direct gaze with a cool, noncommittal look. "It looks as if it might be suicide."

"Suicide?" she said, remembering to react as if she didn't know. "He didn't seem to me to be the type."

Willman's eyes became sharper.

"Funny," he said. "That's exactly what I thought. It seemed plausible enough that somebody else might kill him—he's provoked enough people for that. But suicide does seem out of character for him, at least from what I could tell from the few times I talked to him.''

"Then what makes you think he killed himself?" Linda said, motioning Willman to the sofa. She sat on the edge of a chair facing him.

"He was in his apartment, apparently alone, both doors locked from the inside," Willman said. "Single shot to the head at close range, gun in his hand."

"Sounds like suicide to me, too," Linda said, her back very straight, her mind beginning to turn over more quickly now.

"It was his own gun, too," Willman said. "The downstairs neighbors who heard the shot identified the gun; they'd both seen it before. Nice gun, too. A Baretta .380 double-action automatic." There was a tone of professional admiration in his voice.

"I don't know anything about guns, Lieutenant," Linda shrugged.

"It's just that I couldn't see how Ryter could afford such an expensive gun," Willman said, looking away for a moment. "Then the boys downstairs told me he bought it second-hand last year from a guy who needed money in a hurry. It was all legal, on the up-and-up."

There was a little pause and Linda felt a need to fill the silence.

"So why do you think he would kill himself, Lieutenant?" she said.

"I'm not convinced that he did," Willman said, looking back into her eyes. "I've been backtracking Ryter's actions since I last saw him. He must have left the factory again after I drove away Thursday night, because he never clocked in for work. I don't know yet where he spent the night. But he spent most of yesterday in bars, drinking quietly at first, and then getting more ornery as the day went along. He offered to punch out a bartender who wouldn't serve him a drink. So, I know what the conventional wisdom on this one would seem to tell us: a sexual deviant arrested for kidnapping a child gets out on bail, skips work, and drinks himself into a near-stupor; he grows increasingly agitated and violent; then he goes home, where the combination of remorse, shame, and too much whiskey causes him to impulsively shoot himself. That's what it looks like, but I'm not so sure."

"Why not?" Linda was keeping her voice studiedly calm.

"Well, for starters, shame and remorse don't fit the Ryter I came to know. He didn't seem to be afflicted by those emotions in his past either. And then, there are some oddities about the way it happened, too."

"Oddities?" Again, Linda thought it best to keep her responses minimal.

"Well, his neighbors heard him come home and heard him turn on his television set which was still on when we had to break in. Then he must have made himself a drink because we found it on the kitchen cupboard. But he didn't finish the drink. Then he went into his bedroom, on the other side of the apartment; his body was on the floor just inside the bedroom door. Now what seems odd to me is why a man would turn on a TV and make a drink in one room, and then just walk through another door to shoot himself, not really into the room, mind you, so that he would fall on the bed, or something, but just inside the door."

"Well," Linda said. "If, as you say, he was very drunk, would any of his actions be rational? Maybe all that anger just suddenly turned inward when he was so drunk, and he acted impulsively, the way you said before."

"Yes, that's a possibility, I suppose," Willman said. "But there are some other puzzles. On the other side of the bedroom, we found some bullets in an empty drawer of a bedstand, and next to the stand, there was a cloth on the floor. We sent it to the lab, of course, but it had some stains on it that lookes like they might be gun bluing."

"What is gun bluing?" Linda covered her alarm by expressing a genuine curiosity.

"It's the stuff that's used to keep guns clean and shiny," Willman explained. "So it looks like he kept the gun in the drawer with the bullets. Then he must have crossed the bedroom, taken out the gun, loaded it, maybe, and rubbed it with the cloth. All this before going back to the other side of the room, turning around in the doorway, and shooting himself. Doesn't sound likely, does it?"

"Maybe he went in and out of the room several times," Linda said. "Sort of working himself up."

"Not enough time," Willman said. "As a matter of fact, there was hardly enough time from when he got home to when the boys heard the shot for Ryter to have got the gun and loaded it."

"I see the problem," Linda said. "But didn't you say Ryter was roaming around Holton all day? Couldn't he have got the gun and loaded it, and polished it, too, earlier in the day and then just taken it with him when he went out again?'' Linda felt rather triumphant at having thought of this.

"A possibility,'' Willman said, as if this were not a new idea to him. "But I did some preliminary checking with the neighbors and no one saw his car until about three-forty when the boys downstairs heard him come in.''

"Just because nobody saw it doesn't mean it wasn't there.''

"Oh, yes, I know that,'' Willman said, smiling a little. "It's one of the principles of criminal investigation that we always have to remember. And, of course, he could have taken the gun out to his car before I saw him leave for work. I don't think he had it on him when I saw him, though; it's hard to hide a gun in summer clothes. But another thing bothering me is that cloth we found. It's not like anything else in Ryter's apartment.''

"What do you mean?'' Linda could feel her breathing change.

"It was very white,'' Willman said. "Bleached, you know. Nothing else like it in any of Ryter's kitchen or bedroom drawers. All of his towels and clothes are on the grey side.''

"Well, I suppose he could have picked it up somewhere else,'' Linda said, beginning to feel for the first time that it was strange for Willman to be discussing the case in such detail with her. She decided on a shift in the conversation. "You said when you came in that you were worried about me. Why was that?''

Willman looked a little flustered for a moment. Perhaps, Linda thought, he'd just been using her as a sounding board, thinking out loud, and now was embarrassed at having done so.

"Oh, well," he said at last. "This morning, I began to think it might be just what it looked like, a suicide. And then I remembered how often these things are murder-suicides, and I started to get afraid he might have come after you first and then, when he finally realized he couldn't get away with it, killed himself, too."

"So you came straight over here?" Linda asked, oddly touched.

"Yeah, and all I did was wake you up. I'm sorry about that, and I'm sorry to be going on about Ryter like this, but the whole thing has me confused."

"It's all right, Lieutenant," Linda said, relaxing her back for the first time. "I'm grateful for your concern. I've had so much trouble sleeping lately that I guess I just collapsed last night from exhaustion. I went to bed early enough, so I shouldn't have had so much trouble waking up this morning, but I guess I was more done in than I thought I was."

"I understand," he said, smiling. "You won't have to lose sleep over Ryter anymore."

Linda wondered for a second if there were some intentional irony in Willman's remark, but just as quickly dismissed it as projection on her part.

"I won't pretend to you that I'm sorry he's dead," she said, looking steadily at him. "It's awful for anyone to commit suicide, I suppose, but I can't help feeling relieved that Dana is safe from him."

"I feel just the same," he said. "It was the first thing I thought of when I saw he was really dead."

Linda recognized the sincerity of this speech, saw the relief Willman felt over Dana, and she was almost overwhelmed with gratitude toward him.

"I felt bad about not being able to offer more protection for her," Willman went on. "Or for you, either. I drove by here once yesterday, saw your car home and everything looking calm, but I couldn't find time to do more."

Linda was instantly alert again. Her mind was working very quickly now. Was he testing her? Had he perhaps stopped, rung the doorbell, and got no answer? Then, maybe his mentioning it was a way to trap her into a lie, an incrimination lie. Suddenly, Linda remembered something Willman had said to her about Ryter, how Ryter had discovered that the secret to a successful lie was sticking as close as possible to the truth. Well, she could use that secret, too.

"Oh, when did you come by?" she said. "I was out walking for a while yesterday. When I'm wound up or nervous, I go for long walks. And, frankly, the house seems pretty empty without Dana. It's funny how fast I started missing her."

"I can imagine," Willman said. "I think it must have been a little after two when I drove past."

"I'm not sure," she said, "but I think I was already gone by then. I didn't get back till about four-thirty."

"You *do* like long walks, don't you?" he said, smiling again.

"Yes, I guess it helps me sort things out," she said.

"And you were home for the rest of the evening?" he said.

"Well, no," she said, now ready to tell a complete truth. "I went back out again in the car because I promised the Fishers to put their garbage out on the curb for the pickup. I'd almost forgotten about it. Do you need to know this for some reason, Lieutenant?"

"No, no," he laughed. "I guess I do sound like a suspicious cop all the time. It's a habit that's hard to break."

"Did you mention what time Ryter was shot?" Linda asked.

"It was about three–forty-five when the guys downstairs heard the shot," Willman answered.

"Well, I was walking alone at that time," Linda said. "I doubt that anyone would have noticed me, so I guess I don't have an alibi." And she tried to smile to show that it was a little joke.

"Well," he smiled back. "I don't think anyone needs an alibi yet. But I confess I'm troubled about this one. I was really shocked when the first officers in told me it was a suicide. And there was another bullet in the gun, too. I just can't figure why a man who plans to kill himself would put *two* bullets in the gun. Surely he doesn't think he'll get another shot."

Why *had* she put in two bullets, Linda now wondered? Had she feared that she might miss and then have to defend herself against an enraged John Charles Ryter? Had she instinctively given herself a backup shot?

"But couldn't he have loaded the gun any time before yesterday?" Linda asked. "Maybe there were two bullets left over from some earlier target practice he might have done."

"I didn't think of that," he said, looking at her with frank admiration. "You would have made a good detective, Mrs. Hammond."

"Well," she said, looking away from him in embarrassment. "It just seems to me that Ryter was the kind of man who wouldn't be too careful about emptying a gun before storing it."

"You could be right," he said. "Probably are right. But I just have a funny feeling about this case, so I keep coming back to details that seem odd to me. Even though both doors were locked on the inside, there's a loose screen on one of the windows and the inside window was open."

So the hawk had already seen that!

"But it's a second-story window, isn't it, Lieutenant?" Linda said. "Wouldn't somebody have noticed an intruder using a ladder?"

"No," he said. "The window is inside an enclosed staircase built onto the house. It would be pretty easy for somebody to get up there without being seen."

Now Linda decided to ask a direction question.

"Do you have any reason to believe that anyone else was in Ryter's apartment?"

"Not really," he said. "The state lab is sending someone over this morning, a fingerprint specialist, and I'll spend some time helping him gather physical evidence. Then we might know more. But the two closest witnesses seem to rule out anyone else being there. They saw Ryter come home alone. They didn't hear or see anyone else. One went up one staircase, and one went up the other—there's a staircase inside the building, too. They saw nobody on either side. After they called us, they went outside again and just waited together in the parking lot, and nobody came out of that side entrance."

"Could somebody have waited inside and then gone down the other way?" Linda said. Perversely, she was beginning to almost believe in a crime committed by someone else, and was actually trying to think like a police officer to figure it out.

"Not possible," he said. "There's no window on that side, and the door was chained on the inside. If there was anyone inside, that person had to get out by the side door, right under the noses of the two witnesses."

"So, it does look like suicide from every angle," she said.

"So far," he said. "There's a little unaccounted-for time while the witnesses were inside telephoning the police station. A train was going past, too, they say. The tracks are very close to the house. But somebody would have had to move very fast to get through the window and replace the screen and still get away clean during that short time. I don't know, though. It still feels wrong to me."

"Well, what's next, Lieutenant?" Linda said, still trying to know ahead of time what would be happening so that she could deal with it.

"I have to put together a report for the coroner's inquest in about two weeks," he said. "We'll find what we can at Ryter's house, and I'll interview everybody who might have seen something. Of course, there'll be autopsy reports to look at, too.''

"You have to do an autopsy when somebody's been shot?" She was genuinely puzzled.

"Oh, not for the cause of death," he said. "That's pretty obvious here. A blunt-nosed bullet through the frontal lobes of the brain kills a person pretty definitely."

Linda winced. Was he deliberately being so graphic to see what her reaction would be? Or had she begun to be unnecessarily paranoid? So soon for a new worry, a new nightmare!

"Sorry," he said at once. "Cop talk. We get pretty hardened, I guess. But the autopsy will tell us what angle the bullet went in, how close the gun was held when it was fired. Things like that."

"And what is the coroner's inquest for?" Linda asked.

"To determine cause of death," he said. "To say if it was a probable suicide, or if some other foul play is more probable."

"I see," she said.

"Would you like me to keep you posted?" he said.

Linda was amazed at the question, couldn't figure out the tone. Was he taunting her because of her past insistence of knowing everything, or was he testing her to see how interested she would be in the investigation? Why did it seem to her that his voice was almost wistful?

"If you like," she said, a little stiffly. "But my interest in Mr. Ryter is over now. I cared only about his being a threat to my daughter."

"Of course," he said, looking away. "Well, you can

read all about it in the paper, I guess. I'd better get back to work.''

Linda thought he sounded disappointed. Why would he be disappointed? Because he hadn't succeeded in getting her to betray a suspicious interest? Then she had won, for now. She walked him to the door and said goodbye to him with further expressions of gratitude, all sincere, but making it clear that she never expected to see him again.

Chapter 26

O nly when Willman had driven away did Linda begin to tremble. She sat back down on the chair and rocked herself backwards and forwards for a long time, her arms folded tightly. Finally, she was able to get up and walk into the kitchen. Although she felt no hunger—on the contrary, what she felt was nausea—she knew she would have to force herself to eat something. And she also knew she had better stay away from coffee for a while, though it was the only thing she craved at the moment. Carefully keeping her mind on the task at hand, she made herself two poached eggs and two slices of toast. She poured a glass of milk and cut a wedge of melon. After the first few bites, she found that she was ravenously hungry after all, and she soon finished all of the breakfast, even the milk, which she didn't like very much.

After her breakfast, Linda got dressed and threw herself into a thorough cleaning of the house. It was the best defense she could find against having to think, and it had a calming effect on her that she'd come to expect from such activity. All her adult life, Linda had found housecleaning and tidying soothing whenever she was nervous, a sort of symbolic return to order and balance that appealed to her need for control. Disorder frightened, even disgusted her because it suggested chaos of a primal kind, a confusion in mind and spirit from which any enormity might spring.

By noon, the house was in splendid order, the sun was shining beautifully, and the temperature had risen to near-normal for mid-June. Linda made herself one cup of coffee and curled up on the newly vacuumed sofa cushions. She had slept fourteen hours, had eaten a substantial breakfast, and had cleaned her house on a bright, early summer morning. The return to normality, both in her body and in her surroundings, made her look now at the events of the day before in a new light.

She hadn't considered how she would feel after Ryter was dead. During all the fevered hours of planning and testing and waiting, she had never once asked herself, "Should I be doing this? Is this necessary? Is this morally defensible?" In the realm past exhaustion and terror, the place where something had tipped over in her mind, the answers to those questions had seemed so self-evident that it would have been silly to formulate the questions at all. It had been like the unreal clarity of a suicidal person, who, once having decided on the act, is concerned only with the means, not with the end—"What

will it be like to be dead?''—or with the moral dilemma—
''Is suicide justifiable?'' So, Linda had never thought,
''What will it be like to have killed someone?''

Now, in the tidy middle-class living room with the
sunshine making a bright parallelogram on the carpet,
she was beginning to find out. It seemed to her now that
she had made a horrible mistake. With safety settling on
her like a blanket again, she began to consider that all her
former terror had been exaggerated, perhaps even illuso-
ry. Could anyone be as bad as she had thought John
Charles Ryter was? Willman had said it, she remembered; he'd said, ''Nobody is as crazy as you think he
is.'' So, what had she done? She had let her fear and her
sleeplessness and her failure to eat distort a petty, spiteful, would-be child molester into a monster, a fiend of
such cunning and strength that only death would stop
him. She had allowed a chance remark of his to create,
out of purely circumstantial evidence, the image of a
diabolical killer, the stuff of which yellow journalism is
made. She, a schoolteacher with a master's degree, had
been deceived by a subliterate, undersized lout into
believing that she was dealing with a ''dangerous character,'' and in her arrogance, she had come to believe that
only she could deal with him. When she had seen the
gun, she had thought it confirmed all her ideas about
Ryter, had been convinced that he would use it to hurt
Dana. But now she felt just as convinced that she'd been
mistaken. Wrong, wrong. She'd been all wrong, but it
was too late. Ryter was dead and she was a murderer.

The word revolved in her head like a carnival ride:
murderer, murderer. The coffee remained untouched in

her cup as she stared at the sunshine on the carpet. The only important thing now was that she mustn't be caught, mustn't go to prison for her crime. At the moment, she really didn't care about herself, but she knew such a blow would be likely to kill her mother, and she couldn't bear to think about what it would mean for Dana. No, one thought emerged clearly in Linda's mind: she must outsmart that clever detective; the coroner's inquest must return a verdict of probable suicide. Whatever guilt and horror she was feeling must be pushed inside and kept there, must never be betrayed by a word or a look. She might never be wholly free again, never completely able to banish from her imagination the image of Ryter's staring eye and the trickles of blood descending toward his jaw, but she mustn't go to prison.

The phone rang. Linda jumped, sloshing some of the tepid coffee onto her slacks. She felt oddly frightened, as if the phone had suddenly become a threat. It had rung two more times before she worked up the courage to pick up the receiver.

"Hi, this is Hal."

Hal. Yes, this was Saturday afternoon, and he was back from St. Louis. It seemed months ago that he had gone away. Linda felt almost as if she were hearing from some old acquaintance who was looking her up as he passed through town, someone she remembered only imperfectly.

"I heard about Ryter as soon as I got off the commuter flight," he was saying. "And, of course, it's all over the newspaper."

Again, Linda had forgotten to go outside for her paper,

just as she had forgotten it the morning after Dana was kidnapped.

"How are you doing?" Hal asked.

"I'm fine," she said dully. "A little stunned, but a little relieved, too, I guess."

"How did all of this happen so fast?" Hal asked. "I thought he wasn't even supposed to have that second hearing until sometime next week."

Linda told him briefly about the hearing, about the reduced bail, and about sending Dana to Lake Wheaton with the Fishers.

"God, I could kick myself for going to St. Louis," Hal said. "I had a feeling I shouldn't go. It must have been just awful for you to sit through that, and then to have to face what might happen when he got out."

Linda could feel a sob rising in her throat in direct response to the sympathy in Hal's voice. She suddenly remembered the warm blue eyes, the soft graying hair, even the little scar slanting toward his lower lip. And she knew she loved him, had loved him for a long time, longer than she had admitted to herself. It was a measure of how far from sanity she had strayed since Wednesday that she had scarcely thought about him until now when his gentle voice was bringing her to the brink of weeping.

"Would you like me to come over?" he said. "I can unpack later."

Even before he'd finished speaking, Linda knew she couldn't see him now. She would break down, tell him everything, and that would put on him a burden she had no right to ask him to bear, not now, not ever. Besides, in her present mood, she felt unworthy to be with Hal Lawrence, felt unclean, sullied by what she'd done.

"I'd like that," she said, swallowing the sob, "but I'm leaving town for the Fishers' cabin in just a few minutes."

How smooth she was getting to be at lying, she thought with alarm.

"Oh," he said, disappointment clear in his voice. "Just to bring Dana home? I could drive you."

"No," she said. "I'm going to stay for a few days, through the weekend at least. I don't know if I can make you understand, but Holton has been a very scary place for me lately, and now that the nightmare is over I want to get away from it for just a little while, so it will seem new again when we come back. Sort of like starting over."

She had suddenly become wholly sincere about half-way through this speech and had made up her mind to really go to Lake Wheaton before she had finished it.

"Sure, of course," Hal said. "I understand. I'll miss you, but you need the change of scene, I can tell. I *did* miss you, you know, all the while I was in St. Louis."

"I missed you, too," she said, and she meant it, though not in the way he thought. "I think it would have been so much easier if you'd been here. I would have taken it all much better, and I wouldn't need to get away now."

"I'm sorry I wasn't here."

"I am, too. But who knew, huh? Who knew the world would go crazy in three days?"

"Call me as soon as you get back?" he asked.

"As soon as I come through the door," she said, and came very close to adding, "I love you, Hal Lawrence."

Susan was noisily shocked when Linda told her on the phone about Ryter's death, but ended by saying, "Best thing the little creep ever did in his life, though. I just wish he'd done it a month ago." When Linda asked if she could come for a few days, Susan cackled with delight and promised beer and sunshine as the perfect cure for the "Holton Summertime Blues."

"Oh, and Susan," Linda said. "Don't tell Dana about Ryter. I think it should come from me. She gets the guilts if she's not handled right."

"Sure thing," Sandy said. "But the only guilty party in this whole thing has already carried out the execution."

"Yes," Linda said, her lips feeling numb. "Maybe you're right."

Chapter 27

The Fishers' cabin was a happy combination of the rustic and the convenient. Jerry had built most of it himself and was shyly proud of it. The cedar-board cabin sat high on a sloping hill covered with white birch and small evergreens. Inside, there were carpets on the floors and a fully equipped kitchen and bathroom, but all the rooms opened upward into the rafters and the bedrooms had curtains rather than doors. A Franklin stove dominated the space between the living room and the kitchen—"We get up here in the winter for some cross-country skiing," Susan said—and a long screened-in porch overlooked the lake itself. So huge was this porch that it contained a full-sized dining room set, a porch swing, and a day bed.

Here, Linda sat with Dana Saturday night, trying to find the right tone of voice to tell her about Ryter, conscious of the levels of hypocrisy she would have to maintain while she explained the "suicide." Inside the cabin, the Fishers were making popcorn as a bedtime snack.

"Dana," Linda began, taking her daughter's hands to show her how serious this was. "Mr. Ryter skipped work on Thursday"—she saw the fear leap into Dana's eyes—"and he spent a lot of time drinking in bars on Friday. He must have been feeling very sick and very miserable when he got back to his house, because he took his own gun and shot himself."

Linda felt Dana's hands jerk inside her own hands.

"He's dead, honey. Lieutenant Willman said he died very quickly."

Dana's eyes grew immense, and Linda could almost see her teetering between horror and relief.

"Oh, poor Chrissy!" she gasped at last, and Linda's heart tightened in pain; Dana could think first of the other child, and she, Linda, had never thought of her once. Linda folded Dana against her chest and rocked her.

"It's a terrible thing, honey, but things like this happen when people get very sick in their minds." She was aware that the sentence applied to herself, too. "You know that Mr. Ryter must have been very sick to try to take you away, to tell you you'd never go home again. And you know that grown-ups who touch children the way he touched you are not well. You *do* know that, don't you?"

"Yes, I do," Dana said softly.

"Well, it's this bad thing in their minds that makes them behave the way no normal person would behave.

Then, when you add alcohol to such a brain, the sickness gets worse and sometimes turns against the person himself. What I'm try to tell you, my dear, is that nobody else is to blame for Mr. Ryter's dying except Mr. Ryter himself. We'll be as kind as we can be to Chrissy, but for the rest of it, we've got to put it behind us and forget that his sickness pulled us into his life for a little while. Okay?"

"Okay," Dana said, sitting up. "I know I had to tell what he did, so I can't think it's my fault that he got sad and killed himself, huh?"

"That's exactly right," Linda said.

The cabin had two bedrooms, one for Susan and Jerry and one for Erin and Dana. Linda got the day bed on the porch where she lay awake for a long time the first night, covered by a large comforter to ward off the rather chilly northern air. Her cheeks tingled pleasantly from the breeze through the screens. She thought about Dana, about what a wonderful child she was, what a generous spirit she had. And now she was safe. No one was stalking her, nobody would be waiting outside her school for her or following her to her flute lessons, biding his time. Linda went over in her mind every word Ryter had said to her on the phone, called up the tone of voice, the maniacal singsong. Oddly, the memory comforted her, the way remembering a nice day on her uncle's farm or a triumph at school used to comfort her when she couldn't sleep as a child; it had the same effect, too, for she was soon asleep. Sometime before dawn, though, she had a dream, a confused kaleidoscope of running and water and stairs.

The next day, Linda sat on the dock, covered in Susan's suntan lotion, and watched the others splashing around the raft. She controlled her fear of water by the simple expedient of staying away from it. The sun on her legs and arms felt good; she was beginning to feel strong again.

It was not that the revulsion she'd felt the day before had abated; she still couldn't let her mind turn directly to a memory of Ryter's apartment or of his eyes, first recognizing her and then frozen in death surrounded by blood. If the image came back, even in a glancing way, she felt her stomach contracting in nausea. But she was beginning to rethink yesterday's certainty that Ryter was nothing more than a petty nuisance who, while he certainly needed a prison psychiatrist, didn't deserve to be murdered. She thought again about the gun, the sleek, well-polished little gun that Ryter had finagled away from his impecunious friend. It was all very well to say that his owning it was "on the up-and-up," but why did he have it all? True, he had used no weapon to get Dana inside his car, but that was only because he didn't need to take such a risk as using a gun his neighbors knew he owned. That didn't mean he was an innocent character, only that he was cunning. The gun was no toy.

Remembering his voice on the phone had helped Linda to recall, almost literally call back, the crazy eyes looking at her in the courtroom and the little smile that was more threatening than a snarl would have been. She reminded herself now, as Dana cannon-balled off the raft's diving board, that an observer as shrewd and experienced as Lieutenant Willman had found Ryter unusual, "sadistic," "a cool customer," a defiant and even clever opponent of established authority. And there were those other girls. Could it be just coincidence that Ryter was acquainted with the family of the one girl in Holton who had disappeared without a trace? And Bakerville was so close to Holton; that child's mother had been certain of foul play. A mother knows her child, Linda thought; if Dana *had* disappeared completely two weeks ago, Linda would have known for certain that it wasn't a case of a troubled runaway.

In her first horrified reaction, Linda had been almost convinced that she'd unnecessarily killed a comparatively innocent man. Now, being with Dana again, remembering how close her child had come to being, perhaps, Ryter's third victim, she was feeling again the certainty that her fears had been justifed. Yet, all the while she sat there with the iced tea next to her hand and the reassuring sunshine on her body, the cool, objective part of her mind was saying, *You have to believe Ryter was a monster, or else you can't face what you've done*.

That night, as Linda was trying to fall asleep, she found it harder than she had the night before to keep pictures of the bleeding head out of her mind. It took real determination to turn her thoughts to Hal and to the rest of the summer ahead of them. Maybe she would call him from here and arrange to meet him just as soon as she and Dana got back to Holton. By then, she would have her emotions under control and there wouldn't be as much risk of her breaking down in front of him. He could easily become the best means of putting all this horror behind her, for she sensed already that there was a whole new life to be made with him.

Suddenly, in the middle of thinking about Hal's strong arms and soft mouth, Linda experienced something like a vision; she saw, as clearly as if it were on a television screen, the inside of Ryter's apartment as it had looked that first time she'd seen it last Wednesday when she went to search for clues. She saw the kitchen, and her own bare hand reaching for the handle of the cupboard door under the sink. And she knew, was certain, that she had not wiped that handle when she went back to the apartment on Friday. She had wiped the handles of the upper cupboards, but not that lower one.

She lay there motionless with the fresh breeze coming off the lake onto her face and felt again the freezing sensation settling into her brain, the chill of terror. Willman and the fingerprint expert had been in Ryter's apartment yesterday morning. Had they found her fingerprints and carefully recorded them? What else might she have forgotten? She'd left the towel behind without even realizing it. How long would it take Willman to ask her if he might take a set of her fingerprints for a possible match? How long before he asked to have a look at her stack of bleached dust rags? She must throw them all away. She'd heard that fiber experts could trace materials back to where they'd been purchased. If Willman went on suspecting murder, and if he found evidence that someone else had been in the apartment, it was only a matter of time before he got around to investigating her. She was, after all, a prime suspect, a person who would have wanted Ryter dead. Would it look suspicious that she'd left town? Would it look like running away? Why hadn't she thought about that yesterday?

While she was lying around here in the sun trying to quiet her conscience, back in Holton that tall man with the eyes that could sometimes look like the eyes of a predatory bird was looking and looking, patiently asking questions, calling in experts. He wouldn't accept the easy, obvious answer if any little thing looked suspicious to him. How much had he already learned? She felt a sudden flash of anger at Willman. He knew what Ryter was; he cared about protecting children from such people, she could tell. Why, then, couldn't he just accept Ryter's death as suicide and be grateful that other children were now safe from him? Where did it come from, this passion to question, to pick and pick, to learn what had really happened? Of course, there was a side of Linda that admired Willman's thirst for truth, even unsavory or inconvenient truth, for she was a good teacher and shared a love of truth for its own sake, knowing just to know. But, in her terror, she forgot her admiration, her gratitude for the tall policeman.

Of course she had to go back to Holton. She couldn't stay here playing while Lieutenant Willman was working. Somehow she had to find out what *he* was finding out. He'd asked if she wanted to be kept posted. Now she had to find a way to be kept informed about the case, a way that wouldn't itself arouse suspicion. She didn't sleep much that night.

At breakfast the next morning, Linda suggested casually that she and Dana would be heading back to Holton that morning. Dana's eyes grew wide in amazement while Susan and Jerry exchanged glances.

"Don't be silly," Susan said, and her voice was challenging. "This time, I'd like to see you find one good reason why you need to run back to Holton. There can't be anything you need to know about. Remember, the bogeyman is gone."

Ah, Linda thought, but there's a new bogeyman I can't tell you about. She knew it would be dangerous to insist, though, because Susan already looked suspicious.

"Okay," Linda said with an attempt at a laugh. "But tomorrow morning, we really have to be off. I promised Hal we'd get together about midweek."

Linda felt rather proud of her shrewdness; it was the one reason Susan would accept readily, even eagerly, as an excuse for Linda and Dana to cut their visit short. Yet, while they did breakfast dishes together, Susan showed that she was more perceptive than Linda had given her credit for.

"You still don't look very good to me, pal," she said. "What's eating you? I've never seen you so distracted and, well, I don't know how to say it, so morose. Can't you just be glad that the miserable creep is dead? It solves everything, doesn't it?"

"Oh, Susan," Linda said frankly, "it's just two weeks ago today that Dana was kidnapped, and I've been through forty kinds of hell in that time. I'm relieved that Dana's safe, of course, but I can't seem to work up much joy over somebody's death, even his. I just need a little more recovery time, I guess."

"Sure, sure you do," Susan said, squeezing her arm,

always eager to show her natural sympathy. "And you're probably right that Hal Lawrence is the best prescription you could find for that recovery. I've been waiting for two years for you guys to get together—you're so right for each other—and I'm just ga-ga that it's finally happening."

"Ga-ga, Susan?" Linda said and laughed.

"Well, you know what I mean," Susan said, pushing at Linda with a half-dried plate. "I love romance."

Linda spent the day in the sun, another spectacular summer day, turning first on her stomach and then on her back, sipping iced tea whenever she sat up. But all the time, her blank gaze was looking back into the stuffy apartment, searching for anything else she might have left behind, returning every few minutes to the picture of her hand closing over that chrome handle, the same hand she'd kept so carefully covered when she'd used it to pull the trigger on Ryter's gun.

Chapter 28

As soon as they got back into their house on Tuesday afternoon, Dana wanted to call Jenny Wieland.

"She's going to think I've died or something," Dana said.

Before Linda had finished unpacking, Dana had cleared with her a plan to sleep over at the Wielands' the following night.

"Summer is great," Dana chortled when she got off the phone, "because we can stay up all night and then sleep till lunch the next day."

Then she pitched in cheerfully, putting away her own clothes and dragging out her overnight bag. In just five days at the Fishers' cabin, she had turned a lovely golden brown and learned how to water-ski, both of which she needed to show off about to her "one and only best friend,'' Jenny Wieland. Linda couldn't help noticing that the news of Ryter's death had changed Dana back into the normal, confident little girl she'd been before Ryter had pulled her into his car. The wonderful resilience of an eleven-year-old! And Dana was genuinely unaware that her renewed security and cheerfulness were a direct response to a man's death; it was just a healthy animal reaction to the removal of a threat, and Linda envied it with all her heart. At the same time, she couldn't help rejoicing in it, couldn't restrain a passing thought that Dana's recovery was worth the horrible price which had been paid for it.

Linda remembered her promise and called Hal.

"Are you all tanned and rested?" he said, with a gentle flirtation in his tone.

"A little of each," she said. "And Dana is really her old self again. You'll notice the difference in her, just wait and see."

"I brought you both a little something from St. Louis," he said. "When can I make a presentation?"

"Well, Dana has already set up a sleep-over with her best friend for tomorrow night," Linda answered. "And we're both so yucky from sunning and driving that we have to spend the rest of today putting ourselves to right. There's a ton of laundry to do, too."

"If Dana has a date for tomorrow night, how would you like to have one, too?"

"Sounds lovely. I think I can get unyucky by then."

"Let's pretend that it's like dress-up day at school and do something special," Hal said. "How about dinner at Leon's and a late movie afterwards?"

"Wonderful. When should I look for you?"

"How's six-thirty? A little early for New York, maybe, but, hey, this is the Midwest."

"Six-thirty is just fine. I get too hungry for late dinners anyway."

"Another symptom of our compatibility," he laughed. "See you tomorrow."

All the way back from Lake Wheaton, while Dana slept in the backseat, Linda had tried to think of a way to contact Lieutenant Willman without arousing his suspicions. Nothing very original came to her, and she guessed anyway that too much originality would set off all the alarm bells inside that canny mind. At last, she decided on something fairly simple. But when she called the station, the dispatcher told her that Willman was out; if she would leave her number, he would call her back. She was almost finished with the laundry when the phone rang.

"You wanted to talk to me, Mrs. Hammond?" the familiar voice said, sounding, as usual, a little tired, but kind, solicitous.

"It may sound silly, Lieutenant," Linda said, forcing a little cheerfulness into her voice. "Dana and I just got back from Lake Wheaton, and it occurred to me while we were up there that I hadn't told you I was leaving town. As a matter of fact, I didn't decide to go until after I'd talked to you on Saturday. Then, later, I remembered that you're conducting an investigation into a case that I'm at least indirectly connected with. So I wondered if, perhaps, I should have let you know I would be gone for a few days.'' She had a feeling that she was going on too long, making too much out of it, but there wasn't even a slight sign of an interruption on the other end of the line.

"No need to have concerned yourself," he said when she'd finally wound down. "If I'd needed you to stay in Holton, I'd have told you so. I guessed that you'd gone up to get Dana, and your friend Mr. Lawrence confirmed it for me."

Linda was stunned into silence for a moment. Willman had asked Hal where she was and Hal hadn't mentioned it to her on the phone. What *else* had Willman asked about, she wondered.

"How did you happen to speak to Mr. Lawrence?" Linda said at last.

"Routine," Willman said dryly. "I had to check your whereabouts from the time I spoke to you last Thursday until the next time I spoke to you on Saturday. Unless Ryter is a definite suicide, I have to consider other possibilities."

"And I suppose I must be a prime suspect," she said, her heart pounding. He must have found the fingerprints. Only the fact that her fingerprints were nowhere on file had so far prevented him from making the match.

"Nobody is a suspect at all, Mrs. Hammond," he said calmly. "I'm just going through the numbers, being thorough. Lots of people think police work is like Sherlock Holmes, but mostly it's just legwork, and about eighty percent of it turns up nothing at all. I'm asking around about everybody who knew Ryter, about his ex-wife, the guys he worked with. I'm even considering the possibility that the boys downstairs might have hated his guts and set him up for a fake suicide."

"I see," Linda said. "And how is your investigation coming along? Do you still lean more toward murder than suicide?"

"I haven't drawn any definite conclusions," Willman said. "I like to wait until all the evidence is in before I do that. The lab reports aren't all back yet, and I don't get the autopsy report until tomorrow sometime."

"It all sounds complicated," Linda said lamely, not daring to ask about the fingerprint expert. "But fascinating, too. Like a scientific problem that has only one answer but a lot of distracting data."

"It's a little more like trying to put broken dishes back together when six or seven plates all got smashed in the same place," he said, laughing a little. "The piece that looks like it should fit might belong to a different plate altogether."

"That's a much more concrete way of putting it," Linda said. "Still, it must be interesting work sometimes."

"Sometimes it is," he said. "If you're interested in some of the results from the tests—" and he broke off.

"Yes?" she urged. "What were you going to say?"

"Well," he said. "I usually take my morning coffee break in the cafeteria at Rudolph's Grocery. If you happened to be out Thursday morning, I might have a few more of the puzzle pieces together."

"I have a few errands to run on that end of town," she lied. "About what time do you have your coffee break?"

"About ten," he said.

"Well, I might see you there," she said, trying to sound casual. "If my errands are finished, that is."

That night, when Dana had fallen asleep, Linda brought in all the newspapers from the side porch and began methodically following the story of the death of John Charles Ryter, from Saturday's paper forward, all front page material in the *Holton Post*. The Sunday paper contained a grainy reproduction of what must have been a photograph obtained from Sandy Ryter. It showed a much younger, thinner Ryter in a sleeveless tee shirt, unsmiling, the sun at his back, his hair almost to his shoulders, his eyes simply dark caves under the prominent brows—a fairly common "tough guy" pose of a young man trying to impress his girl. All of the sketchy accounts referred to Ryter's "apparent suicide," but Monday's paper quoted "an officer investigating the case" as saying, "We're considering all the possibilities at this point. Foul play is not ruled out." Linda couldn't imagine Lieutenant Willman saying that to a reporter, but guessed that another policeman influenced by Willman's suspicions had done so.

Linda lay awake for a long time trying to imagine what Ryter might have been like as a boy. How might he have wooed and won Sandy? Had he ever been capable of tenderness or playfulness, the ingredients she herself found indispensible to being in love? Could love have looked out of those eyes once, long ago when he was very young? She wondered, too, who else besides Hal had been questioned about her by Willman. And what could it mean that Hal hadn't told her about talking to a policeman about her? She debated with herself about how wary she should be at Willman's readiness to discuss the case with her over coffee. It might just be a polite continuation of the courtesy he had extended to her when they both feared for Dana's safety; then Willman had seemed to think out loud in answer to her frightened questions, almost as if it helped him to clarify his own thoughts by talking about them with her. But it could also mean that he knew more than he was letting on and was hoping for a chance to trap her into some revelation. She would have to be very careful, very cool.

When Linda woke up the next morning, it was from an odd dream. She had been talking to her father in the kitchen of their old house in Minneapolis. She saw the beloved face very clearly, but he was looking sad and saying, "I wish you would tell me how you hurt yourself, honey. I won't punish you; I just want to know." In the distortion of dream, she could see her own hand and arm, much enlarged, swathed in layers of white bandages while her father was still wrapping, passing a huge roll of gauze around and around her arm. The bottom of the polished white sink was stained with blood.

Once awake, Linda decided that she needed to behave as if everything had returned to normal and, perhaps, she would begin to feel that way. Once, when she was eight, she had developed an intense dislike for her music teacher, and it was her father who had said, "Try pretending that you like her very much. Do and say the things you would if she were your favorite person." After a few weeks of following her father's advice, Linda found that she really did like the teacher much better. So this morning, she roused Dana and suggested a whole day of shopping—groceries in the morning and clothes in the afternoon. If she were feeling normal, she reasoned, she would want a new dress to wear for her dinner-date with Hal, so a new dress was what she was going to have. And Dana, she knew, could use a few pairs of shorts; last summer's were a bit snug in the hips.

When all the groceries were stashed in the cupboards and refrigerator, Linda and Dana had bacon and lettuce sandwiches for lunch, cleaned up the kitchen, and headed for the downtown mall. They both looked for clothes in the first two stores they went into. Dana found several pairs of shorts she liked and even a matching top for one pair, but Linda didn't like most of the dresses she tried on. They seemed to be designed exclusively for flat-chested teenagers, their outlandish colors and designs looking, she thought, ludicrous on her womanly figure. Dana thought the dresses looked "neat" and couldn't understand why Linda hesitated to buy an orange-and-green print crepe with an asymmetrical hemline. They'd left the second shop and were crossing the street when Linda spotted Sandy Ryter.

It took almost five seconds for Linda to react, even to notice that Chrissy was walking next to her mother; they'd just come out of the dress shop Linda and Dana were crossing to. Linda stopped, literally in the middle of the street, and Dana had reached the other curb before she noticed that her mother had stopped. Linda's first impulse was to flee, to just turn around and run. She could see that Sandy had noticed her, for she had reached out to grasp Chrissy's arm, to keep the child from walking away. Sandy just stood there, a box under her left arm, and stared at Linda. The horn of an approaching car sounded and Linda made her decision: what use to run away? Holton was too small a town to allow her to avoid Sandy Ryter forever. She walked firmly to the curb to join Dana, putting her hands onto her daughter's shoulders as she came up to her. Dana had seen the Ryters, too, and was looking a little alarmed.

"Would you go into the bookstore for a few minutes," Linda said softly to her, "and see if there are some mysteries you might like to buy? I think Mrs. Ryter wants to say something to me, and you might be happier looking at books than listening to us. I'll come in for you when we're finished."

Dana made no protest but walked quickly into the bookstore two doors away. For another moment, Linda and Sandy Ryter looked at each other across ten feet of sun-bathed sidewalk. Finally Linda forced her feet into motion and approached the mother and daughter. Chrissy Ryter was a small child for eleven, spindly and pale, her hair and skin and eyes so close to each other in color that she seemed to have no eyebrows at all; her teeth were crooked, piled on top of each other. Linda remembered that she seldom looked adults in the eye, and now the child was staring past Linda, her little face expressionless. Linda didn't think about what she would say, but Sandy saved her the trouble.

"Do you know what we've just been doing?" Sandy said as Linda came up to her; her voice had the same edge of hysteria in it that Linda remembered from their first interview two weeks ago.

"What have you been doing?" Linda asked, trying to make her voice calm, even kind.

"We've just been buying dresses to wear to Jack's funeral," Sandy said, and her eyes reddened. "The funeral is tomorrow. Did you know that?"

"No, I didn't," Linda said, thinking, Oh God, this is what they never show you in the movies; they never let you know that even the bad guys have funerals when they die, and their families have to buy something to wear. "I'm sorry for you and Chrissy," Linda finished, unable to think of anything else to say.

"It's too late for you to be sorry," Sandy said, and Linda could hear the spite that often lies just under the whine. "I begged you to stop lying about Jack, but you wouldn't. You coulda been sorry for us then and none of this woulda happened."

"No one lied about your ex-husband," Linda said, feeling her face beginning to flush. "What has happened to him is something he brought on himself. It might be best not to talk about it in front of your daughter."

Linda had noticed that Sandy tightened her grip on Chrissy's arm whenever she spoke, and that the child had several times tried to get away.

"Don't you pretend to care about Chrissy," Sandy hissed as some people passed on the sidewalk. "It's thanks to you that she's a orphan."

"What do you mean by that?" Linda asked, keeping her voice at almost a whisper.

"If you hadn't a pushed them charges against him, he'd a never gone back to drinking, and then he woulda never killed himself." Sandy had begun with a consciousness of talking to a teacher, but in her anger had returned to her habitual speech patterns. Her pinched face had begun to look almost ferocious.

"If his own behavior brought him to his death, I can't see what that has to do with me or my family," Linda said, again looking at the pale child.

"You come offering your sympathy," Sandy said, "but you don't fool me one bit. You're glad that Jack's dead."

"I regret your pain," Linda insisted quietly.

"You might as well say you helped to kill him," Sandy said, gripping her child even harder. "You might not a pulled the trigger, but he wouldn't be dead if it wasn't for you and your brat."

Linda was beginning to hyperventilate, to feel a little dizzy, but she struggled for calm.

"When you're more rational," Linda said, "you will realize that what you're saying is foolish. Perhaps it's best if we don't talk any more about it right now."

"You can't take it, can you?" Sandy's voice was close to a snarl. "You think you can run away from it. Well, *we* can't run away from it." And she pushed Chrissy in front of her, as if to present her to Linda. The child hung her head, and the back of her neck flushed a dull red. "You don't like scenes, I bet," Sandy went on. "You don't like to hear unpleasant things. Well, here's something pretty unpleasant to think about. They cut her father up in pieces, them coroner people; they just sliced him into chunks, and they never asked me if they could do it, either. Do you know what it's like to think about a thing like that?" And now she was weeping in earnest.

"Oh, think about the child," Linda said, and her voice was almost a moan. "Don't say such things in front of her. Give her some chance to get over this."

Linda wanted to snatch the child away, to grab her and run with her. If she could have this child, raise her to be a healthy adult, it might make some amends—a life saved for a life taken. As it was, she could see the damage already done to Chrissy Ryter by eleven years with such parents, and she could imagine all too well what the rest of her growing-up years would be like.

"We're going now," Sandy said, drawing herself up, on her dignity. "While you go on about your life, you just think about other lives that are ruined."

And they walked away, Chrissy straggling behind, her narrow back already resembling the defeated posture of her mother. Linda stood on the sidewalk, getting her breathing back under control. Then she went to get Dana.

"Come on, honey," she said. "We're going home."

"But you didn't get a dress yet," Dana said, her heart-shaped face filled with concern.

"That's all right," Linda said. "I guess I don't need a new dress. Not really."

On the drive home, Linda stared over the wheel of the car, hardly seeing the streets and the other traffic. So, here was another unlooked-for horror, another thing her plans hadn't taken into account. Chrissy Ryter would grow up in Holton, five blocks from the Hammonds' house. She and Dana would go to the same schools for another seven years. Linda would have to watch the effect on Chrissy of poverty, made worse by the loss of even an inconsistent breadwinner, the effects of being the universally recognized daughter of a child molester and suicide victim. And Sandy Ryter would be there always too, making sure that any attempt, however veiled, Linda might make to help the child would instantly be labeled as salve for a guilty conscience—and, of course, she would be absolutely right. If some sadistic judge were trying to think of a particularly cruel punishment for Linda, he couldn't invent anything to beat this one.

Perhaps, Linda thought, it's just this kind of thing that drives some criminals to confess their crimes, even when there's no evidence against them. Everybody else thinks they're driven by remorse to seek punishment, when actually they might be fleeing gratefully into prison just to get away from the daily reminders of their crimes. Conventional punishment would be such a relief. She remembered reading newspaper accounts about fugitives who had successfully hidden for ten or fifteen years, only to walk into a police station one day to say, "Here I am. I did it. Lock me up." Now she was beginning to think she understood those people.

After Linda had parked the car in the driveway and got out on her side, she heard somone calling her name.

"Linda. Oh, Linda." It was coming from behind the redwood fence that separated her driveway from the Hardwicks' yard next door.

"Yes, Brenda," Linda called back, hiding a sigh. Brenda Hardwick was a silly woman who made herself even sillier by drinking in the middle of the day. Linda had carefully avoided her for two years.

"Just a minute," Brenda said. "I'm coming over."

"Take your clothes inside, Dana," Linda said, "and cut the tags off. Be careful with the scissors."

Brenda came around the fence at the end of the driveway and huffed up toward Linda. She was overweight and smoked too much in addition to her drinking problem.

"I've been meaning to talk to you ever since you got back yesterday," Brenda said, pressing her hand against her ample bosom as she took a big breath.

"Really, Brenda," Linda said. "About what?"

"Well," Brenda said, lowering her voice to a stage whisper and doing a ludicrous pantomime of looking around for possible eavesdroppers. "While you were gone, a policeman came to see me. He asked some questions about you."

Linda was no longer very surprised by this.

"Was he a tall man, bald, with sharp features?" Linda asked.

"Why, yes," Brenda gasped as if she thought Linda clairvoyant.

"That would be Lieutenant Willman," Linda said cooly. "He helped me when Dana was kidnapped—you must have read all about it in the newspaper—and now he's investigating Mr. Ryter's suicide."

"Well, it didn't sound like that to me," Brenda said.

"Why? What did he want to know?"

"He asked me if I had seen you go in or out last Friday. That was the day this Ryter person shot himself, wasn't it?"

"Yes, I believe it was." Linda was amazed at her own control. "The lieutenant has to make sure it was a suicide, and he must consider all the possibilities, as well. He must find out, for instance, if I might have killed Ryter."

"That's just silly," Brenda said, elaborately outraged and smelling of bourbon.

"Of course it is," Linda said. "And what did you tell him, about last Friday, I mean?"

"Well, I told him I saw you coming home from a walk about four-thirty and that you went out again in the car just a few minutes later."

"And did he want to know anything else?"

"He asked me if I had seen you leave on your walk, as if I have nothing better to do than watch my neighbors out of my windows. I mean, really."

"And *had* you seen me leave?"

"No, and I told him so. I only saw you coming back because I happened to be dusting furniture at the front of the family room at the time."

Linda couldn't imagine Brenda Hardwick dusting furniture, and she smiled a little.

"Did he ask you anything else?" Linda said.

"Yes," Brenda said, pulling her eyebrows into a caricature of puzzlement. "He asked what you were wearing when you came home from your walk and when you went out again."

Linda could feel her heart rate increasing. Someone had seen her walking either to or from Ryter's apartment and had described her clothes.

"And what did you tell him?" Linda asked.

"Well, I told him I just don't pay attention to things like that," Brenda said, sounding huffy that anyone might accuse her of noticing such things. "How can I see what you're wearing when you're sitting in your car, anyway?"

"I hope you didn't tell Lieutenant Willman anything but the truth, Brenda," Linda said, beginning to feel reckless, almost savagely daring. "The man is a conscientious policeman, and he's only doing his duty by all of us when he conducts thorough investigations. Now I hope you don't think I need protection from a police inquiry."

"Of course not," Brenda said, almost bowled over. "I told him you were wearing slacks and a long-sleeved shirt of some sort when you came home from your walk, something dark, but I didn't notice the exact color. He seemed satisfied with that."

"I was wearing my purple sweat suit, Brenda," Linda said, carefully planting the lie that was oh-so-close to the truth, "because it was so cold on Friday, remember?" The purple sweat suit was almost brand new and its shirt had no hood.

"Yes, I do," Brenda said. "Yes, purple, that was it. But I really didn't notice what you were wearing when you went out again in the car. Why is he asking about your clothes, anyway?"

"I don't know," Linda said. "Maybe someone was seen in or around Ryter's house wearing a certain kind of clothes, and so he has to ask about clothes. It's his job, Brenda, and he mustn't be blamed for doing it well."

"Well, as long as you're not upset," Brenda said, looking decidedly disappointed that Linda was not more upset.

"You must keep in mind," Linda said, feeling even more dangerously cocky, "that I had good reason to dislike Mr. Ryter, as no doubt other people did, too. So the police are simply checking me out along with other possible suspects. You'll see. In the long run, they'll find out that no other explanation except suicide fits the evidence."

"Sure," Brenda said, and began to get a vague look on her face now that her gossip had fallen short of its target.

"Now, if you'll excuse me," Linda said. "I have to go inside and help Dana get ready for a sleep-over she's going to tonight. And I have to get ready for a date."

This last was a deliberate effort to distract Brenda's foggy brain onto a new subject for spying. Let her look, Linda thought. Let her get her eyes full. In her present mood, having suffered through the meeting with Sandy and Chrissy Ryter, only to find yet another instance of evidence being gathered against her, Linda wanted to shout down the driveway to Holton in general, "Just try to catch me! Do your worst. What can you prove? What can you do to me that can hurt me more than I've hurt myself?"

Chapter 29

After driving Dana to the Wielands' house, Linda prepared for her date with Hal in a dazed and distracted way. She chose a pale beige summer-weight knit dress because she thought it looked all right against the beginnings of a tan she'd managed to acquire in the two days at Lake Wheaton; the sun had also brought out the blond highlights which still streaked through her brown hair. When she zipped up the dress, Linda noticed that it didn't seem to fit right; it bagged a little around her waist and hips. She padded barefoot into the bathroom and weighed herself. At first, she couldn't believe the scale, so she stepped off and back on again. In just over two weeks, she'd lost ten pounds. Linda had never needed to watch her weight, and she often didn't weigh herself for weeks at a time. Looking now at the scale's dial, she realized that she could name with ease the few times she'd eaten a good meal since the Monday night when Dana had been kidnapped.

Stepping back into her bedroom, Linda made a firm resolution to begin eating sensibly again. She knew that lack of sleep and nutrition were enough by themselves to cause mental disorder, even if she didn't also have to live with the horror of having committed a murder and the strain of keeping it hidden. If she was going to deal with Lieutenant Willman the next day—and who knew how many other times before the coroner's inquest made a judgment about Ryter's death—she must remain alert and clearheaded. And she couldn't do that if she went on starving herself and staying up half of every night. Sleeping might be harder to deal with, but nutrition was something she could control, even if it meant forcing herself to eat when she wasn't hungry.

She gave special attention to her makeup, trying to hide the dark circles under her eyes, minimizing the puffiness of her lids with a green eye shadow. Even when she'd finished, though, she thought her face looked gaunt and haggard. No wonder Susan had said she looked bad. Now Linda even imagined that her eyes looked guilty; she could hardly meet her own gaze in the mirror. How long could she carry it off, she wondered? How long before she just screamed the truth at some passerby in the street?

When she opened the front door for Hal, he folded her in a tight hug despite the fact that he was carrying a box in each hand. When he'd given her a quick kiss, he held her away at arm's length and looked at her.

"You look lovely," he said, but Linda thought she saw worry in his gaze.

"Thank you. So do you," she said, trying to smile. And he did look wonderful in his pale gray suit. He'd got a fresh haircut and the sun had made the little wrinkles around his eyes alternately brown and white, an effect that made his eyes look even more good-humored than usual.

"You *did* get a little tan," he said, suddenly awkward. "It looks great."

They stood silent for a moment, almost like teenagers on a first date. Then Hal seemed to become aware that he was holding something in his hands.

"I brought you something," he said, holding out the box in his left hand. "I found it in one of the hotel shops."

Linda opened the box at once—it hadn't been wrapped—and found inside the rustling tissue paper a silk scarf in a tasteful geometric print of red and navy blue. She took it out and let the cool fabric run through her fingers. It was a long, narrow scarf, exquisitely made and obviously very expensive.

"It's beautiful," Linda said, feeling dangerously close to tears. "Thank you so much," and she leaned forward to kiss him just to the left of his mouth.

"I got something for Dana, too," he said. "But I guess she'll have to open hers tomorrow." And he put the box down on the coffee table. "It's a diary. I don't know if eleven-year-olds keep a diary yet, but I figured she'd be able to use it sometime during her teens. Don't all teenage girls keep a diary at some point?"

"I think so," Linda said with a little laugh. "I did."

She looked down at the box and it occurred to her that it was resting on the exact spot where she'd put the gun on Thursday. She jerked her head upright.

"I'll have to buy a special dress to wear with this scarf," she said. "I'm afraid it won't go with this one, or I would wear it tonight."

"Maybe you could wear it to the Carvers' open house Saturday night," he said. When she looked at him blankly, he stammered, "Not that you have to get a new dress by then or anything. It was just my not-so-subtle way of asking you to go with me."

"Good Lord," Linda said at last. "I had totally forgotten about the Carvers' open house. Is it this Saturday?"

"Yes," he chuckled. "The annual ordeal is almost upon us. We'll have to condition our stomachs in advance for Ann's hors d'oeuvres."

Donald Carver was the junior high school's assistant principal, and he and his wife Ann gave an open-house reception every summer for the school's entire staff, a get-together notorious for the weak punch and the stale food. It was a tradition that few of the guests enjoyed, but one they felt powerless to boycott. Carver had ambitions in the school district and, despite his somewhat negative personality, seemed destined to achieve those ambitions.

"I don't feel much like going," Linda said truthfully.

"Who does?" Hal said. "But we've got to put in an appearance and if you go with me, I can whisk you away

to something much more exciting while the evening is
still young.''

His smile was irresistible and, Linda reminded herself,
she'd taken a firm resolution to return to a normal life.

"What a lovely thought," she said. "I think I'll get a
new dress. Won't we just slay everybody by coming in
together, too?"

"That's the spirit," he said. "It'll be the first time in
eight years they'll have something to talk to each other
about.''

Leon's was the closest Holton was able to come to
haute cuisine. Set in a beautifully remodeled turn-of-the-
century building with a magnificent skylight and rows of
hanging plants, the restaurant served a limited number of
excellent entrees, and its wine cellar was reputed to be
one of the finest in the state. Only after they'd ordered
and had a first glass of wine did Linda bring herself to
the subject she'd wanted to ask Hal about ever since he'd
come to pick her up. Even now, she approached it
indirectly, rather than asking a question.

"Lieutenant Willman tells me that he spoke to you
while we were up at Lake Wheaton," she said, trying to
make her tone airy.

Hal blushed immediately.

"When did you see him?" he asked, parrying for the
moment.

"Oh, I called him," she said. "Just to let him know
that we were back in town if he wanted to ask me about
anything.''

"Yes, he came to see me on Sunday," Hal said. "Do you think he ever takes a day off?"

"No, I honestly don't think he does."

"He wanted to know if I'd seen you or spoken to you between Thursday evening and Saturday morning of last week." Hal looked back at her now after seeming to take an interest in the table cloth. "Of course, I told him I was out of town for all that time. Then he wanted to know if I called you from St. Louis. Well, I *did* try to call you during the lunch break on Friday, but you must have been away from the house."

Linda could feel her scalp beginning to tingle.

"Oh, what time did you call?" she asked, managing to sound curious rather than alarmed.

"It was about one o'clock, maybe a little after."

"Oh, that was *you* then," Linda said, taking a quick cue from the words Hal had used: "away from the house." "I was weeding in the flower beds and it was a while before I even heard the phone. By the time I got inside, all I got was dial tone." She had actually done some weeding on Tuesday afternoon after Hal had left for the airport.

"I knew it must have been something like that," Hal said. "Willman said you must have been out for a long time on Friday. He acted like he was checking out an alibi or something and it made me angry."

"You did tell him about trying to call me, didn't you?" Linda said.

"Well, yes, I did," Hal said, and he looked uncomfortable again.

"Good," Linda said. "There's no reason to keep anything from the lieutenant."

"Of course not," Hal said quickly.

"I was wondering why you didn't tell me about seeing Willman, though," Linda said, looking hard at him.

"I didn't think it was necessary to upset you about it," he said, reaching across the table to take her hand. "Besides, I acted like a jerk when I was talking to him."

"How?"

"I told him he should be out looking for real crooks instead of asking questions about good, decent people. And I told him I was glad Ryter shot himself, so why couldn't it just be left that way."

"You were defending my honor," Linda said, her hand cool and limp inside his warm grasp. "That's very sweet, but quite unnecessary. And Lieutenant Willman is just doing his job, 'going through the numbers,' as he says. It doesn't bother me, so it shouldn't bother you. And I'm going to tell you something now that I once said to him. Don't try to protect me by not telling me things. I'm a person who wants to know about what concerns me and mine. I *need* to know, so that whatever happens, it isn't a surprise."

"I'll remember that for all future occasions," he said tenderly.

"You see," she said softly, looking into his blue eyes, "when I learned by accident that you'd spoken to Willman but hadn't told me about it, it made me think that you might have some unresolved suspicions of your own about me."

"That's nonsense," he said, and he was sincerely

indignant. "I think any further investigation of Ryter's death is nonsense. The man killed himself and that's that. But even if something does look suspicious about it, that cop is nosing around in the wrong direction."

"Well," Linda said, withdrawing her hand to pick up her wine glass. "He's nosing in all directions at the moment, and you must admit that I'm at least one likely candidate if Ryter was murdered."

"Willman can think that only because he doesn't know you," Hal said.

Linda felt a sudden flash of irritation at Hal. His answer had seemed so pat, almost smug. She thought of Willman's kind, haggard face, and it occurred to her that Willman might perhaps know her much better than Hal could ever know her.

At the movie theater, Linda and Hal saw several students and ex-students who immediately began to whisper behind their hands when they saw the teachers out on a date. It was inevitable in a town the size of Holton, where supermarket checkout boys, gas station attendants, and fast-food counter girls all sang out "Hi, Mrs. Hammond," almost every day of her life. At any other time, Linda would have found the whispering in the movie theater cute, even flattering, but tonight it only made her remember David Polson.

When the lights went down and Hal took her hand, she wondered whether that slow-witted young man had finally remembered why the voice of the woman in the woods had sounded so familiar. The year he'd been in her class, Linda had worn her hair long and still colored it blonde, so she looked very different now. But a voice was something a person couldn't disguise, she knew, and she hadn't tried to disguise it. How much had she actually said to David? How many words? And if he did suddenly connect the voice to Mrs. Hammond, what would he make of it? Would he wonder why she was driving that road at that time of night? Might he mention to other people, "You know, I was parking with my girl out by Porterfield and I heard gunshots. When I went to look, who do you think stopped to look, too? Mrs. Hammond from junior high. Can you beat that?" If rumors finally reached him that Mrs. Hammond's kid had been kidnapped by a guy who shot himself the day after that night in the woods, might it occur to him that Mrs. Hammond herself might have been firing those shots? How bad would it be if Willman's questioning uncovered David Polson? Surely, nothing more than circumstantial, but added to the rest? What *was* the rest? What did Willman already know?

So it was that Linda sat through a movie she didn't really see, having one man hold and fondle her hand while she thought about another man. By the time she and Hal got back to her house, she was aware of this gap between her thoughts and the occasion, and she was feeling guilty about it. She asked Hal in for a drink, only to discover that she still had no liquor in the house except the brandy from which Willman had made her drink the night of Ryter's phone call.

"Never mind," Hal said. "At least I'm learning that you're not a closet alcoholic. I'll just have some coffee or tea, if you've got some."

While he was speaking, Linda had been staring at the brandy bottle in her cupboard. Liquor, she suddenly thought! There had been some liquor bottles in the cupboard below Ryter's sink. And when she was waiting in the bedroom with the gun in her hand, she'd heard Ryter getting ice cubes out of the refrigerator. What was it Willman had said? Something about finding it hard to believe that a man would make himself a drink, leave it unfinished, and then shoot himself. If Ryter got some liquor out from under the sink, he would have touched the cupboard handle after she'd opened that door, and his fingerprints might have obscured her own.

"Linda?" Hal was saying. "Is something wrong?"

"What?" She turned to look blankly at him.

"You suddenly seem very preoccupied."

"Oh, it's nothing," she said. "I was just thinking that we used to keep liquor around when I was married. I'm sorry."

"No need to apologize," he said. "I get into those memories sometimes myself."

Hal helped Linda to make some coffee and then carried it out to the living room. When they'd set their cups next to Dana's present and sat down on the sofa, Hal suddenly pulled Linda into his arms.

"I won't mind your sometimes thinking about your ex-husband if you won't mind my sometimes thinking about Elaine," he whispered against her ear.

Linda felt petty and mean for having deceived Hal about the cause of her reverie, and her guilt made her feel tender toward him.

"Of course I won't mind," she said, slipping her arms

around his neck. "And I really don't think much about Dan. He's very much in my past now, and I want you to know that."

"Good," he said, and he began to kiss her ear, from the top down to the lobe. Then he nuzzled his soft mouth into her throat, making gentle little nips at the curve of flesh that began to slope toward her breasts.

Linda felt oddly as if she were across the room watching this scene. Objectively, she realized that this was an ideal situation for the development of a relationship she very much wanted to develop. Dana was away for the whole night, until noon tomorrow as a matter of fact. She'd just had a wonderful evening with an attractive man, a man she loved and trusted, a man who was obviously as much attracted to her as she was to him. And yet his kisses and caresses weren't arousing her now. She looked over the silver and blond mixture of his hair as if she saw, on the other side of the room, a tall, stooping figure watching her, judging her with his hawk's eyes, forbidding her to be happy.

Hal sat up and looked at her, his face half puzzled and half hurt.

"Something's wrong, isn't it, Linda?" he said. "I've sensed it all evening. Are you pulling away from me? Is this going too fast for you?"

"It's not that, Hal," she said, and the sincerity of her tone was instantly convincing became she could see the relief in his eyes. "I'm not myself tonight. I don't think I've been myself since before that awful phone call from Ryter."

"But it's over now," he said. "Can't you be relieved and just put it behind you?"

"Susan Fisher said almost the same thing," Linda said, smiling a little. "I guess you're both right, at least from the way you're seeing it. But I still feel on the inside of the whole nightmare. Willman is talking to my neighbors about me, and I ran into Sandy and Chrissy Ryter downtown today."

Hal's eye widened and he threw his hands up into the air.

"Why didn't you tell me that?" he asked. "Here I'm trying to be Romeo, and you've had a lousy day."

"I guess we *both* have to take the pledge not to keep things from each other," she said, and she told him about the meeting in the mall, trying to downplay Sandy's direct accusations, but some of her misery must have come through because Hal was almost moved to tears.

"What a rotten thing to have happen so soon," he said. "She'll see things differently eventually, I'm sure, but right now all she can think of is to dump her own unhappiness all over you. You've got to try to remember that she probably feels some guilt herself that she can't deal with just yet."

"I feel so sorry for the little girl," Linda said. "She's already been dealt a pretty rotten hand in life and now to have this thing about her father hanging over her. Well, it just doesn't seem fair."

"You curl up here and let Dr. Lawrence tell you a story or two," Hal said, indicating his broad chest.

Linda leaned into his arms, pulling her feet up onto the sofa like a child.

"When I was eleven," Hal began, "my eight-year-old brother drowned. He wandered away from us at the beach where we'd gone to picnic on a Sunday afternoon. They didn't find his body for two days—Lake Michigan can be like that. Now, none of this was anybody's fault, but I got some notion in my head that I was responsible for Alan being dead. If I'd stayed with him every minute, I told myself, he wouldn't have got pulled under by the current. If I hadn't played ball with my dad and older brother, I could have been with him and saved him. He was closest to me in age of my siblings, and I even got to thinking that my parents blamed me; maybe they were even sorry that *I* hadn't been the one to drown."

"Poor Hal," Linda murmured.

"No, not poor Hal," he said. "Wrong lesson to take from this story. What I'm trying to say is that this sort of guilt is perfectly normal, even when a person really has no reason to feel guilty at all. It's irrational, but very real, to feel the way I did. Then it all seemed to happen again when Elaine got sick. At first, I couldn't believe it, wouldn't accept it. I fought with every doctor who treated her, trying to find one who would say, 'It isn't true; she's not going to die.' Finally, I realized I was wrong. This awful cancer was sucking the life out of her and I couldn't fight it; I couldn't do a bloody thing about it. It was then that I started feeling guilty; because I was well and she was dying, it must be my fault. If I had done something differently, or if I hadn't done something, she would live. I didn't get all this stuff resolved before she died either, even though she was sick for almost two years. Then, when she died, I got a very serious attack of the guilts. It was almost as if I felt guilty being alive when she was dead.''

"Survivor guilt," Linda said, remembering something she'd read about the survivors of the concentration camps.

"That's right," he said. "And it was all irrational. What you're doing to yourself right now is sort of like that. Your mind knows that Ryter was responsible for his own life and death, and that it has nothing to do with you at all. But your emotions are operating separately from your head. You've let yourself *feel* responsible, as if Dana's being a victim of his sickness had made his suicide inevitable. And now Sandy Ryter has fed those feelings by saying awful things to you today. You just need to get past your feelings, so your good sense can take over again.''

"You must be the nicest man in the world," Linda said, snuggling even closer to him. "I'm just a slow reactor, I guess. I never seem to respond the way I should when something happens. It's only later, in a kind of delayed reaction, that I start feeling things. Will you try to be patient with me?''

"Oh, patience is something a man of my age and occupation has had a lot of practice in," Hal said. "And, as to my being such a nice man, I cannot tell a lie. It's pure selfishness on my part. I want you to get over this so I can have your undivided atttention.''

As he rocked her gently back and forth, Linda thought about Hal's life, his blessedly normal reaction to the deaths of his brother and his wife, marks of his fundamental decency and capacity for sympathy. He was a wonderful man and she was deceiving him. Even her appeal for patience was a kind of lie, because she was letting him think that her guilt was only the humane response of a nice woman to someone else's pain. What would he think, she wondered, if he knew the woman he was holding had committed first-degree murder? Would he jump up in horror and leave the house? She was beginning to think she would never feel good enough to have Hal Lawrence as a potential lover or husband.

Yet, she was feeling comforted in his arms, could feel herself relaxing as he held and rocked her. His chest was a good resting place, a warm shelter, and soon she found herself drowsy, drifting away from her fear and guilt into sleep. This was so gradual that she couldn't say afterwards at what point she'd stopped being aware of Hal's arms around her and of being in her living room. After the drift into sleep, she rode on a long wave of well-being until, many hours later, she began to dream.

In the dream, she was on the second floor of Nash's Department Store, in the children's section, watching out the window for Dana to arrive. Without knowing why, she knew they were supposed to meet at the store. The street below was crowded, many people walking both ways, almost like the worst days of Christmas shopping. Suddenly Linda saw Ryter in the crowd, walking away from her to the south. The short figure with the wide shoulders, the sandy hair, and the rolling walk were all unmistakable. Linda felt a terrible panic, a need to watch Ryter, to follow him, as if some vague horror must be prevented by keeping him in sight. Without any transition, she found herself on the street pushing her way through faceless people, sometimes glimpsing Ryter's retreating figure, sometimes losing him in the crowd. She began to run, feeling more desperate at every moment.

In a twinkling, the street became the long corridor of the junior high, and the people crowding around her were her students, some of whom she recognized. Linda tried to thread her way through the children, sometimes noticing Ryter's head, just barely visible above the heads of the seventh-graders. He was approaching the far door of the school, and Linda felt an increased urgency to catch up with him before he left the building. By staying close to the walls, she was able to avoid colliding with the students and was even able to run a little.

She caught up to Ryter just as he was reaching for the long bar on the door. She reached toward his shoulder, but stopped short of touching him. He turned anyway, turned slowly to his right. When his face became visible, it was the face she had looked at after pulling the trigger: the glazed eye with recognition still in it somewhere, light from the door glinting off the pain tears; a black hole above the eye, oozing blood in long, bright streams that descended toward the waxen smile on his lips. Then the mouth moved, opened, and whispered, "Oh, teacher, teacher."

Linda woke up with her heart slamming against her ribs, perspiration on her face. She was lying on the sofa, covered by an afghan, and light was coming through the windows. It took her several seconds to calm down, to remember why she was asleep on the sofa. She sat up slowly, noticing that Hal must have slipped off her shoes, for they were on the floor next to the coffee table. There was a scrap of paper weighed down by the box with

Dana's present in it. When Linda pulled the paper out, she read, "Call you tomorrow. Hal." She glanced at the mantle clock: 6:00. When she stood up, she ached a little, almost as if the running she'd been doing in the dream had made her legs stiff. Of course, she thought, turning her mind firmly away from the dream, it was from sleeping on the sofa with all her clothes on.

When Linda had showered and put clean clothes on, she remembered that this was the day of Ryter's funeral. She got the paper in and searched all through it for any announcement of the services. There was none. The story of Ryter's death and the investigation surrounding it had slipped to page three and was just a brief summary of earlier accounts. Linda wasn't sure why she'd looked for the funeral announcement. Did she have some notion of attending the services, the black-veiled figure in the back row that always tipped off the detectives in the mystery movies? She could see how ludicrous the idea was, and yet she felt disappointed not to know where and when the funeral would take place.

Of course, she remembered that she had somewhere else to go, another appointment of sorts. Lieutenant Willman would be taking his coffee break at the cafeteria in Rudolph's Grocery, and she must meet him there to find out how much he already knew. And she'd have to be on her mettle, alert and careful. That meant a good breakfast and no morning coffee. So, with her nightmare still lurking around the edges of her consciousness, Linda made bacon, eggs, and toast for herself, swallowing the food without tasting it.

Chapter 30

Rudolph's Grocery wasn't one that Linda ever used; it was on the highway and its prices were always higher than the grocery where she did her weekly shopping. When Linda arrived at 10:10, she found Lieutenant Willman waiting just inside the door. He looked unusually dressed up; he was in a suit and tie, smoothly shaven, shoes shined. Linda didn't remember him being this carefully attired even in the courtroom. She herself was wearing slacks and a knit top, and she felt decidedly underdressed.

"Is this Policeman's Dress Up Day or something?" she said to him, trying to start their meeting off on a casual note.

Willman flushed scarlet and looked away into the throng of shoppers.

"No, no," he mumbled. "Every now and then I like

to look like a professional, that's all, and today is one of those times.''

What an odd man, Linda thought as she walked ahead of him toward the cafeteria. Most of the time he seemed like a cool, hard-bitten detective who had seen it all and couldn't be shaken by anything. But occasionally, he would get all flustered and embarrassed, blushing like a kid. Just now, he had actually seemed offended by her joke. She hoped not. It would be an awkward way to begin.

''I just dropped some things off at the dry cleaners,'' Linda said. ''And I remembered that you'd be here for coffee.'' She actually *had* gathered some winter coats and wool skirts to take to the cleaners, to give a plausible excuse for being out on this end of town. ''I thought I'd find you halfway through your break.''

''Oh, I can take my break anytime I want,'' he said from behind her. ''I'm working even while I'm here because I'm thinking things through.''

Yes, Linda thought, that was wholly believable. Willman was surely working all the time. The tables in the cafeteria were plastic coated, patterned in a bright blue-and-white check, and the benches were blue molded-plastic. As Linda slid onto one of the benches, she noticed several flies take off from the surface of the table.

''What would you like?'' Willman said. ''I'm buying.''

''Just some iced tea, please,'' she said, though the smell of coffee was tempting her to forget her need for calm.

Linda watched Willman go through the cafeteria line, his tall frame towering over the few other customers, his face in profile looking sharp, chiseled. If he had more hair, Linda thought, she might almost think him handsome. He came back with a tray holding a tall glass of iced tea and a metal pot of coffee next to his cup and saucer.

"They know me," he said, sinking onto the bench opposite Linda. "I used to go back for refills so often that they just started giving me a whole pot." And he smiled that wonderful smile that changed his whole face, as if he were becoming a different person before her eyes.

"I'm a coffee addict, myself," Linda said. "Lately, though, I find it's been keeping me awake, so I'm trying to cut down."

"You do look a little tired," he said. "And thinner, I think." His eyes had grown sharp again, his face unsmiling.

"Just a little," she said, playing with the lemon slice on her glass. "Now that the cause of my anxiety is past, I'll fatten myself up again."

"Good," he said, pouring the strong black coffee into his cup. "It's not good for a woman to be too thin. All right for me, but not for you."

Linda watched him take a sip before she turned the conversation.

"Ryter's funeral is today," she said.

"I know," he said. "How did you find out?"

"I ran into his ex-wife downtown yesterday and she told me—among other things."

"Tough?" he asked, and his eyes showed real sympathy and a kind of tenderness she had previously seen him show only for Dana.

"Yes," she said simply. "I'll be glad when this inquest is over and all of us can start putting this mess behind us. When is the inquest, by the way?"

"A week from tomorrow," he said and took another sip of coffee. Linda could see that he wasn't going to volunteer much information unless she asked for it.

"So, what's new in your investigation, Lieutenant?" she asked and gulped some tea to cover her nervousness.

"Lots of little things," he said. "Little things that mount up. The lab boys confirmed my suspicion about the gun bluing on the cloth, but the rag itself is just a piece of dish towel; you can get them anywhere. The only odd thing about it is that there are no others like it in Ryter's apartment and, like I mentioned to you before, nothing else that clean."

"Did your fingerprint expert find anything useful?" Linda said, forcing herself to breathe normally.

"No," Willman said. "The only clear prints in the place were the victim's. We paid particular attention to both doors because the knobs are metal—makes for good prints—and anyone touching them after Ryter would have obscured or smeared his prints, even if that some-one had been wearing gloves. All the door knobs have Ryter's prints on them, clear as a bell, and nobody else's."

Linda could feel her heart steadying. Ryter's need for a drink had apparently blotted out the one place in the apartment where she had left a mark of her presence.

"But the fingerprints search *did* show us something very peculiar," Willman went on after drinking some more coffee. "There were no fingerprints at all on the second bullet in the gun and none on the clip—that's where the bullets go in the gun. And those are all metal surfaces. No prints of any kind on the bullet box either.''

"What do you make of that?" Linda asked, feeling a bit more confident since she'd learned that her prints hadn't been found in the apartment.

"Well, someone wiped that clip down and then didn't handle it again with bare fingers," Willman said. "And the bullets, too. Probably the rag we found was used for that purpose. What I can't figure out is why a man who's intent on killing himself would be so careful not to leave his fingerprints on the inside of the gun.''

"Maybe that wasn't his intention," Linda said. "Maybe it was just his habitual way of handling the gun, sort of keeping it clean while he was loading it. Habits stick with a person, even in times of worst crisis.''

"Maybe," Willman said. "But this particular rag couldn't be part of any habit that man ever had. I don't think he bleached anything in his life.''

"It could be a bar towel," Linda said, suddenly inspired. "You said he spent most of the day in bars. Maybe he just picked it up somewhere and pocketed it.''

Willman looked first surprised and then interested.

"I confess I never thought of that," he said slowly. "I'll have to go back to those bars and check it out. You know, I really think it helps me to talk this over with you. You've got some good ideas.''

Linda couldn't analyze his tone. It seemed sincere, but his eyes were so sharp, so searching, that she went on fearing that he was trying to trap her into a mistake.

"So, what are the other little things?" Linda asked.

"One interesting thing," he said, leaving open the possibility that there were things he knew but didn't consider "interesting" enough to discuss. "We found a pretty clear footprint in the dirt along the edge at that side staircase I was telling you about. It rained pretty hard last Thursday night, you remember, and the ground was still pretty soft."

"Yes," she said. "Now that you mention it, I do remember that the storm woke me up Thursday night. Part of why I was so tired Friday night, I guess."

"Well, somebody was walking pretty close to that hedge. Funny place to walk, too, because there's a graveled parking lot where it would have been much drier for somebody to cross."

"Does the footprint mean anything?" Linda said, closing her fingers around her tea glass to steady them.

"I don't know yet," he said. "We took a plaster cast of it, of course. It was made by someone with smaller feet than anyone living in the house."

"Perhaps neighborhood children play there," she said.

"I thought of that and asked around. Not many kids in the neighborhood and none with feet that size. The print was made by some sort of sport shoe—old, not much tread."

"Well, that doesn't seem very useful," Linda said.

"It isn't," he chuckled. "Unless we find the shoe that fits it."

"So your little things don't add up to much," she said, "if you're still trying to prove Ryter didn't kill himself."

"I'm not trying to prove that," he said, widening his

dark eyes as he looked at her. "I'm just investigating a case, trying to find out exactly what happened."

Careful, careful, Linda reminded herself. She mustn't try to second-guess this man, mustn't act nervous.

"Is your investigation almost over, then?" she said, aiming at a casual tone.

"No quite," he said. "I'm still interviewing people. I learned some interesting things from Ryter's neighbors already. A woman who has the second-floor apartment across the street noticed a light on in his bedroom Wednesday night, and she's pretty sure it wasn't on before that—all the while Ryter was in jail, I mean. It was just a faint light, she said, like a table lamp. Only the overhead light was on in the bedroom when we got in on Friday. Have you got any theories about that?"

"Not a one," Linda said, beginning to feel resentful and struggling to keep it out of her voice.

"Me either," Willman said. "And then an old woman in the next block told me she saw a man walking along the railroad tracks just after the time Ryter was shot. At least she thought it was a man, somebody that tall. The person was wearing a navy-blue sweatshirt with the hood up."

"Oh," Linda said, smiling a little. "So that's why you were asking my neighbor what I was wearing when I came home from my walk Friday afternoon."

"Just routine checking," he said, and he looked embarrassed again.

"I'd be happy to have you check over my wardrobe," Linda said. "You'll find a sweatshirt, but it's purple and it doesn't have a hood. And you may take my tennis shoes downtown to see if they'll fit into your mold." She kept up a studiedly bantering tone through all this.

"I don't think for a moment that you're hiding evidence in your home, Mrs. Hammond," he said, and again she wondered if there were not just a trace of irony in his tone. "I've told you that I'm asking questions about everyone who knew Ryter. I've still got a list of his old acquaintances that I'm checking up on."

"Oh, yes," Linda said. "Mr. Lawrence told me about your questions. If you'd asked me about Friday's noon hour instead of late afternoon, I could have told you that I was weeding in the yard and didn't get to the phone in time to answer it when he tried to call me from St. Louis."

"I hope you'll try not to be offended, Mrs. Hammond," Willman said, looking down at his cup. "I'd almost forgotten about those questions. I finished my check of you on the weekend, and I've moved on to other leads since then."

"I'm *trying* to take it in good part," Linda said, but she was angry with him, resented his probing. The anger came partly from her fear, but partly, too, from a sense that she was in a deadly contest with this man and must be more than a little angry with her opponent in order to win. Like a boxer, she wanted to taunt him for failing to deliver a knock-out punch. Without fingerprints, she thought triumphantly, he could prove nothing against her. The shoes were gone and lots of people had the same size feet as hers. The hooded sweatshirt was gone and Brenda Hardwick now believed she had seen a purple sweatshirt, so Willman could dance his way through her closets if he wanted to. He had nothing concrete, so he really had nothing.

"What other leads have you moved on to?" she asked at last after a pause in the conversation, and her voice was calm and pleasant again.

"Nothing worth talking about yet," he said, and the tone was final. "And I've been thinking a lot, too, about motive. Motives for suicide, motives for murder."

"Don't you ever take a day off?" she said, a little exasperated.

"No, I don't," he said simply. "I don't have anything else to do besides being a cop. Never had any hobbies." He didn't add, "Don't have any family," but Linda could almost hear it hanging unspoken in the little silence following "hobbies."

"So, what have you concluded about motives?" Linda asked.

"Well, suicide has lots of motives, of course," he said. "Despair, remorse, guilt, fear. I just can't seem to connect any of these motives with Ryter, though. But I could be wrong, of course. Now murder I know a little bit more about, having investigated quite a few in my time."

"And what about motives for murder?" Linda said, feeling bold still.

"People kill for lots of reasons, too," he said, leaning forward. "Greed, lust, rage, revenge, fear. Some of them kill because it's the ultimate rush for them, a sick gratification of their weird sexuality."

"Like men who kidnap, rape, and murder children?"

Linda interrupted him, determined to draw his attention
to the kind of man he was calling a "victim."

"Yes," he said, looking at her for a long moment
before going on. "People like that are around, but
they're the exception rather than the rule. Most of the
time, motives for murder are a lot simpler. So, if I have
trouble believing in Ryter as a suicide, I have to consider
what motives for murder there might be in this case. I
figure I can rule out greed and lust right away. Rage
might work if he had died in a bar fight, but if he was
murdered, somebody planned it out pretty carefully, so
impulse based on rage is out. That leaves me with
revenge or fear. I've got to follow up any leads about
people who wanted to get back at Ryter or who feared
him enough to want him eliminated. Or maybe both. He
might have been blackmailing somebody, for instance.
He had a camera and even developed his own pictures,
but we can't find any. So maybe he was using pictures to
blackmail somebody."

"I bet you've worked out a murder theory already,"
Linda said, carefully turning the conversation away from
motive. "One that fits the little bits of evidence you've
been gathering. Would you like to run it past me?"

"Well, just a brief scenario," Willman said, looking
sheepish. Linda couldn't tell if this expression was sincere or disingenuous. "Somebody could have got into his
apartment through that loose screen, somebody wearing
gloves. That person could have been there already on
Wednesday and forgot to turn off the bedroom lamp. That
person could have loaded Ryter's gun, maybe even knew
where it was kept in the apartment. Gloves would have

meant no fingerprints on the bullets or the clip. Then our
intruder could have come back on Friday and just waited
for Ryter to get back from work, waited even longer
because Ryter spent the day in the bars. If this person
we're imagining had stood just inside the bedroom door,
it would have been a simple matter to wait for Ryter to
come into the room, raise the gun, and shoot him at very
close range. The powder burns on his head and the nature
of the wound show us that the gun was no more than
three inches from his head when it went off—maybe
closer.''

"That close range business also fits the suicide theory,
doesn't it?'' Linda asked.

"Sure,'' he said. "But the placement and angle of the
shot are funny for suicide.''

"Funny?''

"Well, when most people want to shoot themselves in
the head, they hold the gun like this,'' and he raised his
right hand to the side of his head above the ear, pointing
his index finger at his temple. "That way, they can't see
the gun as long as they're looking forward. But the shot
that went into Ryter's head went in here,'' and he moved
his finger around to that place above the left of the eye
that Linda remembered from her nightmare. "It's almost
as if he turned toward the shot. And the bullet angled
downward slightly. That would mean that he'd have to
have been holding his elbow almost like this,'' and
Willman raised his own elbow to a grotesque angle.
People in the other booths were beginning to stare at him.
When he noticed this, he dropped his hand to his coffee
cup.

"And he had his eyes open," Willman said more quietly. "I've seen suicides by gun before, and they all had their eyes pinched shut. It's like they were expecting the shot, or didn't want to see anything anymore. Or maybe it's a reflex, like sneezing. But, anyway, none of the other cops I talked to ever saw this kind of a suicide with his eyes open before, either."

Linda was gripping her glass again, having to remind herself that this uncannily accurate account of what had happened in Ryter's apartment was just the lieutenant's theory. He really had no concrete evidence, she told herself over and over, nothing that could be used in court.

"But how could this 'intruder' of yours get away with other people in the house?" she asked, aware that her voice had slid up somewhat in pitch and hoping that he wouldn't notice.

"Very quietly and very quickly," he said. "The guys downstairs aren't agreed on exactly how long it took them to react after they heard the shot. They had to turn off a stereo and then ask each other what to do, that sort of thing. There might have been time for a murderer to put the gun in Ryter's hand, cross the apartment, and get out the open window before the boys got outside."

"But didn't you say they went up both staircases?" Linda said. "Wouldn't one of them have seen this very quiet person?"

"There is one possible hiding place in that side staircase," Willman said. "A thin person could have ducked around a bay window and stayed out of sight as long as the kid at Ryter's side door wasn't looking for somebody hiding. When you're thinking about what might be on the other side of the door, you don't look at other places."

"So you can rule out all the fat people Ryter might have been blackmailing," Linda said, taking grim satisfaction in her macabre joke.

"Right," he said, but he didn't smile.

"But you said those young men stayed outside, or one of them did," she said.

"No, both of them went back into their own apartment to call the police," Willman said. "Not for very long, it's true. But long enough, I think, for someone hiding on the staircase to get down the steps and run along the hedge. Once out of the parking lot, this person wouldn't be seen from the front of the house. There was a freight going by, so the guys wouldn't have heard the footsteps."

"It all sounds pretty farfetched to me," Linda deadpanned; inside, she was beginning to believe that Willman had some sort of a crystal ball.

"Yeah, I know," he sighed. "It sounds pretty farfetched to me, too. Unless I come up with something solid, I'll have to write a report concluding that John Charles Ryter committed suicide. But, like you said when I first told you about it, I just don't think he was the type."

"Well," Linda said, glancing at her watch. "Dana slept over at a friend's house last night and I guess I'd better retrieve her."

"Sure," he said, putting his cup down. "You give that little lady my best."

"I will," she said, standing up.

Willman stood up, too, looking embarrassed again.

"Maybe I'll call you to let you know if anything turns up before the case goes to the inquest," he said.

"Yes, why don't you do that," Linda said, feigning indifference. "I think I'll have an easier time getting my life back to normal once this whole incident is over."

"I'm sure you will," he said. "You can start fattening yourself up again," and he laughed a little at his own lame joke.

Linda began to walk out of the cafeteria with Willman following her.

"I never noticed before," he said from just behind her left ear. "But you're a very tall woman."

Linda's heart lurched, but she managed to keep walking steadily and to keep her gaze forward.

"Five-nine," she said evenly. "I seem to be taller today, though, because I'm wearing these platform sandals."

"Oh, yes," he said. "They're very nice."

It wasn't until she was halfway to the Wielands that Linda began to shake, and soon she was trembling so hard that she had to pull the car off the street for a while. She put her head down onto the steering wheel and drew several long, shuddering breaths.

She simply couldn't figure Lieutenant Willman out. He seemed to have three distinct personas. Most of the time, he seemed like the efficient investigator with a soft spot for kids; a man who seemed to think better when he had someone to talk to about his theories; a man who, for some reason, had selected her as a sounding board. In this role, she felt a deep trust in him and even attraction. At other times, Linda believed she saw the wily fox peeking through, the cunning and experienced hunter who was already convinced of her guilt and who was using his kindly persona as a cover to trap her into a dangerous mistake. When she thought she heard irony in his voice, a mocking of her alibis, was that paranoia on her part? Was her own guilt causing her to see a predator animal where there was just a nice man doing his job? The third persona Linda glimpsed only occasionally was the embarrassed, flustered, almost tongue-tied man who reminded her of a teenager trying to ask for a date. What was that all about, she wondered? Was it just another way to hide the probing, clever mind she knew was lying behind those dark, piercing eyes? It had almost taken her breath away when he'd outlined his "theoretical" murder scenario. Even now, she worried that she might not have kept her alarm out of her face while he was talking.

But he had no proof, she told herself firmly. He had as much as admitted to her that his "little things" amounted to nothing. He was still interviewing people, he'd said, but not about her. Somehow, she couldn't imagine Willman telling a direct lie just to give her false confidence. Whatever the other leads were that he was so reluctant to talk about, she didn't believe they were connected with her. But why had he volunteered to contact her again before the inquest, and why had he sounded so embarrassed about it? Strange, strange man—strange and dangerous.

Chapter 31

Lieutenant Willman hadn't told Linda everything about his investigation. He had reasons for telling her what he did, and other reasons for withholding information. He didn't like to examine his own feelings too closely because he'd become far more involved in this case than he knew was good for him, and good for the job he had to do. Long before leaving Chicago, he'd convinced himself that he had at last achieved the emotional distance that career cops have to have; if they can't get it, they crack, fall apart. And for him, the past ten years had been his most successful in that department: his emotions had stayed on an even keel, his cases had a high conviction rate; in fact, the years had sped by in their sameness, their relative smoothness. In Holton especially, the perks of his office and the lighter schedule had combined to make him feel that it was just a matter of coasting toward retirement.

Now this case had changed everything. He was working almost around the clock, and his subordinates thought he was crazy to do it. From their point of view, Ryter was an ex-drunk and a child molester whose victim had walked away unscathed, so Willman's early doggedness in the case struck them as excessive. Now, the whole department was solidly convinced that Ryter's death was a suicide; a little more sordid than their usual run of cases, but not really very interesting. Willman knew that glances were being exchanged, that junior officers were speculating that the old man must have a screw loose.

And he wanted so badly for Ryter's death to be a suicide! He spent most of his time trying to prove that it *had* been a suicide. He even spent part of his time trying to ignore evidence that led away from that conclusion, despite the fact that ignoring evidence went against the deepest grain of his being. He had become a good detective because of his patient powers of observation, his meticulous attention to detail, and his objectivity; but mostly, his fundamental passion for bringing out the truth and setting forth an accurate report of the facts had been the guiding star of his career. A shoddy approach to facts, a careless or biased attitude toward the truth, offended him profoundly. It had given him a reputation as a cold fish, he knew, a "by-the-booker," but it was simply his character. To be torn as he was now was unfamiliar, even a little embarrassing to him.

He had told Linda Hammond about the footprint next to the hedge, but he hadn't told her about the other prints, the ones he'd found on the morning after Ryter's death when he'd crossed the railroad tracks and found the trampled grass behind those two bushes. Where the grass ended and the edge of the rail bed began, there were several light imprints identical to the one up at the house. He could dismiss one footprint as having been made by some kid using the hedge as a hiding place, but these others, especially there where someone had obviously spent some time moving about on the damp grass, crouching probably in a place where a view of the house was possible—that was too convenient a coincidence. He had shaken his head sadly before starting back up the embankment, unaware that the railroad tie he stepped on was marked on its exposed end by a long scratch.

And he hadn't told Linda Hammond about Nancy Birkin. It had taken him almost a week, but his interviews with Ryter's acquaintances had finally turned up her name. The mystery of how John Charles Ryter had spent his last night on earth had plagued Willman, had begun to seem to him like the key to the whole case. On Thursday afternoon, he'd gone to see Nancy Birkin.

She was wearing a peacock-blue bathrobe, but otherwise looked nothing like the general public's stereotype of a prostitute; Willman knew that very few prostitutes really fit that stereotype. In his years of working vice in Chicago, he'd developed almost a kindly tolerance for "pros," as the officers there called them. It struck him that they were often as much victims as criminals, especially the ones who worked for pimps. Willman hated pimps.

Nancy Birkin was about thirty-five, a bit overweight, a

bit older-looking than her years, but the face could as easily belong to some local farmer's wife, the freckled nose and Scandinavian jaw common in this part of Minnesota. Her blue eyes narrowed, though, when she saw Willman's police identification. When he sat down, she perched on the arm of a chair, swinging her foot in a gesture of defiance, but he could see the fear in her eyes.

"What can I do for the local authorities?" she said.

"When was the last time you saw Jack Ryter?" he asked, quietly, but watching her keenly.

She paled a little but didn't stop swinging the foot; it was almost as if she'd been expecting the question.

"I don't know," she shrugged. "Coupla months ago, I guess. Shame about him plugging himself, but we weren't really close, you know."

It sounded rehearsed to Willman, as if she had considered what she would say if anyone at all mentioned Ryter.

"That's not what I hear," he said, using an old bluff.

"What dya mean?" she said, but the foot had stopped swinging.

"I got somebody who saw him coming out of this building last Friday morning." It was the ultimate bluff, but she caved in immediately.

"So what?" she flared, white patches spreading on her cheeks. "What does that have to do with him dying? Guys don't get depressed in this apartment." This last was said with a defiant lifting of her jaw.

"I wonder why you didn't come forward when you heard about the shooting," Willman said.

"Don't make me laugh," she said harshly, standing

up. "You think I got some cosy relationship with the cops in this town? They hassle me every chance they get."

"Look, Miss Birkin," he said calmly. "I'm not interested in giving you any trouble. You can believe me about that. I'm just trying to piece together how Ryter spent his last twenty-four hours, to figure out how he was feeling and acting."

She folded her arms and sat back down again.

"He was here from about one-forty-five A.M.," she said dully. "I don't know when he left, 'cuz I was sleeping at the time."

"How did he seem to you?"

"In what way do you mean?" she said, putting on an exaggerated leer that made Willman feel sorry for her; she was trying so hard to sound tough.

"What was his mood like?" Willman said gently.

"To tell you the truth," she said, giving up the pose, "I've never seen him like that. He was wild, mad, nervous, chewing on his lip till I thought it was gonna bleed. He wouldn't say what was wrong, but he was churning about something big. He wasn't much for bed either, I can tell you. Not that he ever *was* great shakes in that department."

Willman felt a rush of elation. It fit the suicide scenario perfectly. He had confronted Ryter outside his house and the conversation must have thrown a bigger scare into the runt than he, Willman, could ever have hoped for. Probably Ryter thought he knew much more than he actually did. Ryter had kept his crazy cool for the moment, but he had skipped work and had shown Nancy

Birkin how shaken he really was, so shaken that he spent a day drinking himself into a state where a man who felt himself cornered might easily take the quick way out.

Willman faced squarely the possibility that his midnight confrontation might have pushed the little man to kill himself. He would accept the burden gladly, if only it meant that no one else was to blame for Ryter's death. He could add it to his list of grieving wives, half-orphaned children, shocked elderly parents—all those people he saw in courtrooms when his evidence was sending some man to prison. He was used to it. He could take it.

"So, is that all you want to know?" Nancy said, looking intently at him now.

"Yes, that should do it," Willman said, pulling himself up out of the chair, noting with one part of his mind how tired he felt.

"And you think that makes it all certain that Jack Ryter killed himself?" she said, standing up herself.

"You have doubts?" he said, responding to the mockery in her voice.

"You listen to me, Mister Cop," she said, wagging her head back and forth. "Jack Ryter never shot himself. I knew him pretty well and knew how to stay off his bad side. But when he revved himself up like that, got as squirrelly as he was last Thursday night, it was *other* people who better look out. Jack never got mad at himself. I could believe real easy that he went outta here and shot somebody else, but I don't believe for a mintue that he would ever hurt himself."

"So, what is your theory, Miss Birkin," Willman said

coldly, angry with her now for voicing so clearly his own deepest conviction about the late John Charles Ryter.

"Somebody killed him," she said flatly. "I got no idea who it might be, mind you, but I'd guess there are quite a few people who aren't shedding any tears over him departing this earth. I was scared of him sometimes, I can tell you. He was a mean little guy when he thought somebody had crossed him. So you keep looking for somebody he was after, somebody who thought it was smart to shoot first."

Willman felt profoundly depressed as he left Nancy Birkin's building. He knew that what she had said was closer to the truth than his own biased hopes, and that meant he had to go on investigating, widening his circle of people to interview, probing for something he didn't want to find.

Chapter 32

Saturday morning, Linda went downtown and bought a new dress. She'd taken the silk scarf with her to match the reds, and had found the perfect dress in the fourth shop she went into. The dress was red, a two-piece crepe with a crisscross bodice and soft drapery at one side of the skirt, elegantly simple and flattering to Linda's long body. The scarf added just the right amount of dash to the otherwise plain, collarless neckline. Dana, who had gone along, sat in the dressing room patiently swinging her feet under the corner bench, but when she saw the red dress, she stood up, touched it, and pronounced it "wow."

Linda had spent most of Friday thinking about her conversation with Lieutenant Willman. As she became calmer, she forgot about the nuances of tone and manner which had so concerned her when she was actually with the tall detective and concentrated on the substance of what he'd said. He hadn't one shred of hard evidence against her, and he had turned his investigation elsewhere; these two factors had emerged most strongly, and both were very good news for Linda. Only two days before, she reflected, she'd been terrified that she had left a clear set of her fingerprints at the scene of her crime. Now that fear was gone. Even if Willman could find the shoes and sweatshirt at the landfill, a highly improbable feat, he couldn't definitely connect them to her. Even if David Polson should walk into the police station and announce that he'd seen Mrs. Hammond at a tree farm near Porterfield the night before Ryter was killed, there was no necessary connection between that event and Ryter's death. She could even deny that she'd been there, and she knew she would make a more reliable-sounding witness than poor David.

By Friday evening, Linda had decided that she was safe from prosecution for Ryter's murder: her nightmares, her depression, and her guilt were things she would have to deal with privately—she had begun to be afraid to go to sleep, lest the bloodied head should swim into her dreams again—but, at least, there would be no public scandal. She must work now at getting her daily life and her waking consciousness into a normal routine—child to raise, home to maintain, job skills to keep current, letters to answer, all the comfortable patterns she had established during her four years in Holton.

When Hal had called on Friday evening to ask about "my Sleeping Beauty," she added another resolution to her list: to put her guilt and self-loathing on hold whenever she was with him, to stop using him as a protector, substitute-father figure, and to start thinking of him as a potential lover. It was what she wanted, after all. So, she'd deliberately picked out a sexy dress, the kind of thing she hardly ever considered buying, bought some new perfume, and dug out of her closet the navy blue sling-back pumps she'd bought when she'd just finished graduate school; they had three-inch heels and would make her almost exactly as tall as Hal, but they looked good on her long legs and were a perfect accessory for the lovely red-and-blue silk scarf. Hal couldn't help noticing that she'd built the whole look around his present, and that was a message she wanted very much to give him.

Dana made her usual ritual grumblings about having a babysitter, but Linda knew that she was secretly grateful for the company whenever Linda had to be away in the evenings. The seventeen-year-old daughter of their across-the-street neighbors was a plain, rather dull girl who nevertheless enjoyed playing with Dana's toys and games, and had the added advantage of making it unnecessary for Linda to leave home to get and return a babysitter— an awkward problem that Linda had struggled with the first few years that she was a single parent.

Hal arrived just after 8:30, his little car bounding into the driveway as Linda watched out the kitchen window. It was odd how even the sight of his car made her feel a little thrill of happiness. The thought crossed her mind that the neighbors must already be getting used to seeing his car in her driveway. She smiled, a smug little smile, and walked into the living room where Dana had already let Hal into the house. Her entrance produced exactly the effect she'd hoped for. Hal was literally speechless for a long moment.

"Wow," he said at last.

"That's just what I said," Dana chimed in.

"And we're both right," Hal said, his blue eyes taking on an expression that made Linda's neck tingle a little.

"I have to give you a hug for my present," Dana said to Hal, a little puzzled at not being able to get him to look at her.

Hal turned to her immediately and stooped to get his hug.

"You smell nice," Dana said impulsively.

"Thank you, ma'am," he said, bowing formally. "I'm glad you like the diary. Did you start writing in it yet?"

"Well, no," Dana said, looking at little abashed. "All that nice clean paper is so pretty that I figured I should wait until something important happens before I start writing in it."

"Never mind," Hal laughed. "The nice thing about a diary is that you can write in it whenever you like and even take breaks from it when you want to."

Sharon, the babysitter, arrived, walking in without knocking. She got her instructions, listening with the half-hearted attention that a frequent babysitter develops. Then Linda gave Dana a hug and walked ahead of Hal to his car, deliberately making the spiky heels click on the porch steps. When Hal had pulled out onto the street and put the car into forward gear, he reached out to touch

Linda's dress just at her waist, keeping his eyes on the road all the time.

"Yup," he said. "It feels just as nice as it looks."

The Carvers had a ranch-style house with what Holton natives called a "finished" basement: a huge open room with a bar at one end and bright blue carpeting on the floor. The track lighting in the low-slung ceiling presented something of a hazard to tall guests, but was no problem for either Donald or Ann Carver, both of whom were well under five-ten. When Linda and Hal started down the stairs to this room, she took his arm, partly to steady herself on the high heels, but mostly to show the assembled staff of Holton Junior High that she had staked her claim.

The reception was scheduled to begin at 8:30 and it was after 9:00 when Linda and Hal arrived, so most of the guests were already milling around in a desultory way, occasionally pausing at the long food table that stood along one wall. Ann Carver had already lifted her pale eyebrows when she let Hal and Linda into the house by the back door, and their descent into the crowd below produced something of a sensation. A brief silence fell, and then people at the far side of the room began talking in muted tones to each other, glancing back at the stairs from time to time.

"It's too bad Susan and Jerry aren't here," Linda whispered to Hal as Ann scampered back up the stairs to answer the door again.

"You know," he said, "I think they went to their cabin in June precisely to avoid this little party."

"I wouldn't put it past Susan," Linda laughed. "But at least if they were here, we wouldn't have such a hard time mingling. I hate mingling."

"Come on," he said, taking her hand. "Let's just wade in and see if we can get some punch. Did you remember to deaden your taste buds today?"

They crossed to the table, stopping to greet a few people along the way. Before she'd got her first glass of punch, Linda had been told three times what a nice dress she had on. Hal was far better than Linda at making small talk and knew most of the guests better than she did, so she let him take over for a while. Gradually, she was able to relax enough to join in, especially when she encountered several people whose homerooms were near her own at school. She'd half expected someone to bring up Dana's near-kidnapping and Ryter's death, had even steeled herself a bit to handle it, but apparently the surprise of seeing her with Hal had driven all thought of those other things out of everyone's mind. The party was becoming positively convivial.

George Walters, who taught eighth-grade geography, shouldered up to Linda. He was a big, good-looking man with a reputation for harmless flirtation.

"Boy, Linda," he said, winking and leering. "You should wear red more often. The panting you hear is not the sump pump."

Linda laughed and reached down for Hal's hand. He took her hand in his warm grasp and turned sideways to beam good-naturedly into George's face.

"Someday, George," Linda said, "somebody is going

to take you seriously and then you're going to be in big trouble."

"Never," he said. "That's why I have Ruth to protect me." Ruth was his long-suffering and good-humored wife. "But, if you don't want men slobbering all over you, you should stop waving red flags."

"She doesn't have to stop," Hal said, smiling. "She's got me to protect her."

Linda giggled and leaned into Hal's side. She felt giddy, almost drunk. It was a feeling she remembered, but hadn't experienced for a long time—not since she'd been in love with Dan.

They'd been at the party for over an hour when Hal whispered into her ear, "Donald Carver off the port bow." She turned to see Carver bearing down on them, his duty of chatting with everyone having finally brought him around to them. He was a round, intense little man who looked perpetually worried. His voice, though, was his most unfortunate attribute, a high-pitched, grating voice which never seemed capable of any other inflection except a whine, like a chainsaw heard from a distance.

"How are things with you folks?" he said. "Getting enough to eat?"

"Oh, all we want," Hal said, and he tightened his grip slightly on Linda's elbow to punctuate his irony. Typically, he kept the irony out of his voice, reluctant to wound even Donald Carver.

"Well, it's good that we've had good weather for this get-together," Carver said, and even he seemed to see the pointlessness of this remark, because he flushed a little and forged ahead. "It seems to be going rather well."

"Yes, it is," Linda said warmly, happy enough to want to include everyone in the glow. "We're enjoying ourselves immensely." And it was absolutely true.

Carver fell silent for a moment, his worried look deepening.

"I wonder, Linda," he said at last, "if I could have a word with you in private."

"Oh. Sure." Linda separated the two words with a confused pause. "Excuse us a minute, Hal?"

"Sure," Hal said, his own forehead furrowing as if in imitation of Carver.

Linda followed Donald to a corner of the room, looking back over her shoulder once to shrug elaborately at Hal.

"Linda," Carver began when they had reached the door to the utility room, "I'm not sure what this all means, but a policeman came to see me last Monday to ask me some questions about you."

Linda felt instantly breathless, as if something had struck her in the stomach.

"Lieutenant Willman," she said dully.

"Yes, I believe that was his name," Carver said, and the whinning pitch went even higher. "He said he was investigating the death of that Ryter person, but I just couldn't make any sense out of his questions."

"What did he ask you?" Linda said.

"Well, he wanted to know if you were a sportswoman, participated in any outdoor activities that I knew about. I told him that I didn't know of anything, except that I'd seen you playing tennis a couple of times over the years."

"Anything else?" She felt numb, deflated.

"Well, he wanted to know if your ex-husband was a gun fancier or collector." Carver huffed for a moment. "I told him I had no way of knowing any such thing. I never met your ex-husband or heard anything about him."

Linda stood quietly, absorbing this bit of information.

"What could he be trying to find out, for heaven's sake?" Carver said, and now he looked as if he'd just got a report that a bomb was planted in a school locker.

Suddenly Linda was furiously angry, enraged at Willman as she'd never been before. How dare he go behind her back to her employers? How dare he ruin this wonderful evening? It was just as if he had actually come into the Carvers' gaudy basement to cast his dark shadow over the party. If he'd been there, Linda thought she might have tried to throw her punch glass into his predatory face.

"Well, I'll tell you, Donald," Linda said, a little savagely. "That policeman is trying to find out if I know how to use a gun."

"Oh my!" Carver exclaimed.

"He still hasn't decided if Mr. Ryter really killed himself or if someone murdered him," Linda said, putting her hand on Donald's plump shoulder and leaning down toward his face. "And if someone murdered Mr. Ryter, the good lieutenant thinks it might have been me."

"For God's sake, Linda," Carver said, drawing back from her a little. "You can't be serious. Why on earth would he think such a thing?"

Linda could see that she couldn't go much further with Carver's nerves, and she pulled herself up short.

"It's nothing for you to worry about, Donald," she said more soothingly. "These investigations take in a lot of territory. It's just a fishing expedition. Becase the man tried to hurt my daughter, it follows that I might have wanted to hurt him back. So when he turns up dead, it's only natural that one of the first things the police would consider is that I might have done it. But I've spoken to Lieutenant Willman recently, and he tells me that the evidence suggests only one conclusion—that Ryter committed suicide."

"I hope so," Carver said, "because I don't mind telling you, Linda, any hint of scandal couldn't be tolerated at school. The board would never stand for it, and you don't have tenure."

Oh, yes, Linda thought; he didn't mind telling her. The little slug would have her axed the day he heard of an arrest. Never mind waiting for a trial. Never mind any nonsense about being innocent until proven guilty.

"You worry too much, Donald," Linda said, patting his shoulder. "It can't be good for your blood pressure." And she walked briskly away from him to rejoin Hal.

"What's the matter?" Hal asked after one look at her face.

"Could we leave as soon as we can decently arrange it?" she said.

"Sure," he said. "Stick with me."

He took her hand and towed her through the crowd, pausing every now and then to work in a departure line to a few acquaintances; Linda was too distracted to notice what he said. Finally, after about ten minutes, they reached Ann Carver.

"Lovely party, Ann," Hal said. "Even better than last year's. We hate to hurry off, but Linda has a young babysitter tonight. You know how it is, I'm sure."

Ann turned her rabbity eyes up at Linda, who smiled woodenly and said, "Sorry to run, Ann."

"Well," Ann said. "Next year, you can stay longer perhaps."

"Certainly," Hal said. "Good night, Ann, and thanks again. Pass the thanks along to Don. He's so popular, we can't seem to get near him." And he swept Linda up the steps and out into the cool night air.

She told him about it in the car while he held both her hands.

"God damn that Carver!" Hal exploded. "I'd like to go right back down there and punch his lights out. Why the hell did he have to pick tonight to tell you a thing like that? Why did he have to tell you at all?"

"Oh, it isn't Carver's fault," Linda sighed. "It isn't even Willman. It's me, me."

"What do you mean by that?" Hal asked.

"I've got to be able to take this better," she said, staring out the windshield at the rows of neat houses and carefully watered lawns. "I can't go to pieces every time someone mentions Ryter's name or every time I see Chrissy Ryter in a store. I need to get myself under better control. It's just that I was having such a good time, and I'd almost forgotten all about it."

"Well, it's almost over now," he said, squeezing her

hands. "When the Coroner's Inquest is held, it'll all be settled once and for all."

She looked at him now, at his kind, concerned face. If only it were true, she thought; if only it could be done with once and for all.

"Do you want to go home?" Hal asked.

"No," she said quickly.

"Should we go somewhere for a drink?"

"Do you have a drink at your house?"

"Sure," he said eagerly.

"Well, I think I'd like to see your house."

He let go of her hands and started the car.

It was a nice house, old and roomy, with dark wood-work everywhere. Several of the rooms had been taste-fully redecorated without violating the spirit of the house. The living room had a small fireplace and a slightly worn oriental carpet. The kitchen, where Hal began to get out glasses and bottles, had been designed ingeniously to take maximum advantage of a small space.

Linda was feeling desperate, almost hysterical, as if the strain of the past week had suddenly crashed in on her all at once. She felt a fierce need to flee from her own mind, to hurtle herself into some kind of oblivion. She understood now how some people could repeatedly drink themselves into unconsciousness. While Hal still had his back to her getting ice cubes out of the refrigerator, she thought of another alternative.

"Would you make love to me?" she said.

He turned toward her with the ice cube tray in his

hands. He looked both stunned and uncertain, as if he doubted what he'd heard.

"You do want to make love to me, don't you?" she asked.

"Hell, yes," he said. "All the time."

"Then put the ice away."

He put the tray back in the freezer, but when he turned back to her, he looked a little hesitant.

"It's not just that you're upset about what Carver said, is it?" he asked.

"No, of course not," she said. "I want you. Very much."

He crossed the little room in two steps and pulled her against him.

"You don't mind about it being here, do you," she whispered against his left ear. "I mean, it was Elaine's house, too."

"No," he murmured into her hair. "It's all right. I don't think Elaine would mind either, wherever she is."

Linda slipped out of her shoes, her breasts brushing downward against Hal's chest as she lowered her bare feet to the floor. He kissed her again and again, on her mouth, her throat, her breasts, his hands straining her eagerly against him. Without letting go of each other, they walked to the downstairs bedroom where Hal had slept ever since his wife had died. Both of them worked quickly to shed Linda's clothes, the bright dress falling into folds at her ankles. When she stood back up from stripping off her pantyhose, Hal just stared at her for a long moment in the light that came through the door from the dining room. He didn't touch her then, but began to pull at the buttons of his shirt, though he didn't look down at what he was doing.

She turned and walked away from him to the double bed, where she stretched out slowly on top of the spread. When Hal came to her, he had only his underwear shorts left to take off, a last moment of embarrassment overcoming him until he sat down on the bed. He had a very smooth, hairless chest, the skin there much paler than his hands and face. Linda stroked both her hands over his body, feeling the muscles underneath, her eyes dreamily following the movement of her own fingers. Dan had a lot of hair on his chest, she remembered, but this silky, tender skin was so much nicer. The sound of Hal's breathing made her look up into his face, and she saw, for the first time in her life, a genuinely adoring look, a sweet mixture of desire and affection and gratitude.

Despite Linda's need and Hal's tender eagerness, it didn't go very well. Each of them was awkward, uncertain of what would please the other most, a little clumsy. But afterward, while she held his head against her breasts, Linda thought that it was only a beginning for them, and not such a bad beginning either. They would learn about each other as time went on, explore each other with trust and openness. He loved her—had whispered it again and again—and she loved him; the rest was just a matter of practice, of willingness to give and receive pleasure. When she was a very young woman, she hadn't understood that, and so had often been disappointed in bed. Thank God she wasn't a girl anymore, she thought, smiling up at the ceiling and spreading her hands over Hal's back.

We belong to each other now, she thought, *and you can't hurt me*. It was not God or fate that she was addressing; it was Lieutenant Willman.

Chapter 33

When the doorbell rang at 10:30 on Monday night, Linda thought it must be Hal dropping in impulsively. They had talked on the phone Sunday and once again on Monday afternoon so she could tell him about the arrangements she'd made for Dana to spend Wednesday at Trina DeKaster's birthday-party-sleepover.

"We get the house to ourselves from six P.M. until the next day," Linda had whispered suggestively into the phone.

"Wonderful," Hal had said. "What kind of music do you like? I'll run right out and buy records."

"We don't need music," she had answered. "Just soft lights and some wine."

"I'll bring the wine. You have only brandy, remember?"

Now as she crossed the living room to answer the

door, she was debating with herself whether it would be too risky for them to make love with Dana in the house. At what point would they be ready for Dana to find Hal at the breakfast table when she got up in the morning? But when Linda drew back the curtains from the narrow windows, it was Arnold Willman standing on her porch.

"Don't tell me," she said as she pulled open the door. "You're working."

"Just got off my shift," he said. "You've got to remember that cops don't work just from nine to five the way real people do."

He seemed excited, up, his dark eyes sparkling in the beam from the porch light.

"What can I do for you?" Linda asked, not yet opening the screen door to admit him.

"Well, remember last week I told you I might call you if there was anything new in the Ryter case?" he said. "There's a whole lot new, and I hoped you wouldn't mind my coming by to tell you about it. You've sort of been in it with me from the beginning."

"Come in," Linda said, pushing the screen toward him. She felt the now familiar catch in her breathing, the acceleration in her heart rate. "I could make some coffee if you'd like some."

"No," he said. "I've had enough coffee for today, I guess."

"A soda then? It's a warm night."

"Okay. That would be nice." And he followed her out to the kitchen.

Linda got out the ice cubes and glasses, hunted in the refrigerator for the cans of ginger ale she knew were somewhere behind tomatoes and plastic-covered bowls. All this time, she carefully avoided questioning Willman, terrified that she might betray her panic. Behind her, he commented on the weather and remarked how clean her kitchen always looked, but his voice didn't sound the way it usually did; it was hurried, distracted almost. When she'd poured the ginger ale and sat down across the table from him, Linda felt in control enough to speak.

"Well, what's this news that brings you straight over after your shift?"

"I finally got a real break in the Ryter case," he said, and gulped soda for a moment. "You remember I told you I had a few other leads I was following up?"

"Yes," she said. "I do recall you saying something like that."

"Well, mostly I was tracking down the activities and whereabouts of certain people on the afternoon Ryter died."

Yes, Linda thought, remembering her talk with Donald Carver; she was one of those people. But she said nothing, merely looked at Willman, waiting for him to go on.

"One man kept coming up over and over," he said. "Peter Roblicki."

Linda stared at him for a full five seconds.

"Who is Peter Roblicki?" she said at last.

"Remember the guy Ryter beat up in the bar a few years ago?"

"The one who wouldn't testify against him?"

"That's the guy. And he wouldn't testify because

Ryter told him he'd kill him if he did. That's Peter Roblicki.''

"But what about him?"

"Lots about him." And Willman looked triumphant. "Seems he had a lot to say when Ryter went to jail on the kidnapping charge, and he was saying it in two of his favorite bars."

"What things?" Linda was still very puzzled, looking for a connection to herself in all of this.

"I've got ten witnesses who heard him say he thought Ryter was finally where he belonged and, if he didn't stay there, somebody ought to just 'put him out of commission' as soon as he hit the streets again. Those were his exact words. And he told the witnesses about some town in Missouri where a whole bunch of people just waited for the town baddie to get out of jail and then shot him, and nobody in town ever told who pulled the trigger.''

"I think I remember reading about that case," Linda said, beginning to feel more uncomfortable all the time. "But what does this mean? It's just drunk talk."

"By itself, it means very little," Willman said. "But it's only one piece, only one sliver of the plate I'm trying to put together here. This Roblicki is a friend of Bill Cromett, another name you don't recognize, I know. Cromett lives in the other upstairs apartment at Ryter's building. He told me that Roblicki visited him on two occasions, using the side entrance to go in and out. Cromett and Roblicki work at the same factory, the same shift.''

"I'm still not following this," Linda said.

"Don't you see?" Willman said, leaning forward, his thin face animated. "Roblicki knew the layout of that house, knew everybody's schedule, probably even noticed that loose screen I was telling you about. And its pretty certain that he knew about Ryter's gun because he also knew the guy Ryter bought it from."

"Do you mean to say that you suspect this Roblicki of—?" Linda broke off, her mouth suddenly dry as if she were drinking ashes instead of ginger ale.

"There's more, there's more," Willman said, holding up his hand as if he were stopping her question. "Guess who was not at work on Friday, June twenty-second, the day Ryter was shot."

Linda just stared at him.

"Right," Willman said as if she'd spoken. "Peter Roblicki. He called in sick that morning and didn't show up for work on Saturday, either. And he was seen in Ryter's neighborhood on Friday morning, walking out of a liquor store. The liquor store owner verified it for me; apparently, he knows Roblicki very well."

"It only means that he's a drunk who sometimes skips work," Linda said, and even she could hear the desperation in her own voice.

"By itself, sure," Willman went on as if he hadn't noticed her voice. "But I interviewed Roblicki last week and he has no alibi for any part of that Friday afternoon. Said he was home in bed, no one else around. But he looked worried. I noticed that he looked very worried, and that's what set me to checking his friends and acquaintances."

"He was worried he might lose his job," Linda said,

"if the police poking around got back to his boss about his early weekend."

"He has other worries now," Willman said. "Small arms expert when he was in the army. And guess what size Roblicki is."

"Small?" Linda said. "Small feet?"

"Bingo," Willman said. "I noticed that about him while we were talking, of course. I got the judge to okay a search warrant for the first thing tomorrow morning and then I'm going to have a good look around Mr. Roblicki's place. Now, mind you, I don't think he kept the shoes or even the clothes he was wearing. He probably just threw them in the trash. But I'm betting we'll find other shoes the same size and maybe even some bleached dish towels or rags. That should give me enough to make an arrest."

"Arrest?" Linda's hands were gripping the edge of the table, her knuckles white. "You can't be serious. All of that isn't enough to arrest somebody on."

"Think it over," Willman said. "We have motive, classic motive. Revenge is one I had to keep on my list, remember? The man was heard to utter threats against the deceased just days before he died. We have opportunity— access to the building, plenty of time to set up a plan, knowledge of weapons. We have no alibi for this suspect. And we have physical evidence which could link him to the scene within twelve hours of the shooting. We've got plenty."

Linda stood up from the table, turned her back on Willman, and walked to the cupboard. She leaned on the sink, staring at the darkened window over it as if she were in a trance. Behind her, Willman kept talking, about

Roblicki's experience with guns, about his being an agile person who could move around Ryter's apartment without being heard from below.

In all her planning and agonizing, it had never occurred to Linda that someone else might be blamed for Ryter's death. Like everything else in those terrible hours, it had seemed like a simple set of alternatives: either the police would believe it was a suicide or they would find out that she had killed him. Nothing else had ever entered her mind And since the investigation had begun, she'd been so afraid that this clever detective would discover incriminating evidence against her that she'd never imagined him pulling a net around anyone else.

She had killed a man, shot him to death, and now another man, just because he faked sickness to stay home and drink, because he had a certain size feet, because he might be careful about his laundry or even send his laundry out to a place that bleached towels—that other man might go to prison for her crime. It was impossible. It couldn't be happening. Linda hung her head and was aware for the first time that tears were pouring down her face.

Once again, she was faced with two horrors; once again, she must choose. Her imagination instantly laid one of the alternatives behind her eyes: headlines in the paper about the arrest of Peter Roblicki; a trial, with Lieutenant Willman testifying in that confident, big-city-smart voice; a parade of witnesses saying that the accused had hated and feared the deceased, had openly wished him dead; the defendant himself, inarticulate and helpless on the stand, merely repeating that he was home in bed when the dead man was shot; the coroner's report about the angle and placement of the shot; neighbors saying they saw a light in the apartment and a slight, hooded figure walking away after the shooting; and then the conviction and the sentencing. It was impossible. Just as she'd found insupportable the idea of killing someone else in order to kill Ryter, she now found insupportable the idea of letting someone else go to prison for her crime. She refused to think about the other alternative at all; that would come later when she had plenty of time to think. Now she simply knew that she couldn't let Peter Roblicki be arrested. She would have to stop it the only way she knew how.

Linda hadn't noticed that Willman had stopped talking a long time ago. When she turned back to him now from the sink, she was shocked into silence by the expression on his face. He looked stricken, ghastly pale, as if someone had just told him of the death of his nearest kin. He was sagged in the chair, all of the energy apparently gone out of him, and his dark eyes looked up at Linda from a face suddenly grown old. He knew. He knew everything. She could see it as clearly as if he'd spoken. He had carefully prepared his knock-out punch and it had worked; it had worked perfectly. But he looked as if he'd delivered it to himself as much as to her.

"Lieutenant Willman," she whispered, holding out her hands toward him; in another minute, she would have told him everything.

"Of course," he said sharply, suddenly sitting up straight in the chair. "Of course, the evidence is still circumstantial. I doubt that there would be a conviction without a full confession. So, even if I were to make an arrest, the D.A. probably would be unwilling to prosecute. I guess it would be a waste of my time, after all, to make an arrest." He paused for a second, his eyes fixed with a kind of fierce light on her eyes. "Do you understand what I'm saying, Mrs. Hammond? Without a confession, there really isn't a case."

"Yes," she whispered, her lips numb, the tears still spilling down her face. "Yes, Lieutenant, I understand."

And she did understand. In a sudden burst of insight, she understood everything: understood what he must have felt for her all along when she was too frightened or too distracted to see it, or rather she *had* seen it but had misinterpreted all the signals; understood how the policeman in him must have struggled against that emotional involvement, carefully and doggedly investigating her all the while he was hoping to uncover nothing; understood the guilt he must feel because his interest in her had made him tell her too much at the beginning, because he thought he might have scared her into committing murder. Mostly, she understood the enormity of what he was doing for her now, what he had to set aside in himself to keep her from speaking. She could no longer bear to look into his fiery eyes, could no longer take the combination of pain, concern, and shame she saw there. She turned back to the sink, snatched several paper towels off the roll on her right, and mopped her wet face.

By the time she was ready to look at him again, Willman had stood up and moved to the kitchen door.

"I'm going now," he said, and all the intensity had

gone out of his voice. He sounded very tired and his shoulders sagged. He didn't look at her.

Linda followed him wordlessly through the dining room and the living room, followed him straight out onto the porch. She kept trying to think of something to say to him, some way to let him know how grateful she was to him, how deeply she felt the sacrifice he was willing to make for her. But she intuited that any thanks, any reference at all to what both of them knew wouldn't be tolerable to him, would violate an unspoken pact that had formed between them in those few minutes in the kitchen. If it were ever mentioned, he would have to act, would have to be a policeman.

Willman paused at the foot of the porch steps, his hand on the rail.

"By the way," he said, still without looking at her. "I found the Bakerville connection."

"What?" Linda gasped rather than asked this question.

"When I was sifting through my lists of people who'd ever been associated with Ryter, I came across a guy Ryter worked with on one of his many jobs in Holton. This guy used to live in Bakerville, was living there while he worked here in Holton with Ryter. When I tracked him down on Saturday, he told me he remembered telling Ryter about a family next door to his house in Bakerville, a family going through a messy divorce and a custody fight over a little girl. He said Ryter was very interested, asking questions about the girl, claimed his interest was based on his concern for his own daughter, who was also having a tough time. That was the child who disappeared."

"Then we were right," Linda whispered. "It was true. Ryter took her and he killed her. And the other girl, too."

"I think so," Willman said. "There might even have been others. The pattern was becoming pretty clear, pretty convincing. He was probably the genuine article—serial killers, we call them now. And one who was getting crazier all the time."

"Thank you," Linda said, still whispering; she was afraid that if she spoke out loud, she would sob. "Thank you for telling me." And she wanted to run down the steps to embrace him.

"The trouble is," he said, still not looking up, and now his voice sounded a little angry. "The trouble is that now we'll never know for sure, and those kids will probably never be found, not unless somebody accidentally turns up a body." It was the only time he expressed the frustration of a good policeman who knows the identity of a criminal but still isn't able to close the case.

"I'm sorry," Linda murmured. "I'm sorry for those poor mothers."

"Yes," he said more gently. "It must be the worst thing in the world for a parent to have to imagine something like that about her child."

"Oh, yes," Linda said earnestly to his averted face. "Worse than all the other nightmares put together."

Willman looked up at her now, a steady glance.

"I guess we won't be talking to each other anymore," he said.

"I guess not," she said, and the tears started on her face again.

"Well, goodbye then," he said, trying to look away but not succeeding.

"Goodbye," she said. "I wish—" But there was nothing left to say.

He turned away and crossed the street, his tall body casting a block-long shadow in the path of the street light. He climbed into his car. The starter ground for a few seconds before the engine turned over. And then Arnold Willman was gone, the sound of his car diminishing gradually down the quiet street.

Linda stood on her porch for a long time. She wondered how much of the Peter Roblicki story Willman had made up. Probably some of it was true. Perhaps Willman had learned just enough of those details to make him hope that Roblicki was guilty. Because, of course, Willman had known all along that Ryter hadn't killed himself, knew it in his gut, all his experience as a policeman telling him that it was impossible. So, all along, he'd been looking for a murderer, trying to find a candidate—*any* candidate besides his chief suspect. Maybe he'd pursued the clues about Roblicki with growing hope, wanting with all his tough heart for some addled barfly to be the killer.

But Linda knew now that there was no search warrant, no imminent arrest. And she suspected that Peter Roblicki was not a slight man with small feet, was not acquainted with the man from whom Ryter had bought the gun, probably didn't even know Bill Cromett. In retrospect, it all seemed too pat, too convenient. It occurred to Linda now that Willman had never explained how Roblicki could have known that Ryter was getting out on bail;

only she had been given that information. Willman had invented details to go along with the few paltry bits he had against his new "suspect," had devised the test he felt sure would work. Because he knew her, knew that, if she were guilty, she wouldn't be able to let someone else take the fall for her. He had to find out for sure. Knowing had given him only pain and no satisfaction, had surprised him into acting against all his training, all his instincts, but he had to know. They were alike in that, she thought, in that need to face down the bogeyman, even when the bogeyman was a real monster and not just a childish fear.

Finally, Linda turned back into her house and went upstairs. She sat for a long time in Dana's room, watching her child sleep. Willman loved Dana, too, of course—the quick attachment of a lonely man to a spirited child, an attachment both admiring and fiercely protective, hidden, kept inside like everything else about that strange man. And now Dana was safe from all kinds of monsters, from Ryter, from the specter of a mother imprisoned for murder. They had done that for her, she and Willman, and at what cost to both of them? But they had done it for themselves, too, because the other nightmares were harder to face. She couldn't let Dana be threatened. Willman couldn't let her go to prison; that would have been worse for him than the sacrifice of his professional integrity.

She knew that Willman's report to the coroner's inquest would be factual, but spare, that its details would point in the direction she had originally planned: probable suicide. So he would set her free to face her demons alone and in private, cutting himself off from her just as surely as if she *had* gone to prison.

Such are the ironies of love.